TWICE UPON A Kiss

JANE SUSANN MACCARTER

OMNIFIC PUBLISHING
LOS ANGELES

Omnific Publishing
1901 Avenue of the Stars, 2nd floor
Los Angeles, CA 90067
www.omnificpublishing.com

First Omnific eBook edition, June 2015
First Omnific trade paperback edition, June 2015

The Jarmo archaeological site in Iraqi Kurdistan;
Photographer Linda Braidwood and archaeologist Dr. Robert Braidwood;
Hennepin County Medical Center, Minneapolis, Minnesota;
and the Department of Anthropology, University of Minnesota are
all actual places, people, or entities featured in this novel.
However, the author uses them fictitiously in this book.
All other characters and events in this book are also fictitious.

Library of Congress Cataloguing-in-Publication Data

MacCarter, Jane Susann.
   Twice upon a Kiss / Jane Susann MacCarter – 1st ed.
   ISBN: 978-1-623421-93-9
   1. Romance — Fiction. 2. Time Travel — Fiction.
   3. Anthropology — Fiction. 4. College — Fiction. I. Title

10 9 8 7 6 5 4 3 2 1

Cover Design by Micha Stone and Amy Brokaw
Interior Book Design by Coreen Montagna

Printed in the United States of America

For my immediate loved ones:
Buzz, Mindy, Kent
And to those who come after:
Jake, Ben, Zac, Auden, and Penny

Part One

CHAPTER 1
Entering Dreamtime

Nothing happens unless first a dream.
⮞ Carl Sandburg ⮜
1878 – 1967

Stella

In the garishly lit Minneapolis convenience store near campus, I hear two men — a skinhead and a pimply blond I saw walking in a moment ago — talking in low voices.

Blondie squeaks out a desperate plea to his partner. "But you *said*. You said you were going to *do* it. *Now!*"

I'm next at the till, a giant iced tea in my hand. My anthropology professor, Harry Vale, happens to stand in the queue behind me, holding a pasteboard cup of coffee.

I glance at the unsavory duo from the corner of my eye.

Skinhead glares at Blondie, speaking softly through clenched teeth. His lips are noticeably thick. "Fuck off, Leon."

He has a faint British accent.

Curious, way out here in Minnesota, I'm thinking. So far from either coast.

He catches me watching him and glares, curling his thick lips. He mutters in a voice that carries, "Take a picture, you sodding cow. It'll last longer."

I wince—not because of the menace in the voice, but because the words are true. I *am* rather a cow, although I wouldn't say a sodding one.

Truth be told, I, Stella Denton, twenty-and-a-half year old college student, actually look more like a young, solid-bodied cleaning lady.

For as long as I can remember, I've had a pensive squirrelly face, unfortunately prominent teeth, and precious little to bring to a conversation. If it weren't for my large, light blue eyes—rather lovely *I* think, but what others may decide, I really don't know—I'd start shoveling dirt over myself and be done with it.

No more than five-foot-seven, with sufficient love handles to cause his shirt buttons to strain against their buttonholes, my thirty-something Paleoanthropology 110 instructor tries to rise to the occasion. He directs a lame threat toward Skinhead.

"Watch it, buddy."

Unfortunately for us store patrons, Professor Vale, aka Bucky Beaver, looks as far from threatening as I am far from beautiful, so the duo pays him no mind.

I can't help thinking, *I wish you wouldn't. Leave it alone. Guys like this are liable to do anything.*

Blondie continues his low, frantic whispering. "But I need it *bad,* Wayne, and so do you."

Professor Vale leans in to speak to me in a low voice. "We should leave, now…without our stuff."

We? Before I determine what this we-ness might mean, the duo's whispered voices grow more intense.

Blondie is desperate. "But you *said.* We have to, man, we *have* to."

This time, I turn my head to glance at them straight on. Everyone else in the store does the same.

Again, I avert my eyes from the duo. I don't know what everyone else is doing.

The young clerk behind the counter looks about to shit his pants.

"I'm trying to *think* here, people." Skinhead looks about at the store patrons, myself and Professor Vale included, in a tone that connotes the most reasonable thing in the world. "I'm tryin' to *do* something."

"Then do it and please leave," Professor Vale, requests in a quiet, emotionless voice.

Oh God, Bucky…bad idea. Please shut up.

"When I'm good and ready," Skinhead says in a ridiculously prim voice. "But, what the hell? Guess I'm ready now."

Skinhead sighs deeply, and then, from under the folds of his gray hoodie, he pulls a stubby black pistol from the waistband of his pants. The gun is small and looks cheap, almost like a toy.

In the unreality of the moment, the first thing I think is, *That gun has got to be a fake. It looks like something from the dollar store.*

But it might be real, so I keep my mouth shut.

I don't feel frightened, though — even though I should. Only mild curiosity. I have my reasons for that.

This might surprise people. Not those who really know me, although there are precious few of those. And my thought is: *Looks like I won't need to decide about offing myself after all. Skinhead here might do the job for me.*

Here's the thing about that. Since Mom died, *nobody* really knows me anymore. And that's the core of this problem that people call Stella Denton.

During this millisecond while I ponder matters of life and death, Skinhead waves the gun from side to side in the cheesy manner of a Friday night cop drama.

"Don't nobody push panic buttons or call nine-one-one, nothin' like that, or I'll take you all out. I mean it."

Skinhead is wearing his best Bad Guy hat now.

I have to admit he's got everyone's horrified attention.

Paralysis descends over the few patrons remaining in the store. The ominous sensation feels like ink ejaculated over us by an octopus in dark levels of the sea. Everyone freezes, motionless, and a woman with dark lipstick makes frightened, mewing noises. I don't move.

But I feel myself getting ticked off. If anyone's going to take me out, I want it to be my *own* idea, for my own reasons, in my own time. When I choose. Not some piece of trash with zits and a cheap handgun.

"Show us the money!" Blondie demands. His voice aims for belligerence but comes out in a squeak.

Aiming his gun at the clerk, Skinhead curls his lip in disgust. "Christ, Leon, no movie lines." He looks at the clerk. "Just hand over the cash."

"We…don't keep anything larger than two twenties." The young clerk speaks between stiff lips, parroting lines from his training manual. He's so breathless, he can hardly speak.

"Liar!" Skinhead retorts in a petulant voice. He spews saliva droplets like profanities on those of us nearest him. I'm so close I can see the unwashed smudge of ingrained dirt behind his ear.

"There's a *mess* of cash in there. I saw it earlier." Again, he brandishes the gun in his odd, prissy manner. "So, open up. *Now.*"

Idly, I note that the barrel of his gun is, literally, gun-metal gray. I didn't know they really were, in real life, exactly as described in books and on TV.

At this inopportune time, the voice that lives inside my head—the one I call Squirrelly Girl in a none-too-chummy fashion—chooses this inopportune moment to commence a running commentary.

"What a surreal night *this* is turning out to be!" she says with a metaphorical dig to my ribs. "First Professor Vale's surreal PowerPoint show about Jarmo, and now *this*…"

Without meaning to or even realizing I'm doing so, I inch closer to Professor Vale. Nightmare lights, ugly people, silly toy gun. What am I even *doing* here?

Where is my *real* life, the life I was meant to live? Or is this…it?

Awkwardly, I take a full step backward toward Professor Vale, thinking only of my unvoiced desire for Bucky to dispel the hysteria around me.

Instead, I manage to collide with an adjacent beef jerky rack.

The small metal kiosk topples, glances off a display counter, and slams squarely against the middle of Skinhead's back. I couldn't have done it more effectively if I'd planned it out beforehand with logarithms.

Skinhead turns, yowling in pain, gun arm flailing in a wide arc.

We store patrons crouch low, myself included. Some are already huddling on the floor, whimpering in fear. Skinhead looks down his nose at me in crazed outrage, while Blondie continues to demand of the clerk, "Gimme the *money*, gimme the money *now*…and don't press any buttons, or I'll blow your balls off."

Rooted with fear, the clerk won't—probably can't—even move. The cash drawer remains shut.

As if from a great distance, I hear Blondie's voice rising to a shriek. "Gimme the money, gimme the *money*, hand it over *now!*"

A couple of patrons, bolder than the others, plead with the clerk. "So, give him the *money* already!"

The clerk's eyes are glazed with panic. He opens and closes his mouth like a fish, unable to comprehend that this is really happening.

"Well, fuck this shit," Skinhead says in elegant disgust. And shoots the clerk in the face.

The clerk's face instantly morphs into a crimson azalea, red petals radiating from a hole where his nose has been. He sways on his feet for a sickening millisecond, then falls heavily against a potato chip rack.

In the flailing and shrieking pandemonium that immediately follows, the gunmen wake from their Bad Guy fantasy in dismay and fear. Shit. *Shit…* what has just happened?

Most of the store patrons hit the floor in fear or start running for some kind of cover.

Skinhead looks around in a panic while Blondie scrambles behind the counter and immediately pounds on the electronic cash register, hoping to hit a magic button that will open it. Huddling on the floor, the purple-lipped girl keeps screaming. Overwhelmed by the turn of events, Skinhead shoots toward the front counter again, wildly aimless, in panicked frustration.

Oh *God!* Professor Vale is shot. In the thigh. I'm on the floor next to him and see the resulting blood flow, copper-scented and glistening.

Before Skinhead can shoot a third time, I experience a split second of great clarity, tingling and intense. Harry Vale stares at me fiercely (as if to keep me safe by the power of his gaze alone), grasping his gory leg to stanch the blood flow.

In a millisecond, I see the innocent potato chip bags, cookies, and motor oil, so safe and normal in their crowded rows. I hear the frightened bleats of the other patrons, huddled and shuddering on the floor.

THUK.

The gun's abrupt report fills my world. *Oh shit* is all I can think for one billionth of a second. The THUK sound rushes at me and into my head. Just behind my left ear.

Instantly it's in my brain, already a part of me. The bullet slows from its insane velocity and finally just…stops. It hasn't traveled as bullet-fast as it would have, had he aimed it at me point blank. This bullet must have ricocheted off something metal, altering its trajectory at the last moment.

The bullet entry site feels like black velvet fire. It pulls the rest of me into its fathomless depths.

In a nightmare miasma of screams, blood, shouting, a garish swirl of lights and sudden coldness, I find myself looking down on the scene from a great height. Evidently I'm somewhere near the ceiling.

I grow smaller yet higher in vantage point. Soon I'm only a pinpoint of consciousness hovering somewhere beyond the ceiling.

Then the scene below me dims, obliterated by the sound and odd sensation of rushing waters. A millrace of dark, billowing bubbles surges in, around, and through me. The noise is deep. Soothing. Inexorable. How a pinpoint of consciousness can hear I do not know, but I do hear it—a deep, soft, underwater roaring sound that fills my world.

I realize that the bubbles are moving me toward a tunnel. *The* Tunnel. The one that's said to open up before you when you're about to die.

Then I realize that I don't want to die after all. At least, not just yet.

I want…I want.

I want the silliest, strangest thing!

I'm almost ashamed to admit it to the universe, even when I'm almost dead. If I still had a face and tears, I'd be crying right now. Even as a pinpoint of light, strong emotion shimmers within my life force. *I want to live the kind of life I was* meant *to live.* Like what the professor was telling us about earlier tonight: a life in Jarmo.

Jarmo…

The sound of that name alone draws my formless self deeper into the tunnel where eternity awaits.

CHAPTER 2
Seeking Jarmo

Flow, flow, flow.
The current of life is ever onward.
᠊ Kobodaishi ᠊
774–835 A.D.

Stella, three hours earlier

I look in the mirror. Deep sigh. *Come on, Squirrelly Girl. Chin up, eyes front.*

Comb my hair—chin-length reddish brown, lank as a paper bag—check.

Dust a poof of blush on each side of my face—check. Even though I can't tell much difference.

Change out of my Minnesota Golden Gophers sweatpants and into jeans (my fat jeans at present, since I still haven't lost my Freshman Fifteen, even though I'm a Senior now)—check.

Change my shirt, slip on clogs, grab a jacket and my over-the-shoulder book bag, which holds a laptop and a couple of tampons—check.

I'm trying not to be too noticeably late for my night class, Paleoanthropology 110, a two-credit thing for an hour once a week. Tonight is the last class. The credits for my General Studies major got snarled around the time my mother died, and I missed so many classes. I'm still filling in what's needed so I can graduate this semester.

Locking the door behind me, I start walking briskly from my tiny, off-campus hovel. I should have left earlier. I step along smartly to my latest mantra, silently mouthing the words in time with my steps.

Everything happens…now in my life…in God's perfect order.

A nontraditional student (that older lady I chatted with last week after Social Welfare 250) swore to me it was a Sure Thing. "Guaranteed to sort out what ails you…eventually…"

I repeat the words over and over as I walk the six short blocks to Filsen Hall. I don't feel any better yet. Or different.

I yearn for change. Or maybe obliteration. Which would be so much easier, since there's no one around who really cares.

Yeah, I'm an orphan. How Dickensian is that? Lonely but literary, I give you that much.

Everything happens…now in my life…in God's perfect order.

God. I don't even know if I believe in one…in Him…in it… whatever.

I don't know. Maybe. I hope there's someone. Something. Not just me and the great void.

Most of the time, all I feel is hollow. I have very few friends, but that's my own fault; Mom always told me that to have a friend, you have to be one, and I know that she's right. *Was* right.

It's just that I can't seem to muster the effort. Whatever I do, whatever I try, I feel like I'm living a shadow life. Even my footsteps sound hollow. It's these stupid clogs. What was I thinking? Nobody wears clogs anymore.

Quit thinking so much and step along, Squirrelly Girl chatters at me. *You're going to be late.*

Okay, if I'm being honest here, I'm not *totally* alone in the world. There *is* my stepdad Chuck, thank goodness.

Mom assured me my bio-dad was nobody I'd ever care to know, an inadvertent sperm donor and a non-issue for both my mother and me. Really and truly, I've never missed him.

Chuck married "us" when I was thirteen, bless his heart, and he's been a jewel all along. He covers my health insurance without a murmur, pays my state school tuition, bought me a decent used car, whatever I want or need.

I can't blame him for wanting, and recently finding, a new thirty-something girlfriend.

Last year, Chuck moved to Chicago where he now lives with Laura. She seems like a sweetie, but what do I know, really? I have a hard time even breathing when I think about Real Life, my upcoming life after university. And Real Life for me is coming up pretty fast. The U of M will all be behind me once I graduate next month.

The presence of Laura in Chuck's new life makes it pretty clear, even to someone as clueless as I am, that I've got to start moving forward, too. Make a new niche for myself. Thank goodness for college all this time—you know, a familiar framework where you know what's expected of you.

Chuck always urges me to move into a dorm ("Get to *know* folks, Stella-girl, live a little!") or even to try for a sorority. I ask you, a sorority? I'm sure sororities aren't looking to include bovine cleaning ladies among their numbers. I finally convince Chuck that I'm much happier in my own, private, ratty studio apartment instead. I *think* he believes me. At least he pretends to.

The thought of so much estrogen swirling together at the dorms or a sorority house, all together in one place, rattles me. Because I'm just so…well, slow on the uptake. You know, all that chirpy, witty, bitchy female banter and stuff—I couldn't keep up with it in sixth grade, and I sure as hell can't do so now. Popular girls seldom know, or care, when I leave a room. And men notice even less than that. Living the shadow life that I am, it just doesn't seem like I fit. Or belong. Anywhere.

I just need some motivation to start figuring out my future.

Or to decide if it's all too much for me, and do I even want a future at all.

Bless her heart, dear Mom…how I miss her. She'd be in agony right now (an agony of tenderness and empathy) knowing I was even considering such a final solution. But, sometimes…well, it feels like I'm in the wrong world at the wrong time, with nothing to be done about it except endure—or to check out.

Everything happens…now in my life…in God's perfect order.

Yeah, right…

This neighborhood that I'm walking through is kind of dodgy. I'd drive to this class, but the nearest parking lot is ten blocks away from Filsen Hall. I've just passed the Whistle-Stop convenience store. Only two more blocks.

Finally. Exhaling with relief, I clomp-clomp up the steps of Filsen Hall, then down again to the ground floor partial-basement where the windows are at street level. I'm panting more than I should (Thank you, Freshman Fifteen!). There's not a minute to spare before class.

And there he is, Professor Harry Vale. Harry *K.* Vale. Known to many of us students as Bucky Beaver. Professor Vale and I both resemble members of the *Genus Rodentia.* Round cheeks, recessive chins, prominent teeth, and stolid, stocky builds. More like brother and sister than anything else.

Shit, I'm really late.

I scribble the initials SJD next to my name on the clipboard list by the door. Professor Vale is a stickler for attendance, figuring it into our final grade. I try to tip-toe in (hard to do in clogs) as I seek an empty seat. Every grotty theater seat in the small, amphitheater-shaped classroom is taken, except for down in front. The other students are already in place, rummaging in beat-up backpacks, opening laptops. I slide into a front row seat; my nose is practically within touching distance of Professor Vale's fly. Averting my head, I open my MacBook Pro, turn it on, and look up into his face instead.

Professor Vale starts out the same as ever. A creature of habit, he shoots his cuffs—check. Clears his throat—check. Fumbles to straighten a clip-on bow tie—check. Then he gives me a (reproachful?) glance before he begins.

Probably annoyed that I'm late. He doesn't really know me, though, and I don't really know him. I mean, not *really.* Not hardly. Not like some girls I know who flaunt affairs with their professors, even the married ones.

As if I could ever—I mean, really, as if! As if anyone would ever ask me to.

Okay, yes, so the professor has seen me through all classes in this course—I haven't missed a one, for some reason or another. Strange on my part.

But again, yes, I'm a name on his electronic spreadsheet. My face is a blurry egg under fluorescent lights with few distinguishing characteristics to set me apart from the crowd. But, late as I am, now he actually looks down and sees me.

He looks at me for a moment before commencing to speak—a long moment, actually. Then he clears his throat, takes a dry marker, and in slanting capitals, he writes the words *NEOLITHIC* and *JARMO* on the whiteboard.

My fellow students and I settle in for the duration. The past few weeks, Dr. Vale has managed to transform a potentially interesting topic — the prehistory of modern humankind — into a dry insurance seminar.

Squirrelly Girl starts commenting as Professor Vale makes the dry marker squeak on the board amid the hush of the class.

I should tell you, I don't *really* hear voices; it's just my subconscious talking. From what I can tell, everyone has that voice in their head. And mine is particularly snarky, always looking for dirt to dish about someone...usually me. Tonight it's a running editorial commentary about Harry Vale.

Hmm, he's got to be over thirty. Almost middle-aged. Dorky glasses — not old enough to look new, not new enough to look fashionably old. And what's with the baggy corduroy jacket with leather elbow patches? Which hasn't been hot since 1972. No ring. No woman in this guy's life, I'm willing to bet. No guys either, I'm also willing to bet. Probably teaches extra Adult Ed classes to pay bills. Does the brown bag thing every day — probably bagels with cream cheese and a salted nut roll for dessert. Eats at his desk, then actually saves the lunch bag to reuse the next day.

Sheesh, Miss Denton! He's almost as bad as you.

Professor Vale stops writing, and the dry marker ceases to squeak.

Our instructor draws in a shaky breath and turns to face the class.

His eyes now seem brighter than usual with what appears to be suppressed excitement. For the first time ever he looks...alive.

"The Neolithic Era —" He pauses then, as if to emphasize the momentous news he's imparting. "— is the most important time... in the history of all humankind." Professor Vale stops talking. He looks at us as though expecting a response.

Most of my classmates look dully back at him, exuding a collective, unspoken *So?*

"I've put together a PowerPoint about it. Don't worry; it's short. To, uh, celebrate this, our last class before finals next week. But first, an introduction..."

I see that a laptop is set up on a table in front of the class, plugged in and already humming faintly. A ten-foot movie screen is pulled down, covering the center of the whiteboard.

Finally, something different for this last class in the series.

He puts aside his usual speaking notes. Vale is going rogue.

"So far in our coverage of the Paleolithic, the Old Stone Age, and the Mesolithic or Middle Stone Age, we've learned how both eras were critical in human development. But the Neolithic—particularly that sliver of time just before the Dawn of Civilization—the Neolithic was the most important time *ever*, making us the people that we are today."

What does he mean, the most important *ever*? More important than Google?

Professor Vale's gaze sweeps the class once more, hoping for a response.

Again I feel, rather than hear, the silent drowsiness of the class. *So?*

And then I see it. Something I've never seen on Vale's face before: the faint indentation of a dimple. A single, misplaced dimple on his chubby left cheek.

It's never been evident before because Vale—always so serious, so earnest—rarely smiles in class. At least not enough to show evidence of a dimple.

But he's smiling now, or something very close to it.

"The Neolithic era rose and fell within different time periods throughout the world. But in the Fertile Crescent of the Middle East, in a little village we now call Jarmo, it flourished around 7000 BCE. That's about nine thousand years ago…uh, give or take a few years."

Vale clicks something on the laptop, moves a pile of reference books closer, and turns down the lights. He fusses over a few adjustments, clicks play, and the screen springs to life.

A classical music piece I'm not familiar with starts playing in the background. It's lush and evocative. Compelling. The image of a sunny, grass-covered hill against a backdrop of snow-capped mountains fills the view. The single word JARMO is superimposed over the image in dark blue letters with a yellow drop-shadow.

"Most of us think civilization is pretty damn great, don't we? We think it *has* to be, because we're living in it. Cars, space shuttles, Smartphones, Nine Inch Nails—it's all the world we've ever known. But, as many of you may agree, it can be an exhausting world, too. At least to me."

Some students sitting near me look thoughtful then. They study their hands or nibble at a fingernail.

"Faster and faster, higher and higher, doing more and more work for less and less money. Buying more stuff we don't even need — and don't really want. 'They' just *tell* us we should want stuff. But I'm getting ahead of myself. Let's get back to Jarmo…"

Professor Vale clicks to the next image: an archaeological dig of a prehistoric village, half-excavated, a couple of football fields in length and width.

The partially exposed town crowns the crest of a hill. Along one side, the hill drops off toward a broad river valley; along the other side, forbidding snow-capped mountains jut heavenward in the distant horizon. The land around the village is parched, dusty, and eroded.

I can't help thinking, *Poor little town…what a God-forsaken place to live.*

Vale continues. "Jarmo is…*was*…a gathering place of prehistoric humans from around 7000 to 5000 BCE — deep in the wilderness near present-day Kirkuk in Iraq."

Well, no wonder it looks dreary, Squirrelly Girl decides. *Iraq! What do you expect?*

"Jarmo is just one of dozens — maybe dozens upon dozens — of similar small gatherings in Asia and Europe during the Neolithic Era. Nothing special about Jarmo. The only reason we know about it at all is because of the Braidwoods — photographer Linda Braidwood and her famous archaeologist husband, Dr. Robert Braidwood of the University of Chicago, who, so it's been said, just happened to be the model for Indiana Jones."

Actually, that is pretty cool.

Professor Vale quickly clicks through image after image of the hot, dry dig site, and continues his commentary. "Note the presence of primitive Mother Goddess figures here…one of the earliest sites with decorated pottery…sun-dried bricks…just beginning to grow emmer and einkorn grains, a few plots here and there…note this partial figurine with blue stripes down its cheeks — vestiges of the blue pigment are still evident…"

Another click brings up a Photoshop rendering of what looks like the Garden of Eden — a lush field, surreally green, dotted with red poppies, indigo larkspurs, and wild purple hollyhocks. Heavenly green countryside encircles a tiny, hilltop town—Jarmo. In the background, snow covered peaks rise sharply. Foothills are thickly dotted with both hardwood and conifer trees. Resembling Monopoly game pieces, tiny houses in the village look to be mud brick rectangular with peaked, thatched roofs.

Idyllic. No other word can describe it so perfectly.

"Now *this* lovely place—" Vale indicates the picture-perfect image on the screen "—in addition to the dusty, sun-baked excavation site we've just been viewing, this is *also* Jarmo."

Professor Vale removes his glasses, rubs the bridge of his nose—as if to bring the image more clearly in focus—and replaces his eyewear. "Jarmo, the way it *used* to be. The *world* the way it used to be. Until humans got too smart for their own good and started fucking it up."

Vale is on a high horse tonight. Actually talking like real people talk. Something's afoot…

"I'm going to click through a few more images of Jarmo the way it used to be—designed and Photoshopped, by the way, by a grad student at the University of Chicago. Also, if anyone is interested, the music is 'Andante con Tenerezza' from Symphony No. 2 of American composer Howard Hanson. Check him out sometime.

"In case you're wondering why Jarmo looks so different now, two-thirds of the difference is due to gradual climate change over the years. And one third is due to domestication of the goat, which chews everything right down to the dirt—spawn of the very devil that they are! The Jarmo of 7000 BCE, the timeframe represented in these images, enjoyed a warm, moist, Mediterranean climate. Just about anything could grow there and probably did.

"I'm going to read you some passages from scientific experts who agree with me."

In the dim light, Professor Vale opens the first of a series of books that bristle with Post-it notes. He clicks to an image that looks like Africa's Serengeti, a vast plain dotted thickly with wildlife, then snaps on a penlight to read.

"Listen to educator Richard Heinberg, here," Vale prefaces his reading. "'Our stereotypical image of primitive foragers is of bands of half-starved savages, usually exhausted from searching for roots and berries, or hunting wild animals, engaging in periodic bloodthirsty raids on one another's camps, and living in superstitious terror of the capricious and mysterious natural forces controlling their lives. Instead, however, early myths portray the lives of these peoples as supremely happy. Surprisingly, recent findings of anthropologists and archaeologists tend to support this new, happier view.'"

Professor Vale sets the book aside, then clicks to a scene of a rock-rimmed hot springs, adjoining a rushing stream.

"There was a hot springs at Jarmo in those days. Not now, of course. It's been sucked dry across the millennia. Braidwood's team identified the original location through fieldwork and excavation. Just think, hot and cold running water, abundant wildlife, and plenty of food, ripe for the gathering. At Jarmo, they had it all."

Professor Vale opens another book. "And one scholar, a plant physiologist, says that developing agriculture was the worst thing humankind could have done."

He looks back at us. "I mean, *think* of it! We were never meant to be this way—stressed, depressed, compressed into a megalopolis—multiple megalopolises. Not at all! Humankind was meant to live in balance, like that of Jarmo."

Click to an image of assemblage of painted pottery shards, white snail shells, and a handful of pistachio nuts.

"And here again with Heinberg…" Vale picks up the first book again and turns to another Post-it note. "'Most agricultural societies tend to adopt a diet based on relatively few foods, usually two or three starchy grain crops that by themselves do not provide a sufficient variety of balance of nutrients. Foragers, on the other hand, knew how to obtain a wide range of foods. Paleopathologists, who study evidence of disease in prehistoric human remains, find that the skeletons of ancient hunter-gatherers tend to be larger and more robust and show fewer signs of degenerative disease and tooth decay than do those of the later agriculturalists.'"

He peers at us over the book. "Imagine! In those days at Jarmo, people were stronger and healthier. Their bones were literally thicker. It's a fact. They were more peaceful—in short, happier. The way we were *meant* to be…before civilization corrupted us all."

He clicks another image forward, this time a charcoal drawing of a small, mud-brick, thatched-roof cottage. He grabs another book eagerly. "And *time!* Listen to this. Leisure time versus laboring time. Do you know, really *know*, what slaves we are to this, this…unnatural maelstrom, this rat maze, we call modern life?"

He's got us now. *This* we can understand. Time, we value. Of *course* we live in a rat-maze, stressful and pressured, too often meaningless — we all know that. Has it not always been so, since men, and women, first rose head and shoulders above the apes?

"Consensus among paleoanthropologists now says that hunter-gatherers only devoted some twelve to twenty hours per week obtaining food. Only twenty hours per *week!* The rest of their time was likely devoted to leisure, to family and friends, music and storytelling, and art — *art!* Like this…"

Click to a close-up of a voluptuous mother goddess figurine. "Note what looks to be a letter H on her forehead — it only *looks* like an H, of course, because there was no Western alphabet in Jarmo — no form of writing at all yet. Not for at least another three thousand years."

"Life in primitive, food-gathering societies like Jarmo was one of a stable, loving community, supportive relationships throughout life, a friendly peaceful attitude toward others, and the challenge of direct engagement with nature."

Professor Vale's square face seems to glow from within. The single dimple flashes on his cheek as his words tumble out in a rush. "Game species were at their peak. Fat and sassy they were from abundant forage, *millions* of 'em. So many that the dire wolf and small-eared lion probably left humans pretty much alone, concentrating on the great herds that roamed everywhere. It was a time of lavish plenty, with fruits and nuts, roots and greens. Easy pickings. A morning's hunt and a few days' gathering could keep you in food for a week!"

He shakes his head ever so slightly in reverence and regret. "It was life as it was *meant* to be lived! Not…not life like *this.*"

Vale gestures about him, encompassing the soiled, 1990s-style, tiered theater seats, the growing darkness outside the tall windows, muffled traffic sounds, the sickly sweet smell of sweeping compound blending with the garlic odor emanating from the overused microwave down the hall.

"It was better back then for *all* of us. Better for women especially."

Click on a small, clay figurine. The indistinct clay face is crowned with elaborate braided hairdo, three lines etched down each cheek.

"Dr. Marian Polk writes about the thousands of years when men and women lived together in true partnership. She says Neolithic settlements show no signs of male dominance. How do we know?

One way is by their graves. The graves of Neolithic women and men were equal in size and provision. There were few signs of the rigid, hierarchical social structure that later came to characterize civilization. Human relations in Neolithic times were based on peace, cooperation, and mutual nurturing."

Suddenly, I feel as if I'm holding my breath, and I'm not sure why. Professor Vale's gaze looks from face to face in the dim half-light. He looks into my face for a moment…longer than a moment… then moves on.

"In those long ago days, in what we used to call the Near East, something unique flowered for a time. Scientists call it the Late Neolithic, a way of life beautiful in its simplicity."

Vale's face takes on a private, inward look just then. He looks over the class with quiet earnestness.

"*I* call it the time of the Great Exhale." Vale breathes out softly. Then his face takes on a weary look.

Somehow his dramatic gestures don't seem corny; to everyone's credit, no one snickers. The class seems moderately interested now, listening politely, but no one really seems charged with emotion. Except for Professor Vale. And me.

And I have no idea why. *Am I headed for another panic attack?* The voice in my head sounds a little shaky. It's been at least a couple of months since the last episode. *Oh no. Not here, not now.* Since Mom died, I've experienced these brief but unnerving episodes with increasing frequency. They're no joke, I can tell you. The breathlessness, pounding heart, sweating, heat, then cold, then heat again, and the trembling — so dizzying, making other people's voices sound as if they're coming from inside a conch shell.

I feel my cheeks flush and touch them surreptitiously. My skin is so warm. Too warm — hot, actually to the touch. I try to imagine that Mom is close by, telling me lovingly to *Hush now, hush now. It will be all right. Everything happens, now in your life, in God's perfect order. Hush now, hush…*

Professor Vale's voice sounds somber now. Without knowing why, I find myself leaning closer to catch his words. An odd feeling grows in me, a deep, vibrating thrum.

"The heyday of Jarmo is what I call the Breathing Space," he says, "between the earlier harsh times and the later harsh times to come.

What's conspicuous in most Neolithic digs is the complete *absence* of weapons of war, although there are plenty of tools and pots. Of course, archaeologists haven't excavated *all* of Jarmo yet—there may be levels and clues and evidence of things we know nothing about… not yet. But, given what's happening these days in Iraq, Afghanistan, and Syria, it doesn't seem likely they *will* be fully excavated. At least, not any time soon."

Because I'm sitting close to him this evening, I can see Vale's myopic eyes, bright and blue and shining behind the dated glasses, even in the dim, reflected light from the PowerPoint.

Again, his eyes pause at my gaze for a moment. And I feel…strange.

No guy, not even a nerdy professor like Vale, has ever really looked at me like that. But this one is, and I like the way it's making me feel more alive, too.

I keep watching his blue eyes, which by now have looked back at the screen, and I'm mesmerized by his voice.

"Because later life *was* harsh, you see, once civilization came into being, even though cultivated grains were then plentiful. As we all know, civilization doesn't necessarily mean life is easy. Life *today* isn't easy. Civilization isn't just the wheel, or making pottery, or domesticating horses to pull chariots. Or even inventing writing. Civilization also means warfare and famine, slavery and bloodshed, food scarcities and a befouled environment."

Again, he looks at me shyly, then looks away.

A ferret-faced guy three seats away raises his hand. "But wasn't it good when agriculture came into being, so there was more food for everybody?"

"Just the opposite," Professor Vale replies quietly. "In the Jarmo of 7000 BCE, they were just starting to experiment with planting grains. Not taking it seriously—yet. But eventually agriculture seduced them, and it ended up making more work than ever, more work for everyone. The Breathing Space I'm talking about was that time period just before agriculture really got going. The Breathing Space was an era in balance. It was…Eden."

Suddenly, it all becomes clear to me: *I want…I belong in…a Jarmo kind of life.*

"No modern stress, no traffic, no income tax, and—" he almost glares at the class as he continues "—*no* war. Human beings were too few and thinly scattered for warfare. And they had nothing to go to war about—until that time when resources started giving out."

I speak then without thinking (something I've never done before in class), and my voice sounds swoony, even to me. "But it sounds like such an…easy time!"

A student somewhere snickers, but Professor Vale only looks at me. Almost tenderly. His silence lengthens. At last he says, "But, Miss Denton, that's the *point.*"

He knows my name. He's matched my name with my face. I'm more than astonished. Actually, I'm blown away. I clutch the edge of my seat to settle my inward trembling.

I blunder on, only half aware of what I'm saying. "But, with all that time at their disposal, did they also do something important and memorable?"

Professor Vale's face turns pale and serious. "They did. Eventually. As I mentioned earlier in the PowerPoint, the wheel was invented in Mesopotamia around 4500 BCE, the chariot soon after, and writing a thousand years after that. To the ultimate detriment of humankind."

The professor shakes his head and backs up, metaphorically speaking. "Okay, that's just me yapping there. Another story for another class, maybe. By the time these improvements came along, three thousand years had passed since the Eden time of Jarmo. Their descendants were deep in the throes of agriculture by that time, so they *had* to invent the wheel and *had* to tame the horse. They desperately needed technology to pull carts, plow, drive chariots, and turn water wheels. When the Jarmo folk started taking on the mantle of civilization, they never knew it was already too late."

His voice enchants me into further speech. "Too late for…"

"Too late to keep earth like Eden. Heaven on earth, as it were. Because it wasn't the snake that cast Adam and Eve out from the garden, it was civilization."

More students snicker then, but Vale's face remains impassive.

I persist (Where is this extroversion coming from? It's not my usual style at all.): "So, they didn't build pyramids, or…or dig canals, or do *anything*, rather than just…than just—"

"Just be?" Professor Vale finishes my sentence, looking at me. Silence gains substance in the classroom like a living thing. My heart is going like a rabbit's, and my hands are sweating with barely suppressed panic.

"Just to *be* can be an end in itself," he says softly. "And speaking of endings, you'll be glad to know that this last session tonight is a gimme—we're not going to have a final quiz after all. You'll get points for just showing up." Sudden cheers and fist-bumping erupt in the room. "Not so fast. Final exam is still next Tuesday. Same time, same place."

As if watching Superman transform into mild-mannered Clark Kent, I watch Professor Vale's face resume its former blandness. Professor Vale's body may still be there, but the man of passion I'd glimpsed earlier has gone back into his shell.

As students scramble to leave, Vale unplugs his laptop, grabs the resource books, and shoves everything into his battered book bag. He seems to be pointedly ignoring my part of the room. He waves a casual hand.

"So long, everyone, till Tuesday."

And then, just like that, he's out the door, up the stairs, and gone.

Meanwhile, *my* passion—this strange, persistent yearning for a time long vanished—still flutters against my ribs like a caged bird seeking escape.

And now here I am in the convenience store, just a short while later, blood pouring from my wounded head. As my caged-bird soul seeks literally to separate from my body.

Poised between death and life, I drift inexorably toward the Tunnel of Eternity.

Oh, thank *God!* And right now I do. Literally.

The Tunnel is real, and it's there. And I can see light at the far-distant end of it.

Amid the swirl of gray bubbles, I start drifting in a current toward the light.

Then, without warning, I approach a wide spot in the Tunnel where smaller, alternate tunnels veer off in different directions. *What?* No near-death account I've ever read featured detours like this.

While light still beckons irresistibly from the Tunnel's main branch, I'm abruptly pulled off by a current and shunted off on a kind of side channel.

There's no light at the end of this tunnel. Only a soft, dark-gray mist. Its sides are indistinct, blurring past me so quickly I can't make out what's what, or where I am exactly. And then I'm slowly descending, gently sinking deeper and deeper into a growing darkness. Down, and down, and down. Until I'm immersed in what feels like warm water.

I don't think about whether I have a body or not. Whether I'm breathing or not.

There's no beginning and no end to anything.

I merely Be.

CHAPTER 3
Between Lives

Which is more difficult,
to awaken one who sleeps or
to awaken one who, awake,
dreams that he is awake?
~ Søren Kierkegaard ~
1813–1855

Harry

In the darkness, sirens blare their warning. Instead of waxing and waning with the Doppler effect (the only way I've ever heard them sound), the noise seems to come from inside my head. The siren is probably on the hood of the vehicle like on those medical or cop rescue shows.

But I've never been inside an ambulance before...till now.

I'm lying on a long, narrow bench seat in the fast-moving vehicle, flanked by two serious-faced young EMTs. Someone is driving this tub like a wild man. I never knew there were so many chuckholes in the road. And we're hitting every one in super-quick succession.

On a separate stretcher, one of my students from Paleoanthropology 110, Stella Denton, lies motionless next to me, bloody and waxen.

The third shooting victim — the convenience store clerk — is in a separate ambulance, or so I deduce from a few terse words shared among the EMTs. No need for rushing in the case of the clerk. He's dead.

Dead. Even thinking that word feels like a slap across my face by a vicious hand. Not just one of many plot points like on a TV show. But dead like really *gone*. I don't know why, but I'm always surprised that death is so blithe and heartless. Just like *that*.

And it could have been me. Or her.

The police showed up almost instantly. Don't know who phoned it in. One of the customers probably.

It *did* feel like a TV show then. Police clicking endless pictures everywhere. They took statements from all the living, including me. They even draped the yellow crime scene tape that I've seen in the movies.

I was hyper awake and aware now, quivering with excess adrenaline. My gunshot wound looked fake — ridiculous, impossible. It didn't even really hurt yet, except for an odd dry-ice feeling slowly spreading throughout my body.

The two shooters had battered the cash register until it finally opened, grabbed a paltry handful of bills, then fled the scene. They'll be on the security cameras, though — easy to identify eventually, what with the acne face of one and hyper-real thick lips of the other.

In the ambulance, I try to lift up my head to reinspect my own gore, but EMT One quickly says, "Down, boy!" and firmly presses my head back onto a small, flat pillow.

Meanwhile, we're shrieking down the road like a bat out of hell. EMT Two straps a tourniquet above the bullet entry hole in my leg. I yell in surprise, "Fuckin' A!" It hurts like I imagine acid rain might feel.

"Hang in there, buddy," EMT Two attempts to reassure me. "You're doing fine, gonna be okay. We're almost at HCMC. Just a few minutes more."

That's got to be Hennepin County Medical Center, our megametro medical center where they take gunshot wounds, knifings, and other less dramatic trauma. I have to say, I've never been in such illustrious company before.

"What about her?" I ask, looking at Miss Denton's deathly stillness and the pale green cast to her skin. Although mostly shrouded now by blood-soaked bandages and gauze, part of her face and neck is still visible; I can still see her prominent front teeth as we shoot by under the traffic lights.

As if he can read my thoughts, EMT One inserts a breathing device into her mouth and down her trachea; he adjusts the dials on a green cylinder of oxygen, attaches some type of breathing bag and begins to squeeze it rhythmically. He slowly moves the tube up and down till he seems satisfied the lungs are inflating from the side holes of the device.

Both EMTS are tending to Miss Denton now. Apparently my bloody situation is sufficiently under control. She still isn't moving—my God, how could she?

"What about her?" I ask again. And I sound shaky-querulous even to myself as I try to quell my rising panic. "She gonna make it?"

The EMTs suddenly look evasive. Noncommittal. "Time will tell," one finally says quietly. His worried face makes a weak attempt at a reassuring smile. "At least she's made it this far."

Suddenly everyone but Miss Denton braces as we scream around a tight corner. I think I can see a red-lighted sign, Emergency Entrance, approaching in the distance. Or maybe I'm just fabricating what I want so desperately to see.

Miss Denton's left hand slips off the stretcher, unnoticed in the commotion. Surreptitiously, I gently take it with my right hand. Nobody seems to mind. One EMT sees what I'm doing and smiles encouragingly.

Her hand is medium-sized, not particularly delicate or willowy. But it looks vulnerable, helpless even—if a hand, in and of itself, can be helpless.

She's just one of my students, one of so very many, someone I don't really know. Just another face in a sea of faces. But tonight, I felt a strange connection with her and...damn. Suddenly I felt like I knew her, really knew her, right down to her core. How? Why? And I knew that I wanted her, too. In every way a man can want a woman. Shit—the way I blasted out of class tonight, afraid of making a fool of myself if I stuck around. The first, and only, girl I've ever felt this *knowingness* about. And now, I probably never can again. Never will.

This knowledge makes me feel simultaneously desolate and disgusted with myself, even above the gore of the wound in my leg.

You don't deserve to have balls, you know that? You pathetic excuse for a guy. I'll bet that's what people say: poor old Bucky Beaver. Oh yeah, I know kids call me that sometimes behind my back—he can't ever catch a break.

EMT Two applies an IV drip to my arm, probably something mixed with saline for shock like they do on TV, and loosens the tourniquet around my thigh to allow blood to flow for a bit, and then tightens it again.

EMT One hooks Miss Denton's breathing device to what looks like an automatic ventilator and adjusts the settings, while also applying pad after pad of gauze to the soaked, scarlet bandage at the bullet's exit point. He discards them, one after another, as they turn scarlet. She's still bleeding profusely.

How can she not be dead already? And what will she be like if she manages to survive? I hear a faint beep beeping of a cardiac monitor but can't see it. Miss Denton's heart-sounds seem faint and erratic to me, with a long time between beats, then two or three clumped together.

But hell, what do I know about life and death matters like this? Precious little. I'm only an anthropology teacher. The lowliest of part-time Assistant Professors, not yet even a middle-grade Associate Professor, let alone a glorified Full Professor.

Isn't this just the shits. The voice in my head brings a rueful twist to my lips, part regret and part inward growl. Mediocre at my job, mediocre in my life…and now a girl I might actually have actually gotten to first base with is shot in the brain. It would almost be funny if it weren't a tragic nightmare.

Everybody loses this time, Bucky.

Suddenly I feel tears on my cheeks and hear a guttural sob. Shit, that's coming from me. My inner critic orders me, *Shut up, loser!*

I can't help it. All this truly is a tale told by an idiot. Shakespeare was right. We're experiencing the sound and fury together right now, here and now, and in the end, it will all mean nothing.

"Almost there now. Easy, now, don't try to get up."

City lights still stream by, neon signs and street lights a horizontal blur. A vision of fire ants, chewing their way to my femur, leaves me suddenly cold. My teeth begin to chatter. *Shit, shit…*

One of the EMTs checks Stella more closely and mutters, "Mort, this one's circling the drain. I need a couple bottles of saline or five-percent albumin if you've got 'em."

He jabs a big needle into Stella's IV port and starts the solution.

I squeeze Miss Denton's hand as we finally pull up to the Emergency Room door.

CHAPTER 4
Entering Jarmo

He was part of my dream, of course
But then I was part of his dream, too.
~ Lewis Carroll ~
1832–1898

Stella

Gray. Everything is softly muted and the color of gunmetal. (Again with the gun imagery. I note the irony even here, wherever here may be.)

The indistinct sides of the tunnel blur past me as what feel like bubbles — of course, they can't *be* bubbles, can they? — carry me off to who knows where.

I don't care. I feel no more substantive than fluff on a dandelion seed.

Then I start sinking down, and down, and down. All That Is becomes darker and darker, then inky black. I suddenly find myself in warm…water.

It envelops me. (I don't have a body, how can I feel water?)

My toes touch rounded gravel. (How can I step when I no longer have feet?)

Water gurgles, loudly and uncomfortably, against my eardrums. (Ears?)

Suddenly I gasp and try to breathe, choking and gagging on mouthfuls of water. Where the hell am I? A second attempt to breathe makes things much worse. Which way is up? (Is there such a thing as up anymore?)

I thrash my limbs (yes, I apparently have limbs again) in the dark water, swallowing water, surprisingly fresh but almost hot.

The darkness seems a bit lighter directly above me, and I move toward it. My arms break the surface, but I've little oxygen left to make another strong push. I flail about, gurgling and gagging.

Two pairs of arms grab my hands, pulling me partially out of the water. I'm on my knees on gravel, but at least my torso and rear end are out of the water.

I continue to sputter, gag, and heave for a while, my hands resting on my thighs.

Yes, I have thighs. I have a body again. But it doesn't feel familiar. I feel—elongated somehow. I feel...so different.

The two sets of arms that pulled me out—and the individuals belonging to those arms—retreat back as if afraid. Right now they're just two black, bunched-up shapes against a slightly less-dark background.

God. Shit. Wow.

I don't know what to think. Crap. Oh, crap...oh, wow. I'm woozy with fear and joy, confusion and terror. Shock and Awe has nothing on this.

I look up. A billion stars in an indigo sky arc overhead, while a pale pink dawn gathers momentum behind nearby mountain peaks. Light brightens everything now, more with every moment.

Now revealed by the approaching dawn, the two dark shapes are women. One very young, the other very old. The two stare at me in utter amazement—as if I were a unicorn, a starship pilot, or Bigfoot. For the moment, they're speechless with shock.

I look around me to better ascertain where in the hell I am. I'm kneeling—uncomfortably, truth be told—on some very hard gravel near the shore of what looks to be a large pond with an irregular perimeter. The water is so warm, soothing even, but not mucky, thank goodness. Large rocks rim the shore—put there by humans, I immediately sense; Nature wouldn't make such an arrangement. The pool's perimeter is dotted with clumps of cattails. Cautiously I look about. A rushing stream flows into the pool at one end, apparently moderating the water temperature, then egressing away and down the hill at the other end.

Finally, I no longer sputter or gasp. My breathing slows. A little.

I flatten my hands against my thighs and take a long, cleansing breath. In, out, and sigh...

My hands are slim, long, and tanned. My hands are not mine.

I look up at the women. They look like regular human beings, thank goodness. The gathering brightness of the dawn light shows me they have dark hair and tanned complexions. Like characters in pictures from my late grandma's bedside New Testament.

Although both women are naked, their shoulders are covered by loosely-woven shawls of some kind. Beside them on a boulder is another pile of fabric wrappings or skins or both.

Behind the women, a glorious dawn dims the stars as day breaks.

I attempt to rise to a standing position, but I can't. Guess I'm still wobbly and woozy with unbelief at finding myself here.

Only a moment ago, I was facing a gunman under sickly fluorescent lights in a convenience store. And now I'm...I'm...what?

Well, somebody has got to start talking around here. It might as well be me.

"Um, I seem to be...that is, I'm not sure how..." I'm not exactly covering myself with glory here. "I need a little help here. Would you mind pulling me up?"

Who knows what language they speak, if any. Maybe in this dream there is no language.

I don't know where in the world I am—or if I'm even *in* the world at all. Maybe I'm in an alternative reality that I'm making up as I go along.

I reach up one hand in supplication as I muster a nonthreatening smile.

"*Oh!* We didn't know you could talk!" the younger woman cries in astonishment. And in perfect American English. At least it sounds like English to me, but who knows—it must be telepathy or instant messaging or something. I remind myself that, hey, I'm dreaming. And anything can happen in a dream.

The older woman—she's almost scary-ancient—suddenly giggles and clasps her hands against her chest.

Both women come forward then. Cautiously. As if I'm still not to be trusted. Or believed. Not entirely.

Even so, they lean down to slip their arms around me, lifting me to a standing position and tugging me out of the water by my armpits. "Thank you, thank you," I murmur in relief as I stagger onto dry land between boulders that line the pond.

Looking down, *way* down, at this new body I'm in, I see that I'm tall — and I'm naked, too. But the women seem unconcerned about that, especially since they're mostly naked as well.

Already the sun is higher. Not a cloud is in sight. Everything's bathed in a golden glow.

I observe my slim, concave abdomen (well, it must be mine, since I'm inhabiting it — or at least borrowing it) and dark triangle of kinky brunet hair below. My other body — the one I woke up in this morning, a million miles and a million years away — is straight-up-and-down with pale, freckled skin and red pubic hair.

But now, all is different. My arms and legs are long, slim, and light brown. I reach up to feel the hair on my head — I see that it's long, brown, and wavy as it falls over my shoulders, wet from the pool. When dry, it will probably cascade even past my nipples, a pair of rosy-brown twins set in two perfect breasts. *Oh shit, oh wow...*

I must look, and I definitely feel, like the Blue Girl in the movie *Avatar*, only with no tail and with soft beige skin instead of blue.

"Are you a water spirit?" the elderly woman asks, still suspicious. The young woman stares at me curiously as she bites her lower lip.

"No, I'm just a —" What in the hell am I? "I'm a...girl — I mean, a woman. Like you."

"But where did you come from?" the young woman blurts. "I *know* you're not from around here. I know every single one of us. As far as you can walk in every direction for many days. How did you happen to come here to our hot pool and fall in?"

Best to get things sorted out right off the bat. "I...got lost in the dark."

But I sound like a dork, even to myself. Both women look highly dubious and properly cautious about my mysterious antecedents.

"Well, that is, not exactly." I shift my story to meet their expectations. What the hell — this is a dream (it has to be), and I can do what I want.

"I've come from a...long way away." I repress the urge to add "from a galaxy far, far away."

"You're not an obsidian trader?" they ask. Whatever that might be.

Shaking my head, I murmur, "No."

"You're not one of the People of the East?"

Again, I indicate in the negative. I hope that's the right answer.

Both women continue to look deeply suspicious. Even fearful. The young one crosses her arms over her chest. They're probably not sure if I'm really human or not. Any more than I'd be if Han Solo suddenly appeared while I was taking a bath.

I'd best do a more detailed explanation of things—and fast.

"You see, I…" Okay, I've made a start. Now how am I going to finish this sentence? "I was running away. From my…husband-to-be. Who beat me."

Holy crap, I'm spinning fantasies faster than I can flesh them out. But I've got to reassure these women that I'm not to be feared. Indeed—just the opposite. It's *I* who need their help and direction in this new world.

"He was so cruel; he…hurt me. I just couldn't marry him. So, in a moment when no one was watching, I…escaped. Far, far away into the mountains."

It seems to satisfy them. For a while. Then the ancient crone persists.

"But are you from the East, then? Beyond those mountains? We know little of those people, only what we hear from the obsidian traders. And that is, they're evil."

"No, I'm not from the East, and I'm not evil." I lower my eyes, then gaze at them with what I hope is a supplicating look. "I'm from even further away than that. I'm from where the…sun comes up."

I hope they don't ask me to elaborate. They don't. I must stay consistent with my details, lest I'm called upon to dredge them up later by somebody else.

I'm at a loss as to what to say or do next. I decide to look down at my hands with what I hope appears to be the weariness of a battered fiancée on the run.

The young woman looks more approachable but still dubious. "So, you mean to tell us that you escaped over those enormous mountains…"

I nod, warily.

The young woman continues. "All this way, on your own? Alone, with no visible weapons." She looks around but of course sees nothing like a weapon on my person.

"I lost them. Along the way," I hurry to add. "You know, mis-adventures." After a pause, I add, "It was a *very* long, hard journey."

They continue to eye me suspiciously, and the young one looks at me sideways. "All alone, out among lions, and hyenas, and auroch bulls?"

"I can't talk about it right now." Casting my eyes down, I put on what I hope is a fragile, tremulous expression.

How persistent these Dream People are! And how annoying.

In lucid dreams like this one, I'd always thought I could direct the action, so to speak, if I were ever lucky enough to *have* such a dream—which I never have until now. But these people, dreamish or otherwise, seem not so easily taken in.

"Well, all I can say is—" The crone's face is suddenly split by a broad grin. Several important teeth are missing. "—you're a better woman than I am! Well done, and welcome, and good riddance to any man who'd lay a hand on you!"

She flings her arms around me—the saggy batwings under her forearms brown and swinging—in a heartfelt hug. The young woman appears to capitulate *(oh, what the hell, I'll bite)* and joins our group hug with a tight squeeze around us both.

As we all come up for air, the crone tells me, "Surely the Great Mother has you in her special care. She must have a plan for you!"

"Grandmama, look!" The young woman exclaims suddenly. "Her eyes—they're *blue!* Just like Father's. I thought his were the only blue eyes in the world."

Both women suddenly look at one another. Passing between them critical information I can only guess about. Then they giggle.

"A sign from the Mother. And *what* a sign! What shall we call you? What is your name, strange woman?"

"Um, Stella. That's my name. My name means star. I'm the star from…afar." (Alliterative and dorky—but I like it. Stella the Star. That's what I want them to call me for as long as I'm here in this dream.)

"I'm Maidie, the chieftain's daughter, soon to wed Timon, and this is Grandmama who lives with us. She has no other name but Grandmama—or, if she ever did, we've forgotten it now!"

Both of them laugh, although I don't think it's particularly funny. The very idea—someone actually forgetting your name after living with them for years.

"Come on then, Stella the Star." Young Maidie takes my right hand while Grandmama reaches out and slips her hand into my left. "Let's go home."

Since they're unconcerned about their partial state of dress, I try to be also. I float on the surface of this dream with a bemused smile on my face.

Then I realize they must have come out at dawn for a dip in the hot springs. "You didn't get to take your bath yet. You mustn't let me keep you from it."

I'm starting to tremble a little. Whether from fear, awe, or the cold of the new morning, I can't say.

"Look at her, Grandmama. She's freezing!" The two women snatch up two woolen shawls from the small heap of coverings they've evidently left on a boulder by the pond. They proceed to dress me as if I were a baby or a doll. Maidie ties one shawl around my shoulders, while the old woman ties the second shawl around my waist like a sarong.

From the same pile, the young girl takes two long cured hides and two leather tie-belts. She passes one set over to Grandmama. Both tie them around their middles, leaving breasts only loosely covered by the shawls.

"We can take a bath later. *You* are more important—and exciting—than a bath!"

Maidie and the crone exchange a secret grin and the lift of eyebrows.

Confidentially, Maidie says to Grandmama, "She'll be *perfect* for you know who."

Grandmama laughs and nods her head vigorously. "Oh yes, yes! And high time, too."

Perfect for what? Perfect for who? What *is* this place anyway, and what am I even doing here?

Everything comes hurtling back at me then: the idyllic images of prehistoric Jarmo, Professor Vale's wistful smile and single dimple, the shooter's bullet ricocheting into my brain, the strange branch off the afterlife tunnel.

I'm not in heaven. Not in hell. Not even in purgatory.

Which tunnel branch did I travel to come to such a place?

"Come home with us. We'll take care of you. You must be famished, especially after such a dangerous journey."

Maidie and Grandmama lead me up a dirt trail leading toward the crest of a hill. I follow, wondering what this create-your-own-adventure has in store for me next.

"So…where is it exactly that we're going?" I venture to ask.

All stars have vanished now; the sky is angel-blue, clear, and vast. The sun — piercingly bright, vital, golden — climbs higher over the mountains. A vast, verdant river valley opens up into the distance off to my left, while we climb toward a hilltop village.

Square, mud-brick houses crown the hill like a dusky diadem.

Jarmo.

It can only be Jarmo.

The Jarmo of thousands and thousands of years ago.

I experience the disorienting feeling that I'm in a huge, living diorama in a museum in another galaxy.

Only…the disoriented sensation somehow feels *good.* Exciting. Real.

We walk the winding trail up the hill toward the village. I'm relieved that the trail is hard-packed dirt with a few rocks, not sharp gravel. In my new, barely covered body, I'm definitely what you'd call a tenderfoot.

"Jarmo," Maidie announces, as if in introduction, as we approach the crest of the hill. "Home, where we live. In the Old Language, Jarmo means home. Father lives there, too. He's the chieftain. And he's definitely going to want to meet *you!*"

CHAPTER 5
In Their Midst

A dreamer is one who can find his way by moonlight
and see the dawn before the rest of the world.
⟿ Oscar Wilde ⟾
1854–1900

Stella

The trail parallels a rushing stream that comes down from the high mountains to the edge of town, moving through the hot pool, then rushing beyond.

I keep glancing down at my feet in guilty fascination as we walk. My new feet are slender yet strong, narrow, and brown. And they're way, way down there, since my new legs are long and slender too.

It's crazy…me, being here in Jarmo, which hasn't existed for thousands of years. But I'm not afraid. I just feel *good*.

As we walk, I take stock of myself. At least I still know my own name, know who I am. Stella Denton, university student, twenty-and-a-half years old — younger than most of my classmates because Mom was able to start me a year early with home-schooling.

I know where I was yesterday: Professor Vale's two-credit Paleo-anthropology class, learning about a place called Jarmo. And let's not forget about the bullet. Or the fluorescent lights of the convenience store. Professor Vale's chipmunk cheeks and terrified blue eyes as my brain exploded in fire. I haven't forgotten those. I know *that* really happened. Somewhere. Somewhen.

But this…is *this* really happening?

Squirrelly Girl tries to convince me, but even she sounds uncertain. *This* must *be a dream, you doorknob. It's probably something that happens to some people when they lose consciousness and stay that way for a long time.*

Ah, but it feels good here. Birds are singing; everyone is smiling. I want to see more.

Inside my head, Squirrelly Girl gives in — not her usual style. *All right,* she says, rolling her metaphorical eyes. *You win. Dream it may be, but you'd be a fool not to step into this dream, right now, and live it to the fullest. For as long as it lasts.*

And I answer her with a vow: I will…I am…for as long as it lasts. Even if it goes on forever.

As we walk, the mud-brick, thatch-roofed houses of Jarmo grow closer in my view.

My heart beats faster — I'm excited. It may only be a dream, but it's a dream that feels strong and right and good.

We hike up and over that last bit of the trail. Then suddenly we're there, walking on level ground at the summit.

A young girl digging in a small vegetable patch looks at us, goggle-eyed. She exclaims, "Oh! Oh my!"

Hearing her cries, another woman emerges from a house, a toddler strapped to her back. "What? Who is this? Maidie, wherever did she come from?"

The women gabble like geese. Excited, puzzled, and evidently thrilled by the diversion of…me. I feel like a character in *Stranger in a Strange Land.*

At the sound of noisy babble, more women emerge from other houses. Several men, too. The men say little, open-mouthed as they appear to be — pole-axed yet intrigued — when we pass by. A gaggle of brown, smiling children follow us — me — like the Pied Piper. And I'm thinking, *Wasn't he the one who was hired to get the rats out of town? And stole the village's children instead?*

Grandmama says nothing, just keeps smiling her gap-toothed grin and looking over at Maidie. I observe Maidie looking back at her, again sharing that private look, both of them sporting an I've-got-a-secret grin.

Maidie addresses the gathering crowd on behalf of the three of us, moving with a sense of poised importance as we proceed through the village. "I'm taking her home to Father. Her name is Stella. She ran away from an evil suitor and made her way over the mountains to get here!"

The crowd murmurs and gasps at my boldness, punctuated by a few astonished chuckles.

Pretty soon, the whole town is following us. Thankfully, the air is celebratory, not threatening. It's as if the circus has come to town, and the circus is me.

I glance left and right at the small houses as we pass—my parade shows no signs of losing steam as others join the throng—and I marvel at how charming they appear. Tidy cobblestone foundations. Mud-brick construction. Thick, thatched roofs.

Before us, at the far edge of the settlement, an L-shaped house looms in my foreground. A cherry tree, studded with pale pink blossoms, leans toward the door.

"Father, Father!" Maidie calls. "Come out! Come see what we've brought you!" She's almost hopping from one foot to another, she's so excited. The crowd waits in hushed expectancy.

The little dream house has a door—a stout one, I see, with thick leather hinges, a latchstring, and a stone threshold. Someone, evidently Father, pushes the door open from the inside. Two dogs come bounding out.

"Whitefoot, Trusty, come!" Maidie orders. "Settle." Both dogs race toward her, then discover me and sniff me all over with great interest, especially my crotch. But eventually the dogs obey and settle, while still quivering with excitement.

A figure steps out and gazes in surprise at the crowd. It's a youngish man with chin-length dark, curly hair, and a short-trimmed brown beard. Not basketball-tall but, still, taller than I am. Tall enough. Younger than I'd have thought for being Maidie's father.

"Father, this is Stella," Maidie introduces me formally. "Stella the Star."

The crowd murmurs excitedly. *A star! She's tall…so bold…such big feet.*

"She escaped from an evil man over the East Mountains," Maidie elaborates to the townsfolk. "He was to become her husband."

A collective *oooooh* rises from the crowd.

Everyone watches Maidie's father to take their cues from his reaction. He must be a man of some importance.

I mind my Ps and Qs and keep facing forward politely. I feel like Dorothy Gale newly arrived in Munchkinland. It's as if everyone is reserving judgment about me until *he* acknowledges me. Until he speaks.

"Come forward." Maidie's father speaks with soft authority and looks into my eyes. Using a subtle motion, he beckons to me to step forward.

I take a couple of steps toward him. He continues to stare at me. Intently.

We're at the center of the crowd of townspeople, with Maidie and Grandmama flanking me on either side. I'm wondering if Glinda the Good Witch will arrive in a bubble any time now.

"Closer." He speaks even more softly. His eyes are deep-set, smudged by shadows, yet keenly blue. The most arresting eyes I've ever seen. Yet familiar, somehow.

Nervously, I step closer until I could almost touch him. But I don't.

I keep my chin down but my eyes up…and keep on minding those Ps and Qs.

I'm mesmerized by his wavy hair, blue eyes, and bare chest. Holy crap, all that and six-pack abs, too. Of course, *most* of the men of Jarmo—at least the ones I've seen so far—have six-pack abs as well. They undoubtedly lead a very physical life here.

He's wearing what looks to be a loose-weave wool kilt and sandals with crossed straps to his knees.

"But you couldn't have gotten over those mountains," Maidie's father finally says, playing the logic card. "Not yet, anyway. Too early. Deep snow in the pass for at least another moon."

"I just…stayed beneath the snow line…and kept on walking. And kept the river in sight at all times. Sir." This nonsense comes out of my mouth before I can even think about it. "At any rate, I'm here."

The crowd buzzes with even more excitement. "She speaks our language!"

"Yes, you're here," Maidie's father agrees with a politely raised eyebrow. "But, with what? No hunting weapons? Not even clothes to keep you warm? All alone?" He shrugs with a question in his eyes. "How do I know you're even a woman? You might be an evil spirit."

"But, Father…please, sir," Maidie pleads, hoping her prize will not be spurned.

Again I speak to Father and the villagers collectively. "I'm not. Sir. Not a water spirit or an evil spirit. Or any spirit at all. I'm a woman. Like any other."

Father continues to look at me. He knows something is off. He knows I'm not like any other. Knows I'm like no other person in Jarmo.

"Grandmama and I pulled her from the navel of Great Mother herself, from the sacred pool!" Maidie's argument is evidently an unassailable one, since he seems to immediately reconsider with a shrug and a nod. "Father, I know the Great Mother sent her for *you* so you don't have to wait for Kareli's time of First Blood."

Maidie's father keeps looking at me. Considering her words. He obviously likes what he sees before him. Conversely, I like what I see before me, too. But he's so young! How could he be the father of a teenager?

"Are you hungry…after your long journey?" he asks me politely. Still gazing. He still looks highly dubious of my story, but his expression now looks less like consternation, more like admiration. Or maybe inspiration.

"I'm famished!" I can't help blurting.

"Then we'll eat," he says. With the quiet confidence of a leader, Maidie's father turns to the crowd. "Leave us now. We'll definitely learn more of this matter, but first this traveling woman shall be fed, and I will hear her full story. You shall hear my full report in due time, probably in three days at the pairing ceremony—a double ceremony, now."

The crowd erupts in cheers, whistles, and glad exclamations.

What?

It sounds as if there's a wedding in my future. My very *near* future—in just three days' time.

CHAPTER 6
Learning the Ropes

Happiness is not only a hope, but also
in some strange manner a memory.
☙ G.K. Chesterton ❧
1874–1936

Stella

You'd think a little mud-brick house might be dark inside, but it's not. Inside the chieftain's house, open windows all around, flanked by upward supports and stout shutters, let in freshness and light.

After Father, Grandmama, and I enter the house, Maidie closes and latches the door behind her, effectively closing out the eyes of curious neighbors, at least for now.

I look around a bit apprehensively at my new…dream home.

Banked coals glow dimly in a fire pit at one end of the room. What looks like a hard-packed clay sink stands beside it. A canopy made of deerskin (or maybe the pelt of some animal I've never heard of) channels the fire pit smoke, venting it through a hole in the wall to the outside.

There's very little furniture, just rough-hewn shelves made of small split logs lying atop pegs pounded into the mud-brick wall. More pegs hang with homespun wool fabric and treated skins. Primitive pottery plates are in evidence; they look unfired, as if they'd readily dissolve in water. There's an array of animal bladders, full of liquids, tied off at the top and hanging from pegs. Stone grinding bowls contain mysterious dried objects. A few large bowls carved from wood are stacked beside the biggest window. The floor's hard-packed earth looks as if some amendment has been poured onto and mixed through it — maybe animal blood — giving the floor the serviceable aspect of cement.

On shelves along one wall, in a place of honor and importance, are the hunting weapons. Several wicked-looking spears, even a couple of spear-throwers. Atl-atls, I marvel, remembering Professor Vale's term for them from his earlier lectures, only I thought he said their use died out many millennia before the time of Jarmo — guess he was wrong. A long, blond-wood bow lies in the place of honor on its very own shelf, its quiver of arrows nearby. Several obsidian knives with bone or wooden handles, pressure-flaked and glassy black, lie in a tidy row on another shelf.

A small altar dominates one corner. A dusty, gnarled bit of bone, about as big as my fist, rests on one side. Spring flowers arranged in a whorl seem to rise from a wooden cup of water in the middle. A small statuette of the Mother Goddess is situated on the right. On her forehead, the pervasive symbol of Jarmo — the H with daubs of red, above and below — is plainly visible.

Beside the fire pit there's a raised bed, not very big, but still plenty comfy enough. It looks inviting enough to bounce on, though — but of course I don't. The bed's framework consists of rectangular mud bricks, plastered together with mortar that looks suspiciously like animal excrement mixed with clay. But, hey, it's up off the floor and away from the cold, which is the point. Sleeping on a drafty, hard floor would get old fast. What I presume to be the mattress looks lumpy, covered by a tan animal skin with the fur still on it. A heap of mixed furs lies to one side. I see red fox, plus others I can't identify. They appear to be patchworked together with sinew. A quilt of thick fur. One could do a lot worse, at that...

Maidie catches me looking at the bed. "That's where Grandmama and I sleep — for now. In three more days, I'll be in my own house with my own husband. Just across the way."

"And where..." I begin hesitantly. "Where will I be...staying? And Grandmama? What about her?"

"Grandmama will stay here part of the time, and the rest of the time with me and Timon. She likes to keep house for Father — you'll be helping her, of course," she adds nonchalantly. "She'll stay in this bed. You'll be back there." She points toward the other wing of the L, where a second, larger raised bed is tucked under the eaves at the far end of the room. "With Father."

"I don't think—"

I'd better speak up, better say something, before I'm railroaded into I don't know what. I know it's all a dream, but still, I don't want events to start getting out of hand. But no one pays a mind to my dithering.

Instead, Maidie's father asks his women, "Is anything left from last night's dinner?" His voice is pleasant, non-authoritarian. Hopefully men in Jarmo are not like Old Testament patriarchs with their women. This one doesn't seem to be.

"Oh, yes, a great plenty." Reaching for a small wad of wool, Grandmama uses it as a hot pad to grasp a large wooden bowl near the glowing embers. Maidie sets out several large shells—they look like freshwater clams—each the size of my hand. Then four spoons, made of smaller shells tied to sticks by something white—sinew, perhaps? The table looks to be made of rough slabs of pine, pegged together into a square. I can't help marveling how stone tools can even make such a thing. So clever, so inventive. Four rough stools complete the dining room ensemble.

The table faces a good-sized open window. The day grows even more glorious, if possible. Sunny air wafts in, carrying a faint scent of new grass, spring flowers, and the rankness of goat and urine—just a little, not so much to be off-putting.

Two stools, probably Maidie's and Grandmama's, are situated together at the long side of the slab table. The other two seats, which must be for Father and me, are at the two shorter ends of the approximate rectangle. The opposite long end is pushed up against the open window.

But first Maidie beckons me to a corner of the room where a few garments hang from pegs and several pair of sandals, all somewhat worse for wear, are stowed neatly in the corner.

"Here, you can wear these for now. These, too." She hands me a well-worn, loose-weave shift and a pair of stout leather sandals. "They're mine, but we'll make you some new ones."

Modestly, with my back to the group, I drop the homespun shawls, and slip a roomy, short, sleeveless shift over my head. I feel heavenly in it, especially with no underwear to bind or constrict. Maidie and Grandmama change clothes, too, into something equally comfortable. I feel like a middle school girl, trying on clothes together with friends at the mall. Something I should have done in those days, but never did.

I stand, dressed and ready, by the table, waiting for the women to join me before I presume to sit down.

"Sit, eat," Maidie's father urges all of us once we're assembled.

Grandmama and Maidie bring some mystery dishes to the table and commence the meal.

"Tell us more of your dangerous journey—and your plans for the future," Father, the chieftain, says to me.

Grandmama hands me the warm-to-the-touch wooden bowl, including the wool holder. I peer at the dinner mixture it contains. Hunks of stewed meat—I'd rather not know what kind. A few lentils, and some kind of mystery roots, hacked into chunks. Looks like wild onion, too.

I pause, embarrassed because I'm not sure of proper protocol in how to get the stuff out of the bowl, or where to put it when I do.

"Scoop it with the shell," Grandmama explains kindly. "Like this."

I wait until everyone is served before I venture a taste. *Damn, it's good!* It's even salted. *I thought it would be flat and gluey.* I'm so surprised and starving, it's all I can do to not wolf it down.

Between bites, Maidie's father says politely but dubiously, "Now tell us more about your…escape…over the mountains from an evil husband."

"Husband-to-be," I correct him politely. "I'm not married yet."

"You're awfully old to not be married yet." The chieftain looks at me with more than a little interest as he speaks in a polite, conversational tone. Maybe it's just the truth. Maybe I am pretty old to be a new bride…in Jarmo.

The chieftain takes another scoop of stew. "People have come here before, to Jarmo, over the years. Not just the obsidian traders—they *always* come. But I mean other travelers. Loners. Strangers. I can count the number of such travelers who have come here in my lifetime on my two hands. And none of them spoke our language the way you do. How is that possible? Your husband-to-be must have been truly evil to drive you to such…desperation."

"Actually, I don't know how I happen to speak your language. It's because…it's also *my* language. Since I was born." I shrug and smile. Weakly. "My people must have a connection with Jarmo that goes way back."

I'm winging it here, but I figure I'll just tell the truth. Whenever I can.

"But why no husband?" asks Maidie's father. It seems a sensible question, even to me. "You are a beautiful woman. Ripe and ready for plucking. Why no husband? What's wrong with the men of the east, anyway? Why did you have to make such a journey? Was there no one else to take you to his fireside?"

I answer slowly, trying to think in advance what the proper response might be. "The man who was chosen for me was despicable. He beat me whenever he could. And I knew it would only get worse. Besides, where I come from, women marry late. I myself have, uh, seen twenty seasons pass."

Maidie's father sniffs dismissively — what a ridiculous idea and waste of a perfectly good resource.

"How lonely for you." Maidie looks at me pityingly. "Here in Jarmo, you'd have a husband to keep you warm by the time of your First Blood. Mine happened in the last moon after fourteen summers, but it comes earlier to some. What are your people waiting for, anyway?"

What indeed. Or whom?

Who am *I* waiting for? I often wonder. And does anyone wait for me?

The chieftain notices that I look uncomfortable. He rises from the table, looks around at us all, and tells his women, "I'm taking Stella the Star for a long walk now. Just the two of us. After I bring her back, I'm heading out with the hunting party for two days to bring in more ibex for the wedding feast."

He holds out a hand to me, looking at me encouragingly. I take his hand without a word, glance back with a bemused smile at Maidie and Grandmama, and step forward into my new life.

We walk leisurely toward the highest point of the hill of Jarmo. It's a foothill, actually — exposed and separate on two sides. One side drops off to a cliff, not very big but still enough to be dangerous. The fourth side leads to still higher foothills, with more hills beyond that.

The levels continue, up and up, into the most forbidding mountains I've ever seen.

The chieftain continues to hold my hand, but that's okay. His hand feels very nice in mine. Reassuring, non-sweaty.

There's a broad dirt trail where the stream's cataract passes directly under the Jarmo hillcrest on its way down to the hot pool and beyond. We follow it for a short way, then cut off to the right and sit under the branches of a low tree with lacy, palmate leaves. I think it's a nut tree, but can't be sure. It's still springtime. The leaves have only been out for a short while.

We lean against the trunk. There's plenty of room in the shade for both of us.

"You know my name—Stella—but what is yours?" I spread out my hands in mock helplessness. "I certainly can't keep on calling you Father! I will call you Chieftain, though, if you'd rather."

"Hari," he says, looking over at me. His eyes are so blue, and a wormlike scar bisects one eyebrow. "I am called Hari."

He pronounces it with a short *a*, hah-ree, and somehow I just *knew* this had to be his name. The face of Professor Harry Vale flashes before my eyes. I wonder why; the two men look nothing alike. Except for their eyes. And perhaps they share the fact of a single dimple? I wonder…I'll probably never know because any dimples are hidden behind Hari's close-trimmed brown beard.

"I am the current Hari. Of many, many other Haris of Jarmo who came before me. Since the time when the Great Mother walked upon the earth, there has always been a Hari at Jarmo to keep things…safe."

I smile at him and nod. Then my smile deepens, and I cannot look away.

We recline, relax, and chat for what seems like hours. It feels like hours, but I can't be sure. There are no clocks in Jarmo, that's for sure. And there won't be for thousands of years.

I feel so relaxed with the chieftain, as if I've known him forever, as if I always have, always will. I don't feel rushed or stressed or anxiously nervous about the time—or about anything.

There is no time to worry about here. There is only now.

I ask him about his duties as the Hari of Jarmo.

"What does a chief do here, exactly? Give me some examples."

"Well, for one thing, there was the strange sickness that foxes and jackals got a few years back. That sickness that made their mouths foam, and their bites bring death. I led the hunters to exterminate all that we could before they could attack anyone, especially the children. There have been other crises, too, many of them, like the terrible floods of two years ago that swelled our little river and almost destroyed the hot pool. We had to rearrange the boulders. And the terrible drought two years before that, when many of our people needed extra help to find food."

Then he smiles and admits, as if telling me a secret, "Mostly, though, I pretty much do what I like. I do a lot of mediating. That is, I direct the goods and services of the obsidian traders—they come through our village twice a year—to make sure they're being fair in their dealings with our people. I act as judge between disputes. Even if there aren't really that many disputes. It mostly happens when two men want the same woman. Or two women want the same man. Or when people drink too much wine and get into fights. And so, although I'm the Chieftain of Jarmo, I still have a lot of time left for other things."

"What kinds of things?" I am curious.

He thinks for a moment. "Things like hunting, or thinking up new songs, making designs on pottery, and getting my need satisfied whenever I can. The wives of Jarmo are generous with their kindness, and there's always someone around willing to…to help me out until a girl comes into her time of First Blood, and I can take another wife."

He can't resist a sheepish, one-sided smile.

"But you have no wife now?" I can't resist asking the question. "No…consort?"

He keeps his answer brief on this one. "Not at present. But I shall take a wife very soon."

This could mean any number of things, so I take a new tack. "Your eyes are so blue, and so are mine. But everyone else in Jarmo seems to have brown eyes. Why is that?"

"It means I was born like this," he replies grimly. "The weak-eyed one, they used to call me. Who can know the mind of the Great Mother to mark me in this way? I myself think it was an accident of birth. Something that just…went wrong. I should tell you that there are people, right now here in Jarmo, who do not fully trust me, just because of my blue eyes. They're afraid I might be up to no good, although I've never failed my people yet. They're just afraid because I'm different. But now there's you and *your* blue eyes. Now there's someone here like me. An ideal match…"

He flashes me a momentary grin.

I find him most unassuming. He's very laid back for someone who's supposed to be a tribal chieftain.

He tells me about the obsidian traders who make a circuit through Jarmo twice a year — from the east in spring, from the west in fall. "Their arrival is always a reason for great feasting and celebrating. Very rarely, sometimes a small group of hunters from a faraway tribe may cross our land, but they always move on after a day or two. It's no matter; there's abundance for all to share."

And I'm thinking, *For now* there's abundance. *For now*. The thought of later harsh times and the warfare that Harry Vale talked of draws a momentary veil over my contentment.

"What does the name Hari mean? Among my people, we say Harry, not Hari. But it's an old, historic name where I come from — the nickname of royalty. And the name Jarmo — what does that mean?"

I truly want to know. "I thought you and your people might have names like White Cloud or Running Stag…something like that."

Hari looks mildly annoyed. "Why would my parents name me after a cloud? Or an ibex?" He sniffs dismissively. "We use the same names of the Old Ones, names that have come down to us for generations, from the First People. From mother to daughter, father to son. They have no other meaning, just in and of themselves. We seek to preserve the old names of Jarmo down through the generations. So our children will always know and remember."

"And Jarmo?" I persist. "What does that name mean?"

"We don't know who first called it that name. Some grandfather-of-a-grandfather-of-a-grandfather may have heard it from the lips of the Great Mother herself. Who knows? All we know, and all we *need* to know, is that Jarmo *is*, and forever means, our home."

"Maidie is your daughter." I speak not a question, just this statement of fact. He nods. "Do you have any other children?"

He looks away as if peering into the far horizon. But I think he just doesn't want to meet my eyes. "I did. But they're all dead now. Nine."

"Nine children?" I repeat in quiet horror. Nine children—it doesn't seem possible. He looks so young. How can he bear the loss?

"Maidie is my oldest child," he explains. "Daughter of my first wife, Crixa. My only child who survived. Crixa died in childbirth—and the second baby with her—and so, as soon as another girl, Davi, came into her blood-time, I took her for my next wife."

He strokes my hand with his thumb and doesn't look me in the eye for the rest of this story. "Davi is…was…a very headstrong, passionate woman. Wanted my seed all the time!" He barks a couple of laughs, then looks uneasy and sad.

"Nine times my seed grew in her belly. Mostly they were born much too soon. Still too small, covered with blood and fluids, never taking even one breath. One of the babies—the last one, a boy—did make it through the span of eight moons and was born. He even gave a gasp and a cry, but then he died soon after that. He just…wasn't ready, and the Great Mother called him back."

He swallows, and I see it's hard for him to talk about this. "With all of the babies dying, Davi became…intense. Crazy and wild with grief. As anyone would be, of course. She raged against the Great Mother. And especially, she raged against me. She was not a very… comfortable person to live with. Again, understandably."

"And where is Davi now?" I must not be so nosy. It's a terribly private matter, after all, but I want to know. I *must* know.

He speaks with his eyes cast down, tracing lines in the dirt with a stick. I see it's the Jarmo H.

"Last winter, when the baby boy died, she arose from her sick bed and gathered him up. Went into the village with the dead child in her arms. She blazed in fury at me in front of everyone. She told me, and everyone, that my seed was rotten, no good. That it could never take hold and grow properly. Then she jumped to her death off the crest of the hill, the cliffside, with the dead child still tight in her arms."

He looks up at me then. "That's when I started seeking a new wife. To banish the sound of her words in my ears and, hopefully, to have someone who could be my friend…in my bed. But up to now, I've had to wait. Wife candidates in Jarmo are not always plentiful. I had been waiting for young Kareli to come into her time of blood, but it may be another year or two yet."

Young Kareli. Hmmm. She sounds very young indeed.

I picture her with a round baby face, big brown eyes, and light-brown hair snarled gently about her face like a halo.

"Of course, I could always go exploring over the mountains for a woman—and I may come to that yet! But I haven't had to wait to fill my need. The wives of Jarmo are happy to do that until a wife can be found. With the blessings of their husbands, the wives take care of things like that, as is their way with widowers here in Jarmo. And widows. They take turns so I'm always satisfied. That's never a problem, although being gracious to so many women wears me out! But still, I'm ready now—more than ready, actually—to sleep in my own bed again in my own house, once more tucked around a wife of my own, and keep the door closed for a while. And then, maybe after a year or so of just enjoying ourselves for a while we could try again for a baby."

I exhale a deep breath I didn't realize I was holding. That's a lot for me to take in.

"And so…babies. You want more babies, but not necessarily right away?"

"Not yet." Hari is serious, quietly adamant. "Sometime, yes assuredly, but not right now. I want to enjoy a happy wife for a while. With little chance of tragedy or loss because of dead babies. I've had enough of that to last a lifetime."

I shudder to think of what he's been through. And still, he's kept his cool. Kept his mellow temperament and sense of fairness—and not demanded his *droit de seigneur*, his rights as king of the castle, to take another man's wife as his own at the expense of the other man.

I cast around for a somewhat lighter subject. "Um, Maidie, your daughter, she has seen, uh, fourteen seasons? And who is the man she's marrying?"

"Yes, fourteen turning of the seasons. An age, the perfect age, to become a wife. Her First Blood was in the moon just past, and she's marrying Timon, a man of fifteen seasons. Her dearest friend since they were babies. A good boy, good family."

"Speaking of babies…" I must ask this delicately. "In Jarmo, how do you keep them from…taking root?"

I'm definitely curious. In olden times, babies seldom waited to be invited. Even in the twenty-first century, they'll just show up if you're not careful.

"Have you not the purple-leaf plant where you come from in the east?"

I shake my head, wondering where the conversation is heading next.

"It's low to the ground and extends with tendrils and vines all over, small oval leaves. I'll show you," he promises. "It's supposed to be a Women's Secret." He rolls his eyes at me — just a little. "But everyone knows of it, including the men. Just chew a few leaves each day from the purple-leaf plant, and it keeps a baby from taking root in your belly, simple as that. It's a good thing our winters are moist and mild. The plant stays alive year-round and grows thickly in summer. We'll look for some on the way back to the house and pick some. You'll be needing it soon."

I will, will I?

When I look at him inquiringly, he gives me a look. And then a wink. Who knew that Prehistoric Man knew about winking?

"So, it's true then?" I blush to even mention it. "You're thinking of…marrying me?"

"I'm not thinking, I *am*."

Hari's look turns me crimson, so much so that I place my palms against my cheeks to cool them off.

"But you don't even know me!" I can't help laughing helplessly.

"But I will. Soon." Hari smiles, takes my two shaking hands away from my cheeks and grasps them in his own. "So, it's settled then. You will be my wife, and I will provide for you, kill game for you, and protect you. And our children."

Oh, brother! I squirm inwardly. But still…

Hari lifts my chin so I can look in his eyes when he says, "All right, then? Yes?"

I'm sure he doesn't have to ask. I'm sure he can take what he wants. But still, he is a gentleman, through and through.

I murmur without even thinking. "Yes."

It's my dream. And I'll do what I want to. And I want…

Oh, yes, I *definitely* want.

I think of the double wedding, coming up in three days' time. Suddenly my hands grow clammy, and I feel an odd, gathering feeling — I don't know what else to call it — deep down in my belly.

But the thought of putting up a fuss about this wedding never crosses my mind. *Oh, no, I do* want. I may be nervous, but I still want to experience it all.

This dream of Jarmo is my *dream, and I want him.*

"Hari, how many turning of the seasons have you seen?"

He thinks for a moment. "Twenty-nine." Still so young to have lived so fully and bear responsibility for so many.

"There!" Hari cries suddenly. "The purple-leaf plant. We'll gather some leaves. Dried leaves or fresh-picked, it doesn't matter. It still works. Good thing this plant is so common and grows readily. Else our women would have picked it bare to the ground long ago!"

We crouch to gather some pickings—not all of them but enough to give me several good doses for many days. Hari puts them into a small pouch hanging from his belt, and we continue our homeward stroll.

And then I feel another sensation, from another part of my body, a sensation that I've tried to ignore for the last fifteen minutes, but it's inexorable, and growing, and will not be cast aside.

"Um, Hari, y'know…when you've had a meal? And then later your body wants to…well, go to the bathroom? The thing is, I don't know where your bathroom is. Or if you even *have* a bathroom. An outhouse, maybe?"

"What's a bathroom? Sounds to me like you might need the ditch. You know, to…dispose of excrement."

"That would be the one, yes," I agree, too much in need to mind about bluntness. "Is it nearby?"

"Just over the stream. Downstream and downwind of the village." He points to a flat, weedy area. "I'll show you."

He steps from boulder to boulder across the rushing stream, from rock to rock, in his leather sandals. The taut lacings up his calves keep the sandals straight and stout. I follow behind him as best I can.

In the latrine field, I see a freshly dug trench amid what looks like sagebrush. Nearby are other trenches that look recently filled. Some mounded-over trenches look much older. A little boy straddles the current trench, looks at me curiously but unconcerned, then lets fly from his nether region. When he concludes his business, he kicks dirt over it from a row of earth that was excavated for the present ditch.

"This should be what you need," Hari says encouragingly. He looks like he's waiting for me to do my business, right then and there. There seems to be nothing like toilet paper in evidence. No broad-leafed plants, even.

"But you're not going to *watch* me!" I protest in horrified severity. "Go! Go home. I know where it is; I'll meet you back there."

"No, I'll be leaving soon with the men for the ibex hunt. Here…"

He gives me the pouch with the purple plant leaves. "You'll want to have some of these. I'll see you soon…at the wedding." He gives me a look then and an irresistible private smile, then heads back to the village.

I'm still shimmering in the afterglow of his company, but there's urgent business to attend to. I wait until the little boy departs, then furtively do what I need to do. There isn't anything to use for toilet paper, so I hoist my short, loose shift and crouch in the stream—again, downstream from the village, thank goodness—and thoroughly wash below my waist.

I do miss twenty-first century toilet paper. But, so far, nothing else from my century of origin.

CHAPTER 7
The Engagement

Each night, when I go to sleep, I die.
And the next morning, when I wake up,
I am reborn.
~ Mahatma Gandhi ~
1869 – 1948

Harry

I'm holding the hand of Miss Stella Denton. She's my fiancée now — and she hasn't the slightest idea.

She doesn't know *anything*, really, because she's still in a coma at HCMC.

It's night — still in the first few hours of our nightmare. We're here at Hennepin County Medical Center, the metro hospital where trauma patients are delivered, along with drunks, druggies, down-and-outs, and lots of ailing run-of-the-mill folks too. Stella was shot in the head at close range, and I've taken a hit to the left thigh.

From the ambulance, I'm wheeled from the ER directly to OR for surgery.

Stella is taken to another operating room. I don't know what happens next to either of us, because they give me general anesthesia for the procedure.

Next thing I know, I'm waking up, groggy and stiff, in Recovery. All the nurses will tell me about "the girl who was brought in with me" (as I describe Stella to them) is that "she's still in surgery."

I eventually learn that Stella went straight from the ER to the lab for a CT scan—not an MRI, I am told, because the bullet and its metallic/magnetic properties can give misleading readings. The CT scan is just to get baseline information for a second operation, a craniotomy, wherein the neurosurgeon, Dr. Elbert Fanning, removes a three-by-six-inch, football-shaped portion of Stella's skull.

Removes it temporarily, that is.

A craniotomy is supposed to evacuate blood and relieve pressure on Stella's injured brain so it can swell without being restricted by the cranium. And swell it does—more about that momentarily.

I learn later that the removed cranial segment was whisked away to be frozen in solution, hopefully to be reattached to Stella's skull at some future date.

With half of her head shaved, part of her skull removed, and wearing what looks like a hockey helmet, Stella is now gurneyed into a private room in ICU. Here she gets specialized nursing care round-the-clock.

I wake up in Recovery around eleven p.m. The police show up yet again to take additional testimony from me about the shooters—where, what, when, and presumably why.

After they leave, I can't sleep because I'm too zoned-out on drugs. Plus, I keep wondering and worrying about Stella.

Too many unreal things have happened tonight—and might still happen. Who knows? It all seems a weird, fluorescent dream to me, with floating soft voices and beeping/pinging technology.

I'm starting to feel queasy. I don't know if it's the anesthesia wearing off or what. Maybe it's just the thought of a bullet actually passing through my body. A metal slug, pushing aside tender bloody flesh in my leg. But thinking about Stella Denton, thinking of a metal projectile in one's brain…My skin crawls, and I refuse to think of it at all.

But back to the fiancée thing—it happens totally by accident. Or fate. A positive kind of fate, I hope. A kind of fate that takes me by the scruff of the neck and hustles me out of this gory confusion, into someplace peaceful and positive where no further questions are asked.

To police and hospital officials, I identify Stella Denton as the name of the victim so that University Admissions can check its records, determine her next of kin, and contact them.

By four in the morning, the man I later come to know as Stella's stepdad, Chuck Denton, flies in from Chicago. The flight takes less than an hour, and fortunately there are at least a dozen flights a day between Minneapolis and Chicago. He grabs a taxi to the hospital, and his arrival here is the catalyst as to why and how Stella becomes my fiancée.

It's like this: In the fluorescent light of Recovery, I watch as a good-looking, fifty-something man, whom I soon learn is Chuck, approaches the nurses' station. I can see him plainly since the nurses' station is centrally located in the room, and I'm there in the middle of it as well. Only side privacy curtains separate the Recovery beds. Although the nurses' station is brightly lit, the rest of Recovery is dim and shadowy, and most everyone is asleep or unconscious. I sit up in bed because my leg feels better that way. Plus, I can't sleep anyhow.

Bleary-eyed and rumpled, Chuck Denton somehow manages to look simultaneously kindly yet expensive, like an ad in an upscale fly-fishing catalog. Chuck speaks softly to the nurse behind the counter.

"I'm here to see Stella Denton? I'm her dad, her next-of-kin. I was told she might out of surgery by now?"

A nurse takes his hand and pats his shoulder awkwardly. They murmur quietly together. I can't make out distinct words. Yes, of course I'm watching and listening. Who can sleep when Life and Death are all around me?

Finally, I hear Chuck asking, "Was anyone with her when she was shot?"

More indistinct murmurings. And then both nurses and Chuck quietly pull my privacy curtains to one side and step quietly to my bedside.

You know how it is that hospitals are never really dark, even in the middle of the night? I am fully awake, despite being full of pain meds. I've never been a sound sleeper anyway. Always too nervous. Too insecure to let go and just be.

"Hello!" says Chuck in a low, soft voice. He's surprised to see me sitting up in bed. "They told me your name. It's Harry Vale, I mean Professor Vale, yes?" He extends a gentle handclasp my way. "I'm Chuck Denton. Stella's dad—that is, her stepdad. They tell me you were with her when she was shot? You were both shot, first you, then Stella, right? After the clerk was—you know…" His voice trails off.

"Yeah."

Chuck continues in a low whisper. "And you were shot in the…"

"Thigh." I lift the sheet to show him the considerable bandage. "Right here. A quick in-and-out, apparently. I'm so drugged up right now I can't feel a thing. I'm guessing I'll sure feel like hell tomorrow, though."

We exchange a nervous almost-but-not-quite chuckle. *Whistling in the dark when the devil walks over our graves.* Then Chuck has the decency to look somber. Not sure of how much I've been told about Stella's status (which is almost nothing, due to privacy laws), he proceeds to fill me in.

"When I called earlier, they said they just don't know about Stella's prognosis. Though she seems to have stabilized, she's still intubated and on a ventilator, just in case. Still hanging onto life something fierce, though. They've scheduled brain scans for tomorrow to see where the bullet is seated and how much gross damage there is."

"Whoa." I speak the ineffectual word in an exhale. It's a lot for anyone to take in. Especially as loaded with pain meds and antibiotics as I am.

Chuck exhales too, exuding a bone-deep weariness. It's almost four a.m. "I'm going to stick around a few days to make sure everything is being done for her. To see if she wakes up…" Then, in an altered tone, he adds, "I live in Chicago now, you see."

A faint timbre of wistfulness comes through in his voice. It sounds a bit forced and false to me. Chuck quietly rattles on. "I'm crazy-busy, you see, doing fundraising for international NGOs. Always on the go. Jeez, I'd feel so much better about leaving her here, if only she just…" He's quick to add, "I mean, to leave her here once she's stabilized and on the mend, of course! I just wish she had some folks close to her here. Someone, anyone…"

Before I can comment, Chuck sighs again and continues. "She's become such a loner, especially since my wife, her mother, died a year ago. I'll fly back here whenever I can, of course. But I'm just not able to, you know, stay here every day given my situation. Also, I'm about to remarry—in three weeks' time, actually. Plus I'm inheriting a new young family…"

Chuck's monologue rambles to a stop. Perhaps he wishes he'd worded his explanation differently. Too late now. He has run out of wheedles and excuses.

And then I do something massively stupid; I speak again. "Actually, I'm her fiancé. Stella and I, we just recently became…engaged. Don't worry. I'll take care of her."

Chuck looks at me in honest surprise. I'm a good thirteen or fourteen years older than Stella Denton. Not by any stretch of the imagination a likely catch. But then again, neither is Stella.

Silently I acknowledge that the two of us, Stella and I, could hardly be called attractive under the most generous of circumstances. Chipmunk-cheeked, yes. Nervous and eager-to-please, certainly. Forgettable, most definitely.

"I'm actually her teacher *and* her fiancé," I amend my earlier declaration hurriedly. "We just got together this spring. I know the university frowns upon teacher fraternization with students, but you see, today…well, today was our last class together, our last as teacher and student. And then, tomorrow—today—we were *supposed* to be just regular civilians who could be legally open about our relationship."

I'm lying like a madman.

I'm watching myself do it but can't seem to shut off the flow of words. What's making me talk like this? I feel like a stranger in my own body, peering in at the strange inhabitant of my hospital bed. Unbidden, the thought comes to me: I am comprised of many different selves who all call themselves *me*. It's a sobering thought.

"Oh, thank God!" Chuck exhales in relief. "Then you can look out for our girl. And, um, congratulations under the circumstances. Stella is a singular, very special individual."

And I agree: of course, of course.

Chuck takes a deep breath, lets it out. He's steeling himself to ask me the huge favor. Or maybe not so huge under the presumed circumstances. "Please watch over her, will you? Look out for her? But of course you will!" Chuck answers his own question. "I'll be back on weekends whenever I can. You know, to check up on things, help with the rehab. That is, once she wakes up…"

The unspoken word between us is *if* she wakes up.

I feel a shift. A moving of tectonic plates in my life.

Suddenly my life doesn't seem so meaningless to me anymore. I'm no longer just a freshly baked professor on the next-to-the-lowest rung of the university hierarchy, teaching entry-level classes at night, doing teaching assistant stints whenever I can, with university tenure only a dream.

Now, somebody *needs* me. Even if she doesn't know it. She really and truly does need me. I need her, too.

And to me, being needed is just as good as being wanted. *Maybe better*, I decide.

"Oh, assuredly," I answer Chuck and lay my hand reassuringly—for just an instant, but it is enough—on his forearm. As I agree to this, I willingly change the vibration of my days, the future pathway of my life, forever.

I look Chuck in the eye with drugged but avowed sincerity and elaborate on my newly forged agreement. "Of course I will, Mr. Denton…Chuck. Count on it. While I'm still a patient, I'll keep an eye on her here. And once they spring me from this place, I plan to…" I cast about hastily for some proof of my devotion. "I'll stay by her bedside for at least a couple hours each day. More if I can. I'll bring my laptop, grade papers, prepare lessons, that sort of thing." Inspiration strikes. "I'll play music for her on my iPod—Hanson's 'Andante con Tenerezza,' for starters. Books on tape, that sort of thing. Whatever the doctors allow. And I'll talk to her. Lots of talking. She'll need to hear the sound of a human voice, my voice, guiding her back into life."

There's a deep sigh of satisfaction from Chuck. Now he can return to his new, fast-paced Chicago life without a guilty conscience. We chat a little more, then he bids me farewell with excessive, guilt-driven gratitude.

And I…well, curiously enough, drugged and blood-sullied as I am, I'm also feeling more hopeful than I have in years. *I have a purpose now, and it's necessary and meaningful and right.* Holding that thought, I finally drift into a deep, healing sleep, despite the beeping of machines and nurses' soft-soled shoes shuffling about the nurses' station.

Stella Denton has a fiancé now, and I am her intended.

CHAPTER 8
The Fiancé

Sometimes our fire goes out,
but is blown again into instant flame
by an encounter with another human being.
~ Albert Schweitzer ~
1875–1965

Harry

My days have a new rhythm while I'm still at the hospital: wake up; earn a little money via online tutoring through the university; rest my bum leg, which is still healing too slowly for my restless self; then spend time with Stella.

No more classes for me to teach just now. The last session of my last course was the night of the shooting, with the final exam on the following Tuesday. A higher-up Anthropology professor generously handled that for me.

Late spring now morphs into early summer, and I feel free. No more job responsibilities for the next three months.

Thankfully, under my current university contract, my annual salary is portioned out into identical (albeit depressingly small) paychecks year-round. They show up in my credit union account once a month. I'm especially glad of the money now. It means I'll have lots of time for convalescence and visiting Stella.

I definitely need it. My leg still throbs like a bastard.

After our initial time together in the ER, Stella and I are sent to different floors. Stella is wheeled immediately up to the ICU (for who knows how long.)

After an initial look-see at my leg, the doctors send me to surgery.

My first five days pretty much revolve around changes of my surgical dressing (it gets nasty pretty fast), dosing me round the clock with strong antibiotics, and forcing myself to watch bad soap operas (it's either that or HGTV). It's scary because I'm almost getting to enjoy them.

During those days, Stella and I couldn't see one another at all. Stella was far too critical, plus she was unconscious, and I was on a different floor.

But now, finally, I'm permitted to have someone roll me in my wheelchair up to ICU so I can convince the nurse manager to let me see Stella.

"I'm sorry, sir." The nurse manager speaks to me firmly but with real regret. "HIPAA laws forbid us from allowing in any visitors except family."

I look innocuous and non-threatening even in the best of times, even more so now that I'm temporarily in a wheelchair. I plead my case. "But I *am* her family. I'm her fiancé. The only family she's got here in the Twin Cities," I tell them. "Her father, Chuck Denton, lives in Chicago, but I'm sure he left instructions with administration here that I'm an official member of the family. Please do feel free to call him, if you wish. Stella's patient advocate has his contact information."

As I observe from afar a hushed discussion at the nurses' station, I'm not sure who says what to whom, or why. But suddenly I'm ushered into Stella's room with a smile. Ever since then, I've not been challenged or questioned again in any way.

Besides, everything I've told them is true. Well, at least, from my side of reality.

And there's no reason to believe that it won't become true someday when—if—Stella returns to normalcy.

I'm giving destiny a swift kick in the pants in hopes it will start smoothing things out for us in the highest and best possible way.

Before I wheel myself into Stella's private room to see her for the first time, I ask at the nurses' station about her status. They tell me that when the bullet entered her head, it wasn't going at the speed of light as bullets usually do. Doctors say it must have ricocheted off something else first—metal, brick, whatever—and changed trajectory, slowing its travel before it entered her skull.

That's why this foreign metal object is still inside her head—and, miraculously, it hasn't killed her yet.

I approach Stella's bedside for the first time. With so many tubes, drips, and wires connected to her, it's hard to even see her at first amid the lump of blankets and technology.

I wheel in closer. The close-up view turns my stomach. She is definitely altered—quite possibly forever. Her face looks a bit like a multicolored pumpkin; the skin there is simultaneously black and blue, yet also somewhat swollen and shiny. She's an off-putting sight.

I mentally call myself all kinds of a shit for even thinking that, but I can't help it. *Oh, Stella. Oh, my dear Miss Denton, where in hell did you go?*

Stella also wears a protective helmet. They tell me that half of her head has been shaved and the rest of her hair is clipped short. *Joan of Arc hair*, I think to myself. Only probably not like in movies, I suspect. *It's probably a lot more ghastly under that helmet.*

"If you can wait awhile, the doctors should be coming in soon on their rounds," Stella's afternoon shift nurse tells me.

I tell her I'll wait. I'm antsy and eager to talk with them.

After more than an hour, during which Stella's inert body is turned frequently and ministered to by a variety of staff, two fifty-something doctors in knee-length, white coats enter together.

We introduce ourselves. The tall, barrel-chested neurologist, Dr. Montrose, is forthright and hearty, while the wraith-thin neurosurgeon, Dr. Fanning, is taller still and barely talks above a whisper.

"This must be such a nightmare for you," Montrose begins with a kindly handshake. The conversation quickly turns to sympathy for, and commiseration with, Stella's situation—and mine.

"Tell me, please…" I'm not sure where to begin with all this. Stella looks so ravaged on all fronts. "Tell me what's being done for her at the present time. And please tell me about the…helmet."

"We had to do a craniotomy on Stella to help relieve the brain trauma—that is, the massive swelling," Dr. Fanning murmurs almost inaudibly. He sees my confused look. "We had to remove a piece from one of the bones of her skull. They call it a bone flap procedure. It's just temporary. For a few weeks…"

Weeks.

"…until the swelling can be managed. For now she has a hole in her skull, covered over with just a flap of skin. That's why the helmet is essential for her own safety."

"Let me see a little closer." I nudge the wheelchair's footrests to each side and attempt to stand up. My good leg obeys; the gunshot leg howls a silent protest, but I hold onto the side panels of the wheelchair and push myself to a standing position.

Stella looks even worse up close. Dr. Montrose, the neurologist, halts any further examination on my part. "No, you probably don't want to see her any closer than that. There's a pretty big opening in her skull just now. She'll have to be on constant, strong antibiotics to preclude brain infections from taking hold. It's really hard to treat because of the blood/brain barrier. No two ways about it, she's going to face challenges."

I can't help blurting, "Please, doctor, what do you mean challenges? What kinds of challenges?"

Dr. Fanning interjects his own cautions. "We'd like to warn you, Professor Vale…Harry…that she's going to look a lot worse before she gets better. In days ahead, she'll be facing all kinds of challenges — things like brain infections, possibly bladder infections, probably lung problems. Bed sores are common because she's got to be turned all the time. There could be tissue necrosis at the surgical sites. And that's just for starters."

The doctors know that Stella's ailment list is plenty long already. I can't take any more just now, so overwhelmed am I by our mutual medical immensities.

"But," Dr. Fanning tries to cheer me and only partially succeeds, "all things considered, she's actually doing quite well. Truly. When the danger of brain swelling is over, when all the drains and tubes finally come out, when we reattach the bone flap to her skull, then we'll finally be making tracks on her journey back toward a normal life."

"Some coma patients make it back in an excellent fashion," Dr. Montrose adds. "More often than not, though, they don't. Sometimes they become a lesser version of themselves or someone totally unrecognizable to loved ones."

Some things don't bear thinking about.

And so the weeks pass. I am finally declared healed (enough) and am discharged from HCMC. I drive back each day to visit Stella — a solitary pastime for me since she remains unresponsive. My only vocal companions are the nurses, therapists, aids, and occasional doctors who come in to minister to her needs.

On the definitely positive side, I'm told that Stella is showing signs of proper brain function, including intact reflexes like a good, strong cough (the doctors especially like that one), as well as her spontaneous breathing that no longer requires supplemental oxygen. They keep the trach intact, however, JIC—just in case.

Periodically, Stella goes in for more CT scans and EEGs. Each one looks marginally better than the last. She's moving in the right direction, and it's not quite been two months yet.

By the start of month two, Stella is successfully weaned off the ventilator as her reflexes start returning. Another excellent sign.

Three months! That seems to be the universal benchmark in this process. Most progress is made within the first three months. Nurses and doctors repeat this to me constantly, always hastening to add, "And even after that, progress still continues. Remember, the factor of youth always helps!"

Stella's physical therapist shows me how to gently but firmly grasp Stella's ankles; carefully rotate her bare feet with the palm of his hand; and bend her arms and legs, gently and gradually, in a semblance of exercise in her inert body. But more often than not, now that he has carefully taught me all the moves, the therapist works with other patients and lets me do Stella's PT instead.

I am family now and treated accordingly. I can ask most any question I want, and people will answer readily. Giving me positive answers if they can. Or evasive replies if they can't.

I can massage Stella's hands and feet anytime I want, play music for her, tell her long pointless anecdotes, and it does me good.

If I had to tell you *why* it does me good, I couldn't really tell you. Don't know. But just helping her, being her devoted fiancé, makes me feel better than I have in years.

Every third evening, someone—usually the three p.m.-to-midnight shift nurse—comes in to do the coma stimulation test on Stella. Sometimes I'm there when this process occurs. The test assesses how deep the coma is at present. There's a list of things to do: first, ring a bell by each of the patient's ears to see if she reacts, poke at the patient with a finger (quite sharply too) to test for possible reactions, flutter their finger by the patient's eyelashes (whether eyes are closed or open, clear or unfocused).

Then there's the dreaded sternal rub.

Oh, that one's the shits, that sternal rub. Uncomfortable for me even to watch. It always makes me cringe. The nurse makes a fist and uses her knuckles to (putting it delicately) "aggressively rub" the sternum area, that place where rib bones meet together over the heart. It's said to be very painful procedure, used to determine the level of patient responsiveness.

If you don't respond to a sternal rub, you're pretty close to hopeless.

But today, for the first time, Stella responds.

It's only a soundless grimace—she can't make a real vocalization with her trach in place. But it's enough. And it happens every time the nurse knuckles her today—hard. The nurse emphasizes what a positive sign this truly is.

"See? That's marvelous! We must let Dr. Montrose know. He'll be over-the-moon glad, and you should be, too. When patients start grimacing at a sternal rub, they're on their way back."

Lately, I've even seen Stella cough. "That's fantastic!" Dr. Montrose is jubilant about that, too. "A very promising sign!"

Not only is Stella coughing to clear her throat and responding to painful stimuli, her eyelid reflexes start responding when the nurse gently touches her eyelashes. I'm told it's so she can subconsciously, instinctively help protect herself, at the most basic level, from eye injury mainly—a very rudimentary but very strong reflex. Those that don't have it are deemed to be deeply comatose indeed.

RNs frequently suction out the trach tube, injecting saline to liquefy any thick secretions. This very necessary process used to make me queasy during that first month, but now Stella is healing so nicely they hardly have to do it anymore.

Still I watch, whatever the procedure, and still I help if I'm allowed to.

I watch and learn. *And wait.*

Every day there's the bed routine. They're constantly raising and lowering Stella's bed. Physical Therapist Bill constantly monitors Stella's muscles and tendons, leaving standing orders that she's to be turned every two hours, twenty-four-seven. This I can do while I'm by her side. Together or individually, we gently move all of Stella's joints through a complete range of motion. We do this several times a day to help guard against deep vein thrombosis — the dreaded, and often fatal, DVT.

Since the beginning of this ordeal, Stella has been wearing what look like small, bright blue catcher's mitts. She wears similar gear on her feet, too, fastened with Velcro straps. It's to prevent her hands and feet from becoming misshapen. Early on, a friendly, freckled nurse named Kelly explained it to me. "You know, to keep her hands and feet from clawing-up like crab legs."

Stella's gastroenterologist, Dr. Wu, supervises anything to do with her stomach feeding tube. He and I chat often, as Hanson's "Andante con Tenerezza" plays quietly in the background.

"My job's not sexy," he explains to me, "but, hey, somebody's got to deal with lower G. I. tract." Some things don't bear thinking about, so I just smile and nod and go no further into that subject.

Besides producing an occasional cough and grimacing against painful stimuli, Stella also occasionally opens her eyes. It's a surreal sight and one that floods me with adrenaline, since I assume she's waking up. But her eyes still look dim and glazed over. Whatever world she's seeing, it's still an inner one. She obviously doesn't see me.

I'm continuously surprised that a mostly inert body requires so much care, just to keep it alive.

During the first weeks of our mutual hospitalization — Stella's and mine — I am plied with real food, lots of it too, while her body exists on IV lipids and Hyperal, a liquid vitamin and energy electrolyte solution. Once the stomach feeding tube goes in, Stella's dinner choices get slightly more interesting. But not by much.

Stella's chipmunk cheeks are much thinner now — I wish mine were. Despite the trauma of my gunshot wound, my appetite seems unimpaired.

When I visit Stella, I play the "Andante con Tenerezza" over and over — sometimes for thirty minutes at a time on a closed loop. It must drive the nursing staff crazy. I guess I could put ear buds in her ears, but I like to listen along with her, so I'm permitted to set up the iPod with a tiny speaker on her bedside table.

Many people passing by give me reassuring, approving smiles. They see me working away on my laptop as I make occasional notes on future lectures. The lush Hanson "Andante" plays. I want Stella's brain to start remembering me and our last class, when I showed the images of Jarmo. Other times, I take pity on the staff's forbearing nature and mix up the playlist: early Nora Jones, Bonnie Raitt, Basia, even contemporary tracks by Paloma Faith and Adele.

Not long after I start keeping vigil by Stella's bedside, her patient advocate checks in with me. She's a kindly woman with a soothing voice, and she speaks with gentle persuasion. "Talk to her, Professor Vale. The music is wonderful, of course, but still, please talk to her even if she doesn't respond. She might be hearing every word we say. Most coma patients don't, but some do. We must keep her stimulated, engaged with life."

Stella still has to go to the third floor for follow-up CT scans and EEGs. After each series of scans, I eagerly pelt Drs. Fanning and Montrose with questions. "Any changes? Improvements? Anything?"

It's hard to get much out of Fanning; he's too busy and can't be bothered. But Montrose loves to talk.

"Nothing new to report. Everything looks super-promising except the gamma wave function. They *should* be moving in a pattern of neural oscillation with a frequency between forty and a hundred Hertz."

"But they're not?"

"Not yet. But they must…and they *will*. Soon." Always so positive, Dr. Montrose.

Seeing my blank look, he explains. "Scientists believe that gamma waves are what creates the body's unity of conscious perception—where we experience ourselves as a separate being in the universe. Where we come to experience us as *ourselves*…as a soul, if you will…and not an inanimate object or nothingness altogether.

"Stella's biggest problem is that her bullet is lodged next to the thalamus. Big problem. Huge! Because it's the thalamus that emits those gamma waves—the ones that aren't behaving in Stella's brain just now. If the thalamus gets damaged even a teensy bit, this wave stops and consciousness stops, and the patient remains in a coma. There are different types of brain waves, of course, and Stella is doing great on all of them—except for the gammas. And the gammas are the main essential wave for the return of consciousness."

Suddenly, he sighs. Deeply. "You do realize that by the end of three months, if she's still not awake, she'll probably have to go over to Bethesda, the long-term care facility?"

No, I did not know that. Somehow I have the idea that she'll still be here in the HCMC, with me, until she gets better. Or dies.

"Coma patients can't stay here forever," Dr. Montrose explains this unwelcome news. "I only wish they could. But we've got to free up the beds for patients even more critical than she is. Eventually, she'll be moved over to Bethesda Hospital in St. Paul. It's what we call an L-TACH, long-term acute care hospital. They're great at what they do, the best in the Upper Midwest."

I visualize Stella's bullet alongside her thalamus, an extremely delicate, critical area. The doctors dare not touch it. Inflammation is still going on there, big time. Montrose goes on to explain that the human body will work to rid itself of foreign objects, naturally, gradually moving the bullet toward outer dermal layers until it's cast off, or out, by the body itself. Like a sliver of wood in one's thumb or a piece of shrapnel.

I think about Stella's body, trying to move this bullet within her brain via impossibly tiny, incremental movements by mechanisms I can't possibly understand.

Suddenly Dr. Montrose pats my shoulder; he's ready to head out. "You're doing great, Harry. What you're doing here with Stella is an immense help to her. Huge."

He really likes that word, *huge*. I just nod in farewell, and the doctor shuffles off down the hall, eager to move on to a patient with a more positive prognosis.

Once the doctor is out of earshot, the patient advocate pops her head in for a few words with me.

"Remember, Harry…" We're on a first-name basis. "Stella is *not* brain-dead."

I sigh deeply. "Well, she's certainly giving an excellent impression of it."

She strives to be gentle with me, and calming. "The term brain-dead is used only when the brain *stem* is unresponsive. That's the most ancient and primitive part of the brain, the part that lets you breathe automatically. If she no longer breathed on her own…well, that would definitely indicate brain death. But she's breathing quite well and could go on as she is for years yet, or could wake at any time."

She pats my arm and strolls away, just like Dr. Montrose did ten minutes before.

I shudder. *Years* for Stella in this black and featureless void. Or maybe it's something…more?

CHAPTER 9
The Foursome

Large as life
and twice as natural
❧ Lewis Carroll ❧
1832 – 1898

Stella

It's my first night in Jarmo, and I'm in bed — Hari's bed. But he's not in it tonight. Only me. Before he left with the hunting party, Hari told me to use his bed while he's away. His bed — our bed — looks lumpy and itchy. None too clean. (*Bugs?* I wonder with a sudden sinking feeling). It looks warm, though, with plenty of furs.

I wish Hari didn't have to leave so soon. I must get to know him better, before…

Can a person, can I, really come to know someone, know them enough to — you know — after only a few hours' conversation?

Hari makes me feel like a schoolgirl, in all the best ways. I still *am* a schoolgirl, God knows. But somehow he manages to also treat me as a consort-to-be. Someone important, worthy of respect. Very unchieftainly of him, and I'm glad.

In the short time we've known one another, Hari doesn't seem to mind my blushes, fidgets, and strange questions. He doesn't seem to have anything to prove. He seems perfectly happy just To Be. So far, he's treated me like a fully-fledged member of the community, an attractive, grown-up woman with the ability to take things as they come. Like this bed.

In the twenty-first century, I'm a rodent-faced nonentity, perpetually on the periphery of things. It feels so much better to Be Somebody here in Jarmo, stepping forward into life on my own terms for a change.

After spending just a few hours with him, I believe Hari is, and will continue to be, exactly what he appears: kind and sensible, responsible and mellow, and severely good-looking.

I'm not used to having a hunky older man *(twenty-nine years old!)* look at me with such frank and positive appraisal. It's never happened before. Truly. Never. I'm not even sure how to act around him. He's going to have me, body and soul, in just three days. Should I should be coy? Play hard to get? Pout and keep him waiting, or what? Just… dive in? I've never faced this situation before.

But then I reassure myself. "Hush, Stella. Remember, it's only a dream, you know, so do what you want."

The words not only calm me, they cause my lips to curve into a Mona Lisa smile. In this dream, I can be what I want, do what I want, go where I want, with whomever I want. And when I wake from this dream — as I surely will, eventually, although this is beginning to be a *very* long dream — all will be forgotten. It will be as if it never existed. There is no predetermined right or wrong here. Only what my heart tells me to do.

Before Hari leaves to join the hunting party — they're meeting together soon in front of the Gathering Place — he looks at me speculatively, a little shy, then his short, trimmed beard crinkles as he smiles.

"Goodbye, then, Stella the Star. I'll see you again in two days. At the pairing."

And before I can worry, gasp, or wonder, he's kissing me. Thoroughly. I didn't know kissing had been invented yet. I guess it's been around for a really, really long time.

I haven't been kissed, even half-assed kissed, since I was fifteen and once played Suck and Blow at a tenth grade party. I didn't get invited to many parties in those days (I still don't), so that was supposed to be an A+ night for me. It was different, all right, and I learned a lot, but afterward I only gave it a C. Maybe C minus.

Suck and Blow is where you pass a piece of paper around from person to person, mouth-to-mouth, using only suction. If the paper falls, you're now kissing the person who was passing it to you. I remember there was a lot of saliva involved, and most of it didn't taste very good.

But this time, now with Hari, it's like, whoa. Everything is so different. I'm older and more aware, for one thing. My nerve endings shimmer all over, and Hari's kiss tastes like field grass and mint leaves. Neutral. Clean. Delicious. His tongue explores everything in my mouth, especially my tongue, before I even know what's happening, and so I go with the flow. And it's amazing. I feel like I'm rafting down an unexplored river. One with unexpected lurches, exhilarating turns, scary rapids, impossible-to-resist currents.

Before he leaves, he tells me, "Don't worry. The women will take care of you while I'm away."

"What women?" I manage to ask. I'm still too bemused and dazzled to say any more.

"Maura, Nydre, Kerki, and Koral. Maidie and Grandmama, too, of course. I've asked them all to watch over you. To feed you. And not let you get into mischief." He smile deepens, and I'm lost.

And with that, he's off and gone.

I check out Hari's brick bed frame — my bed, *our* bed — and find it stuffed with reeds and dried grasses. It's not half bad at that. There's even a homespun-covered pillow of sorts. We'll have to devise another one…

As afternoon shadows lengthen, Maidie and Grandmama return to the house from wherever they were off to. Maidie stokes the fire pit with fresh fuel, which also serves as the sole source of light in the little house, and we eat the rest of the leftovers for our evening meal.

As darkness falls, Maidie tells me as she prepares for bed, "You can close your shutters if you want, to keep the bats out, or leave them open if you like. I'm leaving ours open; I like to hear the crickets. Oh, and be sure to sprinkle some dried parsley on the bed to keep the bugs away. Not sure if you do that in your land beyond the mountains."

"I will," I promise, not offering further editorial comment about my supposed place of origin. "Good night, Maidie, Grandmama."

They both murmur pleasant, sleepy replies, then snuggle in together in their raised bed by the front entryway, close to the fire pit.

Bats? Nah, never been too worried about bats. Bears, yes, but not bats. Or spiders either, thank goodness. My personal bravery in the face of insects and small mammals should come in very handy here in Jarmo.

I lean out my window and gaze out into the darkness. Framing both sides of the window opening, stout shutters of split logs hang from leather hinges.

I decide to leave the window closest to my bed open, too. I'm in the far side of the L, out of the line of sight from Maidie and Grandmama, which thankfully affords me a little privacy, as well as a good view of the glowing reflection on the wall from the fire pit, which is already banked for the night.

Just like there were this morning at the hot springs, a billion stars hang in the indigo sky. I can still hear a few murmuring human voices. A few bleats of goats, a dog barks in the darkness, then all is still.

Quiet. All of Jarmo is asleep. Only a sea of crickets replays their endless closed loop of chirps.

I climb into the surprisingly large, surprisingly comfortable bed. I watch the reflected flickers of the firelight on the wall, and then I know no more.

The next thing I know, I hear three young women's voices cheerfully calling my name. When I open my eyes, four teenaged females hang over the open window, so close I could touch them.

I sit up in bed and look at them in amazement. Three of the women laugh. One of them, a sultry dark-haired beauty with a lopsided smile, just smirks with ill-concealed annoyance.

I look at them and repeat slowly from memory, pointing at random as I go, "Maura…Nydre…Kerki…and Koral."

The merry young women laugh even louder. Hearing the commotion, Maidie ambles into my wing of the L. The strangers greet her, "Good morning, Maidie!" then turn their attention back to me.

"No, *I'm* Kerki; *she's* Nydre!" A cheerful, round-cheeked, dark-haired girl with a smile as broad as a watermelon points to a skinny, grinning young woman with a pregnant belly.

"And I'm Maura." The proverbial fat girl with the pretty face, Maura is indeed lovely. She reaches through the window to squeeze my hand in welcome.

"And this is Koral," Maura adds, her eyes sliding toward the fourth member of the welcoming committee. Koral appraises me frankly;

I come up short in her estimation, I can just tell. Koral's eyebrows remind me of the feelers of a moth, only much darker and thicker. A dark, dangerous, gorgeous moth. I'd best steer clear of that one.

"Hurry up, out of bed, Stella! The sun's been up for ages, and we've lots to show and tell you!"

"But, um…" I hesitate, then add frankly, "My mouth tastes terrible. It probably smells terrible, too. I need to, uh, clean my teeth. Somehow. With something."

"Use this." Maidie takes a small twig from a pile in a stone dish. "Like this…" She takes a twig herself and demonstrates a quick up-and-down rubbing motion on each tooth. "Then chew mint leaves afterward. The bush always grows outside everyone's door."

"We're coming in," Nydre calls, and the girls clamber nimbly through the open window and surround my bed. "We're walking you down to the sacred pool first thing so we can all take a bath! Then we'll plan out our day from there."

I spring out of bed, already dressed since I didn't bother to take off my shift (well, Maidie's borrowed shift) before I went to sleep.

Maidie grabs up two squares of brown, homespun material—beach towels—while Grandmama calls out, "Have a good soak!" as we troop out the front door.

I am still cleaning my teeth. I am surprised; the twig method of tooth-brushing feels surprisingly clean.

"Remember the mint leaves, Star Girl!" Koral reminds me, with her arched eyebrow and superior gaze. "Using the twig without the mint leaves, you'll still smell like the ass-end of a goat."

Oh, shit, yes, got to have the mint leaves, or it'll be morning breath all day long.

I quickly snatch up a handful of mint leaves from a large, knee-high plant by the door. The flourishing mint thicket has obviously been growing there for decades. Even longer.

I glare at Koral's back as we walk. I don't feel like Squirrelly Girl at all. I feel strong. Energized.

Back off, Moth Bitch. Remember, two can play that game. I've never played it before, but I know I can learn.

CHAPTER 10
Enduring the Moth

It's no use going back to yesterday,
because I was a different person then.
~ Lewis Carroll ~
1832–1898

Stella

Over the next two days, the foursome shows me the ropes. Young Maidie joins us often but more as an acolyte; she's at least four or five years younger than we are. "We" being the Young Wives group—or wife-to-be.

I now call the young women my foursome: sweet Kerki with her broad grin and almond-shaped eyes; giggly, pregnant Nydre with stick-like arms and legs; kindly Maura, undeniably tubby yet pretty nonetheless; and Koral, the Moth Bitch. All of them have husbands already, thank goodness, so The Moth hopefully won't be stalking my future husband anytime soon. But I still don't trust her.

There's so much laughter here in Jarmo. And singing! Lots of singing. The people of Jarmo break into song for most any reason. Even a task as simple as bringing home the goats merits a song. So does skinning rabbits and staking out the skins to dry in the sun. Even little children—who run in packs, in and out of the houses and around the small garden plots—are always singing about something. There's so little arguing. No sniping, whining, or shoving. Well, maybe the latter a little bit, just in fun.

Koral finally asks me, straight out, "How is it that you're so ignorant? You're a grown woman, you ought to know better. You should know…more."

It's a reasonable question. One with no easy answer to give. But I try. "Where I come from, over those mountains, there was always someone else to…do the work. You know, hunt the ibex, make the meals, and find fuel, that sort of thing."

"So, what were you doing, all this while? We thought you had a mean suitor who beat you." The Foursome looks puzzled and interested in my answer.

"I…I did. But most of the time I was actually a student." Seeing their puzzlement, I attempt to explain. "I was learning many things from…elders…who had, um, great knowledge and power."

They nod to one another. That's got to be right, they figure. I'm a new, strange person. Very strange, at times. Sometimes I'm perceived as childlike, but other times I'm seen as suspect and possibly dangerous (who knows?). In any case, I'm definitely someone to be reckoned with.

"We'll tell the Wise Ones about your special powers," Nydre pipes up seriously, as if sharing important information. "There may come a day when you'll do us good."

"Let's hope so." I look away as my thoughts are suddenly awhirl. Images of the university night class, the convenience store gunman with the British accent, Professor Vale's piercing look of horror just before we were shot, all tumble together in the kaleidoscope of my mind, mingled with images of Jarmo's brilliant sunshine and fresh air, the laughter and singing of its people, the bleat of goats, and the trill of grassland toads.

"That's probably the one reason the chieftain is willing to take you for a wife," The Moth declares with a carefully noncommittal expression. "Even though you're awfully old for a bride."

"He just wants a wife of his own," Kerki quietly concludes the conversation. "It's perfectly simple. His wife dies, he needs another, then you show up, obviously a gift from our Great Mother, so why should anyone wait? Neither one of you is getting any younger." She pats my forearm reassuringly. "Don't worry. The chieftain is a very skilled lover."

Suddenly, I have a horrible suspicion. "How do you know? For sure?"

"My husband shared me with the chieftain a couple of moons ago," Kerki replies complacently. "He had the need, and his wife was dead, so I helped him take care of it."

"Me too," adds Nydre. "A few times last fall."

"And I, also," giggles Maura. "Once in the winter and once a few moons before. My husband doesn't mind. It's an honor to care for the need of the chieftain."

I glare at The Moth, and she smirks back at me with a shrug that indicates *me too*.

"What of it? It's always been that way in Jarmo. A widower, or widow, must never go without because of the need. It's only right that we should all help. It's unhealthy and even dangerous to go without."

"She's right," Maura reassures me earnestly. "Why wait?"

Why indeed. It comes to me suddenly: Jarmo is so small and the prehistoric world so vast. There just aren't that many potential mates in this tiny community amid a limitless wilderness. Sometimes you have to wait a long time until a mate becomes available. Plus, you don't ever have the option of being choosy. You take whom you can get.

"And so…" I arrive at an embarrassing conclusion. "Everyone here has…um, had sex with my husband-to-be…except for me?"

"Well, yes…" Kerki answers, then qualifies her statement. "Just for taking care of the need, of course. Not to be his mate. We already have husbands of our own. But we must keep our chieftain strong and healthy. Until a new wife can be found."

The other girls nod in agreement.

Something else occurs to me. "But, are there no babies afterward? Do you eat of the purple leaf plant first?"

Koral lifts one eyebrow, and her lips curve into a knowing smile. "What do you think? Of course we do. Unless we *want* a baby to grow."

She rubs her hugely pregnant belly proudly. "My husband would beat me with a bulrush stalk, had he not planted this seed himself! But most men don't like to be reminded about it, you know? That we have this power from the plant to keep a man's seed from growing. So, we don't talk about it. We just quietly…do it."

Later, my foursome and I sit in a patch of shade that overlooks the hot pool, sorting and opening pods of wild peas together, singing while we work. But my thoughts drown out the high, cheerful voices. I stop singing and keep my eyes on my work.

My stomach suddenly clenches with nerves. All of this talk about making babies…My shoulders bunch up together under my ears when I think of my own rapidly approaching wedding night.

Aside from some stupid, literally distasteful kissing games when I was in tenth grade, I have experienced nothing in the realm of sex. Nothing. No Thing. No groping, no stroking, no fingering, no sucking. And certainly not that word that rhymes with sucking. I don't even know what he will do, exactly. I feel myself quailing before the mystery of it all. Yes, I know. I've always been the Odd Girl Out.

My mother was so sick for so long before she died, and I was her mainstay through it all. All throughout college, I could always find excuses—no, "worthy reasons"—for not seeking and nurturing friendships with girls or flirting with nerds in my own lowly league. Not that anyone was looking my way, in either case.

And even if I *had* made the effort, so to speak, who would be interested in me, a squirrel-faced girl with a blocky figure? My teeth alone were enough to put off the guys in the kissing games. Kind of hard to kiss around those teeth. (Yes, I wore braces for two years. They helped—some. You should have seen me before.)

But now my Jarmo teeth are perfect. Well, at least they feel perfect when I run my tongue over them.

I look down at the hands I have now—so long, lean, lovely, and tanned. But whose hands are they really? I know I'm only borrowing them, but from whom? My legs are beautiful; my arms are beautiful. Even the flatness between my pelvic bones is perfect. Just a tiny bit concave, enough to hold a tiny reservoir of water between my navel and dark triangle when I lie perfectly still just beneath the surface of the hot pool.

Sometimes I feel a tiny thrill of fear that whoever owns this body will someday want to return to it and will oust me like the traveling spirit that I am. But that may not happen for a long, long time. Maybe never.

No matter what happens on my wedding night, I figure my husband will not be all that displeased with me, even with my ignorance and clumsiness.

Suddenly, I can't wait for Hari to return.

CHAPTER 11
Becoming a Bride

Rules for happiness:
something to do,
someone to love,
something to hope for.
❧ Immanuel Kant ❧
1724–1804

Stella

I think of Professor Vale's last lecture, the one before the shooting, where he tells us about the primitive lifestyle in Jarmo.

One might assume such a life would be difficult, boring, or harsh. I don't know. Buggy too, probably. Full of dirt and mouse poop.

But now that I'm living in it, I realize it's not like that at all. Instead, it's just so *abundant* in every way. Wild fruits and vegetables, protein on the hoof. Heavenly weather and climate. Friendly, laidback people. And, fortunately, a population that's in small enough numbers so they don't mess things up too much.

The closest neighboring settlement is more than a week's journey away on foot. And foot is all we have in Jarmo. Only goats are currently domesticated. For some reason, they haven't quite gotten around to sheep yet. And the era of the horse lies far in the future.

The same goes for the invention of the wheel.

Here at Jarmo, it's just us and a great big mysterious world out there. *World without end, Amen.*

The words of the old prayer drift, unbidden, through my mind. There's something about Bible verses and Jarmo. I don't know why; they just seem to go together.

It starts creeping me out if I think about it too much, how isolated we are here, how infinitesimal in the grand scheme of things. But no one else in Jarmo seems worried. About anything, actually. All I hear around Jarmo is singing. Or laughter. Always someone is laughing somewhere around the village.

"Wake up, Stella. They're back! The hunters are back, loaded with meat!" Again, my foursome pokes their heads through my open, unshuttered window, tickling my nose with long strands of wild wheat. Well, three of them greet me…Nydre, Maura, and Kerki. Koral is nowhere to be seen.

I hear industrious sounds of chattering voices and the occasional clatter of unfired clay dishes against mud bricks. And, yes, I hear laughter, and I think, *Oh shit*…it's my wedding. Now. Tonight. It's almost showtime.

Already all of Jarmo is busy preparing for the double wedding ceremony and feast.

I'm too full of dread, excitement, and adrenaline to stay in bed any longer. Too excited to be hungry. Maidie and I run outside to meet up with my foursome (still a threesome) and prance along with them excitedly along to the Gathering Place.

Already a happy gaggle of Jarmoites — women, men, and little kids — surrounds the hunters, and Maidie presses a stone knife into my hand. "Come on, Star Girl. Time to prepare the meat for the pits!"

I'm thrust along in the crowd to a place where seven dead ibex lay, glazed-eyed, on the ground. They're a strange-looking, furry mammal, like a cross between a goat and an antelope. These ibex carcasses are dusty, covered with flies, and unbearably odorous.

"Sit by us, Star Girl, and help us skin one out." Clusters of women already surround six of the dead ibex, and my threesome and Maidie start dealing with the seventh.

I watch as Maura takes a wicked-looking obsidian blade and carefully slits a female ibex from her vagina to her neck. She looks like she's carefully attempting to remove a coat from the animal. The others huddle in close with their own knives—some obsidian, others pressure-flaked stone—and start making gentle chop-chop motions between the outer dermal layer and the red, clammy carcass below as they gradually free the animal's outer hide from its body.

Nydre looks at me questioningly ("What are you waiting for?"), so I take a deep breath and take the handle of a stone knife that Maura holds out to me. I pull a handful of loose hide taut and away from the ibex's body and commence chop-chop-chopping. My hands and nails become bloody instantly with ibex blood, thankfully not my own. Every worker is bloody now, but no one gives a damn. Someone starts a song, sings a line or two sweetly a capella, and the rest of us sing it back to her. I even start singing myself, though I have to fake my way through the words.

But all the while, I'm looking for Hari. Looking for the groom. Where is he, anyway?

I also think, *I hope I get a chance to clean up before the ceremony. After all, I am one of the brides.*

The ibex hide is rubbery and tough. With their strong, sun-browned hands, some middle-aged women gut the animals, removing different organs into separate piles, including a big spaghetti-like heap of intestines. Oh yes, everything will be used one way or another. Nothing goes to waste in Jarmo.

They replace the bloody organs with what looks like some kind of root vegetable. And onions. Lots and *lots* of onions. Dried sage leaves, too. And handfuls of salt—excellent! (Where on earth did they get ahold of that?)

Hari, where *are* you? I just want to look at him again. See if he's as desirable-looking as I thought he was three days ago.

And suddenly, I do see him. He sees me, too, and gently but firmly elbows his way through the crowds until he stands before me. Very close. And looking very happy.

"Hello, Stella the Star," he says quietly. Then he envelops me in a deep kiss, simultaneously grabbing my ass and pulling it toward his groin. I cannot breathe, even if I'd wanted to. The crowd cheers their approval; I'm not thinking about breathing just yet.

His short, trimmed beard tickles my face. His tongue seeks mine. *Strange,* I think. So wet and slippery and strange, but I like it. I feel a surge of tingles. Deep down.

But in the middle of our kiss, soon the men of Jarmo start a cheerful caterwauling. "Chieftain! Hey, Chieftain! Beer and wine and a soak! Beer and wine and a soak!" Other men take up the chant, good-naturedly, evidently eager to get started on the day's libations.

Kerki explains to me what's happening. "The men get to go first to the sacred hot pool for bathing. When they're done, then we women have our turn. You know, to clean off the mess, get dressed, and ready for the weddings. It's tradition that the men always bring pots of wine and beer with them. Dried meat, too. They'll stay at the pool most of the afternoon, drinking and telling stories, and laughing their asses off."

As most of the men, and young boys too, amble off to the hot pool — carrying Hari and young Timon aloft on their shoulders, singing at the top of their voices — four teenage boys reach around us women to lift and carry each skinned, gutted, vegetable-stuffed carcass into several deep pits. We follow their procession just to watch, and I glimpse glowing beds of coals in the pits, ready to receive the ibex. Older children cover the carcasses with broad leaves, then scrape sandy soil over them, effectively covering the meat with a lid, so to speak. The seven ibex will slowly cook all day and into early evening, until the meat falls off the bones tonight at the celebration.

It should be a beautiful night. The moon is supposed to be full and rising early tonight — so say the girls — and right now it's another beautiful day in Jarmo. Perhaps they're all beautiful days here, I conjecture, being days in a dream…

But another thought crowds closely in on my initial one. One that elicits in me a faint shiver of dread: I hope I don't awaken from this dream anytime soon.

No. My mind refuses to believe it. *I refuse to go there. Not yet.*

Oh please, not yet. Because I like this dream.

I love this dream.

I've never felt so alive in my life as I do right now in Jarmo.

After joining a chattering cluster of females for a lunch of cold cooked rabbit and pistachio nuts (salted! — they're delicious), we retire to our own little homes for much-needed naps. And I'm thinking there's going to be precious little sleeping done tonight.

CHAPTER 12
Becoming a Wife

Who in the world am I?
Ah, that's the great puzzle.
🙠 Lewis Carroll 🙢
1832–1898

Stella

The gathering of women at the springs is even more hilarious than the men's before it.

Mid-afternoon, while we younger women and children watch from the crest of the hill, five old women, Grandmama among them, walk solemnly down to the hot pool and start chasing the men away. The men leave slowly but good-naturedly, many of them already tipsy on their feet.

"Out, out!" the old women demand in loud voices. They pick their way among intermittent boulders lining the pool and shove the men who don't leave fast enough. They're smiling, but they still mean business. "Go! It is the Time of Women now. We must make ourselves beautiful and talk of secret women things."

Laughing and joking, the mostly naked men and older boys eventually start trooping up the trail, while the younger females watch from above, snickering and giggling, making none-too-subtle editorial comments about the length or girth of this one or that. Koral finally shows up for that part of the action. I note that she's quick to show up for the fun stuff. No trace of ibex blood on her.

I'm feeling slightly dizzy, having never seen that much male nakedness in one place at one time. I can't help looking, goggle-eyed, at the variety of sizes and shapes of the male organ, as well as such broad variations in pubic hair.

Actually, I've not seen any of this at all before, except for pictures of Michelangelo's *David* and diapering for a few babysitting customers years ago.

I scan the crowd for Hari to see if he's as naked as the rest. He is, but I can't see anything (ahem) because the gang of men headed back to the village is again carrying aloft the two grooms, and there are arms and legs all over the place. No doubt they'll sample the beer, tend the fire pits, and drink, then drink some more.

If I remember correctly from Professor Vale's lectures, both beer and wine are relatively recent inventions in this late prehistoric era—an exciting new slap upside the head in the otherwise innocent, responsible lives of Jarmoites.

As we females traipse down to the pool, most with homespun towels or cured hides wrapped around us, I see that some women are also carrying wrapped bundles of…something. Guess I'll see what it is shortly.

A few women carry nursing babies, but most of the children remain up with the men, whether either group is happy with this or not. This is one of the few occasions when Jarmo women can actually be alone with one another, and they aim to take full advantage of it.

We enter the broad, steaming pool with soft exclamations of contentment and pleasure. *Oooh, this feels so good!*

These women must have uttered these same exclamations thousands of times before, as did their mothers before them, and their grandmothers before that. But still, how can they help it? It always feels so good, so new. No matter how much a part of their lives the sacred hot pool is—and always has been, always will be—the pleasure remains fresh.

After we loll about and chatter leisurely for a while, one woman takes it upon herself to announce, "Hair time!"

The women who brought the mysterious bundles fetch and unwrap them. I see large wooden combs, thin leather strips, ornaments fastened by sinew to bone hairpins.

Young, old, and in-between, the women arrange themselves in a circle around the perimeter pool. We're in a daisy chain, half in and half out of the water, all facing in the same direction.

I'm sitting next to my new friends, my foursome, with Maidie close by. It makes me feel so good to be part of a friendship, part of something bigger than myself. All that time, back in my old life, when I was nursing loneliness so close to my heart, I could have been sharing with others—and, by doing so, diminishing the pain.

"Maidie, Stella!" Grandmama calls us over with a smile. She takes our hands and tugs us toward a smiling, forty-something woman. I look back at my foursome with a hesitant smile. What is the old woman cooking up now?

"Stella, sit here in front of Lati. And Maidie, you sit here by Hana. The best hairdressers in Jarmo! Soon you two shall be the most beautiful brides Jarmo has seen yet!"

Each woman starts fixing the hair of the person directly in front of them, and someone starts up a song. Other voices chime in, singing something about migrating birds and secret sweethearts. Their blended voices are incredibly lovely. So relaxed and natural, unselfconscious. So happy.

Grandmama hands me a wooden comb and several thin leather ties, then sits nearby while two little girls start fussing with her hank of long gray hair. I see the back of some strange woman's head, thick with frizzy, mahogany-colored hair, waiting for my ministrations. The head turns toward me. I see a flash of a smile and a missing tooth.

"I'm Leyne."

"Stella." I smile back at her in introduction and take a deep breath as the woman again faces front. Slowly I start to comb the long hair on the back of Leyne's head. Simultaneously, I feel a soothing, combing motion on my hair. I turn my head to smile at my own hairdresser, Lati *(the best in Jarmo!)*.

"Hello, Lati. I'm Stella," then I face front again.

In a leisurely fashion, punctuated by much a capella singing by my pool mates, I create a series of French braids in Leyne's hair. Thankfully, it's uncomplicated, and the knack of it readily comes back to me from my Girl Scout days.

I'm not sure what Lati is doing to my hair, but it must be something fancy. Besides using the bone ornaments, both Lati and Hana make a quick detour into a nearby field to pick masses of spring wildflowers. My hairdresser threads the longish stems into my elaborate hairdo.

I see Maidie similarly adorned. I'd give anything for a mirror. But they won't be invented for ages yet.

Shadows lengthen, the air cools infinitesimally, and my nerves kick into high gear. Suddenly I can't stop my knees from quivering.

The singing peters out, and the talk turns to sex, punctuated by high shrieks of laughter.

Koral (who will always be Evil Mothra to me) casts me a patronizing eye. "You know that our chieftain is, as they say, insatiable. Be prepared, Star Girl! Tonight there'll be nothing left of you but your fingernails." Everyone laughs uproariously.

I'm ashamed and too mortified to tell everyone that I'm still a virgin. They'd be shocked, pitying, maybe scornful, unbelieving. They'd never let me live it down, in any case.

And, besides, maybe this body that I'm inhabiting isn't a virginal one after all. Who knows where it's been, what it's done? But my *mind* is certainly virginal, and my mind is me — my soul, or something like it. Whatever it is, I know that I'm more than just my body, no matter how sultry this body might be at present.

Suddenly, Grandmama stands before me again. Grasping Maidie's small hand in her left hand, the old woman leans over and lays her right hand gently on my shoulder. "Stella, it's time."

The other women come out of the water and gather close around us. Many are wrapped in their towels now against the coming chill, while others tough it out in their nakedness and endure their goose bumps nonchalantly.

Four other gray-haired women flank Grandmama on either side. They are all smiling. Knowingly, kindly, even a wee bit sad. It's an enormous turning point in our lives (even if one of us is only dreaming.)

Whether dream or reality, this marriage is looms large in my life. How could it not?

"Kneel and receive the symbol of Jarmo," Grandmama says softly in a voice that still carries strongly in the peaceful birdsong air. "Now you are no longer children, but grown women, with the rights and privileges, and responsibilities, of a daughter of the Great Mother."

I kneel on gravel in the shallow water. It's distinctly uncomfortable, but I'd best not refuse. Maidie kneels beside me.

I see Maidie in my peripheral vision. *A grown woman,* or so they say. Subconsciously I sigh. The girl looks younger than her fourteen years. And can't be more than ninety-two pounds dripping wet.

Grandmama continues. "You have a responsibility to the community now, as well as to your husbands. To replenish Jarmo with new babies. To make new households. To help keep us, *all* of us, well and strong and safe from harm. To keep things in Jarmo as they are... as they should be...as they always will be."

Everyone is as still as a mouse—no fidgeting or whispering now. I look into Grandmama's eyes and see that this is a serious covenant. A partnership between Jarmo and me.

I am moved to utter a certain word that I haven't spoken since my mom died; it passes my lips before I have time to think about it.

"Amen." When the women look at me curiously, I add, "That means 'so be it.'"

The five old women smile then, and Grandmama nods. So does Maidie. She doesn't seem to be able to speak for herself at the moment.

Grandmama repeats the words, "Receive the symbol of Jarmo."

She dips her gnarled right hand into a small pot of sticky-looking, black substance. Whether ink, tar, or crushed minerals, I cannot say.

In the middle of our foreheads, Maidie's and mine, Grandmama draws with her finger the distinctive Jarmo H.

I know the symbol, from the image on the pottery shard in Professor Vale's PowerPoint about Jarmo. And here I am now, living the dream that's now realer than real.

"Let us go," Grandmama speaks for us all. "It's time."

Everyone exhales then, and cheerful chatter breaks the silence once more as we gather our things and start sauntering back to the village.

I remain silent. My thoughts are long, long thoughts. This is happening; this is real. There is no past, no future. Just the Eternal Now.

CHAPTER 13
Plow My Field

Behold, this dreamer cometh.
~ Genesis 37:19 ~

Stella

It's just after sunset. I'm sitting in what I call the women's section of the outdoor Gathering Place, wearing a borrowed wedding dress, and trying not to drip grease on it as I gnaw the meat off an ibex rib.

The dress is Grandmama's from long, long ago. It's from when she married the first of several husbands, all of whom she has long outlived.

The loose-fitting, sleeveless shift is decorated with red and blue pigments. Snail shells, sewn with sinew, line the hem of the dress — where a hem would be if it had one. Apparently the originator of this fabric just stopped weaving somewhere along the line. On me, the perimeter of the shift is above the knees. It was probably much longer on Grandmama when she was young; she's much shorter than I am, and I feel so tall in this body. I must be at least five-foot-eight, although there's no way to know for sure.

My elaborate hairstyle, lavishly dotted with spring flowers, remains in place by willpower — and maybe a little mud or grease, I'm guessing, for hair spray. While the top and sides are elaborately braided, swirled, tied and pinned up, the back falls free like a waving brunet cape to the middle of my back.

It's been a hell of a wedding — make that double wedding — so far. According to my foursome, Jarmo has never celebrated a double wedding for as long as they can remember.

We're quite a crowd, all one hundred twenty-three of us—no, one hundred twenty-four now, counting myself: men, women, kids, and babies. Laughing, singing, dancing, gorging ourselves on ibex barbecue. Except for the babies, everyone drinks beer and wine. Even the little children take sips.

The president of my grade school's PTA would hardly approve of *that*—nor do I—but, hey, who am I to go against a custom that's decades, maybe centuries, old?

I get the low-down on things from my foursome. They tell me that the party always commences with a sex-segregated barbecue first, females on one side of the giant bonfire, males on the other.

I see Hari watching me from across the crowd. I smile and make a little wave, not sure if it's the thing to do or not. He smiles back and nods. And keeps on watching me.

My girlfriends tell me that dinner is followed by circle dances around the bonfire, first men alone, then with women whom they pull to their feet to dance within the ring of dancing men. With a sentimental sigh, Kerki concludes, "Then the Wise Ones perform the words making the marriage binding, and after that, it's time for the First Bedding. Then we drink and dance until dawn and fall asleep in heaps and piles."

Quite the blowout.

Everyone tells me I look so beautiful tonight, so it must be true. It feels…surreal. I've never been beautiful before, of course. Only supremely average or a somewhat below. As in "forgettable in a crowd." I feel so beautiful now that I truly believe I must be, but still…

I feel like I'm doing a kind of sleep-walking-beautiful thing. Like I might wake at any moment and find all this to be a dream. Or the product of my fever-ravaged brain.

On some unseen cue, many Jarmoites bring out wooden and reed whistles from wherever they'd stashed them earlier. Others fetch wooden drums with taut leather surfaces. Still others brandish gourd rattles and other noise-makers. Let the dancing begin!

Male voices, lusty and loud, sing the words to songs older than time itself. It's hard for me to make out the words—most folks are tipsy, or well beyond it—but I catch the general drift. Something about "New husband, take your new wife, plow her ground, plant your seed."

Jarmoites don't have actual plows yet; that comes later, with the rise of agriculture. But they do have pointed digging sticks for their garden plots.

Not unlike Native American dances, the men skip, dance, and prance in a counterclockwise direction around the fire. I'm entranced by the leaping firelight, gyrating dancers, and hypnotic whistles and drumming.

Then it's the females' turn. As the men dance by the place where we of the Estrogen Club wait, poised and ready, a man will spot his own wife—or girlfriend, or young female friend if the dancer is a young boy—reach out his hand to her, and pull her into the dance. Only the women don't dance counterclockwise with the men; they must start a new, clockwise circle inside of the dancing males and much closer to the fire.

Female after female gets snapped up, joining the laughing, singing, and clapping dancers. But still I stand. Partnerless. And so does Maidie.

We stand close together, as befitting a pair of dual brides, and I look at her inquiringly (Why am I not chosen yet?). Maidie whispers, "Don't worry. The bride—brides—always get picked last. It's the custom. Right before the marriage words."

Suddenly a warm, brown hand with long fingers grabs mine, pulling me into the circles of dancers. Hari. I see young Timon pull Maidie into the ring, as well.

Hari grins at me in the firelight. He looks like a very happy man. That makes me happy, too. I can't seem to suppress this foolish grin.

The two huge, concentric rings around the bonfire make one more revolution, before the Wise Ones—three old men, five old women—step over to a rough stone altar.

A carved stone image of the Great Mother, almost two feet tall, dominates the altar. The statue is flanked by many smaller spiritual images.

Some represent the Mother herself: indistinct face, huge pendulous breasts, generous belly, and a prominent female triangle.

Other figurines look oddly like aliens, with three downward stripes, carved or painted in blue, on each cheek.

The crowd must know what comes next, because it quiets and shifts almost immediately, forming a semi-circle around the Wise

Ones. Hari finds me in the crowd, takes my hand, and leads me to where Timon and Maidie already stand before the gray-heads.

First the old men talk. Actually, only one of them speaks, and the other two stand quietly beside him for moral support. The old man mumbles softly; it comes out in kind of a whistle because of the absence of various teeth. I can't quite catch what he's saying. Then the old man does what looks to me like a churchlike laying-on-of-hands, first to Hari and me, then to Maidie and Timon. Again, I have an overwhelming desire to say amen at the conclusion of his speaking, but I keep it to myself this time.

Then it's time for the wise women, the Crones of Jarmo, to do their part: old Betta, Grandmama, and three other women whose names I still haven't caught. Smiling Grandmama (she looks to be the second in command) holds a small stone bowl filled with some type of pigment. Betta beckons us to come stand before her, Maidie and Timon first, with Hari and me, his bride, close behind as the main attraction.

Betta dips her thumb into the bowl, pulling out red pigment, and presses a red thumbprint both above and below the horizontal cross line of the H. "This is the blood of the marriage bed. Plow her garden, plant the seeds. You are now partners together on this journey through life."

A third crone steps forward with two very thin, leather straps. Using one strap per couple, she binds our wrists together, carefully but with sufficient slack for movement, Hari's left to my right.

Mentally I repeat the old twenty-first century saying: *No one's getting out of this one alive.*

Suddenly everyone is singing loudly. Yet again. With Maidie and Timon in the lead, the crowd surges slowly forward in a procession toward Maidie and Timon's just-built little house, closer to town than Hari's.

Than ours.

"New husband, new wife. Now walk a new way together in your life! Blessings on the husband, blessings on the wife. May the Great Mother bring many children and watch over you always." The song goes on and on, repeating over and over, with little regard to keeping in tune or in time, off-key and out of rhythm, but always heartfelt.

Timon opens the door of their tiny cottage. Together, Maidie and Timon grin at the crowd and close the door behind them as the Jarmoites cheer heartily.

I figure that's it for Bride and Groom Number One, but no, there's more to come. Much more. Everyone remains milling about in front of the house, drinking and laughing.

Hari and I are still holding hands (of course we pretty much have to—we're tied together at the wrist, after all). I incline my head toward Hari's, look into his blue eyes, and ask, "But isn't everybody going to give them some, uh, privacy?"

"A wedding is no time for privacy, Star Girl." He smiles at me, seeing my apprehension. "But it's all right. The people of Jarmo want to make sure it takes, the wedding and the bedding. Babies must be created sometime, if not immediately, if Jarmo is to prosper and endure."

"And so we wait here until…" I look at him under raised eyebrows.

"Until the joining is completed, and there are blood spots on the wedding cloth. Of course, at the wedding and bedding of a widow, there wouldn't be any blood spots, like there will be with Maidie. But there *will* still be laughing, jokes, and songs."

He looks down at me reassuringly. "The youngsters will come out when they're done and show us the blanket spots. And then receive the blue Lines of Marriage from the Wise Ones. That makes it official."

Some ten minutes later, the front door opens. A great cheer goes up from the crowd. A grinning Timon and shyly smiling Maidie carry out a small, gray homespun wedding sheet, displaying for the wedding guests its few tiny spots of blood.

From a different stone bowl this time, Betta anoints both groom and bride with three blue stripes on each cheek. She then paints the tied wrist band with blue pigment too.

"You are now husband and wife," Betta announces solemnly, but she can't help smiling. Everyone else is whooping and cheering at the young bride and groom as they wave goodbye to the guests and close the door behind them.

Hari squeezes my hand, looks at me a little anxiously, and takes a deep breath. "Ready?"

Oh shit, *shit*. We're next.

Suddenly it's showtime, and I'm really nervous. Dream or no dream, there's no backing out now.

My breath starts coming in short gulps and gasps. I feel as if I'm on stage before thousands of people, blinded among the footlights, glazed with panic.

The crowd quiets suddenly. They know that the opening act has successfully concluded, and the main attraction is about to start.

As Betta dips the fingers of one hand into a pot of red pigment, she intones, "May the Great Mother bring blood to your marriage bed, symbolizing the fertile soil in which the chieftain's seed will be planted." She dabs the center of our Jarmo symbols with red paint, directly above and below the cross bar of the H.

The singing, cheering, rhythmic clapping, and constant joking is now higher-pitched, stronger, and louder even than it was for Maidie and Timon. Everyone is pretty wasted from beer, wine, and barbecue. Many are unsteady on their feet, but still experiencing a fever pitch of vicarious sexual pleasure. Even the little children dance about, shoving one another and giggling, enjoying the antics of their elders.

Hari opens the door to our own house, now as dear and familiar to me as if I'd lived there always. With the arm that is tied loosely to mine, Hari clasps my hand and leads me inside. As he closes the door, the singing and cheering grow louder still.

Oh shit…dear God…Hari already knows I've not had a husband before. But does he know that I'm still a virgin? Does he *hope* that I'm still a virgin? I'd better say something. Quick.

My hands and feet are clammy and freezing on this warm spring night. I'm not sure if my legs will hold me up for much longer.

The singing, laughing, and chanting outside the door grows louder. It's starting to give me the willies. Won't they — please, please — just get tired, or drunk, and go away?

In desperation I blurt, "Hari, you know…" I slow my words and try for a semblance of calm. "You…must suspect…that I've never done anything like this before. I mean, well, of course I know how this whole thing works. It's just that I won't know how to…please you…because I haven't…"

"Of course you'll please me," Hari says softly. "You please me right now." I know he's trying to set me at ease. "I wouldn't be doing any of this right now if you didn't please me."

He takes my two hands in his and looks into my eyes. We're in deep shadows. The fire pit's flame is low.

"You please me just by being. You don't have to do anything at all."

He squeezes my hands, then releases one to add a couple chunks of wood to the fire. The fire flares up cheerfully; its shadow dance against the wall somehow reassures me. But still I can't stop trembling.

Hari looks at me uncertainly, assessing the situation.

"Come here," he finally whispers, gathering me close with his right arm; being tied to my right wrist temporarily hampers his left arm. We allow the tied arms to hang down and clasp our hands.

He just holds me, rocking from side to side just the tiniest bit. And holds me and holds me, stroking my hair, whispering, "Shh…" for the longest time.

"Come," he says, gently leading me toward our bed. I can see the firelight's erratic yet comforting gleam. Outside, the music and laughter continue, fueled by alcohol and the lateness of the hour.

"It's all right," he tells me, and slowly I start to believe him. "Just remember, it's all right…it's all right. You can do no wrong here. There's nothing you have to do at all. Just relax and trust me. Once I start knowing you intimately, I'll take care of the rest."

I do feel I can trust him, but all that singing is making me nuts. Like a tea kettle coming to full boil. Soon I'll start whistling, or shrieking, or something — ready to blow my top…

He pulls me down gently so that we're kneeling, then lying, on the bed.

The music, cheering, and chanting grows higher and louder. It makes me want to scream. Hari notices, but he just holds me closer to him with his right arm.

"The singing…I can't bear it anymore." I'm close to panic.

"Shh. Hush now. All you have to do is look into my eyes…and keep looking until the sound grows dim."

I comply with his request. And his magic starts to work. His eyes are so beautiful, such a light, clear blue, ringed by smudgy shadows. Up close, I see how shockingly good-looking he is, how comfortable he seems in his own body, how at peace with his world and his place within it. He keeps looking into my eyes, as if to mesmerize me.

It's working. I exhale. Slowly but deeply.

"No matter what happens, just keep looking into my eyes. I won't do anything that you don't want me to do. Just…float upon the music…and dream."

Then slowly, ever so slowly, his free hand starts caressing me. First my neck and shoulders. Then ever-so-gradually down to my backside, slowly massaging each cheek.

Float upon the music…It's true; it works. The music outside seems more muted and faraway, no longer annoying, no longer distinct. I keep floating.

Hari's caressing hand is now around my waist, moving up to my breasts, still covered by the homespun shift.

It's true what they say about one's wedding day…I do have Something Old: my old brain, which remembers both of my worlds equally. Something New: a new husband in a new world. Something Borrowed: this lovely, vintage wedding dress with the snail shells. Now I only need something blue.

Then I realize I *do* have something blue — Hari's blue eyes. And mine. And the blue-painted cord that binds our hands together.

"Do you realize now how beautiful you are?" Hari speaks suddenly, softly, in my ear. I emit a tiny whimper, my last vestige of apprehension.

"Star Girl, it's all right," Hari softly insists. "Now and forevermore. You do trust me, yes?"

I nod, wordlessly. He plants a very gentle kiss then draws back, still looking into my eyes.

"Then keep looking at me, until…well, until you can't anymore. And by that time, everything will be all right. Do you believe me?"

I nod.

"Do you trust me?"

Again, I nod yes. I look at him in trust and keep on looking… looking…floating on the music and blocking out the raucous noise outside our door.

We're on the bed now. Horizontal.

Hari's blue eyes hold mine in a place where there is no time.

Then I feel his hand moving between us, gently pulling up my shift, and then he's touching me between my legs.

I feel a sudden clutch of panic when I think of dirty, snaggled fingernails touching me there. I flinch, but I keep on looking into his eyes. And there's no pain. I remember seeing Hari's fingernails as he ate lunch with us in his house; his nails were short and clean, most likely trimmed by a razor-sharp, pressure-flaked obsidian blade.

There is slickness between my legs. Holy crap, how did that happen? For a while I can't think at all; there's only sensation. And then… oh shit, oh wow, I seem to be receptive. Two fingers enter me, moving slowly in a circular motion, then pressing toward the front strongly but gently…then moving gradually in and out, in slow motion.

After four or five rotations (or revolutions? Whatever the hell it is, it's exquisite!), I hear a soft groan. *Oh God…that's me.*

"Augh…" I utter the sound again in a higher pitch, a moan instead of a groan this time.

Wordlessly, he keeps doing what he's doing. Again, and again, and again. "Keep looking…just keeping looking into my eyes." His voice is more ragged now. He keeps doing what he's doing, and I keep looking into his eyes.

A pressure seems to be gathering deep within me, and my legs stiffen to attempt to arch my body. I don't know why, but I cannot help it.

I'm wondering…Could it be, can this be the…? Is it really, finally the…?

I look into Hari's eyes for a millisecond…surprise, wonder, embarrassment, excitement, *oh shit, oh yes!* Then my eyes squeeze shut of their own accord. My entire body squeezes like an arched fist as a delicious fire pours throughout me. *More,* I plead wordlessly, *moremoremore, please don't go…*as it gradually subsides.

"Yes, Star, yes." Hari is kissing me now, hard and deep, and I'm still making inarticulate, aftershock noises into his mouth. Then I feel him remove his fingers and suddenly, not roughly, but slowly and deliberately, he thrusts his man part into me. A sudden pinching sensation, deep down there, causes me to gasp, but he keeps on kissing me and doesn't stop. He keeps moving in me in a strong, measured, yet careful motion. I keep my eyes closed now, feeling the sensation. It's like Hari is asking me a question, over and over, and I arch closer against him to wordlessly answer *yes, yes, yes.* Soon he is moving faster and faster, then suddenly he cries out in a strangled tone. He clutches me, shuddering and vibrating in a release of energy and fertile seed.

I feel like I've gone over Niagara Falls. It's all so much to take in — the passion and adrenaline, the gasping and excitement, so much of the great unknown and yet unknowable.

It's the single most incredible thing that's ever happened to me… in this world or the other. I've had to come to this world of Jarmo to become truly alive.

This knowledge is suddenly my bedrock fact: I will crave this union with Hari again, and again, and again, world without end. I clutch him close and kiss him again.

My eyes open slowly. Heavy-lidded Hari is smiling at me. The firelight flickers low and lovely. Neither of us wants to move.

But we have an appointment to keep. Outside, where the Wise Ones await beside our door.

The crowd noise is loud as ever. No let-up in sight. "I suppose we'll have to go out," Hari says with soft reluctance. "Eventually…" He smiles and kisses me softly. Literally and figuratively he's still buried deep within me, and I pull his backside closer to bring him as deep as possible.

"Stay," I plead softly.

"I wish I could now," Hari replies. "Next time, for sure."

He looks deeply happy. Sated.

The singing has reached a crescendo pitch.

"Come, they're calling for us." Hari gently pulls me to my knees on the bed, then to a standing position beside it, arranging my shift properly over my nakedness. He carries the wedding sheet closer to the firelight. I am surprised to see a couple smudges of blood on it — tiny but legal enough for the Wise Ones.

"That's good," Hari remarks, examining the tiny spots. "I'm glad we have something to show them." He puts his free arm around my waist and draws me close. "Ready?"

I nod, and Hari opens the door.

The crowd cheers wildly and sings even louder. The three old men smile broadly. The five old women grin as well. Everyone seems deliriously happy.

We are making all of this happiness together, Hari and I…and Maidie and Timon too. Together, someday we'll make more candles against the darkness, new little ones who will grow and thrive and hold back the shadows in the wilderness.

Still, deep down, I'm glad I secretly chewed a handful of purple leaf plant leaves this morning.

Hari extends the wedding sheet to the old women. They examine it, then hold it aloft to the crowd who cheer as if on cue.

Assisted by Grandmama, the crone Betta intones to us both as the crowd hushes. "Come forth, New Husband and New Wife, and receive this, the marriage covenant of Jarmo." From a stone bowl, Betta dips her fingers into blue pigment and draws three lines down each of our cheeks, both Hari's and mine.

Now I have another thing that's blue.

My eyes behold Hari as a glorious wild man in a simple tunic. His flower-studded dark hair waves around his jaw and stands out around his face like a lion's mane. His eyes burn like blue coals. The red-and-black Jarmo symbol stands out brightly on his forehead. The blue streaks of marriage painted across his oblique cheekbones disappear into his short-trimmed beard.

Betta then dabs blue pigment onto the narrow leather strap that binds our wrists together. "May you multiply and be fruitful together for the glory and honor of Jarmo. Our home, always and forever."

Amen, I silently add. It needs an amen to make it real.

Amen. So be it. Forever and always, world without end. Amen… amen…amen…

With the happy cheers of Jarmoites ringing in our ears, Hari clasps his hand in mine, guides me back into the house, and closes the door—and closes out the rest of Jarmo.

CHAPTER 14
New Wife, New Life

There is a place like no place on earth.
A land full of wonder, mystery, and danger.
⟩ Lewis Carroll ⟨
1832 – 1898

Stella

I have a new life now. And whenever I acknowledge this fact, whether it's verbally to my new compadres or silently within the privacy of my cerebellum, my heart crinkles with foolish love of it.

In my previous life, if anyone had ever told me that I, Stella Denton, raised in a metropolis of nearly four million people, would find myself living amongst just one hundred twenty-three individuals — and loving it — I'd tell them they were crazy.

And if they'd also told me I'd be living in a strange, remote land on the other side of the world, well, I would think *poor me*. How inexpressibly boring they'd think it must be.

Well, save your pity. I'll happily take your congratulations and envy, though!

Life here isn't boring at all. My Jarmo life is full. Full to the brim with sex, friendship, sex, happiness, sex, community, passion, and love. And more sex, laden with so much irresistible lovemaking that I literally prance through the days with a foolish grin permanently pasted on my face.

Hari's at the heart of it. *My* heart. So calm and centered, he doesn't fit the typical village chieftain persona at all. Thankfully, neither does he have a "big fish in a little pond" complex. He's attractively deliberate, calm, and unhurried. After all, what could there be to hurry about—or worry about—in Jarmo? At least, the way it is now?

All I demand from him, and receive, is a lot of lovemaking. He readily complies, and then some. A lot of the time, I feel like I'm moving about on rubber legs, so bone-deep satisfied am I after my frequent workouts with Hari. After the wedding, on our first morning together, we both awoke to spring birdsong, the blue paint streaks newly dried on our cheeks, and we came together again in the best way we knew how. He was incredibly patient and skilled at teaching me how to meet him more than halfway.

Each day, we awake and have lovely, leisurely morning sex, and then move blithely through the days. Sometimes busy with our own separate pursuits, me learning new tasks from young women far more capable than I, and Hari off with the men, hunting or tending to issues of state, such as they are.

But sometimes we're just off together. By ourselves.

Grandmama now divides her time between the two houses, Hari's and mine, Maidie's and Timon's. At first I was hugely embarrassed that the old woman could hear us from her bed in the main part of the house, even though she couldn't see us.

"Why?" Hari asked me in genuine, placid puzzlement. "Does it worry you? It shouldn't. It's…well, the core of life, who we become when we come together. Why should that make you embarrassed?"

And the old woman, obviously eavesdropping—there's nothing wrong with her hearing—pipes up in the darkness. "Yes, I like to hear it! Why be embarrassed? I'm not, and you shouldn't be either. Ah, it makes me feel young again."

Somehow, now that I live in Jarmo, that seems to makes perfect sense, and I no longer worry about the sounds wafting out from our part of the L-shaped house.

Hari teaches me not to be embarrassed by outdoor lovemaking either. Sex is such a natural part of life here that people do it pretty much wherever and whenever they like. Young children take it all as a matter of course—something that the big people do, no big deal, except that it makes their parents smile, which is a good thing.

Let me qualify that a bit. It's true that people don't have sex in the middle of a crowd, but maybe they will under a pistachio tree at the edge of town when they think nobody else is around. Or snuggled together under furs around a campfire, say, or on the crest of a foothill near the hot springs. Not in the center of town, no, but certainly around its edges. Even in midstroke, they'll still wave an unembarrassed greeting at folks passing by, and the passersby will return their own cheerful acknowledgments.

I'm getting more nonchalant and daring about this myself. It's such an addictive pastime, and time is so abundant in Jarmo. As I happily drift on the current of passing days, I sometimes feel as if I'm floating inches off the ground—so happy, so loved, so safe, so unstressed. So satisfied with life and with the two of us.

Living in Jarmo is like—what? Being retired, maybe? Being only twenty-and-a-half years old, I wouldn't know. But I know that it does feel like summer camp, all day, every day. A very special, romantic summer camp. Needless to say, I sleep like a just-nursed baby most every night.

Although there are heaps of tasks to be done each day, there's such a mind-blowing abundance of everything in Jarmo—berries, fruits, birds' eggs, meat, fin, and wing, wild root vegetables, edible gleanings, goat hair for weaving—that no one, not even the laziest Jarmoite, ever goes hungry. Jarmo's climate is perfection itself, mostly Mediterranean, gently temperate year-round, with little difference between summer and winter (or so I've been told; I haven't experienced winter yet), and green things just keep on growing. No one suffers very much from winter's cold since it rains only sporadically, and it only snows higher up in the mountains. Jarmo is truly Eden where one day follows another…*world without end, amen.*

From the girls, I learn when, where, and how to pick pistachio nuts. Pistachio trees grow everywhere here in small thickets, halfway up the mountainsides. The girls show me how to soak them in water, then salt them (from our stashes of salt that we bargain for with the obsidian traders, who show up twice a year), and bake them around the perimeters of our indoor cooking fires.

I learn where to find snails and how to cook them (I gagged on them at first, but now they're downright addictive, especially when simmered in goats' milk butter and a little wild garlic). The girls instruct me on how to shear wool from Jarmo's small flock of goats and from carcasses of a certain sheep species they call argali, and how to spin it into yarn. I learn how to gather eggs (which, where, when, and how), how to set traps for rabbits and pikas, how to skin game and prepare strips of meat into dried jerky, and how to make water pouches from ibex stomachs and needles from the fine bones of small mammals.

I even accompany Hari on hunting parties sometimes — ten to twelve persons usually, both men and women — seeking the wild cattle that Jarmoites call aurochs. But we're also on the lookout for horses. Yes, wild horses. To *eat*. Of all things…

I haven't seen any yet, though. That horses are actually a prey species here makes me astonished and more than a little queasy at first. "You actually hunt horses and *eat* them? But why? Why don't you just ride them instead?"

"Ride them?" Hari raises one eyebrow and can't help laughing. "Not possible, Star Girl. You'd have to catch one first! Which I doubt the horse would put up with for long. They're just too fast, strong, and dangerous to bother with that way. Except to chase off a cliff and then roast over a fire pit. Ibex or young aurochs are much easier all the way around."

As Hari first makes his equine excuses, I'm accompanying him on a small hunting party — just eight people today, men and women both. We'd set out together this morning, and we're presently scouting for game south of Jarmo along the Great River.

At a deep level of my mind, I know that Jarmo will eventually become part of the Fertile Crescent, the Cradle of Early Civilization. *Right here in this very place…*

Hairs on the back of my neck rise as a shiver of unease ripples through me.

Thankfully, my Squirrelly Girl inner voice reassures me — see, she still can show me her good side if she wants to. *Don't worry, Star Girl, it's not happening yet. Jarmo won't become part of the Cradle of Civilization for another thousand years at least, maybe two thousand. I know you love Jarmo exactly the way it is. Remember when Vale said that the Old Ones first domesticated the horse pretty much around here? Yes, folks did it in other places and other cultures too, but they did it here first. Just remember, that's all still far into the future. Until then, or unless some human changes things earlier than we'd thought, horses will remain a dinner item, not a game-changer of civilization.*

Hari and I, along with the others, stretch out beneath a huge, spreading oak on the crest of a small hill. It's very hot. Flies buzz erratically. Not a cloud in sight. High summer has well and truly arrived. Hari gathers me in close with his right arm. Despite the heat, it feels wonderful to be close to his sweaty side. And so safe.

Hari speaks softly since our fellow hunters doze in the shade. "Stella, look. You've been wanting to see horses, and finally I've got some for you. About a dozen, walking our way."

Hari points out a small herd of equines, ambling and grazing with apparent unconcern near the Great River.

The horses are stocky little things, gray-brown and taller than a burro but shorter than modern horses, at least ones I've seen in pictures. As a (former) city girl, I really don't know squat about horses, modern or ancient.

These have a soft-looking, grayish-tan manes, tails, and coats with a black stripe delineating their spine. And look at that—zebra legs! Yes, actual black stripes from their flanks on down. Big blocky heads, compact, and strong. And I'm thinking, *They've sure got a long way to evolve.*

The broad valley before me goes on forever, mile after mile, to the horizon and beyond. I'm so transfixed that it's hard for me to breathe. It's a vast diorama before me, rich with living species. So many animals graze peacefully before us, some familiar to me, most of them not, as far as the eye can see.

Hari points them out to me with an understandable pride-of-place; he obviously loves it here, loves the animals, and loves his place in this natural world.

"See?" he says, pointing toward the river's edge. "There, a couple of four-horned antelope, by those boulders. And over there, look, short-eared elephants, and further down the valley, those tiny dots? They're ostriches."

I ask what the large animals are that I see ambling toward a nearby wetland. They look like cows on steroids.

"Aurochs," Hari says. "Remember when I told you about them? Their calves make great eating. As you yourself well know, since we had auroch backstraps for dinner last night."

I recall the name auroch now from Professor Vale's lectures: a huge, wild cattle species that once flourished here, now long dead for some two thousand years. I observe the brownish-black bulls and reddish cows stepping about sedately on their absurdly long, slender legs, their massive horns broad and elongated.

With Hari's arm around my shoulder, we lean against the oak tree's broad trunk and savor its shade. Hari warns me there are also big cats in this country: the wily short-eared lion, as well as black cheetahs and long-tailed tigers. Cave bears, too.

"They're not out right now because of the heat," he explains. "They're resting, as we are. But they're likely watching us right now from their hiding places, even as we keep an eye out for them. That's why we puny humans always travel in packs."

With high mountains to the east and a cluster of foothills to the north, the river valley looks like the African Serengeti Plain, only fuller, richer, even more alive. In perfect balance exactly as it is.

The voice in my head sounds wistful as her commentary meanders into a sad quagmire. *And now, most of these species have disappeared from the earth…for all these many thousands of years. Hari is gone, too. And so are you. Dust on the wind.*

No. *No.* I stir against Hari's side in sudden panic. I gasp and look about wildly for a moment. Hari's eyes meet mine with concern, and he draws me in closer.

"It's nothing. I was just…thinking," I quickly fabricate an excuse. But still, I look up at him, my eyes wide with concern. He kisses away the horrors.

"Everything is all right, so try not to think too much. Stella, you always think too much. You need to just…be."

I nod and hug him tightly, shutting my eyes and shutting out the immensity of an uncertain future.

Hari is my refuge, now and always. His presence helps me endure the screaming mimis of deciding whether I'm sane or insane, whether the Jarmo world is real or unreal. His presence keeps me from worrying about what can truly be known *for sure* and what remains an unknowable mystery.

"I'll always take care of you, Star Girl."

And so I choose this life. *This* life. This is not a long time ago. This is real.

The Other, that is the dream. This is Now, the Eternal Yes.

Much later, before we head back to Jarmo, our hunting party takes down two young auroch calves with bows. The eight of us carry the two carcasses home, tied to poles by hemp ropes, leather straps, and sinew. It's sad to think of the two auroch mothers losing their babies to our relentless, rapacious species, but I know it's the way of Nature. Kill or be killed. Eat or be eaten.

If given enough time and space to do so, Nature in Jarmo always manages to replenish her species in her own good time. So far, anyway…

I look out over the endless, peaceful herds feeding on lush grasses that are always there through winter rains and summer snowmelt, appearing so effortlessly and endlessly across the valley.

Hari says not to worry. Hari says there'll always be more when we need them. There will always be more. Or so he says.

CHAPTER 15
Obsidian Traders

Where was I? Did I wake or sleep?
Had I been dreaming? Did I dream still?
☙ Charlotte Brontë ❧
1816–1855

Stella

Here in Jarmo, as high summer slides inexorably toward autumn, I'm learning. A lot. At least it feels like a lot to me. I feel like I'm starting to deserve the title of Hari's consort.

I'm becoming more useful to Hari, and to the village, in more ways than just serving as his official bed partner, although that's still my favorite role. I'm still careful to surreptitiously nibble a few leaves from the purple leaf plant each day. I'm so happy just the way things are; I don't want to risk a pregnancy just yet.

Even Hari seems ambivalent, at least for now, about the question of babies. Natural, I think, given his tragic history concerning his stillborn children. He's perfectly content to just let things slide for a while.

Sometimes I wonder…would it really be a real pregnancy, or only a dream one? Would my baby even be real? Am I really here?

Or is everything in life — either life — truly a dream? And if so, who is doing the dreaming?

But this line of thinking can lead me to madness.

So, I refuse to go there. Instead, I just hold my head high as I join in the flow of life at Jarmo, as we laugh, work, and sing our way through the days.

Only one thing scares me a little, and it's something I truly love: the sacred hot pool from which Maidie and Grandmama dragged me as they ushered me into my current life.

Might there be a wormhole in the pool, a passageway from the twenty-first century into prehistoric Jarmo? How did I get here, really? And who am I really? Could the hot pool pull me back down again (into…where?) if I step in too deeply?

I can't resist the delicious hot water of the pool, nor can most other Jarmoites, so I find myself succumbing daily to its irresistible temptation. As the Squirrelly Girl voice reminds me, *Don't overthink things, Denton.*

However, I'm careful only to loll around in the shallows of the pool's perimeter; I don't walk out past my knees. I know for a fact that, while it's mostly shallow, it's very deep in some places, and I don't want to tempt fate to suck me away again.

One glorious late summer morning, I suddenly hear a neighbor woman cry out, "They're back! The obsidian traders, they're back!"

Suddenly the village is a swarm of activity. *Visitors!* Such a novelty to see familiar but different faces for a change. We've been expecting them for some time now. The obsidian traders travel a regular trading circuit, spring and fall, but of course there's no way of knowing in advance exactly when they'll show up.

Hari is off supervising, and no doubt lending an occasional hand with, the digging of a new latrine ditch. He'll hear the news soon enough — pretty much everything is within earshot in Jarmo — so I race outside looking for the girls, my clique of young wives, the group that unfortunately also includes Koral.

However, as much as we dislike one another, Koral has been part of this clique forever, herself born and bred in Jarmo. I'm still the newbie and must be content with my place in the hierarchy of friends. There frankly aren't enough people living in Jarmo for anyone to be finicky about whom to invite into one's group.

I locate the girls among the chattering throng surrounding the traders, who include three bearded men, two women carrying toddlers in slings, a boy who looks about fifteen, plus two gray goats held by lead ropes with loaded panniers across their backs, and three excitable herd dogs. Our own dogs, Trusty and Whitefoot, are in the throng too, barking with the best of them.

There'll definitely be feasting and stories, as well as gatherings each night, until the traders move on southwest, following the Great River.

I'd never seen obsidian objects before, close-up, until coming to Jarmo. Our people are keen to trade items—from animal pelts to stone bowls, bags of dried berries to woolen tunics, anything—for the exotic blades these people create and trade.

An obsidian blade is a beautiful thing, razor-sharp and highly prized among our people. Not only do the traders barter obsidian blades and tools, they also trade arrowheads of multi-colored flint and hammer stones made of shiny gray chert for making flaked projectile points. The two visits by the obsidian traders each year are times we greatly anticipate, like the Fourth of July or Christmas.

I thank my lucky stars that I took Intro to Geology as a sophomore to fulfill a science requirement. I still vaguely remember hearing how lava sometimes extrudes sideways from a volcano, and if it cools rapidly with minimum crystal growth, shiny blackish lumps of glass are the result. Since it's naturally very hard and brittle, obsidian can be purposely worked, causing it to fracture into pieces with very sharp edges. These pieces make great cutting and piercing tools, as well as arrow points that kill cleanly and fast.

Because there's no obsidian to be found anywhere near Jarmo, there's keen demand for the obsidian traders and their desirable skills and products. The traders obtain their raw materials from a mountainside near an enormous lake to the northeast, over the big mountains.

Over the next few days, most every Jarmoite will line up to trade, goods for goods. The obsidian traders allow Jarmoites to watch while they ply their skill, called knapping, at shaping the raw obsidian or flint into flaked tools. Obsidian knapping, flint knapping, the traders do it all with great pride and skill.

Yes, our men of Jarmo *could* learn this skill if they set their minds to it, but it takes a boatload of practice to become good at it. Plus, we have no flint, agate, or obsidian anywhere around here. It's easier to leave it to the experts and save our wish lists for the traders' twice-yearly visits.

After the big barbecue and blowout tonight, the first night of their arrival, the members of the obsidian trader band are farmed out, in singles or pairs, to various family homes so they can sleep indoors for a change.

As apparently has long been his custom, Hari invites the teen-aged boy—Ashur is his name, Hari knows him well and has watched him grow over the years—to bring his sleeping furs into our home.

Although Ashur is short for his age, he seems like a bright boy with a good-looking, beardless, olive-skinned face. He seems overly curious, though. He checks out everything and says very little, but his keen black eyes miss nothing. After the eating, singing, and drinking start winding down, he makes himself a fur-lined, indoor sleeping nest near the apex of our L-shaped house. That means he's clearly within sight lines of both Grandmama's bed on one side and Hari's and mine on the other.

Ashur keeps looking at me, which makes me a little uncomfortable, but I just smile politely and say nothing. But after we're in bed, with Ashur snoring away quietly in his corner, Hari tries to explain.

"Ashur means no harm. He just needs to look. At a woman. He'll soon become a man, one of these days, and he'll need to learn what to do. And how to do it properly."

I wonder aloud (but not loud enough to awaken Ashur or Grandmama), "And so…how *will* Ashur learn to do it…um…properly?"

"Just like we always do here in Jarmo," Hari tells me, quiet yet unembarrassed. "Have you not wondered why young Tork is staying with a different family than his own for a while? Or why Derk's son has moved in with Nia and Kirt for the summer?"

"Not exactly." I don't know if I want to go where this conversation seems to be headed.

"An older woman must teach him for a while. For a few months, until his own prospective bride is ready."

I am aghast. "But, what does the older woman's husband think?"

Hari smiles at me in the semi-darkness. "He doesn't mind. It's how he himself was taught years ago, and his father before that, and the grandfather before him. It pleases the Great Mother, showing the next generation what to do and how best to do it."

I look at young Ashur as his chest rises and falls in a gentle, peaceful rhythm. He sleeps on his side, toward Hari and me, with both hands tucked under his cheek.

I whisper to Hari and splutter in dismay. "But he's…he's nothing but a child, for heaven's sake! It's…well, it's indecent, is what it is."

"Shhh, don't wake Ashur." Hari effectively shuts me up with a kiss and a whispered final explanation. "Most likely, when Ashur returns to their real home in the southwest, one of the older women will teach him. Not a relative, but someone else. Someone with at least twenty seasons or more. Someone they like and trust to show their son the right way of things, so that when he takes his own bride, he'll know what to do."

After a welcome interlude of showing me exactly what he means, Hari is soon breathing rhythmically beside me as starlight pours in through the open window. Ashur continues to breathe noisily into the night. I'm thinking with grumpy annoyance, *That boy certainly needs his adenoids removed.*

I consider the concept of taking such a young stripling into one's bed, and I don't know what to think. I lie awake for a long time, staring into the darkness at the overlapping reeds that comprise our ceiling.

Then suddenly, not aware if I'm still awake or sleeping, I feel a sudden, searing pain in my head, just behind my left ear.

"Aughhhh!" I emit a noise that sounds like a grunt, a groan, and a cry, mixed together.

"Stella?" Hari is awake in an instant. "Star? What is it?"

All I can do is cry out a second time, then a third. Finally, I can manage to gnash out the words between clenched teeth, "My head. Oh, Hari, it hurts…right now…really bad!"

Dimly, I'm aware of young Ashur and Grandmama moving about, talking in concerned voices. Someone puts more wood onto the fire so they can see better.

The stabbing pain jabs again and again. It feels like someone impaling a screw driver into my brain. Twisting it around, and around, and around.

I hear someone crying out, and it must be me. Hari examines me closely, fear radiating from his face. "Stella, Stella! Did something bite you or sting you? Show me where it hurts. What happened? What can I do? What *should* I do?"

Grandmama and Ashur also draw close to my side, worry showing plainly on their faces.

The pain grows even worse. I feel like my brain is being tugged out of my body by a crochet hook through a thumb-sized hole behind my left ear.

Fumbling through unbelievable pain, I try to feel behind my left ear with my left hand. There's nothing to be felt there but my hair. My sensitive eyes seek relief in the firelight shadows from this assault on my senses.

My ears then fill with a disturbing gurgling sensation as if I'm underwater, like that of many bubbles, trying to carry me up, up, and away.

Then I experience a sudden vision of harsh *(artificial?)* lights, glimpsing objects that look metallic, square, and strange. Tubes hang from some of the objects (not possible, there's nothing metallic or square in Jarmo, only natural shapes of natural things). I seem to be in a narrow bed with a white, waffle-weave blanket, and there's someone sitting next to me. Someone, I can't quite make out who…

No, not *that.* Not *again!*

I continue to cry out as I feel my body become simultaneously rigid and rippling with vibrations. I must be having a seizure. Part of me observes this clearly, I've no idea how.

Through the bubble-sensation, I feel Hari clutching me in his arms, crying out, "Stella, Star! *Star!* Tell me how to help you, tell me—"

Mentally, I cling to the sound of his voice. *Don't let go, don't follow the bubbles. Hari, keep me safe! Hari, keep me safe! Hari…Hari…Hari…*

Miraculously, my brain seems to obey this mental command. Gradually, ever so gradually, the pain in my head subsides. My body ceases its rigidity and vibrations. The bubble-feeling subsides. Finally I open my eyes.

Above me, I glimpse the dear, familiar, thatched-reed ceiling. I see Ashur's and Grandmama's faces in the firelight, panicked and helpless. I exhale, long and slow, and my face relaxes.

Dear Hari hugs me fiercely, tighter than tight, his voice rough with simultaneous fear and relief. "Oh, Star, *Star,* you're back. Thank the Great Mother you're back. What happened? What was it? Where did you go?"

The pain in my head is gone. But I know what's happening. Suddenly I know with a sureness beyond space and time.

It's my old life trying to pull me back again.

It's that bullet in my brain, that God-damned bullet. Trying to drag me with it and out of Jarmo, away from everyone and everything I now love.

"It's gone, stopped now." I look up at Hari as I whisper-croak the words with a faint, crooked smile. "It—"

I close my eyes and give a faint shake of my head. My skull, as well as the gray matter inside it, doesn't hurt me anymore. I don't know why. I'm just glad the pain is gone. For now.

Hari looks fearful, unconvinced.

I try to explain. "It's from an old injury. To my head. Sometimes it just…comes over me. But I'm all right now."

I repeat the words with a bit more force. "I *am*. Just…keep me safe…please?" My last sentence sounds tremulous, even to me. "Just hold me. I'll be all right now if you just keep holding me."

A few neighbors call to us from outside the front door. They've heard my cries and wonder what's going on. Grandmama tells them I've had a bad dream and sends them away.

Eventually (what can they do, after all?) Grandmama and Ashur creep back to their beds and into an uneasy sleep. Despite the night already being so warm, the fire pit is kept stoked to make things easier to see, should I start crying out again.

And finally, Hari and I fall back asleep too, wrapped in one another's arms. We share a fevered sleep with jarring, unsettling dreams. Finally, at morning birdsong, I awake into blessed normalcy. *Thank you…* That's all I can think just now, but it's enough. And I mean it to the core of my being. *Thank you for bringing me back.*

I know where I am again. It's where I'm supposed to be. Here in Jarmo where I'm Real. Where it's always Now.

Harry

One afternoon, while I'm helping conduct a paleoanthropology workshop (and picking up extra cash in the process), my cell phone vibrates in my pocket while I'm lecturing.

I manage to give it a surreptitious peek as I speak. The ID window displays a number I know by heart: the nurses' station in the Step-Down Unit at HCMC.

Holy shit. Something must have happened to Stella. Something's wrong or something's right. Something—

I cut my lecture brusquely short (let 'em sue me), sprint into the hallway, and press the speed dial number for the nurses' station on Stella's wing.

"Professor Vale, you'll want to come quick!" the nurse manager gushes at me with breathless excitement, pleased to be first with the news. "It's the most amazing thing! Brace yourself—Stella is starting to regain full consciousness! She did for almost a minute today before sliding back under. But the doctors are confident she'll regain consciousness again very soon, and this time it'll probably be for good."

So stunned am I that I can only stupidly utter, "Uh, what?"

"Stella! She's awake. That is, almost. Just out of the blue, she started moving her arms, like in swimming motions, you know? As if she were drowning and trying to come up for air. She made sounds, too, and we rushed to put the plug in her trach so she could speak aloud if she wanted to. She just kept making these sounds, and then she went under again. She's quiet at present, but Dr. Montrose is sending her down for a follow-up EEG. Oh, aren't you excited, Professor! Stella's trying to rejoin the world!"

Suddenly my feelings are all over the map, conflicted as hell. There's simultaneous joy and a thrill of fear at her responsiveness. I also feel shame and internal abasement at my widespread deception as her "fiancé." I'm suddenly afraid of what Stella will say to me, if anything, when she wakes and decides to stay. Or what *they* might say. I even harbor an odd, wistful regret over losing this quiet yet companionable time together with Stella. Who the hell knows what I'm thinking? I really couldn't tell you.

But I know it's time to act.

"I'll be over immediately. Fifteen minutes, tops."

CHAPTER 16
Perchance to Wake

There are as many worlds
as there are kinds of days…
⟩ John Steinbeck ⟨
1902−1968

Harry

Traffic is a nightmare. Plus there's a car accident on I-94. Not a deadly one, thank goodness. I see both drivers standing around looking dazed; two highway patrol cars are already in attendance. No time to give it much thought. I've got other matters of Life and Death waiting for me at the hospital.

Driving into the city on Friday afternoon from a workshop in Eden Prairie is a dicey prospect at best — rush hour starts shortly after lunch, I swear — and I arrive at HCMC long after I promised the nurse manager I would.

I literally sprint out of the elevator on Stella's floor and try not to clomp too loudly on the gleaming tile floor as I head for her room.

Various nurses and aides smile and wave at me as I pass by. I'm such a fixture on this wing, most everyone knows me by now.

"Come and see!" The shift nurse is already halfway around the nursing station counter. "She moved her arms a lot, then *looked* at us. And actually *saw* us. We put the trach plug back in case she wants to talk!"

I flop my briefcase and laptop bag onto the guest chair beside Stella's bed, then lean over and peer at her intently.

Except for having shorn hair and wearing the black hockey helmet, Stella almost looks like Stella again. *Even better, actually.* No more swelling, no more pumpkin head. Her cheeks are thinner than they've ever been. Her shaved hair is starting to grow out. She looks surprisingly fine…and so close to regaining consciousness.

I take Stella's hand. The blue anti-clawing mitts are off. A frown line creases her forehead between her pale, untidy brows. She looks distressed. Worried, even. As if she's not liking her dreams but is unable to wake and escape them. Her white Shiley trach tube seems to glow in the fading sunlight through the window.

Seeing her like this—even as close to consciousness as she is—she still looks so vulnerable, so helpless. So at our mercy regarding what we might do with her.

Most coma patients do not look pretty. Or even normal. Some photos of long-term coma patients that I've checked out on-line look ghastly. Contorted, twisted, mouth agape with intermittent drool to be wiped away.

Oh, Miss Denton, I think with a wave of pity. *Are you going to finally be my partner? Are you going to come back and take me with you as we move forward together into life?*

"Stella," I speak softly but distinctly, close to her ear. "Stella, it's me, Harry. Sorry I'm late for my visit. There was a backup on the freeway."

I watch her intently for any motion, sigh, twitch, cough. There's nothing.

"Well then, darlin'…" I call her darling, partly because I'm supposed to be her fiancé and partly because it just feels good to say it. "Well then, darlin', I'll put on some music—the usual—and tell you about my day."

I take out the iPod and miniature speaker from my briefcase and set it up close to her ear. The lush, romantic theme of "Andante con Tenerezza" soon infuses the air. I think of it as our Jarmo song since I used it as background music in the PowerPoint presentation about Jarmo.

Dr. Montrose suddenly stands over me. Thank God he's not gone home yet, because I want to hear details. Stella's neurologist looks simultaneously excited yet cautious, hoping against hope.

I'm afraid he's going to tell me something like "Let's not get overconfident, brother!" but he doesn't.

I turn Stella's music down very low and eagerly grill Montrose, pleading for specifics: when and how did the brief awakening happen, what did she do exactly, were there any witnesses—and how can we make it happen again?

I can't help asking, "Doctor, this has *got* to be a good sign, right? Especially after her being out these past three months. How can we get her to open her eyes again, and stay that way?"

"I'm the first to admit to being blown away by this myself," replies Montrose. "And I must still advise some caution here, Harry. Remember that she's been in a coma for more than twelve weeks. Even if she awakes at this very moment, there will be a long recovery plateau for her, several months at the very least. The longer folks are in a coma, the longer it takes for them to return to something like normalcy. But I've got to tell you, her EEG brain wave test just came back, and damn! It's exciting!

"Of course, being a neurologist, I may be showing partiality to my favorite organ, but the brain has *got* to be the most complex and exciting organ in the human body."

I can't argue with him there.

"From here on in for Stella," Dr. Montrose adds, "it all depends on her brainwaves."

"How so?" I ask.

"The brain emanates its activity in brainwaves, and human beings have five different kinds of 'em. Let me show you. Got anything I can scribble on?"

I quickly rummage in my bags and come up with a few sheets of copy paper and a cheap ballpoint.

"The kinds of brainwaves humans experience most of the time are betas—normal waking consciousness."

Dr. Montrose makes squiggles on the paper that look like a printout from an oscilloscope. Lots of peaks and valleys, sharply up and down. Anticipation still courses through me; I can hardly sit still, hardly listen to him, but I manage to stay in my seat and look intent.

"Betas are pretty fast brainwaves, mostly up-and-down zigzags. You experience beta waves when you're talking, hanging out, working, even sexually aroused. Regular stuff."

I muster an encouraging sound, and Montrose continues.

"Next we move into alphas, which are slower than betas but with higher amplitude. More up, more down. When you're very relaxed." Dr. Montrose makes more pronounced, vertical squiggles on his brain wave schematic. "Everybody loves those alphas. You know how people always talk about being in alpha, and, yeah, it's a good thing. We're in alpha when we take time out to relax or meditate. It's when we feel calm and peaceful.

"From here on, though, things get wonky. When you start to daydream or blank out on the world—you know, like when you've been driving your car, but you suddenly realize you can't remember the last ten minutes of the drive? Drowsy and drifting. That's when you've moving into theta. Theta waves are slower than alphas but can be higher in amplitude. Being in theta means you're in a complete break from conscious reality."

I look at Montrose's sketchy diagrams, and suddenly I feel overwhelmed. It's a whole new world for me, all this jargon, all these brainwaves. A world unknown to me: the inner world of Stella Denton's brain.

"Ah, but there's more! And it gets even stranger," Montrose continues. "Once you go beyond thetas, you move into deltas. Very slow brain frequency and very high amplitude."

He shows me his sketches, and I nod. His voice sounds as if it's coming from a great distance. I wonder what brain wave I'm experiencing just now.

"Deltas occur in a deep and dreamless sleep with complete loss of body awareness. Rather like Miss Denton, here. But beyond that, beyond even the deltas, alphas, and betas, there is still something more. Far and away beyond it all. And that's the gamma waves, small and fast, originating from the thalamus of the brain."

Montrose looks thoughtful just then, and looks away from me as he speaks. He keeps his eyes fixed on Stella.

"Gamma waves are simply…mystical. No other way around it. They're associated with perception and consciousness. They're what make us who we are as a person…or as a soul. They're associated with higher mental activity, a feeling of inner peace, unconditional love, an interconnection with all things. They happen in REM sleep and are also present during the process of…awakening."

Awakening. There's that word again.

I think of how many times, too many to keep track of, when I've whispered the following imperative into Stella's right ear, then into her left, "Awake, Stella. *Please.* Wake up. For me."

Montrose looks about to see if anyone else is listening to us. No one is. Nurses and aides move back and forth, taking no notice of two unremarkable-looking men making notes by Stella Denton's bedside, the entire scene bathed in late afternoon sunshine.

I try to explain my concern to Dr. Montrose. "Look. Don't you think she looks different somehow after this episode? See, it's like she's frowning. Or afraid, maybe. About something over which she has no control."

"Maybe," Montrose considers. "Don't tell my fellow saw-bones about this, but personally I believe that she *is* thinking. Right now. The EEG test results show that she's finally producing gamma waves. This tells us she's still in there. Alive, awake, and aware. And ready to come back at any time."

Again he looks around to make sure no other doctors are listening. With so much close contact between us over the past weeks, Montrose knows I've got an open mind, something many doctors don't possess. So, the neurologist speaks to me with surprising frankness.

"And so, Harry, the long and short of it is…I believe that gamma waves are…" He laughs in embarrassment. "Connected with the beyond. It's gamma waves that make you recognize your own consciousness. I mean, if you believe in that sort of stuff. Of course, there's a scientific bickering about this like you wouldn't believe!" He laughs again, an explosive unhappy bark. "Believe me, nobody can argue with more rancor than one doctor to another, scientist versus scientist."

"I'll bet." I can't deny that one, silently acknowledging the rampant sniping and malice in my own corner of academia, paleoanthropology.

Suddenly I'm very tired. "You're getting way beyond me, doc. Guess it's something we each must decide for ourselves. But what *I* want to know is…" I look at Montrose as I attempt to draw the conversation back from the brink of the unknowable immensities. "What can we *do* — actually, tangibly, right now — to help bring Stella back to consciousness?"

"Two things, actually," replies Montrose promptly. "Things I never would have advised doing, even as recently as last week. But now, with her sudden move toward consciousness, I say let's go for it!"

He pulls a bottle of pills from the pocket of his white doctor coat and tosses it toward me.

I catch the pill bottle and read the name of a popular commercial sleep aid on the label. "No way!" I can't help laughing; it's so implausible.

"Wild, isn't it?" He laughs with me. "But sleeping pills have been shown to be really helpful at restoring consciousness—in some cases. We'll add a crushed pill periodically to her feeding tube. It's the latest science now, no kidding. Sometimes it can bring them back. Not like in the movies, of course. But gradually, and sometimes effectively. Over time. And if that doesn't work, we can also try implanting electrodes in the brain since we now have evidence of her increased brain wave activity."

I shudder on Stella's behalf. That sounds horrible. But it may be necessary if we want her to return to life.

"Let's try the pills first," I tell Dr. Montrose.

"We have to remember that, in Stella's case, it all goes back to that bullet in her brain. And it's still there, still touching her thalamus. We always come around to that thalamus again, and that's what makes things so maddeningly difficult."

Montrose gives a little shudder. So do I.

Suddenly I blurt aloud in a pleading voice, without thinking first, "I…I just hope…that she's dreaming now. Thinking or dreaming something good. And not just existing, brainless and thoughtless, in the dark."

"Me, too," says Montrose. He speaks quietly. "You know, scientists used to say that dreaming only occurs during periods of rapid eye movement. But now we know better. Dreaming occurs during other times, too. And, so, may her dreams be sweet ones."

Montrose stands up suddenly. "Well…" he concludes. Our private moment is over. "Until later. We'll be watching her like a hawk and will call you ASAP if she starts wakening again."

I look down at Stella's troubled face and take her hand in mine. It still hasn't wasted away into something delicate and willowy. It's still squareish. But it seems even more vulnerable than usual.

Dear Miss Denton, my inner voice speaks into the void with aching need. *Oh, Stella, where have you been all this time? And are you ready to join me among the living?*

CHAPTER 17
Death Comes to Jarmo

As the generation of leaves,
so is that of men.
❦ Homer ❧
800 BCE – 701 BCE

Stella

"I'm fine!" That's what I keep telling everyone in the days following what I call my head episode. "Really. It was just a...recurrence of an old injury. I slept it off. It's gone, over and done with."

Folks tiptoe around me solicitously for a few days; then they take me at my word and start forgetting about it. Except for Hari. He continues to watch me. Keenly and with doubt. And he continues to worry.

One morning, not long after the incident, Jarmo's typically idyllic weather takes a nose-dive. It sleets and blows, causing the obsidian traders to begin preparations to move on.

Once the brunt of the blustery weather passes, the obsidian tribe moves out into weak-looking autumn sunshine. They're leaving town, heading north over the mountain pass. They have to go before it starts snowing again, effectively sealing off all travel in either direction for months.

Young Ashur claims a hug from me — too long and much too close, but what the hey — before they head out. Most of the population of Jarmo comes out to bid them goodbye as they head off on their circuit. First they'll travel far to the north and east to obtain more obsidian raw materials near Big Lake, then west, trading with other tiny settlements scattered thinly throughout the wilderness, and finally south, along the lower Tigris River, where they'll spend the winter in their comfortable seasonal camp, working the raw obsidian into the objects of trade that is their livelihood.

About Ashur…oddly enough, yes, I'll miss him particularly. Miss those inquisitive black eyes that see everything. Miss his laugh. Half-boy, half-man, almost a head shorter than I am.

I lean my back against Hari's chest. Hari, my Biblical "ever-present help in times of trouble," wraps his arms around me as together we watch the obsidian traders move slowly yet inexorably along goat trails toward the Shining Mountains to the northeast. The snows could come any time now. They must make it over the pass, plus a few days more—nearly a week—to reach the People of the East. There, they'll need to rest and replenish their food before cutting north toward the Big Lake and the obsidian foothills.

We watch until the traders are mere dots against the terrain. Suddenly we can't see them at all, as they vanish against the immensity of the countryside.

On the following day, a string of heavenly days settles in over Jarmo, bringing with it golden light and surprising warmth. Twelve halcyon days in a row. Fall wild flowers spring up where none had been a few days ago.

Everyone in Jarmo seems happy, even Hari, who relaxes his vigilance over me a little to let me go where I will. First, to the hot pool with my girlfriends, then on pistachio nut reconnaissance treks with several family groups, and finally he takes me with him on an extended group hunting trip, which I adore.

The land of Jarmo looks more beautiful than I've ever seen it. If I were back in Minnesota, I'd call it Indian Summer, but here it's just business as usual, and I love it.

I'm lulled into a sense of complacency and happiness once more. And I think, winter won't be coming for ages yet. And even when it does, everyone says it doesn't amount to much, just a little rain.

After the last of the golden days, on the thirteenth night, I awake in pre-morning darkness to a throbbing head. My bullet, or what I sometimes call The Ghost of The Bullet, reminds me of its unwelcome presence in my head.

Reminds me from the inside.

A strum of panic ripples through me at the sudden pain. Dear God, not again…

My feet and palms start to sweat. But I can't acknowledge the situation just yet.

I can't. *I just won't.*

I can almost feel the bullet shifting. Seeking release. Escape.

Like it won't give up until it's out in the light of day.

Tears well in my eyes. But I refuse to tell Hari about it just yet. *Hush now…hush now…If I don't tell him right now, it'll probably go away. Like before.* I order myself to *just give it time, don't give in to the pain.*

I wrap myself around Hari's sleeping self like a vine, close my eyes, and will myself to sleep…sleep…sleep. And amazingly I finally do.

I wake to an uncharacteristically cloudy sky. A stiff, cold breeze blasts in through the open window. Hari sleeps on, deep in his bed furs, sleeping the sleep of the blessed.

As I rise to close and fasten the shutters from the inside, my head gives a warning throb. First one throb, then another, more powerful and erratic than last night's pain. Yes, it's undeniable. The pain is still there. Shit, oh *shit…*

I aim for what I hope is a neutral expression, trying to suppress the pain's evidence from my eyes, as I sleepily move toward the fire pit. The house is cold to the bone. I stir last night's embers, adding some sphagnum moss for tinder and sticks to reanimate it. Then I move slowly about the place, head still throbbing, as I start shuttering the other windows.

Before I close the northeast window, I look toward the Shining Mountains. A unseasonably early storm shrouds the peaks in whitish-gray mist. I note with surprise that it's actually snowing up there. I've never seen real snow around Jarmo, snow on the ground that is, only as picture-postcard, blue-white coverlets over the highest peaks.

Then I see something else. Out of the misty whiteness, a dark dot appears, making its way slowly down from the heights.

The dot grows larger.

No, it's two dots, joined together. Two persons. Clinging together, stumbling down the goat trail from the mountain pass. Who would voluntarily be out traveling in such weather?

Eventually they're close enough for me to recognize two of the obsidian traders, one of them Ashur. The other is his uncle, Samon.

Both are stumbling slowly, gory with blood and looking exhausted beyond belief.

"Hari! Hari!" I screech. "It's Ashur! He's coming back. Quick, something's wrong!"

My head gives another warning beat of pain, as if in caution: *Pay attention to me.* But my feet are already flying, back to rouse Hari. I hurriedly strap on my calf-high sandals and grab a fur-lined cloak.

Sensing our agitation, our outdoor dogs emit a furious volley of piercing barks, causing other neighboring dogs to do the same. Within seconds, the neighborhood is wide awake, with folks pouring out of houses, wondering what the fuss is about.

Meanwhile, I make no mention of my pounding head as Hari and I scramble up the goat trail to meet the two fugitives. At least they look like fugitives to me, wounded, bloody, and beaten.

Amid an exclaiming crowd of Jarmoites — they're suddenly afraid: *Who could have done this to our friends? It's like an attack on us* — Hari and I, with help from others, manage to guide the two escapees, sometimes dragging or literally carrying them, back toward the village.

Hari calls for more furs and bedding for Ashur and Samon. Food, too. Lots of whatever is available and ready. Ashur and Samon probably haven't eaten in more than three days.

Hari also orders an outdoor bonfire to be built nearby in an open grassy area and a temporary bed of sleeping furs made up for the two beside the fire.

He knows that we can't secret the two fugitives away in our home just yet. All of Jarmo is now gathered around the runaways, dying to hear the news, now that the two have wolfed down some food and water.

We're all collectively horrified and clamoring for explanation. What calamity spurred their escape?

"It was the ones who call themselves the Shield People who'd moved in on the People of the East," says Samon. He speaks in a weak, gravelly voice; in fact, he's close to passing out altogether. Even saying these few words exhausts him.

Samon is mottled with dried blood. Below the knee of his right leg, broken bones, yellow-white and garish, protrude from the mortified flesh. Ashur is blood-sullied, too, but only by association with Samon. Otherwise, he seems to be unharmed, just bone weary and scarcely aware of what he's doing.

"Let them rest a bit first," Hari orders. He speaks in a voice that carries with calm authority, but he looks shocked. Evidently, this is a situation he's never faced before. "Bring food and drink, keep them warm, whatever they want. And somebody fetch Neti and the girls."

Neti and her two daughters are Jarmo's healers: herbalists, bone-setters, midwives, and more. I figure they must be good. I've not yet seen any real sickness here in Jarmo and only occasional minor accidents or broken bones.

Finally, the two fugitives have collected themselves enough to speak. Still lying pretty much prone on the makeshift sleeping nest under a mound of furs, Samon speaks so weakly and softly the crowd can't hear him. From the crowd comes a sibilant buzz: "What? What's that he's saying? Hush, I can't hear him…"

And so, seated on a block of wood beside his uncle, wrapped in a wolf pelt, with his belly full enough, Ashur speaks up. "Don't bother my uncle. I can tell it all. I was there too."

He swallows a couple of times before proceeding. Gathering his thoughts, no doubt. Steeling himself to relate the horrors. He projects his voice to carry across the crowd.

"It was King Vizla," he says, but doesn't explain.

"Start from the beginning," Hari tells Ashur with more than a little impatience.

So, Ashur begins. He tells of their journey up and over the mountain pass (uneventful, still snow free, four-and-a-half days of travel) and their arrival at the village of what we and the obsidian traders call the People of the East.

"And the place has really changed since our last visit. It was always kind of dry around there, but now it's *really* parched. With nothing much left for gathering. Hardly any ibex or auroch for hunting, either. Nothing for meat, only the goats."

Ashur tells of seeing familiar faces among the People of the East. But more of them are strangers now from even further afield. The ones who call themselves People of the Shield. They've come there with their king, a man named Vizla.

"They arrived in the village just a short while before we did. Act-ing friendly with the native folk, at first. You know, eating their food, smiling at their women from a respectful distance, asking many questions, appearing to help without really doing anything—stuff like that. Their king, Vizla, he seemed to…fascinate them. Such stories he told! He was so…so confident. And so…what is the word? Smooth. No one ever questioned him. He…charmed them."

Ashur looks bemused, even now. Then he clears his throat and continues. "Then we obsidian traders showed up, and they started asking even *more* questions of everyone, and smiling even more."

Ashur's voice sounds wobbly just then, but still it carries clearly over the silent crowd. "They acted like they were everyone's best friends, until one night, when…"

He pauses again to articulate his painful thoughts.

"One night, after laughing and joking around a big bonfire, we all went to bed. And then, in the middle of the night, King Vizla and the People of the Shield came to murder us all, People of the East and obsidian traders alike."

The crowd gasps, bursting out in horrified speculation. But Ashur isn't finished.

"Quiet! Let him talk, let him tell it all," Hari orders, and the crowd falls silent.

"I should have said, they came to murder the men and the grandmothers, little children too. But *not* the younger women. Those they raped. Over and over. And they decided to keep those who were still alive. It was like nothing I've ever seen. Just…horrible. My uncle and I could see it all in the light of the bonfire which was stoked and burning brightly. Probably on purpose so the Shield People could see where to find us all in the dark. There had to be a prearranged signal. *Had* to be, so that, after the rest of us fell asleep, the Shield People would move through the village and kill us in our beds as we slept. Like I said, everyone but the young women."

A voice from the crowd calls out to Ashur. "What about your father and your other tribesman, your mother and aunts, and the babies?"

He looks down at his feet and shuts his eyes, then looks away. Silently he shakes his head.

"But why? Why would the People of the Shield do this terrible thing?" Other voices are shouting now.

The clamor goes up, and a gaggle of different voices competes to be heard. "Yes, why? We've all heard of one man killing another man in a fight or over a woman…but killing *every* man? For what reason? Why would anyone do that?"

"Hush!" someone shouts. "Samon wants to speak!"

The gravely injured Samon struggles to rise to his elbows. It costs him a great effort, but he does so just the same. Ashur stops talking in deference to his uncle.

"It was because they had…spoiled it all." Samon's voice is bitter yet quavering.

The crowd is silent, listening. The wind blows the bonfire into wild peaks and valleys.

"They'd spoiled their home, and their food, and wild game…and they wanted to take over somebody else's. Simple as that. The man who tried to kill me said so. Before I killed *him*…"

In a halting voice, Samon relates his version of the night of horror.

"Ashur and I were sleeping in our furs apart from the big bonfire, away from everyone. Probably because there was no room close to the heat. We had our own tiny campfire and were just drifting off when I heard the screams. Suddenly, out of the darkness, a little fellow with a big knife came at me, armed with one of our own obsidian blades!" He laughs at the irony, but the smile doesn't reach his dead-looking eyes.

"So, we tussled something fierce. You know I'm not one to go down without a fight. I yelled for Ashur to run for cover and don't stop running. I still didn't really know what was happening yet. But I finally managed to wrestle the knife away from my attacker and pin him down. And before I stabbed him, I had to know, so I yelled at him, '*Why?* Why are you doing this? Just tell me and I might not kill you.'"

Samon looks beyond exhausted but manages to continue. "It was hard to understand him because his words were strange, somewhat different from ours. But I could still make out what he said. So, I kept him pinned down with the knife at his throat as he told me, 'Because we *can*.' Can you believe it? I yelled at him again, 'What? Because you *can*? That's no answer!'"

Samon pauses to expel a wad of phlegm. It's mixed with blood. Then he continues.

"So, he said to me, 'We're taking over this East Mountain land right now, poor and worthless as it is, to use as a base of operations.

To rest up, and recuperate, and prepare. Because, next spring, soon as the snow melts, we're going over the pass to conquer the land they call Jarmo.'"

Samon exhales sharply, a man with little hope. "I still had my knife at his throat, and his arm was all twisted up behind his back. I figured to keep him talking a little longer till I got the answers I wanted. I asked him, 'Why Jarmo?'"

Samon pauses to take a shaky, shuddering breath. All this talking…It's depleting what little reserve he has left.

But he rattles on, talking more weakly but even faster now. Lest he pass out—or pass on—before he can finish his report. "They call it the Land of Promise," Samon says.

I think of Jarmo, so lush and green, rich with women and game species, food for the gathering—everything an invader could want.

Samon's voice is soft and fluttery now. Like the gentle rattling of an autumn aspen leaf.

"Then…then he says to me, 'Spare me now, and we can escape together tonight. We'll head for Jarmo and beat the rush.' I killed him then, of course."

He shows no emotion whatsoever except immense weariness. "I met up with Ashur. Eventually. From the light of the big bonfire, I saw many bodies on the ground. All our men dead. Wives too… including my Alix. All dead, except Ashur and me. Even the babies."

Samon stops talking for a while. He starts choking on another wad of bloody phlegm. Ashur pats him on the back until the coughing fit subsides. He must be coming to the end of his tale. How much worse could it get?

"We took off running the same way we'd come into town, only a few days before, back toward Jarmo. We managed to escape during the night. But around dawn, I took a wrong step. Squirrel hole. We were still trying to run. I pitched over into a gully. Heard a snap when the leg broke. It hurt like…like a…"

Too weary to speak anymore, Samon falls silent.

I look at his exposed leg. Ravaged and purplish like spoiled meat with tinges of green. The tip of a yellowish broken bone protrudes from the skin.

But no. Samon has another sentence or two left in him. "It's snowing in the high country now. Snow'll be deep on the pass. No one is going up *or* down till spring. But once that snow melts…"

At last Samon exhales, nods weakly *(There, I've done what I came here to do)*, and drifts off to sleep. Or unconsciousness.

The crowd doesn't know what to think, what to say, what to do. Even Hari seems nonplused. Or thunderstruck. *Both,* I think.

But I know what I think, and I think it with cold horror, down to my bones. *They're coming. They're coming to take Jarmo.*

CHAPTER 18
Remembering

Touch has a memory.
~ John Keats ~
1795 – 1821

Stella

W e finally put Samon and Ashur into a real bed — both of them on Grandmama's pallet at our house — and build up our household fire to a comforting roar. Almost instantly, the two refugees fall back into an exhausted, shock-induced sleep.

We start dispersing the crowd, urging everyone back to their own homes and pursuits. No one knows quite what to do now. The news is too awful. Unbelievable. We have nothing whatsoever to compare it to in our experience.

The day continues cold and raw. Many men and even a few of the women gather to talk more about this imminent threat to Jarmo. Since the two surviving obsidian traders are now asleep in our house, the group moves several doors down to Maidie and Timon's cottage. At least fifteen of us crush together inside while Timon stokes the fire.

Then we hear an old woman's voice, calling out into the cold air. "Dead! He's dead!"

It's Grandmama. And then there she is, banging open the door and looking around at us all, her tanned face a sorrowful mandala of wrinkles, as she repeats the words. "He's dead. It's Samon. Samon has died in his sleep. Ashur doesn't know yet. I let him sleep."

Everyone looks to Hari to tell us what to do next. And surreptitiously, before he speaks, Hari glances over at me. I close my eyes in sympathy and horror, but still, I nod at him to continue on. As our tribe's headman, it's Hari who must provide direction.

Hari curses softly under his breath. Samon, gone—broken bones, blood poisoning, utter exhaustion. It's a wonder he lived long enough to make it back to Jarmo. Now Ashur is truly the last man standing of his tribe.

"May the Great Mother receive him joyfully into the next world." Hari intones the words like it's a prayer, and for all I know, maybe it is.

My head is still throbbing, but nonetheless I'm impelled to sidle over to Hari. I wrap my arms around his waist and whisper in his ear, "Let me help. I can tell our people about them. I know things about the enemy."

Hari shoots me a quick look of concern *(What is my mysterious wife coming up with now?)*, but he nods.

Hari continues; not even the death of Samon can delay what needs to be said.

"All the more reason for us to talk of war now. To face it head on. My Stella is the one to tell you. She was born far beyond the Shining Mountain country, and she knows the evil these people do. As for me, I know that one man can, and will, go up against another man to the death. When I was younger, a man of Jarmo, someone we all knew, stabbed another man over a woman. In those days, we didn't have enough women, and tempers ran high. But I'm still not sure…Why would *all* of the Shield People want to fight against all of *us*, people they don't even know? Stella knows the ways of strangers, what would cause their tribe to rise up against us. And she knows what to do about it."

He looks at me hopefully, wordlessly urging me to take center stage.

In my old life, millennia in the future now, I've rarely been one to speak up in class. I don't even like the sound of my own voice. So nasal and hesitant even to my own ears, it typically makes me cringe.

But now, with our very lives at stake and the future of dear Jarmo weighing in the balance…well then, what possibly I *can* do to keep it from harm, I *must* do.

And I *will* do. No matter what it may cost me.

My head throbs ominously again. *Shit.*

I silently order unhelpful Squirrelly Girl, who still lurks deep inside my head, chattering away and poking her lacquered fingernails into my cerebellum: *Just stop the pain. Stop it, please. I don't have time for this crap right now.*

My brain responds with a constant, low-grade pain that pulses with each heartbeat.

Ignoring the pain as best I can, I muster all of my memories from Professor Harry Vale's Paleoanthropology 110 class. I stand up, and my very presence commands the hard-packed, earthen floor.

I speak slowly but my voice is surprisingly loud. It carries throughout the room.

I'm relieved, and oddly touched, to find that people are actually listening. Listening to *me.* Stella the mush mouth. No, Stella the former mush mouth. Now, Stella the Warrior Princess. For real — not some seventies TV character.

"My people — my *original* people — lived much further from Jarmo than the Shining Mountains People or even the Shield People. But I've been taught the history of both tribes, and I know. This horrific attack happened because of greed and the need for self-preservation."

I pause for a moment to give my words more weight. "After living many years far to the northeast of Jarmo, the Shield People are now experiencing a change in weather patterns, bringing with it a prolonged drought. Over time, the Shield People have become wasteful and shortsighted. Just damned *lazy* is what it is. Killing too many animals, too often. Acting thoughtless and heedless regarding the plants of the fields and woods, gathering way too many, far too often. Not leaving enough to grow back for future days and generations. So, they're starting to get hungry. Running out of animals to hunt and foods to gather.

"And goats!" I add, almost accusingly, looking from one face to another. Ever since coming to Jarmo, I've detested the goats: their increasing numbers, the stink, the way they strip a plant of its leaves in the blink of an eye. "The Shield People have far too many goats, as *we* are starting to accumulate, too. Damned goats anyway, eating every living plant in sight! The land of the Shield People is now dry and barren. Even the goats have little to eat, and the Shield People don't know how to fix things. So, they just decided to take over another tribe's hunting grounds and homes. *Ours.* Since they had spoiled their own."

A sudden hit of pain roils behind my left ear. I close my eyes for a millisecond until it passes.

"And when we of Jarmo don't want to give up our land without a fight…well, that's going to mean war."

Everyone remains speechless, even Hari. I can see from many faces that they don't really know the meaning of the word.

"War means…killing. Our men and women against other men and women. Even the little children. It's either killing or slavery, with someone else forever being our master and using us as they will. When things get out of balance, and the Great Mother and her gifts are no longer respected and loved, war always results."

Still there is silence. No one knows what to say, what to think, what to feel.

My head throbs, slamming me hard, and I wince. I must conclude what I want to say; it's important. I need to finish…and then lie down.

"The Shield People want our very home and lives, because they've already used up theirs. We have to prepare to fight them. Any way we can."

The people seem dazed, incapable of understanding just how serious this threat is. If, indeed, it even *is* true and not the gabbling of a desperate man trying to cheat death. These people know nothing of war. It has never happened in Jarmo before. There was always plenty for everyone.

Hari speaks quietly then, subdued and uncertain. "Stella, is there any way to avoid this coming war altogether?"

"No." There's no way to sugarcoat the message. "No way to stop the war. But we might be able to *win* it. *And* keep our homes and land."

A faint aura of hope pervades the room. Faint but palpable.

"It's going to take every one of us to go against them with everything we've got. And some things we don't even have yet to win such a war, things we have to find, or do, or…invent."

I can't help it; this fact must be brought into the light of day. "You *do* realize, don't you, that there *will* be bloodshed? As in blood that is, literally, *shed*. Killings. Many deaths. And even then, when it's all over, things will never be the same as they were. But we can still prevail. *If* we prepare. If we prepare ahead of time, before they arrive—"

"But how should we prepare, Stella, specifically?" young Timon asks plaintively. "How can we win this war?"

Just then a sickening wave of nausea passes through me before I can reply. My head is pounding so hard, it makes the gray light coming through cracks in the shutters seem piercing, so bright I can hardly bear it.

Suddenly I'm dizzy and shuddering. Convulsing. My legs collapse beneath me. Oh no, *oh shit, not me, not here, not now…* Hari moves like a flash to grab and hold onto me before I hit the floor.

Even in the refuge of his arms, I windmill my limbs and flail about. The pain is so intense, I don't know what I'm doing. My world is nothing but pain that keeps pulsing and pulsing and pulsing.

Dimly I hear Hari calling my name, "Stella, Stella!" as gray bubbles seem to swirl about me. It's hard to breathe. My head feels about to burst. I'm making inarticulate noises, voicing my pain in a scream.

And then I am dissolving into a pinpoint of light. Again. And rising toward the ceiling.

Again.

As a point of light, somehow for a while I'm still able to see everything below me. I view things dispassionately: the little mud-brick house, Hari hovering, frantic with worry, over my limp body, the crowd of neighbors squashed cheek-to-jowl around us.

My pinpoint of light continues to rise. Soon I'm above it all—and the little Jarmo house is a million miles and a million years away. I move, upward and forward, through gray mist into a shadowy tunnel that seems to beckon.

A male voice calling, "Stella, Stella!" permeates my consciousness.

I don't know if it's Hari. I'm not sure where the voice is coming from, but somehow it's a comforting sound.

The voice changes somehow as the indistinct walls of the tunnel blur past me.

"Stella, Stella!" The voice sounds louder now and different in tone. Still male, but less frightened, somehow deeper.

I feel something, or someone, plucking at my hands (I have hands again), touching my arms (I have arms), stroking my cheek (I have a face).

I also have eyes again, because I can feel myself opening them and looking out onto a twenty-first century world.

CHAPTER 19
Returning

Remembrance of things past is not necessarily
remembrance of things as they were.
↝ Marcel Proust ↜
1871 – 1922

Harry

"Stella, Stella!"

It's finally happening. Right now, before my eyes. For once I'm at the right place at the right time. Stella Denton is awakening at last!

It shouldn't take me by surprise, though. For the past couple of days, Stella's been restless. Making occasional humming sounds, even faint moans. Dr. Montrose and the pulmonologist ordered her trach plugged since she's breathing well on her own. They want her to be able to talk audibly whenever she's ready.

Each day, Stella receives crushed particles of the prescription sleep aid, along with "medicinal food" (in other words, nasty looking gruel) into her feeding tube. This crazy cure seems to be working. The more of these meds she receives, the closer she approaches consciousness.

Stella shifts her arms and legs about in apparent aimlessness, so much so that they have to be gently restrained with small bungee cords. They probably have an official medical name, but they look like bungee cords to me.

Up until now, her eyes have been opening halfway, looking dully at nothing, and then falling shut. She even moves her helmeted head a bit.

Whatever she's experiencing in her inner world, she's concerned and restless.

It might be silly and unscientific, but I can't help thinking that she's between two worlds right now and she must choose. The inner world or this temporal one. And neither world comes with any guarantees.

I'm here by her bedside on a late Monday afternoon for my daily visit, nervously pecking in lecture notes on my laptop, while the "Andante con Tenerezza" plays softly in a loop on the iPod at Stella's bedside.

All of us, everyone connected to Stella in any way, are just waiting for her to wake up. And stay that way, if possible.

Chuck Denton paid Stella a visit this past weekend, bringing his new wife, Laura. Both of them clucked and cooed over Stella, and were friendly and personable enough with her doctors, the nursing staff, and me. They even brought a huge box of designer bakery items as thanks for the staff's invaluable help over the past three months. But I could tell Chuck and Laura were secretly relieved to exit the hospital and return to their own normal, healthy lives.

Shortly now, my life will be full as well. I'm moving up to full time work very soon. It's fall, and the university is giving me more classes, more hours. It's about time.

Stella's restlessness excites yet unsettles me. It's so strange to observe her apparently aimless movements on the bed. I keep asking the nurses, "Are you sure she's still in a coma? That she's not in pain? Can she hear me? Shouldn't we be doing something?"

They reassure me that this random movement is quite normal for a coma patient, as well as being an excellent sign of improvement.

"She still doesn't know who she is or where she is just yet," the nurses reassure me. "It's pretty much reflexive movement. But it won't be long until she opens her eyes for good!"

"I can't wait!" I say with feigned pleasure. But still I worry. What will happen when Stella wakes? Will she be normal? Will she even know who in the hell I am? Will she buy my story of being her fiancé? Why did I ever launch such a lie into the world?

But I know the answer to that one without having to ask it of myself: I wanted a purpose. I wanted a partner. Someone to love. Who would hopefully love me back.

I wanted a partner for Stella, too. Someone…well, someone like me. And maybe she'll learn to love me back. Eventually. So long as I don't mess things up by providing TMI.

Earlier today, I worked on reassuring myself by reiterating what doctors and staff have told me over these weeks: "When she finally does wake up, just remember that it won't be like in the movies. It's pretty much gradual. In stages. She'll still be terribly confused. Probably grumpy as all get out. And very, very tired just from the business of *thinking*—she won't be used to that, remember. Don't be surprised if she doesn't remember you. Or her apartment, or teachers, college friends, any of that. Her old memories will be far more intact than recent ones. Plus, remember, she'll have to relearn how to walk again. Oh, so many things! Most of all, she'll need that bone flap screwed back into her skull."

I'm waiting for Dr. Montrose to stop by on his late afternoon rounds. We're usually his last stop of the day. He's got to see this. Stella has never been so close to wakefulness.

In a clear voice, in what I hope is a calm, reassuring tone, I lean in close to her ear—her good ear, not the one damaged by the gun blast—and call her name.

"Stella! Stella! Stella, wake up, darlin'. Stella…Stella…" Finally I order her, "Open your eyes, darlin'. Stella, open your eyes!"

With her eyes still shut, she finally answers me.

"No." It comes out sounding very normal, strong even.

I can scarcely breathe. "Stella! Stella, darlin', wake up and see me. See the world. It's still here. We both are!"

"No!"

Well, her *no* sounds emphatic, all right. Very clear, too. Her next words are a bit slurred, petulant and wistful at the same time. "I want Hari. Where's Hari?"

She's saying my name…I think. But why? She has not even opened her eyes yet, can't really know it's me. And why *would* it be me sitting here beside her? To her, I'm just one of her professors. Another face in the crowd, but I hope she at least thinks well of me.

She's saying my name funny, too. Hah-ree.

Suddenly Montrose is here, too. Instantly he takes in Stella's condition, looks at me in astonishment, then sheer glee. He takes one of Stella's now-unmitted hands in his own and looks at me as he smiles broadly. "Hello and ahoy there, Stella! We're so glad you're awake, my dear. Welcome home!"

"Hari," Stella murmurs. "Wanna see Hari. Wanna go *home*."

Already she's tired from the effort of just these few words. She still won't open her eyes.

Dr. Montrose reassures her. "Harry's right here, Miss Denton. Stella. You'll have to open your eyes if you want to see him. He's sitting beside you. And *has* been, most every day since you've been here."

I add my plea to his. "Open your eyes, darlin'. Harry is right here."

And finally she opens them fully and looks about, following the sound of our voices.

Her eyes are a little bloodshot, tinged with yellow from antiseptic drops, but still a brilliant blue. I'd forgotten what lovely eyes she had. *Has.*

Without too much difficulty, Stella manages to focus her blue eyes on mine.

"Hari?" She sounds, and looks, horrified. I can see she suspects I'm an imposter—anyone but the real Harry.

Could she be seeking another person named Harry? But, I mean, how likely is that? After all, she's pronouncing the name funny… sort of foreign…

"Yes, Harry's here." Dr. Montrose grins broadly and wills everyone else to be jovial, too. "Sitting right beside you."

She seems on the edge of panic. "No! I want *my* Hari." She starts calling for him a fretful, frightened voice that gets progressively louder. "Hari? Hari?" She strains at her tethers and attempts to sit up. "Hari! Where is he?"

Oh, Jesus. This isn't the way I'd imagined her awakening. I rush to soothe and gently try to restrain her. As I do, a trickle of nervous sweat slides from my hairline along my forehead and down to the bridge of my nose. That makes my glasses slide a bit sideways, so I rip them off impatiently and drop them on the end table. I lean in close to Stella and take her hands in mine.

"I'm here, Stel. Harry is here…"

The sight of my naked face obviously rattles her, and she becomes even more agitated. She starts to cry, huge wracking sobs, turning her head from side to side. Looking for something, someone, she doesn't find.

I look at Dr. Montrose helplessly. All he can do is shrug and whisper, "It may be best to move back a bit."

But I don't comply. Instead I move in even closer so that my blue eyes are just above her own. Gradually she settles, growing less agitated, and gives me a searching look.

"Hari?" she asks. Seeming to hope against hope.

Why this odd, faint accent? Where does *that* come from?

All she can see of me are the blue of my eyes, up close and personal. Suddenly tears gush from her eyes once more, but she smiles crookedly.

"Hari!" She says it again twice more—once as if asking a question, and finally as if giving the answer.

I look closely at her and repeat my name: "Harry." I use the regular, flat intonation of this not uncommon yet still pretty dorky name.

"Hari," she echoes, using the other pronunciation.

"Harry," I correct her. Gently, softly. In a non-threatening way.

"Hari…" Again she repeats the name her way, but wistfully, in an uncertain manner.

Then her face crumples as it starts reflecting inner heartbreak and desolation.

"It's Harry…Harry, darlin'…Harry Vale?" A sudden inspiration makes me add, "You remember me, don't you? Harry Vale? Of Jarmo?"

I don't know what makes me say that. But the words seem to sprinkle stardust over Stella Denton, because instant comprehension dawns on her face. Simultaneously, Stella's face reflects enlightenment, then desolation, brave resignation, and finally reluctant acceptance.

"*Professor*…Vale." She stresses my title, then repeats my full name slowly. She looks at me now as though she really knows me. Knows who I am, without a doubt. "Professor Harry Vale."

"You…you brought me to Jarmo." She sounds very tired now but accepting of that fact. "And for that I am…so grateful."

"Well, you're welcome." What an awkward thing to say. Actually, I must break the news to my engagement to her soon…the sooner, the better.

"And remember, I'm not only Professor Harry Vale, I'm your *fiancé* Harry Vale. We're engaged, Stella, don't you remember? We're going to make a new life together."

"New life…" Stella repeats the words. "I already did."

It's so weird to hear her talking, hear her audible voice. It's like hearing one's dog or cat in conversation — strange, surreal, and amazing.

Dr. Montrose speaks up. It's time for him to start being The Doctor now, not just a happy onlooker. "I'm going to ask you a few questions now, Miss Denton, and then we'll let you rest, okay?"

"All right." Her voice doesn't sound too rusty, even after three months of disuse.

"Stella, what city do you live in?" Dr. Montrose asks. He's hoping she'll give him the right answer, which is Minneapolis.

"Jarmo." Stella now speaks slowly. She's starting to sound tired again, slurring her words, but we can tell that she's trying. "Not a city. Village."

The doctor looks amused at this and lifts his eyebrows at me. "Well! What village do you live in then?"

"Jarmo," she says again. And the hairs on the back of my neck stand up.

"Hmm, Jarmo," Dr. Montrose repeats. "And where is Jarmo located?"

"So very far." That's all she'll say on that subject. Already she's exhausted from the effort of talking.

"Who is the president right now, Stella?" Dr. Montrose tries a different approach.

The effort of awakening and talking again has worn her almost back to unconsciousness again. She's almost asleep.

"The president of the United States, who is he?" Dr. Montrose persists in a hearty voice.

This might all be too much for her. Finally she replies softly: "He's…brown…"

"That's right," Dr. Montrose replies with a smile in his voice. "And how many fingers am I holding up?"

She opens her eyes briefly and whispers the correct answer.

"Just one more question, Miss Denton, and then we'll let you take a nap. What year is it?"

That one seems to throw her. The doctor repeats the question. "Do you know what year it is, Stella?"

"It…I don't…" Her strength leaves her. She looks weary, confused. Lonely. Finally she whispers, "It's a long way off. So…far."

"Yes, Jarmo *is* far," I reassure her softly before Dr. Montrose can speak up. "Long, long ago and far, far away. Right, Stella?"

The Star Wars comparison must fit the bill, because Stella looks at me, then slowly nods her helmeted head once.

I squeeze her hand, and she squeezes mine back. Weakly. Then she closes her eyes. The interview is effectively over for today.

After leaving fervent instructions with nurses to call me if anything, *anything*, should change in her condition, I leave Stella to her dreaming and head out for a brief consulting job.

The next day when I come to see her — shortly before dawn, because I'm so nervous and excited — she's fully awake, lying quietly in her bed, her hands crossed over the feeding tube in her abdomen.

She gives me a searching stare. Still doesn't say much.

Still wondering, possibly, who the hell I am.

"Engaged?" She says it softly, like a question. "You are engaged… to me?"

"Even as you are engaged to me," I reply, taking one of her hands in mine. I'm not wearing my glasses. She seems to interact with me more fully when I'm without them.

She looks at me then with a wistful longing that breaks my heart.

"You can't remember? Us getting engaged?"

Her big blue eyes tear up again as they look into mine. She shakes her head slowly as if it's too heavy for her to move.

I feel like a shit for forcing such a bare-faced lie on her, but I can't help it. I'm going to go through with it. If she'll let me. If she'll have me.

It's another big day in another way, too: today Stella gets fitted with wheels. With three of us assisting (nurses on each arm and me managing her legs), we leverage her into a soft-sided, reclining wheelchair. We strap her in carefully and thoroughly. Evidently, wheelchairs for recovering coma patients, or any type of brain trauma, must keep the patient reclining back so they don't get light-headed and pitch forward onto the floor.

Stella's Foley catheter is removed today. Ditto her stomach feeding tube, which was removed earlier this morning since she's readily taking soft food by mouth now.

She still looks pale and distracted, exhausted much of the time, but she's finally looking closer to normal, except for the helmet.

I wheel her slowly up and down the halls.

"Let's take a tour of this joint!" I decide cheerfully. With the doctor's permission, I even wheel her outside under the shade of river birch and soft maples on the narrow strips of sod by the busy road that literally runs under the H-shaped hospital.

When she gets really tired, sometimes she forgets, and starts asking, "Where's Hari?"

As she starts doing right now. "I want Hari. I want to go home. Why won't they let me go *home?*"

"You'll soon go home with me, darlin'. With Professor Harry Vale."

"But you're not Hari." She gives me a pitying look of knowing, then, and I know she's one-thousand percent awake and aware at last. She knows that this isn't Jarmo. Jarmo is gone. It's dead and buried under nine thousand years of dust, decay, and forgetting. And she knows I'm not Hari, that Other Guy she thinks she loves in Jarmo. But now she really knows that he's gone too. That he's deader than the tombs of Egypt. It's as if Jarmo and Hari had never been, never existed, never flourished once upon a time.

I park Stella's wheelchair under a tree next to a bench where I slump in surrender. Cars continue to whiz by us, smelling faintly of exhaust, but their low hum feels therapeutic and hypnotic, not distracting.

I look at Stella. There's a lump in my throat when I ask her, "So, will you tell me, then, Stella? Tell me how it really was in Jarmo. With Hari. There's so much I'd like to know. And this is as good a time as any to talk."

And so, haltingly at first, then gaining momentum, Stella tells me everything.

She doesn't treat me as the near stranger that I was and in many ways still am. She knows that I am somehow more to her and treats me accordingly.

She tells me about her new body, so stunning and alluring. About the Jarmo people and their lifestyle, so carefree yet still so dependent on the tenuous abundance that surrounds them.

And she tells me about Hari. Chieftain from a long line of family heirs. How good and wise yet unflappable he is. I get a sense that even the once shy, reclusive Stella believes that Hari should speak up more. Be more assertive about securing and protecting Jarmo's future.

She also talks about Hari the husband. Although she's more circumspect about divulging this part of her new life, I get a strong sense that she has utterly embraced the primacy of sex, along with the man himself.

Her eyelids are now at half-mast. She looks unutterably weary. With stabbing guilt, I realize that I've worn her out. "You're tired, poor dear. Sorry to keep you talking so long. I'll take you back to your room."

With assistance from the nurse and aide assigned to her care today, the three of us manage to get Stella back into her hospital bed, all tubes and wires reattached.

When the others exit the room leaving me alone with Stella, I assess her tiredness to see if we're indeed done with talking for the day. Her weariness is replaced by a thoughtful look. Her mind is millennia away.

I risk making Stella the following proposition: "You do know that I…*could* be Hari for you. If you just give me half a chance."

She looks at me but doesn't reply.

I get an inspiration and make Stella another offer. I'm not sure if it's half-assed or not, but I'm going to put it out there on the table, along with the other one.

"I know that…you want to go home to Jarmo. I'd like to go with you to Jarmo. If only I could! If only we could together. But we can't. Jarmo is gone.

"But I'll do the next-best thing that I can. Do you remember when I showed you that PowerPoint presentation of Jarmo on the last night of class, just before we were shot?"

She nods.

"Would you like to see *that* Jarmo again?"

"Oh—yes!" She manages a faint smile and looks more alert.

I know I shouldn't overtire her so early in the awakening process, but this is important.

I set up my laptop on the wheeled, over-the-bed table, which I've adjusted in front of her wheelchair. The speaker should still work fine from her bedside table. I click Play.

And there it is again: the image of the sunny, grass-covered hill against a snow-capped mountain backdrop. The single word

JARMO superimposed over the image in dark blue with the yellow drop-shadow.

I've not opened this document in over three months.

One by one, the slide show moves through the familiar images as I slowly recite the lecture by heart.

Stella watches. Tears blur her eyes. But she smiles tremulously.

She keeps up a soft-voiced commentary on each image. "Oh, it's the Gathering Space. That picture is wrong; the stream flows on the other side of the village. The houses have higher rooflines, but you've captured the look of them. Three blue lines on the face mean a wedding…"

Then she sighs deeply, turns her face away, and feigns sleep. But not before she gives my hand a squeeze.

Finally she falls asleep for real with dried tear tracks still evident on her cheeks.

Time for me to leave her to her dreams.

CHAPTER 20
The Call of Jarmo

The true paradises are the
paradises we have lost.
∼ Marcel Proust ∼
1871 – 1922

Harry

In just three days' time, Stella's skull will be made whole again.

To me, this celebrates and symbolizes the fact of Stella's true return to life. To *this* life.

It gives me hope just to think of it: Stella Denton — now alive, awake, and aware — will soon have all of her missing parts rejoined in one living, breathing being.

I'm hoping she'll be a woman whose interest is piqued by this big, amazing, external world of ours. And by me too, of course. Instead of stubbornly pining for an inner one.

For the past six days, Stella and I…Somehow the two of us are living a lifetime together. In just one week.

Stella now strives mightily each day for full consciousness, and most of the time, she actually gets there. For the past six days, we've experienced a compressed lifetime together of talking and sharing, memories and possibilities, and hope.

Over the span of a week, Stella tells me everything she remembers about her Jarmo existence. *All* of it.

But finally she takes my hand in hers and tells me, "He's *you*, y'know. Hari. He's you in an earlier lifetime."

"Me…" I repeat parrot-like, but secretly I'm saying *yes, yes,* and again *yes.*

"He's you. And you're him. Just in a different body. I just *know.* I can tell by your goodness. And your blue eyes."

I have no words for that, so I kiss her hand and press it against my cheek.

She seems to thrive on my presence, my affection, when I stay by her bedside for hours, while we talk about the world of Jarmo and the Eden-like richness of it all.

Is it this tale of Jarmo true? Did she really go back, really connect? Part of me aches to think it's real. Part of me believes it *is* real, that it *has* to be. Another part of me is jealous—Why can't I go back to Jarmo? Why only Stella? Do you really have to almost die to get there?

Still another part of me thinks it's all nuts.

I want to keep her happy. I want to very badly, so she'll go home with me and start our new life together. After all, she has no other place to go.

Neither do I.

I don't think Drs. Montrose or Fanning, or any of the nurses or therapists, have the faintest idea of the full extent of Stella's true vocal and mental recovery. Only I do. When Stella is in their presence, she speaks very little, although she talks intelligently and coherently when called upon to do so. Her doctors are beyond pleased.

When she's around Fanning and Montrose, Stella intentionally dons the mantle of the typical coma patient: confused, forgetful, fretful, still drifting in and out of consciousness, gradually making her way toward something approaching normalcy—if she's lucky.

But when the two of us are alone, Stella pours out to me her anguish over the upcoming fate of Jarmo. Well, it's sort of upcoming, even if they've all been dead for thousands of years. It's because we don't know, we'll never know now, whatever became of them all.

"I want to help them. I have to. I *must!*" Again Stella's eyes are brimful with tears.

No, you need to come home and be with me.

"They've never known war. They don't know how it changes things forever. They don't know what to do to protect themselves and their way of life. I must help them somehow. Please help *me* to help *them*, Professor! Somehow…"

It feels like a punch in the gut, hearing her call me Professor and not Harry.

"I have a name, don't forget. It's Harry. And I hope you haven't forgotten you're engaged. To me. Because *I* haven't forgotten…"

I kiss her hand. Tenderly. Again and again.

She amends her words. "Yes, I know you're Harry…and also Hari."

She dips her chin and gives me a sidelong glance under her lashes. But she's not finished yet.

"I know that we're engaged, although *that* still seems strange to me. I never thought I could forget such a thing as actually getting engaged, no matter what world I was in! However, it appears that I have." Then, in a rush, she adds, "I'm *so* sorry about the…the not-remembering. But that doesn't mean I don't want to marry you in this life, because I…do."

"You do?" I sound more surprised than I should for an engaged man.

"Yes. I do." Already, it sounds like she's speaking a wedding vow. I aim to make it so just as soon as we can.

But after this week of healing and rest for Stella, as well as more meaningful conversations between the two of us, Dr. Fanning turns things up a notch.

"It's time, Stella."

Dr. Fanning meets with the two of us today, at his request, and makes a strong case for Stella's next procedure.

Stella sits in her hospital bed, half-reclining, half-propped-up, while I lean forward, listening intently, in the bedside chair.

"It's time. And almost *past* time," the neurosurgeon continues. "If we keep your cranial bone out for too long, it'll start losing its ability to regrip and grow. And if it won't stick, so to speak, then we'll have to remove it and put in an acrylic plate—custom made for your particular skull, of course. But this doesn't always work out, and if that's the case, then we have to use permanent mesh. Your own bone is always best, of course. That's why we want to get it back in again as soon as possible. How does that sound to you, Stella?"

Stella just says, "Okay." She smiles politely and tries to look positive, but says nothing more. Again she's miles away.

Dr. Fanning probably assumes she's still experiencing coma confusion. The brain surgeon doesn't press her. Of all people, he knows just how confusing this whole situation is to us all, especially the patient.

He gives her knee a pat and continues. "We're going to put your missing puzzle piece back in and keep it there with little pieces of mesh about the size of a dime. The mesh coins lay over the corners of the flap and skull, and we'll keep them in place with tiny screws. Yes, we're actually going to screw them right into your skull with a little hand-held, battery-powered screwdriver. Don't worry! You won't feel a thing. And then, after you wake up, no more helmet!" He touches her hockey headgear in gentle emphasis.

"One more thing, though. Be forewarned that after this particular procedure, you might feel like you've gone fifteen rounds with Mohammed Ali. No, not because it's painful—it's not. Not directly, that is. It's just that coming out of general anesthesia can be…" he coughs delicately "…can be a bit…challenging…for patients so recently out of a coma."

Fanning explains how general anesthetic is actually a controlled, intentionally-induced coma in and of itself. He relates how brain trauma and stroke patients react more deeply than people with so-called normal brains. That is, with very little anesthesia, they can fall deeply into the coma state again, and their awakening from anesthesia is often very slow and difficult.

"We've got you scheduled for late Friday morning. And by Saturday, if you're doing as well then as you are now, we'll move you to a unit requiring even less critical care. And that's a very good step on your road to getting out of here."

Stella looks at him with her big blue eyes and says in a determined voice, "Let's do it then. Let's light this candle!"

I think that's an old movie line, but I can't quite place it.

With heavy-lidded eyes and a faint smile, Stella looks at us then, one to another, then closes her eyes. Almost immediately, her breathing becomes slower and more regular. She's asleep again. *Just like a coma patient.* All the better for her to keep on healing.

Just then, Dr. Montrose comes in from his late afternoon rounds to join us. Three of us men—Fanning, Montrose, and Vale—stand together in the vestibule, half in and half out of the doorway, volleying soft chitchat for a while. We try not to awaken Stella, who needs all the sleep she can get.

Then Montrose raises something that's been bothering him. He keeps glancing at the sleeping Stella as he speaks. Evidently, there's something he doesn't want her to hear.

"I'm more than a little concerned that she's going to take a humongous dip on Friday after the bone flap replacement. Can't tell you why, since she's been doing great lately. But it's just this feeling I can't shake…That she's not quite ready yet."

Fanning and Montrose do a quick, informal consult together, laced with professional jargon. They don't mind that I keep standing there, listening. Phrases and catchwords are pitched back and forth doctor-to-doctor. *Possible occurrence of bacterial meningitis…severe pain after craniotomy requiring a morphine drip…prolonged lack of appetite…strong possibility of post-traumatic epilepsy.* I keep my mouth shut, listen, and try to remember what I hear.

The procedure doesn't sound as easy as Fanning described it to Stella. It sounds both daunting and ghastly. But it has to be done. It would be far worse for Stella to have to live with a hole in her head.

After the doctors take their leave, I linger awhile in the doorway, mulling over my own deep thoughts. Then I hear a quiet voice from behind me.

"Professor Vale…Harry…"

Stella is awake. I quickly return her bedside chair and take her hand in mine.

"I woke up and heard you guys talking. About the cranium operation." She takes a deep breath. "And I want you to know…that I've decided that it's probably all for the best. That it's probably a…sign."

"A sign of what?"

"A sign that I won't be coming back here again."

"Here?" I repeat. "Here as in…here in this hospital?"

"No. Here. As in…here in this existence."

She looks spent. It still makes her tired to engage in too much conversation, especially one so fraught with emotion as this one.

"Not coming back? Of course you're coming back," I retort, feeling a shiver of fear. "Dr. Fanning wouldn't consider doing it yet if he thought you were in real danger. Don't even think of such a thing!"

But Stella looks calmly resigned. "No, Harry, I don't intend to die…not just yet, if I can help it. But maybe I'm just meant to…

go. *You* know where. Besides, maybe death is just a dream too, and soon I'll awaken…somewhere else. And you'll be there, too. As him."

"But how can you know?" I plead with her. "Know where you'll go…know if you can even choose something like that?"

"If I can, if I get the chance to choose, I choose Jarmo."

To Stella, it's as simple as that.

"But what if you, I don't know, go back to a different time period in Jarmo—a thousand years earlier, or a thousand years later? Or what if you go somewhere else altogether?"

"It's a chance I'm willing to take."

How brave she is, whether the Jarmo world is real or not.

She smiles then and takes my nearest hand in both of hers. Her smile quirks up on one side, tremulous. "Just remember, you and Jarmo Hari are two sides of the same cosmic coin…karmic coin…whatever, somehow. Remember, you have the same eyes and the same loving heart."

I reach out and embrace her then, hockey helmet and all, but carefully because of her vulnerable brain. I bury my face in her neck. "Please stay, Stella. Please, for me. Remember, I stayed at *your* side, day after day, week after week. Can't you please just stay a little while longer by *my* side…just for me? Just remember that love is all the stronger for being learned over time."

She starts to cry then, noiselessly but with little spasms. She turns away from the door so passing nurses can't see. She holds me and whispers between sobs, "I'm sorry…I'm *so* sorry. But I've got to go. They need me."

There's nothing I can say to that. Except, *I need you, too.* Only I don't say it. Pleading doesn't seem to help with Stella, and I'm getting so weary of carrying this load.

"Please help me with this, Harry," she whispers. So very tiredly. "I can't even get my fingers to work right yet, let alone work a laptop. I need to…Google things…take information back with me."

"Darlin', I just thought of something." I pull back from her a little and look into her eyes. "Bugs."

"Bugs?" She repeats the word, startled out of her misery.

I continue. "Bed bugs. Mosquitoes. Chiggers. Ticks. Leeches. Cockroaches. Every place has them, especially prehistoric places. Do you remember those as part of your dream, too? It couldn't be a real place and not have those."

"I don't know." She replies in a plaintive voice, suddenly uncertain and tired to death. She also looks lost and helpless. "I don't remember."

Why am I picking on her when she's down? There's only one thing she really wants. And that's to stand beside the other Hari on the hillside in Eden and live out their lives in happiness together. Whether it's real or not.

And so I tell her, "That's okay. It doesn't matter."

Suddenly I envy her with a pang that makes my heart ache.

"Please?" she whispers. "Montrose and Fanning aren't going to let me out of this bone flap operation. And I know it's more serious than they're letting on. Please help me to look things up, battle stuff, you know. Just in case I…don't come back. Tell me about it, read the info to me. I have only three days to commit this stuff to memory. It might not make any difference in the grand scheme of things, but still I have to try."

My heart feels like lead. *I'm losing her.*

Not that I ever had *her.*

I try to be positive but don't really succeed. "Don't be too sure you're going to slide into a coma again. You'll probably come back here whether you like it or not. The body does what it wants, you know, and we just have to roll with it."

She just keeps whispering, "Please…"

Enough.

I take a deep, ragged breath, open my laptop, and boot it up. Then I tell her, "You'll need to start with the wheel."

For three days, Stella and I give Wikipedia and other sites a run for their money. The doctors and nurses are pleased to see us talking together so much, even working on a computer together, even though it seems like some very strange stuff we're looking up.

Unfortunately, Stella isn't a quick study on subjects of ancient warfare and technology. Her brain is still fragile and fried. She knows nothing about the concept of the wheel and axle, one of the six universal simple machines that allow heavy objects — men, chariots — to be moved easily while supporting a load or performing labor. Together, we look up, print out, and try to study (in the most generous sense of the word) articles on chariot design, function, and operation with a single horse or tandem team; the capture, training, and taming of wild horses, both for riding and for pulling chariots; weapons, chiefly bows, spears, and atl-atls, to make sure we haven't left any competitive technological edge untried; as well as the cultivation of prehistoric emmer and einkorn wheat to have a food supply closer to the village.

Whether we're inextricably playing with time travel or not, thereby changing the nature of reality as we know it, I don't even want to speculate. I just do what Stella wants. I'm past worrying about the ramifications. I just want to make this desperate young woman, *my* woman, happy.

On Thursday night, the night before Stella's cranial surgery, we're both exhausted and suffering from sensory overload. She's as ready as she'll ever be, which means she still only has a hazy idea of what to "invent" and what to implement. But we're satisfied that we've done all we can, and the rest is up to Stella's old mantra. She told me about chanting it in time to her steps when she walked to class that last night.

Everything happens, now in my life, in God's perfect order.

I don't know if God has a hand in all this or not. We're truly on a journey, even if we don't yet know the final destination.

My dream of a fiancée and, eventually, a bride of my own looks like it will remain only that — a dream.

"Stella, can I —" I'm rambling on here, but I must ask her. "Can I kiss you goodbye now…before you go — *if* you go?"

"I would be heartbroken if you didn't," she replies softly.

I look her all over then: cheeks made hollow by illness, her pale blue eyes large and clear against her light freckled skin. Her unremarkable nose bisects her rather nice lips over undeniably prominent teeth. *Just like mine,* I remind myself. *Just like mine.*

Helmet be damned, she reaches out for me then with both arms, and I gather her close, heedless and resentful of the barrier covering her skull, and meet her halfway in a kiss. Somehow our two sets of beaver teeth don't get in the way at all.

It's long and deep and explorative as kisses go, one that speaks volumes to one another about our shared emotions. About physical desires not acted upon. Together, our kiss tastes of mint toothpaste and the chocolate chip cookies we sampled earlier this evening. The kiss also tastes of regret and of the road not taken. Lives not lived. Lives that never *will* be lived together. Not in this existence, anyway.

When we finally come up for air, she just says, "Maybe. Just maybe…"

Around eleven fifteen on Friday morning, just before the scheduled time of Stella's operation, a September thunderstorm starts rolling through the city.

Wordlessly, Stella and I watch the sky together from the tall windows of her private room. Strange, this storm wasn't predicted at all on last night's news and weather.

I even ask one of the transport nurses about it when a duo arrives to transfer Stella to a gurney and wheel her to the OR. "What if the electricity goes out and you lose power during the operation?"

I'm told it's no problem, emergency generators just kick in, and "you won't even know the difference, except for maybe a momentary flickering of lights."

Still, I worry.

After an elevator ride, they wheel her down a long corridor with west-facing windows along one side. I'm allowed to follow the gurney for a while, and I don't let go of her hand.

"Ready to get this helmet off, Stella?" It's Dr. Fanning. In his whispery voice, he talks to us with a reassuring smile before leaving to prepare himself for surgery.

"Yes." She looks like a soldier about to enter battle. And so she is. "I'm ready."

But they aren't quite ready for her yet in the operating room, so the three of us — one of the transport nurses, Stella, and me — remain parked by the windows for a while. Stella and I are still holding hands; we don't let go, and together we wait.

Chubby and cheerful, the second transport nurse chatters to break our nervous silence. "Get a load of that sky, would you! Looks almost green. I know it wasn't predicted for today, but that's *got* to be bringing in one heck of a storm."

"Yes," says Stella. She looks up at me then. Searchingly, saying goodbye. "Yes, it will be. One hell of a storm."

I nod at her and hope my eyes convey what I'm thinking and praying: *Come through this healthy and strong, Stella. May you either find your Hari on some Other Side—and remember your memoriza-tions—or come back to me in one piece so we can make our own Jarmo right here. Either way, give 'em hell from me.*

The first transport nurse comes back to us then. "They're ready for you now, Ms. Denton."

Together they start wheeling her down the corridor, then left to the double doors of the OR wing. I'm not permitted to go beyond those doors. Stella must face this part alone.

Stella keeps looking at me, as long as she can, until the double doors close behind her—and close her out of my life.

Probably forever.

Or...not? Who can say? Forever is an awfully long time, and I'm willing to wait. And see.

Part Two

CHAPTER 21
After the Operation

Hope is a waking dream.
 Aristotle
384 BCE – 322 BCE

Harry

"**W**hy is she not awake yet? You all but promised — okay, I know, I *know*. You can't make promises in medicine! But you strongly suggested she'd regain consciousness by now."

Dr. Montrose responds with a weak, "Well…"

Try as I might to reason it down, my inner panic rises.

We look down at my unconscious fiancée. Stella's skin looks like ivory wax. She looks sickly, vulnerable, not quite alive.

It makes me feel queasy just to look at her head, again so thickly wrapped in gauze. A breathing tube, just in case, bisects her lips and is held in place by surgical tape, the kind that doesn't tug skin when it's pulled away.

It's two hours post-op for Stella now, here in the ICU, and they've finally allowed me to sit beside her. As her closest official relation, I can sit beside her for a long time, so long as I behave myself and don't mess with the equipment.

Worry prevents me from catching my breath fully. I can't keep the faint quaver out of my voice as I ask Dr. Montrose the same question, just repeated in different ways.

"Everything went so well, you said. But, hey, it's going on three hours now."

Dr. Montrose is brisk and reassuring in his reply. "Now, now, she's still well within normal limits." But he furrows his forehead faintly. Even he seems to secretly will Stella to come back *now*.

Montrose tries to calm my agitation. "Remember, having a missing piece of your skull reattached, after so many weeks without it, is a real shock to the system."

Montrose clicks on the TV near the ceiling, keeping the volume off as captions flash across the mute screen. "Here. Watch something else instead of the monitors for a change. Pass the time while you wait. While *we* wait."

The news flashes on, drones through its allotted time, and after thirty minutes it morphs into a sitcom.

More hours pass.

Interns and nurses glide in and out of the ICU, murmuring together *sotto voce*, checking Stella's vital signs. They're starting to look worried, but no one will voice their concern. Just yet. She's breathing just fine, but...

No response from Stella. Not even a twitch or flicker of consciousness. Shit. *Shit.*

I can't suppress a deep, shuddering sigh. *She must have found that rabbit-hole and made her way back.*

I'm mesmerized by the bedside monitor's output: green, gray, blue, and red electronic lines with their regular, and often irregular, patterns of ominous peaks and mysterious valleys. The soft beep, beep, beep sound underlies everything; I can feel it deep in my sternum. Beep, beep, beep...heartbeat, blood pressure, cranial blood flow, saturated oxygen and carbon dioxide in the blood. Unfortunately there's no brain monitor for me to watch like there is for the rest of the body.

But every twenty minutes or so, a nurse comes in to do another EEG test on Stella to determine her current brain activity. I can't help but notice that some activity registers on the printout. Not a lot, but enough. I figure that some activity has got to be better than *no* activity. And so I wait.

Although Stella's soul essence is probably in Jarmo, I know that part of her is still alive *here*, too. And could return to this century at any moment.

I've learned a lot sitting around this hospital. But I've not be-grudged it. Not a particle. My…devotion, I guess you'd call it…gives my life meaning and purpose. I'm here because she needs me.

Okay, it all sounds nuts, I know, but I still believe in my heart of hearts that Stella told me the truth. *Her* truth. Jarmo still ex-ists—somewhere, somewhen—and now, she's there too.

Stella, damn it! Please wake up. Please come back. Don't leave me alone here again in this twenty-first century world that no longer feels like home. Wake up, Stel, and this time somehow take me with you to Jarmo.

I can become that Hari for you.

I'll be any Hari that you want. Just don't leave me behind.

CHAPTER 22
Returning to Jarmo

A kind of light spread out from her.
And everything changed color.
And the world opened out.
 John Steinbeck
1902 – 1968

Stella

I hear a man — older than me, I think, but still youngish — calling my name. His voice sounds funny, electrical and tinny. Almost robotic. Then it grows louder and more normal. Still, it's high and tense, as if on the edge of panic. Is it who I hope it is?

"Stella? Stella!"

As he calls my name, I'm rushing at warp speed through the gray tunnel. For the second time in this lifetime.

Moments ago — or was it really a lifetime ago? — I lay wide-awake on an operating table, trussed-up like a chicken with various anesthesia IVs and electrical leads. It's a big day for me, a nerve-racking day, because I'm having my missing bone flap reattached to my skull.

Bone flap is what they call the removed bone, now kept in-definitely in the hospital's cold storage, the skull bone that took the brunt of the bullet.

I've been out of the coma now for more than two weeks, grow-ing stronger and more lucid each day with devoted Professor Harry always by my side.

But I know where I want to go, where I want to be. And it isn't here.

Not anymore.

As loving and loyal and dear as Harry Vale is to me—he's my fiancé after all, although this fact still seems strange to me—he will somehow always be The Other Guy. I must return to my chieftain and his people who I've come to know and love. I hope to help save them from the invaders.

During my precious few times alone with a laptop in my hospital room, I've Googled "bone flap replacement surgery" and "patient reviews." I know it's not uncommon for patients like me to experience what euphemism calls a "huge dip" after such surgery. Some even slip back into a coma. Some never come out. I'm hoping that will be me.

A masked woman with friendly brown eyes—I think she's the anesthetist—touches my hand. "This Versed will relax you, honey. You won't remember a thing."

She's right. I remember nothing. Not even leaving my body. Suddenly I'm just suspended in the tunnel of gray.

I suspect that's due to the fact that my brain waves aren't behaving properly yet.

Dear, obsessive/compulsive Professor Harry researched all manner of things regarding my upcoming procedure. Gently but relentlessly, he inundated me with information—classic TMI—until I had a decent understanding of all my possible outcomes.

According to my fiancé-professor, "Researchers who study anesthesia find that certain ones—including Propofol, which they're going to use on *you*—can cause a reduction in gamma waves. It's gammas that permit the brain and body to create their own conscious perception…wherein you know that you are *you*."

Gamma waves. Yes, I remember Harry telling me more about gammas during one of our many bedside chats as he crammed me with knowledge of how to help Jarmo. I visualize gamma waves originating deep in the thalamus part of my brain, bathing the brain in a rolling wave, front to back, over and over, forty times a second. And so…am I just whatever gamma rays tell me I am? Or am I infinitely more?

That remains to be seen.

I'm in the tunnel now. Moving toward…something.

Suddenly I'm yanked to the left—again—into a side channel. The gray walls of the branch tunnel take on a warmer hue, soft and reddish-tan. Sort of like the inside of my eyelids when my eyes are closed against the sun.

The male voice keeps calling my name. Then I feel him jostling me, gently at first, then with something approaching roughness, trying to rouse me back to life.

"Stella, Star, wake up! I'm here. We're all here. Come back!"

It sounds like…It's got to be…

I open my eyes when I hear other voices, too: tremulous, astonished, hopeful voices, yapping none-too-quietly above my head.

Several faces peer down at me. Concerned, loving, dubious. But a man's face—haggard, hopeful, sun-browned with a short-trimmed, black beard, beautiful—moves in closer, crowding out all others.

It is Hari. Jarmo Hari. Chieftain Hari. My Hari.

Above me, he looks down into my eyes, his face turning radiant with fearful joy. His eyes are bleary with unshed tears. Far overhead, I glimpse a brown ceiling of interwoven thatch.

Jarmo. It's got to be Jarmo.

I'm home.

In that first split second, when I look at Hari, hear the buzz of conversation, and before I even speak, the Squirrelly Girl Voice screams in my mind, and the words reverberate through my brain. *This time, remember, dammit! Remember who you are and why you came back. To be the savior of this precious, little world. If you can. If you dare.*

Mentally I vow, *Yes, yes, yes. You* know *I will. If I can.*

I'm home again, and it's for real.

Surreptitiously, I finger the rough wool blanket over me, a furred animal skin pulled over it. The cool, dryness of dust is everywhere, along with the scent of cooked lentils and *eau de goat.*

I look into Jarmo Hari's eyes while my lips part slightly. For a millisecond Jarmo Hari's dark-smudged blue eyes are superimposed on a different face—the plain but friendly, acne-scarred face of Professor Harry. Who also has blue eyes and the elusive single dimple. The double vision blurs for a moment, then is gone. It's only Jarmo Hari's face that looks down on me now with vast relief and yearning.

Is his beloved face part of my future? Or my past?

Somehow my head doesn't hurt at all. I am hyper-awake. Still lying covered on the floor, suddenly I smile hugely at Hari and state the obvious.

"I'm back."

He grabs my hand to kiss it, makes an inarticulate exclamation of joy and relief, then leans down to gather me up in his arms. So close. Even closer. And buries his nose in my hair.

I raise my right hand to caress the back of Hari's head. *Yes, my beautiful hands are back.* Light tan, ethereal prayer hands like on statues of the Virgin Mary. With my other hand I fumble in my hair, bringing a long lock before my eyes. The hair is dark brown, luxuriant and wavy. I'm the Jarmo me again, the me I feel — I know — I was meant to be.

I release my lock of hair and hold Hari close with one arm while my other hand remains fervently imprisoned in his own.

Hari keeps embracing me while I'm still lying on the floor. We're both on the floor now but, oh, so happy. The villagers who still hover over us now crow and exhale with happiness and relief. Hari takes my face in both his hands, gently yet seriously.

"Don't ever do that again, wife. It took all of our prayers to the Great Mother, over and over, to bring you back this time, but what if your…illness…happens again?"

"It won't." I won't *let* it happen again. I've made my decision with destiny, and I am already moving forward into this life.

Hari still looks so worried that I tell a white lie. "The Great Mother told me while I was…away…that I'm back here to stay for good."

But so much has happened, I remind myself. Days and nights, weeks and months. How much time has passed in Jarmo since I've been gone?

"Is it still…the same day?" I ask, afraid that months and years may have passed. At the same time, my rational mind tells me I couldn't survive for more than a few days without food or water.

"It will soon be sunset, but, yes, it's the same day," Hari reassures me. I hug him even tighter, still smiling.

"Thank goodness." I mean it with all my heart. Others in the room talk more loudly among themselves now, joy and relief clear on their faces.

My twenty-first century life was real. And it still exists simultaneously, somewhere, somehow.

But this is *more* real to me.

This is now. This is mine. Time for life to begin anew.

"Hari, can you please take me home? And does Grandmama have any lentil stew in the fire pot? I'm starving!"

Hari laughs and then cautiously guides me to a sitting position. I don't even feel dizzy. I could move mountains, jump tall buildings in a single bound—if there were any buildings here to jump over.

With Hari's help, I manage to assume a not-too-shaky standing position. I feel fantastic.

"Go home, everybody," I tell everyone in as strong a voice as I can muster. It sounds pretty good, even to me. "And thank you all... so very, *very* much...for caring about me and caring *for* me."

Now I speak kindly but new resolve. "Everyone, please go home now and eat. Pen your goats for the night. But know that tomorrow we start preparing for war. We must. And we will."

I look back at Hari with a question in my eyes. He suspects I'm going to say something momentous—or dangerous—but still he nods.

I give voice to my thoughts (and a loud, determined voice it is, too). "Everybody, spread word around the village to meet at the Gathering Space tomorrow morning, shortly after sunrise. All right?"

I look at Hari for corroboration, and he nods. He's only too glad to grant me anything at this point.

"The invaders are coming. Six moons or less. And we haven't a moment to waste."

CHAPTER 23
What We're Going to Do

Necessity may well be called the mother of invention
But calamity is the test of integrity.
❧ Samuel Richardson ❧
1689–1761

Stella

It looks like the entire village—in other words, our whole world—has turned out for our self-styled town hall meeting at the Gathering Space next morning. Fortunately, the autumn sun starts taking the chill off things in short order.

The villagers' faces look expectant, receptive, and eager. Even so, we'd better come up with a good reason for all of this disruption of their lives.

Without further preamble, Hari begins. That's one thing about living in a small, easy-going tribe. No lengthy rituals or elaborate hoops to jump through when making decisions. Life is breathtakingly immediate here. The chieftain facilitates things, of course—at least *our* chieftain does, bless Hari's heart, no totalitarianism here—and all adult men vote with a show of hands on any major decision. (Voting rights for women have another nine thousand years to wait.)

"As you all know, my Stella was born far beyond these mountains. She knows about important, powerful things of which the rest of us know little to nothing—like children. If these invaders are truly coming to overrun us in the spring—and if their numbers are greater than ours, which they very well may be—we can never start too early to prepare. And that means *all* of us, every person older than ten turnings of the seasons, must shoot with a bow and must be ready to fight. Women too. We must prepare a hiding place for the little ones with our grandmothers to watch over them. We must stockpile food and weapons. Make a plan. Make *alternative* plans, just in case. Stella will tell you how."

Before I can pick my jaw up off the ground—I didn't think I'd have to pontificate so soon—Hari steps to one side and urges me forward. He nods at me encouragingly. His blue eyes assure me that he's confident in my superior knowledge.

I only hope I'm up to the task.

The "information helpful to Jarmo" that Professor Harry crammed into me in the hospital now whirls in my brain. Where do I even begin?

Despite Professor Harry's private lectures to me about how Jarmoites can tame wild horses, design chariots, apply ancient battle tactics within our tiny army-to-be, will I actually remember enough to instruct our people when the time comes? It all seems so futile now, all of this cramming of…what? Random historical facts, tidbits of knowledge? Can it really help us to hang onto what is ours: our land and resources and homes…our very lives?

We'll find out soon enough.

"Intimidation." With this one word I start my speech to the crowd. In a voice that carries.

I can almost feel the collective *huh?* emanating from everyone.

I find my voice. My *true* voice, which grows louder and more decisive. A voice I never knew I had before. And to think it was waiting, quiescent, within me all the time.

"We must use intimidation, and I will soon tell you specifically how. Dear people of Jarmo, trouble is coming in the spring. True, we don't really know the day or time, but it's definitely coming. There will always be somebody coming over that hill, sometime…and we must be ready."

Many Jarmo faces are sober, others downright somber. After all, invasion, warfare, mass deaths and destruction has never happened in Jarmo in their collective memory. We've never been tested. We don't know how to prevail, don't know what we're going up against.

"These invaders—I'm going to call them the Bad Guys, because that's what they're called where I come from—anyway, the Bad Guys are coming and bringing their families with them to cast us out of Jarmo. They want to take over our homes and land and food and hunting grounds and, well, everything. They'll make us all slaves, or kill us, or chase us out of Jarmo and into the wilderness.

"So, what we need to go up against these Bad Guys is something my people call intimidation—make them so scared they'll shit themselves."

This doesn't sound like mousy, reclusive Stella Denton talking at *all*. But I'm only just getting started.

Although the crowd still looks confused, some folks start to look marginally hopeful.

"We're going to throw those Bad Guys completely off balance. Distract them, for starters. Scare them away. Fill them with awe and dread."

"So they'll run away…" one skeptical man pipes up. "But what if they come back at us? Again and again?"

I reply quietly, but still my voice carries perfectly throughout the crowd. "Because when they come at us that first time, we'll intimidate them with our superior weapons, fill them with fear, and then *we* will keep coming, and coming, and coming at *them*, until finally we kill them all, unless they surrender."

My bloodthirsty words cause the Jarmoites to stand speechless. In the moment, I've forged ahead, trusting my momentum to carry me forward with a strength I don't myself yet feel.

"That's what we'll do when they come to take over Jarmo. And here's how."

I inhale deeply, mentally line my ducks in a row—that being, my mental notes that Professor Harry crammed me with during my brief respite after the first coma—and begin.

"We must do five things." I look to my Hari for corroboration. Again, he nods back at me. His glance is sober but determined. How inexpressibly relieved, how *safe*, I feel when Hari has my back, even though secretly I fear that Hari is too easy-going to be an effective tribal chieftain in wartime. We shall see.

"We're going to designate five committees, or troops. That is, groups of warriors to work on five specific tasks. Everyone must, and will, participate. No holding back. We need you all."

The villagers know by now that we're deadly serious about this. And so are they.

"The first committee is the Horse Troop. They will catch and tame several horses…" I don't even pause at the collective gasp that runs through the crowd "…and make them accustomed to us, like dogs. And then some of us shall learn how to ride on their backs."

The crowd gasps some more, while some even snicker and others guffaw. "Why?" a voice in the crowd calls out. "What good will *that* do? Why ride 'em when you can eat 'em? One would feed my family for days!"

Several laughing voices chime in with agreement.

"We need to ride horses for several reasons. Just hear me out."

I frown at folks who continue to titter at the ridiculous idea of riding a horse, then I stare them down. The tittering stops. Horseback riding may be as strange to them as riding a cow is to me. Actually, both are pretty weird concepts to me, since I've never done either. A big city girl born and bred, all of my life I've lived in a metropolis of about four million people. Although, by now I've discovered that sleeping on fur-covered hay can be quite comfortable, and I've started the long road toward mastering the art of cooking over an open fire.

"All around this land, as far as you can see and even farther, *all* peoples will eventually be carried on the backs of horses—one of these days very soon! But we shall be the first and lead the way. Don't doubt me on this. You know that I know things from afar. Do you know what it'll do to the Bad Guys to see us on the backs of horses? First it will scare the shit out of them, then it will *awe* them. Intimidation, remember? These things I'm telling you today will, how shall I say, throw them off balance, actually and mentally. Then we'll have an easier time of killing them. Before they can kill us."

Finally, I'm starting to see some interested agreement on the faces of our people.

"Those who join the Horse Troop will also learn to shoot arrows while galloping on horseback into the crowd of invaders. They won't be able to shoot back at us effectively, because we'll be coming at them faster than a man can run."

"Put me in the Horse Troop. Please! I want to ride a horse and kill the enemy more than anything!" Maidie's voice rings out clearly. She pushes her way toward the front, quivering with resolve and sudden bravery.

This is a very different Maidie than the one I've come to know and love. That slight-boned, happy-go-lucky young girl is morphing before my eyes into a deadly Amazon. Suddenly I feel a deep yearning over, and great fear for, Hari's only living child, his daughter, his firstborn.

"Done!" I call out. I look over at Hari, and he nods reluctantly. Looking stalwart but still worried, his face is so easy for me to read. "Before we disperse today, we'll assign everyone into committees and start working right away."

"I'll be in the Horse Troop too," another voice calls out, a male voice this time.

"I will…"

"Me too…"

More voices chime in until there are five in addition to Maidie.

I exhale. Just a tiny bit. Momentum is building. At last.

"Committee Two is a very important committee. Crucial to our success. This will be called…" I pause impressively. The Jarmoites hang on my every word. "…the Wheel Troop. And your job will be to…"

Again I pause. I want them to get a sense of how big a deal this really is. "Your job will be to invent the wheel. And make a four-wheeled cart. Hopefully, even a chariot or two."

The crowd looks absolutely blank. No one knows what I'm talking about. Not even Hari. Many look frightened or suspicious. Or both.

"Don't worry. Together we'll be learning all of these things. I'll teach you. Don't let words like wheel, chariot, or cart unsettle you. Soon we will all be tapping into their awesome power. Learning how to construct these war tools and devices that will help us vanquish the Bad Guys for good. Here, I'll show you what a wheel looks like…"

I look around for a possible drawing tool (a small stick will do), then kneel on the ground and take the stick in hand. I start drawing in the smooth bare dirt of the Gathering Place.

"This…" I draw a large round circle with five spokes "…is a wheel. A spoked wheel. But first we'll make wheels of solid wood." I draw another large circle, bisected by a single line to designate two half circles, making marks to indicate where the two halves are pegged together.

"You know how heavy objects can be moved more easily if something round, like a fallen tree log, is placed under it and the object rolled over it?"

Several folks nod, although they still look dubious.

"I myself have seen the men of Jarmo men tie several slabs of wood together with leather straps, all facing this way—" I try to demonstrate with my hands "—then fasten wooden runners to the bottom, squared-off small logs or large poles, facing the other way, see? Like this…"

Again, I draw diagrams in the dirt.

"Where I grew up, this was called a sled. People here call it a sledge, and you use this…device…to move heavy objects for a long distance, pulling the sledge over the tops of several logs. I call those the rollers. So the sledge, and its cargo, is pulled from roller to roller to roller."

I'm not getting through to them yet. Although their faces display interest and possibility, there is still too much confusion in their expressions.

"What does this sledge and roller arrangement have to do with inventing the wheel, you're wondering? It's because this arrangement is the *mother* of the wheel! This round wheel was born from the concept of roller logs and sledge, only it's *so* much easier. And faster. Those in the Wheel Troop will find out just how much."

Finally comprehension dawns on a few faces around us. Keener interest, too. Several voices pipe up simultaneously, bidding to be in the Wheel Troop.

"You'll learn how to make wheels yourselves, and work with the Horse Troop to learn how to strap horses to wheeled carts, each carrying two or three warriors with bows and arrows. And maybe even build a two-wheeled chariot that a horse can pull, carrying a driver and an archer, going as fast as the wind!"

Additional voices chorus their assents to learn the mysteries of the wheel.

Feeling my personal mojo increase with growing excitement from the crowd, I press on.

"Committee Three will be the Wheat Troop. In charge of growing more readily available food for our people. Because, with war coming, we'll need to stick closer to home, need to keep watch, and have a more reliable source of food instead of hunting and gathering all the time. We will call this the Wheat Committee…the Wheat Warriors."

This doesn't sound as exciting as horses and wheels. It isn't. But it's necessary.

From thousands of miles and thousands of years away, I feel Professor Vale's dismay over what I am doing now: starting mankind on the long road to a restrictive agriculture society—not without major unintended consequences. But I have to; I have to do this *now*. If I don't invent settled agriculture, someone else will eventually, somewhere. And it might as well be us. We must have more food, and it must readily at hand.

"You mean that whiskery grass with the golden heads that I munch for a snack?" A voice from the crowd sounds dismissive, even a little derisive. What on earth could this plant have to do with warriors and warfare?

"Yes, that very plant. Two of them, actually. One is called emmer—the one with bigger kernels—and the other is einkorn. Both are types of wheat that grow naturally around here. The Wheat Troop is going to gather ripe wheat heads—there are many out there right now—and *not* eat them, but instead plant the kernels ourselves, on purpose, around the edges of the Gathering Space, because the dirt is already bare and loosened. We'll make sure they have enough water to sprout and grow, carrying water to them personally if winter rains don't cooperate. By next spring, we shall harvest our first crop of winter wheat. Then we'll separate the seed heads from the chaff and grind them with our grinding stones into a meal that can be baked into bread or cooked into cereal. When war comes, we'll be glad to have ripe wheat, ready and waiting, to feed our people without them having to hunt or gather."

I'm surprised when two old men speak up to join the Wheat Troop. Several older women also agree to join in this endeavor. We'll also be assigning lots of children into this group.

Speaking loud and aiming to keep things moving along briskly—I fear my audience is growing too restless, and I might lose them altogether—I almost yell the next words. A distant part of my brain summons a fleeting vision of Professor Vale. Trying to galvanize his phlegmatic class into action. Or at least maintain their interest. I never knew how hard it could be to inspire interest in people.

"Archer Troop! That is our fourth committee."

Now I've got their attention again. And then some.

"We're setting up regular, compulsory practice sessions with the bow and arrow. For all men who have completed their manhood ceremony. For all women who've completed their time of First Blood. And for the older children, too, if they're tall enough. For *all* of us.

No one who is tall enough is exempted from this. Many of you are already skilled with the bow, the spear, the atl-atl. You will be the ones who will teach the others, and drill them and drill them, until we become a united fighting troop. You are *all* members of the Archery Troop, in addition to your other troop specialty."

I look at Hari questioningly. Does he really want me to go ahead with Committee Five? Hari steps forward himself to talk about the last committee.

All Jarmoites fall silent in respect for their usually easy-going chieftain. Today, Hari is seriousness personified.

"The last committee, Committee Five, the Death Troop, will be comprised of all those who are good at fighting, but mostly they will train the rest of us in the best ways to kill. Whether it's hand-to-hand fighting with a knife, chucking a long-range spear from a distance, stabbing with a short-range dagger, strangulation, suffocation—whatever you can do, and however you can best do it, that is what we *all* will learn to do to protect your own lives and that of your fellow villagers."

I'm in my Jarmo bed tonight thinking long thoughts. Deep thoughts.

Hari dozes lightly beside me. Ashur and Grandmama have been asleep for hours.

I can't help thinking about things Professor Harry told me in my other life. About Jarmo.

During our cramming sessions at the hospital, Professor Harry told me that the Jarmo settlement won't be abandoned until around 4950 BCE. Why will the villagers abandon it? Famine? Fire? Earthquake? Invasion? We'll never know what brings about its end.

But I *do* know that Jarmo has two millennia in which to flourish. Two thousand years of abundant wildlife, fresh water, and a mild, sunny climate. But where are we now along the Jarmo continuum? Are we toward the beginning of our flourishing times? Or nearing the end?

That, as the saying goes, is the question.

I want to ensure that it's our line—*my* line, Chieftain Hari's people—who'll continue to populate Jarmo and carry it into the future. Let our people enjoy Eden while we can. Before the resources give out, the water dries up, and the weather starts see-sawing between harsh extremes of heat and cold.

The Jarmo archaeological site contains least twelve known levels of habitation, Professor Harry says. Twelve! Built up over the two thousand plus years of its existence. Holy crap. That's way more history than the United States has, even more than England had as a separate nation.

For more than two thousand years — *years* — this little community will shine its tiny candle flame of community and civilization into the darkness of the wilderness.

It's not going to be obliterated on my watch.

My thoughts roil on, keeping me awake and staring into the darkness.

But how do I know that future residents of Jarmo are descended from my people? What if they're descendants of the Bad Guys? Does it even matter in the grand scheme of things? Do I really even care?

Hell yes, I care.

I care because…because it matters to *me*. All of these dear, familiar, beloved people of Jarmo. *My* Jarmo: Terren, the mighty hunter. Grandmama soaking her ubiquitous lentils. So many little children. My girlfriends Kerki and Maura. Dear little Maidie. But does it really matter who will ultimately vanquish whom? Other mighty hunters, friends, and grandmothers will take the place of the fallen. Other hunters, other lovers.

In the dark, I'm thinking that while I've a breath in my body, I can't let our people be mowed down. Yes, I know everything morphs, everything changes. I've certainly changed, and the process continues. But I'll fight or kill to keep us safe as long as I can.

I'm going crazy with too much thinking. I start to stroke Hari, just the way he likes it, and he slowly starts to smile in the dim firelight. Before we know it, I am initiating a session of wild and sweaty sex, seeking, seeking, seeking to receive the answer to the question our bodies are asking, and quickly drifting off to sleep after finding the answer in a mutual cataclysm.

Not too many weeks later, I awaken to feel the room spin, and a little while later I throw up my breakfast of lentil stew. Soon after, for days the smell of raw butchered ibex makes me dry heave. I feel like all I want to do is sleep. Then eat. Then throw up again.

"You forgot to take the purple leaves. It can only be a baby," Hari explains to me with a grin, and he certainly ought to know. I think of the many miscarriages and stillborn babies Hari had with his second mate, but I don't mention them. As for Hari, he looks happy and excited, but more than a little concerned.

Holy crap. I've been so distracted lately that I haven't even thought about it, but now—too late—I suddenly remember the purple leaf plant, natural contraceptive of the Jarmo countryside and trusty remedy for every Jarmo woman of childbearing age. With a sinking feeling, I realize I haven't ingested any in a while. With so much else going on, I just forgot.

My heart gives a lurch when I realize I must be pregnant. I can't remember the last time I had my period. I'm not feeling dread, because I'd *love* a baby of our own. But a pregnancy just seems, and is, so inconvenient and immediate just now. So fraught with unknown perils.

As firelight flickers over Hari's shadowed face, I see happiness fighting with concern. Ashur is softly snoring. In the other part of our L-shaped room, Grandmama rustles and sighs in her sleep.

"Depending on snow pack in the mountain pass and how quickly it melts," Hari tells me in a low voice, "you could still have a big belly at the time of the battle. I'd thought we would wait until after the…war…before growing a baby. What was it? Did you forget to chew a purple leaf or two?"

He looks at me sideways. And I look sideways right back at him.

"Or…" Hari continues his soft-voiced inquiry, "do you just want to live dangerously?"

He draws me to him then, kissing me thoroughly. I guess he doesn't care if we live dangerously or not. But he does tell me, "*You* are a most inconvenient woman!"

But then I straddle him, and Hari quits talking. He needs his energy for something else.

CHAPTER 24
The Beginner

A good man is always a beginner.
∾ Marcus Aurelius ∾
121 – 180 A.D.

Stella

Ashur is looking at me again. Looking at me like *that*.
It makes me a little uncomfortable. Not a lot, but, yes, I'll admit, some.

The sound of sex doesn't seem to faze anyone in Jarmo, no more than the *blaat* of goats or the cries of migrating cranes. It's just part of life.

But I'm still enough of a twenty-first century girl to wish for privacy when we're doing private things. We'd thought Ashur was already asleep in his corner nest, so Hari and I made more noise than we should have last night. Guess we woke him up with the involuntary noises coming from the big bed. Also, the firelight keeps things bright and easy to see: erotic shadows dancing on the wall. Even Grandmama, hidden behind the wall in the other part of the L, sighs and giggles a bit in her sleep—or her not-so-sleepy sleep. She says that listening to sounds of sex sooths her; it reminds her that she's still close to the mainstream of life, even if she's no longer an active participant. Not that she wouldn't join in if asked. She'd definitely attempt to rise to the occasion, if anyone offered, but the absence of several important teeth keep any potential suitors at bay.

"Hari," I whisper. I snuggle behind him, spoon-fashion, and cup his sex in my hand before he falls asleep. It's too cold to sleep with the windows open anymore, so the shutters are closed. The room grows dim as the firelight subsides.

I raise myself up on one elbow and whisper again. "Hari."

My husband's eyes slowly open; a flame of firelight glints in each one. His eyes are so beautiful, pale blue yet somehow dark-smudged. Before he can slide back into sleep, I whisper, "Ashur's been watching us again. You know…"

Hari looks over at Ashur, who has now closed his eyes again, although the latter's forehead remains furrowed by the immensities of life. I don't think he's shamming. He really does look like he's drifted off again.

Ashur is definitely a strange one, skinny and scrawny. I think he's about fifteen, but nobody knows for sure. He likes to follow us around, Hari and me. He tries to go where we go, do what we do. Thank goodness the kid's not afraid to work. He can snare rabbits and marmots like anybody's business and bring down a water bird with one throw of his bolo.

The kid still broods and grieves a lot, though. As anyone would who has been recently orphaned and his tribe decimated. Hari told me how the obsidian traders came through Jarmo twice a year, heading north in the spring and south again in the fall. That's how he came to know Ashur and his family so well. That's why Hari feels so sorry for Ashur and somehow responsible for his well-being.

Fortunately, Ashur speaks our language, albeit with an odd accent. He tells us it's actually *his* language, and *we're* the ones who speak it funny.

I no longer ponder the conundrum of language in Jarmo. To me, everyone in Jarmo sounds as if they're speaking American-accented English, minus a lot of the idioms, of course. I know this can't be true. Although I haven't thought about this for months, maybe this whole place and time *is* just a dream after all, and I, Stella Denton, am the one who is the dreamer.

And so, yes, Ashur's our problem child now. Except he's not a child any longer. Children don't have the beginnings of a skimpy beard, hairy legs, or a slightly musky smell. The question of what to do about Ashur seems to have no answer. He certainly doesn't feel like our son. Or another man.

"He looks at me all the time," I tell Hari in a hushed voice. "Like he wants to…be with me, you know? What can we do for Ashur, anyway? How can we help him? He's not exactly a man yet, so we can't just marry him off."

Hari props himself on one elbow. "Not yet…" he says in a low voice. Together we stare at Ashur's dim form in the darkness.

Very quietly, Hari explains. "He still needs to fulfill two tasks of honor before he can be judged a man, take a wife, make babies, and head up his own household. And neither task is easy. So, no, we can't just marry him off. Not right away."

"What kinds of tasks?" I'm curious, wondering if it involves skin piercing or doing a vision quest alone in the wilderness.

"For one, he must kill an auroch bull. All alone, by himself. And the second, well…" In the low light, I see Hari's lips curve into a faint smile. "He must be able to call forth the joy hidden in a woman and make her cry out."

"Joy…" I repeat, cuddling close to him in contentment. "That's what…somebody I used to know called it." Actually, it was author James A. Michener describing sex among Hawaiian missionary couples. "Sanctified joy, he called it. Sanctified because it's a gift from the Great Mother."

"Sanctified joy," he repeats. "A good name."

I snuggle closer to Hari and start caressing him in ways he likes. He nuzzles my right ear with his nose and lips, and starts to respond, but I see that he's also still watching Ashur. Deciding pros and cons in his mind.

Ashur gently snores on into the night. At peace, at least for now.

Finally Hari speaks to me in a tender yet altered tone. Softly and seriously, like we're going to have a talk between grown-ups. And Hari is nothing if not persuasive.

"Stella…" He takes a slow, deep breath and speaks just above a whisper. "You want to do something for Ashur. I'll tell you how. We've taken Ashur into our home, and with that act comes responsibility on our part. Not because he's a child, because he's not, but he *is* part of this household now. Part of our tribe. He has no one else. He's not yet a man, but very close. As we do with all young males, an older man of our people is now teaching him our ways of hunting auroch and ibex, red gazelle, horses, deer, all of our prey. And Ashur needs this training because he's been an obsidian trader and flint knapper all his young life, and hunting is pretty far down on his list of skills. But now he's learning the ways of the hunter from Helin."

After taking a deep breath, Hari forges ahead.

"In order to officially enter manhood, Ashur also has to learn the ways of a woman. Only an experienced, fully-grown woman can show him how to be a proper husband. A wise and loving woman. Like you."

"Like...*me*." I repeat the words without expression. "Me? But I can't. I'm already married." I look at him pointedly. "As you yourself well know..."

Hari pauses. He looks at me with understanding and, again, great tenderness. "But that has nothing to do with it, wife. All our grown women who teach our boys a husband's role, they're already married, all of them. They have to be. Every woman must be some man's wife. You know we don't have enough people here to allow any of us to lie fallow. A woman's womb is like the earth. It must receive the seed and be watered well so it can bring forth a bounty of new life. Only an experienced woman knows what to teach a boy so he can learn to please a younger woman who'll be his wife."

"So, you're really asking me to..." I don't know how to finish the sentence. It's simply unbelievable. Fantastical. Unthinkable. "I can't believe you're trying to talk me into this! Besides, I'm not...from around here. It isn't my custom. At all. My people were—are—very, uh, private and proper. This—what you're proposing to me—*this* isn't proper at *all*. And Ashur is still so young. I think it's kind of creepy."

Hari looks surprised, crushed. Even puzzled. I can tell he doesn't have a clue what *creepy* means; Jarmoites aren't big on idioms.

"But, Stella, don't you see, it would be an honor for us both to see that he learns the proper ways of being. And living. And being a good husband."

Hari's voice becomes more audible now. Ashur still looks asleep, but I wouldn't be surprised if he's shamming now.

Hari rambles on softly in innocent simplicity. "It's an honor to pass along knowledge from one generation to another. It's *always* been this way in Jarmo; it's how knowledge of adulthood is passed. And among Ashur's people, too. It is the right thing to do. And this is the right time and place. If it's not you, it'll just be some other married woman."

"Good!" My voice is harsher than necessary. But really, I am totally creeped out. "Some other woman can do it. Someone who grew up with this…this custom."

I can't believe my own loving mate would suggest I do such a thing. But then, as I've often told Hari, I'm not originally from around here, and it shows all over me, in what I say and think and do.

Hari nods, leans on his right elbow on the bed, and raises both palms in silent defeat. "All right, if you wish, we'll get someone else. Because of your hesitancy. But I know Ashur is really hoping it'll be you, and I think it should be, too. A boy cannot dawdle with learning about such things. We have young girls who will probably bleed within the year. We need young men ready to marry them and treat them properly."

"But…" I don't know whether to be affronted, horrified, blasé, or furious. "But don't you care about having me stay…faithful…to you and you alone? You mean to tell me you wouldn't mind?"

Hari's smile looks helpless, faintly pleading, and still hugely mystified. I'm sure he's thinking, *what's the big deal?*

"Please. I know it can only be you for the both of us. You *are* being faithful to me, don't you see? By doing this kindness for him, a kindness that I'm asking you to do, you're showing your faith and support and honor. It honors me, and the tribe of Jarmo."

Pole-axed as I am, all I can ask is, "For how long?"

"What?" Hari isn't sure what I'm talking about.

"So, how long do you want me to…service this…teenager?" I ignore the fact that I'm still close to the teen years myself.

Hari answers me then with a gentle, soothing smile; I can sense it in the darkness. "Not long. Just for a couple of moons, or less. It shouldn't take him long to learn how to bring forth your…sanctified joy." He adds with a dubious glance into the distance, "Just so he can kill a bull auroch—he still has to do that before he can wed—but at least you don't have to help him kill the bull! The other hunters and I will teach him everything he needs to know about that."

Then he pulls me against his body, skin to skin. "Your joy lies always very close to the surface. Very close, *very* close…"

And all discussion about servicing Ashur is forgotten. For now.

The following morning, I have a hard time believing we even *had* that conversation. How outlandish. And ridiculous. *And* creepy. Surely, it must have been a dream.

But apparently it wasn't, for later today Hari reminds me (followed by a kiss), "When Ashur comes to you tonight, it will be from behind. Don't worry. I talked with him this morning and gave him suggestions. Told him to wash his hands and trim his nails. Young males still in training, so to speak, are not permitted front to front, skin to skin, until he learns to call forth your sanctified joy in the way all other animals do. Once the joy comes forth, then you can know him in other ways. And *then* it'll soon be time to marry him off. Once a girl is ready."

Hari seems so unconcerned about it all. Sex, faithfulness, and doing the right thing all must occupy completely different spaces in his brain, in his heart, in his life. He sees my obvious hesitation and reluctance over the whole idea, and though he doesn't understand it, still he sees it and tries to set my mind at ease. He also kisses me again and looks deeply into my eyes.

"It's the way I was raised in my youth. And my father before me, and his father before him. How else are boys to learn?"

How indeed? For once, I have no words.

That night, I remain rigidly awake, waiting for some move on Ashur's part. Next to me, Hari is drowsing, and eventually I too am lulled into a half-twilight place between wakefulness and sleep.

When suddenly I feel them.

Two fingers. Slow. Hesitant. Careful. Down there.

Instantly I'm jerked awake, but I don't jerk away. I'm hyper-alert, though. First I remain perfectly motionless and hold my breath. The fingers are finding my—

Hari must have given Ashur very specific instructions because, so far, he's being careful. Deliberate. Unhurried. And it feels…

I'm surprised. It feels nice.

Better than nice. After a while, I find myself moving slightly against the fingers. Part of me wonders what in the hell I'm doing, but the rest of me starts relaxing. And going with the flow.

Then I feel something hard against my backside, something pausing, poised for entry, hoping for an invitation before proceeding further.

Squirrely Girl speaks into my head just then and, for once, she takes pity on me, my fears, my squeamishness. *Don't overthink things too much now, Denton. Just relax.*

Before I can think of a hundred reasons not to do so, I don't think at all as I reach between my legs. I find myself guiding that part of him into the secret part of me that is more than ready. As he fills my length, Ashur utters a wordless, happy sound, something between a moan and a growl. And starts moving.

Way too fast at first. "Slower, slower," I urge him softly in the darkness. But it's too late. I feel him come within me like a landed fish, flopping, shuddering, and then finally clutching my hipbones.

"It's all right," I whisper to him without turning around to look at him. I couldn't look into his face now if I wanted to. The fire has gone out, and darkness reigns through throughout our house and all of Jarmo. "Next time, um, take it a bit more slowly."

He rests his forehead against my exposed shoulder and breathes deeply. "Yes, I will." And then, so quietly I have to hold my breath to hear it, he adds, "Thank you."

"You're welcome," I whisper, then bite my knuckle hard to quell a sudden fit of giggles. I shift my body involuntarily, and he pulls out of me—also involuntarily, I am sure. In the dark, I sense him shuffling off to his own bed. As he does, I feel other, more self-assured fingers seeking me out. Hari has awakened.

And then it's Hari filling every inch of me with something better than fingers, and I can feel his mouth smiling against mine in a kiss. Soon sanctified joy overcomes me, and I happily lose myself in the sensation, riding it for as long as I can.

The next day, Ashur moves his pile of sleeping skins next to mine. I now feel like an Oreo cookie: a girl in the middle with raging testosterone on either side of me.

It must be the sounds of too much sex that finally causes Grandmama to offer to move to Maidie's and Timon's house for a while. She has a good excuse, though; Maidie's young husband broke his arm in a hunting accident and needs extra tending.

Now the nighttime sounds—daytime sounds at times, too—are noisy with pleasure and satiation. My queasy pregnant belly finally settles.

What shocks me to the core is the fact that everyone seems to be happy these days in the House of Hari. Even me.

CHAPTER 25
The Horse

A man on a horse is spiritually
as well as physically bigger
than a man on foot.
— John Steinbeck —
1902–1968

Stella

I know where to find horses around Jarmo. Everybody does. Especially Maidie. She's now queen of the Jarmo horses.

Horses are common in our valley, usually grazing beside the Great River where grass grows thick during our cool, wet winters. That's where we're headed now, the Great River. The Tigris, Professor Harry told me, although it won't carry that name yet for thousands of years.

Six of us comprise this initial scouting party, our first official Horse Troop field trip. Meanwhile back in Jarmo, the other members construct the impressive round pen of stacked fieldstone, about fifty feet in diameter, a short ways from the village on the downhill side.

It's kind of funny. I didn't think so many Horse Troopers would actually fear horses. Well, *I* do, of course, city girl that I am. But then I'm not an official member of the Horse Troop. Hari and I are honorary members of all the troops, and no one cuts us any slack on anything. They assume we must know it all, and so we try our best to project a confident image, even if we haven't many clues about what we're doing.

Twenty-first century horse whisperers, usually men, insist that a round pen is essential for the kind of horse training we plan on doing—what we *hope* to do in the very near future.

Most Horse Troop members are men, but there are a few women too. And Maidie is one of them, the most excited and confident of us all. Like I said, she seems to be the only Horse Trooper, male or female, who isn't distrustful or afraid of horses. Horses enchant her, mesmerize her. She loves everything about them.

For that reason alone, Hari publicly appoints Maidie, his only living child, barely into her teens, to take on the role and responsibility of Prime Dominant: the sole individual who will gain dominance over the horses and direct the horse program as it progresses from there.

There's a new look these days on faces in Jarmo. Confused. Worried. Resigned. Usually all three. They look much like twenty-first century commuters in Cincinnati or Minneapolis, Seattle or Long Beach. Places where too many folks must endure working at what they don't like to do all day long and where they can do what they like to do only for a few free hours after dark. Like I say, it's Jarmo's new normal.

I worry. Oh God, do I worry! I can't stop thinking about it. My mind keeps coming back to this: It's all just a crapshoot. Win, lose, or draw, it probably won't make much difference what we do beforehand, here and now. But still…

But still.

And this horse business! I'm definitely biting off more than our people want to chew here. What do I know about wild horses anyway? And presume to teach to neophytes even greener than I? Less than nothing. All I *do* know is that horses are big and scary, usually wanting (and getting) their own way.

My mental sparring with Squirrelly Girl usually ends just before I fall asleep exhausted after reaching the following conclusion: As beautiful, idyllic, and safe as the world of Jarmo initially seemed to me, I have to admit that it's not. And never really was.

I know it's just nature being nature out there. A nature that neither smiles nor frowns. It just *is,* and if we humans can't keep up with what destiny sends our way (famine, fire, invaders, dangerous wildlife), well, tough-titty-said-the-kitty. Eventually I fall into an exhausted sleep. And awaken tomorrow, unrefreshed, when my worrying starts all over again.

There's danger in doing nothing, danger in doing something, danger in *everything*.

But we're not going down without a fight.

And so, here we are on day one of Project Horse, six of us on a small hillside far below Jarmo. Here to select the wild horses whose lives we're going to be changing forevermore. And whose lives will soon change ours.

We'll probably have to wait a good while before we spot any. And a long time it turns out to be. Afternoon shadows already lengthen, and it feels like we've walked miles—we probably have—before we finally glimpse a small herd.

"There! Just coming into view now." A tall young Horse Trooper with a spidery black moustache and sparse beard is the first to spot them. A good herd of five—no, six—five mares and a stallion. We follow his hand direction with our eyes.

There they are, the valued subjects of our quest.

We watch the horses feed peacefully together in the pale winter sun. Their manes are dark and wavy, not unlike my own Jarmo hair, only much shorter. Their stocky, dark legs are mottled with pale markings like reverse zebra stripes. A line of dark fur runs over their spine, even through the mane and tail, while a dark shoulder stripe bisects the spinal stripe, forming a cross.

It doesn't take long to identify the stallion or the dominant mare either. Especially the mare. She's a broad-beamed, dusty horse with a blocky head, low shoulders, strong legs, prominent scar on one hindquarter. And she's got a take-no-prisoners attitude.

We approach our herd slowly and cautiously. Definitely keeping a long, safe distance from them so as not to cause panic, among the horses or us. This first trip out to the horses is just a reconnoitering one, to see if the horses are still here (yes), determine which animals comprise their herd (five mares, one stallion), and to decide what to do about the stallion (take him out—surreptitiously and unobtrusively with volleys of arrows or a spear chucked via atl-atl from a secluded spot).

Since the grass is unusually lush here, our troop figures the horses will stay around this area for a few days. But it's late, nearly sunset. We back away from the horses and head for home.

The following day, we try to make ourselves noiseless as the horses approach—sort of. They're wary yet curious. We don't move and scarcely dare breathe. They know we are here.

Boss Mare is what my grandma used to call a piece of work. Not above giving a shove, kick, or serious nip to any lower ranking mare who attempts to test boundaries of the rules.

Although twenty-first century equine research says that any boss mare is truly the ruler of the herd and the stallion is only window dressing, Professor Harry warned me not to believe it, no matter what the prevailing wisdom might be.

"Make no mistake, that stallion is still King Tut of the herd. Don't even think of trying to tame him."

I feel sorry for the stallion. He can't help it if he happens to be the wrong sex for our needs. He paces the perimeter of the group on perpetual lookout for danger from large predators (as are we all), as well as challenges from other males who lust after his harem. By living on the periphery of the herd, perpetually on high alert, the stallion endures a rough-and-tumble existence.

Unwisely on my part, I decide to go out with the Horse Troop today to kill the stallion. First we cover ourselves with tanned auroch hides to obscure our human form from the mares. From a natural bunker of boulders and brush, an experienced hunter launches a short hand-spear with his atl-atl. It slices the air as if shot by a Howitzer. The projectile penetrates the stallion with an audible *thuk* behind the horse's right shoulder.

The horse falls to his knees, then flops over sideways while emitting an ear-splitting squeal. Groaning and writhing, he attempts to right himself. His piteous vocalizations make me want to cover my ears, so I do. Okay, I'm a wuss, but I feel so bad for him. Still "needs must" as Grandpa used to say. Finally the stallion's large gray head falls to one side, his sides heave a few times, and then all is still. While the stallion is dispatched, the mares gallop off in confusion and disarray.

After the mares hightail it, the six of us quarter the stallion and bring what we can carry back to Jarmo for (ugh) dinner. Upon reflection, though, I have to admit pony boy is surprisingly tasty.

I'm hugely thankful to see the horses still remain in the same general area, day after day, especially after the stallion's...ahem...assassination. The mares are still around. Not by the stallion's gut piles, because jackals are already devouring those. But at least they're close, just one small hill away.

It's official now, but not without whining and more than a few protests from male Horse Troop members, that Maidie will definitely be the first one to ride the beast. Nobody really wants to go first — except Maidie. Even her young, devoted husband, Timon, is nonplussed at his wife's courage and confidence. So, it's Maidie who will tame the mares and lead them back to Jarmo. Eventually. From this day forward, until such time as the mares are coaxed into the round pen, only Maidie and Timon will work on this project: Maidie as the Dominant Human, Timon as the hidden lookout and the one watching Maidie's back.

I can almost see Maidie's brain working a mile a minute. She ticks off tasks on her fingers. "Timon is coming with me, of course!" She looks up at him gratefully with an ear-to-ear smile. "With a bow and a spear as my lookout. And early tomorrow, could you please have the Horse Troop cut and gather more sweetgrass, making five separate piles inside the pen? Each mare will want her own portion of food. There'll be fights otherwise. And could you also, please, post a couple of watches on the village-side of the pen to keep random people away from the direction in which the horses and I might approach Jarmo? I don't want anybody or anything to startle those horses. They'd probably never come back, and we'd have to start all over again with a different herd."

Truly, I'm in awe of this gutsy young woman. I admire her more than I can say. That such a slight little person should be so brave and seemingly unconcerned in the close proximity of unpredictable wild horses. I'm about a head taller than she is, but there's no way I'd have anything to do with a horse.

The following day, I just can't help it. I have to wait and watch for Maidie, from a safe, hidden distance, of course, to see if she can really bring the wild mares home.

No matter what else I have to do — and, together with Hari, there are heaps of tasks on our mutual plate — I simply have to see Maidie's moment of triumph. Indeed, triumph for all of Jarmo, and the first concrete sign of Jarmo moving forward toward ultimate victory over the invaders.

Beside the growing success of the Horse Troop, the other troops are, thus far, less than illustrious in their progress. They're running into new snags faster than Hari and I can sort them out.

The Wheel Troop has had no luck finding a likely slab of downed timber for the making of one wooden wheel, let alone four. So far, the Wheel folks spend most of their time sharpening stone axes and telling stories. We'll definitely have to light a fire under that bunch.

The Archer Troop is up and running smoothly, but we haven't found a way yet to keep up with their need for a ready supply of arrow points. Although each projectile point is carefully saved, stored, cleaned, sharpened and tended to, eventually some are lost in the course of hunting and target practice. Ashur is really starting to earn his keep here. Right now he's the only man — well, soon to be a man — who knows how to shape flint and quartz into precision stone arrowheads: the timeless, critical skill of knapping. He's teaching the archer group knapping skills much of the day, when he isn't off learning valuable skills from more experienced hunters.

The Wheat Troop, mostly grandparents and young children, has carefully sowed last fall's dry, ripened seed heads. First they carefully thresh it by hand using grinding stones to separate the kernels from chaff. They sow it in the loose soil around the perimeter of the Gathering Space. At least it's rained sufficiently to sprout the seeds. We're all watching for green shoots to break the surface. No sign of anything just yet.

And the Death Squad? This group hasn't even met yet. The three group leaders — one of them, Boze, even has a unibrow while the two others sport equally menacing countenances — are coordinating this group together. But all they'll say yet is, "We're still figuring out what to teach. We will let you know when we do." I don't like the sound of that at all.

By mid-morning, I can't resist the urge to slip away to watch and wait for Maidie. I have no idea when she's coming, of course. Anything could happen, and most generally it does.

I park myself under a cherry tree not far from the village. It's a wild cherry, of course, and I've become familiar with its tiny, dark, incredibly sour fruits. I'm still close enough to the village to be safe from predators, yet far enough out to be able to see the opening in the round pen clearly, even though it's still at a distance. The cherry tree's bare branches provide a surprising amount of shade for something with no leaves. I make myself comfortable in the underbrush beneath the tree, settling in for the duration.

And I wait. And wait. And eventually doze. Not a good idea in wild country.

I'm awakened by a reproving kiss on the lips. Before I can yell or even get my bearings, I see that it's Hari and start kissing him back.

But he's glowering at me, looking worried and relieved at the same time. "Why did you run off like that? You should have told me where you were going. Hyenas sometimes approach this close, and I don't want you anywhere around here when they do."

"I'm waiting and watching for Maidie." I kiss him again in an attempt to smooth his frown.

A voice suddenly speaks close by. "Wait no more, Chieftain's Wife."

I almost jump out of my skin, and so does Hari, although he tries not to show it. It's Timon, well-wrapped in an auroch hide. Evidently, he's shadowing Maidie's movements, staying well away from her horse maneuvers, yet close enough to provide deadly force should she require it. He must have come up the hill in advance of her arrival.

Timon inclines his head to the downhill slope. "She's coming up with them now. Be still." His voice drops to a whisper, and he motions for us to stay down within the obscuring underbrush.

Them? I hug myself with excitement and crane my neck to see. Hari searches the horizon too, although all three of us make ourselves as invisible as possible.

The early afternoon sky is so blue, it almost hurts to look at it. If any horses follow behind Maidie, today's moderate breeze blows in an ideal direction to keep the reek of human habitation far from the equines. So far, so good.

Then I see her, a tiny, sun-browned shape walking slowly up the hill.

And she's not alone. A single, mouse-colored horse follows her. Cautiously. Stopping from time to time, neck tensed, ears alert and forward.

As Maidie pays her no mind and keeps walking, Boss Mare takes a few brisk steps to follow the two-legged creature, then stops again. As member of a prey species, a wild mare can't be too careful in the wilderness around Jarmo.

Maidie still brandishes her ever-present willow switch, I see. I watch as the girl turns and approaches the Boss Mare again, her right hand held high as she swishes the slender switch back and forth. Just enough to intentionally force movement on the part of the Boss

Mare. The horse retreats, then stands to watch with interest what her Human Boss will do next.

Maidie turns her back on the mare, then brings her left hand across her abdomen with closed fingers, and slowly walks through the rock fence opening into the round pen. Professor Harry told me that these are all intentional movements, calculated to gradually make the mares submissive to Maidie.

She pays the mare no mind whatsoever and enters the pen alone.

A minute or two pass, during which Timon, Hari, and I wait with bated breath, Boss Mare, with visible trepidation, peers around the open gate of the pen. She clearly sees her Dominant Human, who is not so strange anymore, in the pen turning deliberately away from her. Yet again.

After many moments of decision, when caution fights with bluff and bravado, Boss Mare enters the pen herself. Now both human and equine are out of our field of vision.

What are they doing in there, anyway?

Then, suddenly, come the other mares: three adult females and a smaller filly who must be a yearling.

They're following their own inborn imperative to follow wherever Boss Mare leads them. And Boss Mare is following Maidie.

No doubt by now, Boss Mare has found one of the hay piles in the pen and is happily chowing down. She's the first one to eat, her right by virtue of her prominent position, her intelligence and confidence, and hard-earned herd wisdom.

The contented rest-and-digest sounds of Boss Mare's chewing, audible through the open gate, no doubt reassures the other mares. Cautiously, they too, with no thought of disobeying their equine queen, enter the round pen, following her lead.

I see Maidie exit the pen, unhurried and straight-backed, tall as her four-foot-eleven inches will allow. Deftly, Maidie swings the slatted gate shut without a sound on five very surprised but probably no longer alarmed mares. Five piles of delicious, fresh grass inside the round pen are a powerful soothing agent against fears of the unknown.

Maidie then bars the gate by fitting a thick, rough-hewn, rectangular slab of wood into two wooden upright holders, held in place by stout pegs, on the outside of the gate. Five mares are now safely and securely at home in the round pen.

Confidently, joyfully even, Maidie starts walking toward the village. We come out from our hiding place and start running toward her. She runs to meet us, too. We meet together in a welter of joyful shrieks, arm waving, and hugs.

Holy shit, she's done it! My arms may be hugging, my voice laughing and praising joyfully, but mentally Squirrelly Girl is already moving to the next order of business. *Now that she's gotten the horses for us, she and the others must learn to ride the fucking things. That's a whole 'nother stewpot of fish.*

Plus, we still have to make those damned wheels. I still can't visualize a workable axle to save my life. *Oh, Professor, dear, good Harry Vale, I don't want to fail you now! If you can sense my comatose brainwaves, please send me a reminder hint from beyond, okay?* And then there's that harness we've still got to figure out for the cart. And we still have to learn how to shoot actual human beings with bows and arrows—shoot to *kill*.

Indeed, our warfare journey has only just begun.

CHAPTER 26
The Bow

In preparing for battle I have always found that
plans are useless, but planning is indispensable.
~ Dwight D. Eisenhower ~
1890–1969

Stella

Make the arrows. Make *more* arrows.

Day in, day out, my world is now comprised of arrows. That is, when I'm not vomiting up my breakfast or falling asleep on my feet like many a pregnant lady before me.

I now work on the arrow assembly line at least two hours a day, sometimes more, when I'm not otherwise monitoring the horse-taming project, helping to water the wheat, or cutting leather patterns to make arrow quivers. Soon the Death Squad will get its act together, and then I'll start learning how to fight to the death with another human being.

How I miss the lovely, leisurely Jarmo of my early days here: lounging in the hot pool, singing with the girls, arranging one another's hair, gathering berries and nuts, and giggling over the incomprehensibility of men. But leisurely Jarmo is gone, at least for now. Life is so damned busy. Everybody works long and hard. It's mandatory. Everybody who can walk or work has at least one job to do, usually more.

The sheer scope of what we need to accomplish keeps me awake most nights. First off, we've got to make a mountain of arrows. Heaps and heaps. Enough for everyone tall enough and strong enough to pull a bowstring and carry a quiver of ten arrows, hopefully more, slung bandolier-style over the body. And that describes most everyone in the village, except for a few toddlers, babes-in-arms, our three designated Graybeards, and five designated old wise women (the Crones, we call them—and Grandmama is one). The Crones will serve as babysitters and bodyguards of our little ones.

Arrows and, holy shit, arrow*heads!* We'll be needing mountains of these, too. And arrowheads take a lot of time. And skill. And talent.

Even Hari sheepishly admits that, for decades, our people have become dependent on the obsidian traders to supply our arrowheads. We assumed because they always *had* come through Jarmo twice a year, they always *would* come around. Forevermore. We never dreamed they'd all be massacred in a single melee. All but one scrawny teenaged boy.

Who is fast becoming a man in every way he can.

The only obsidian trader left alive, Ashur teaches our men, who are eager to learn the tricky skill of flint-knapping. Flint will have to do. Ashur tells us that the nearest obsidian is more than two weeks away on foot and therefore too dangerous to attempt without a sizeable group. We're just glad and grateful to have a ready, easy supply of plain old flint around here. Flint arrowheads don't look as intimidating and wicked-beautiful as obsidian, but they can kill you just as fast.

Nights at home by the firelight, I work on a list. I write furtively with a piece of charcoal on a large square of tanned deer hide. It's our Jarmo Manpower list—People Power, I should say. Who are the best shooters, who'll be the best killers, how many arrowheads, bows, arrows, quivers, shields, spears, atl-atls and darts will be needed.

Since Hari, Ashur, and Grandmama can't help observing the strange squiggles I'm drawing, I've sworn them to silence on the matter. "These are magic markings. Known only to me and the Great Mother. Say nothing about this to anyone outside of our family," I caution them, and they agree without question. They always suspected I was more than a little strange, someone to step carefully around, probably not quite fully human, and now they know it for sure.

I feel so weary sometimes. So tired of the drama and uncertainty of it all. Sometimes I feel pretentious and more than a little ridiculous. Like Xena, the Warrior Princess, from the old TV show.

My mind constantly churns with *what if.* What if all this is just a bunch of hooey? What if Ashur overheard wrong, and the invaders aren't coming after all? What if they've given up the whole idea or never intended such a thing in the first place? What if the Great Showdown never comes to pass, and I've made our people work so long and hard for nothing? Or what if the strangers are simply friendly? And their great evil is vastly overblown? What if they just want a little piece of our action here, a small portion of our resources?

That wouldn't be so bad. Would it?

I can almost talk myself into downplaying my worries. Almost.

But at other times, battle cries prod me awake in my dreams. And I think, *Shit! I'm not worthy! I am not enough. I'm a fake. A fraud. A nothing and a nerd from the twenty-first century with no idea what I'm doing here. Am I actually leading these people—my people, my dearly beloved people—over a cliff? Am I warping their society to such an extent it will affect future generations, future actions, future decisions—perhaps irrevocably?*

This is why I toss and turn at night, long after the love-making is over, when my men are already snoring gently into their sheepskin pillows.

Although our people don't know it, the possibility exists that Jarmo, right now, may be on the cusp of want and scarcity. Professor Harry has told me many times how the Jarmo settlement endured for nearly two thousand years. Which is pretty freaking amazing. I can't help but hug myself with pride, even though I've had nothing to do (up to now) with Jarmo's continued success.

But there's no way to know if we're still at the beginning of our good times—or close to the end. Yes, we still have plenty of resources to take care of our own. For now. But what if our numbers should suddenly double, from one hundred twenty-two to two hundred forty-four, or even say three hundred, four hundred, immediately? What then?

How friendly would the newcomers be? How friendly would *we* be if we had to make do with less than half of the bounty and resources we're accustomed to?

Each morning, still sleep deprived and frequently nauseated, I continue to slog through each day with resolve. *Damn it, I can only do what I think is best with the knowledge I have. So, strike me dead if you want to, God, if this isn't good enough.*

At night, at home by the firelight, as Hari and Ashur work on flint-knapping together at the far end of the room and Grandmama hums off-key tunes as she prepares her kefir milk cultures, I match names with jobs, with occasional solicited coaching from the sidelines, and list them under the following categories:

63 males

~ 28 adult males

~ 14 pre-teen males

~ 15 little boys

~ 3 Graybeards

~ 3 baby boys (infants to toddlers)

59 females

~ 28 adult females (ones who have started their periods)

~ 9 pre-teen girls

~ 10 little girls

~ 7 grannies/Crones

~ 5 baby girls (infants to toddlers)

I'm figuring everyone, from children on up, needs their own bow to shoot, custom-made for their own size and strength. Assuming that our adult men, pre-teen males, and little boys already have their own bows, that's going to be at least five hundred seventy arrows.

Deep in my brain, Squirrelly Girl can't resist reminding me, *And that's just for the guys!*

I write the names of our forty-seven able-bodied females. That's four hundred seventy more arrows. Counting everyone who'll need them, that's over a thousand arrows! With hardwood to be located, selected, cut, hauled home, seasoned, and shaped. And more than a thousand new broadhead projectile points to be carefully knapped, then hafted, onto the arrow shafts.

And bows! So many new bows are needed too! Since Jarmo females typically don't use bows very often—only slings, snares, and bolos—they currently have none of their own. But now we must all learn to use bows and arrows, or be mowed down in the end.

I mutter and figure, cross things out, and sigh. A lot. Words swim in my head: bows and arrows, the wheel (we've got to move faster on that), horseback riding (we're still gentling the mares, and not even Maidie has ridden yet), the wheat field still shows little in the way of green, and then there's daily archery practice. And, no matter how scary and revolting, we must soon learn from the Death Squad leaders about hand-to-hand combat and how to kill.

Chieftain Hari now goes around with a perpetual furrow between his mismatched eyebrows. Men come to our house to learn flint knapping from Ashur and add to the slowly growing heap of broadhead arrowheads.

I must admit that Ashur is starting to look like a man now—and is now treated like one, fitted out as he is in leather apron, thigh cover, chest protection, and a precious wealth of arrowhead knowledge critical to our survival.

Hari and I check in with each committee daily. Two days of work, followed by a day off for necessary hunting, gathering, and soaking in the hot pool for restoration, then two days on again. We try to coddle reluctant folks along, praising them when their fumbling early efforts become more assured and skilled. We pitch in and do more than our share of plain old grunt-work: cutting, sharpening, scraping, watering, and hoeing, just for starters.

Today, after grabbing a quick breakfast of leftovers from our fireside's stone stewpot, Hari and I walk through Jarmo's narrow lanes to the home of Tarek, his wife, Sua, and their three young sons.

Tarek is what Jarmoites call a bowyer. He's the best bow-maker in the village and admired by all, hands-down. The home of Bowyer Tarek is prosperous by Jarmo standards, with a substantial mud brick house with large, shuttered windows, flung open this morning to the new day. Within the home's sun-dappled interior, three men, two women, and Tarek's three sons laboriously scrape at long, narrow lengths of hardwood—bow staves—using obsidian blades. Another woman braids together three long strands of wet-looking, off-white material.

The sight of Tarek's bow assembly line unsettles me. Nothing like it has ever been seen before in Jarmo. I feel slightly nauseated to see row upon row of so many bows already taking shape. It makes the coming battle all too real.

The Archery Committee is a very big deal in Jarmo. Already it has split into four subcommittees. Headed by Tarek, the bowyers make new bows for women and older children, plus additional back-up bows for the men, created specifically to each person's height and strength.

Coordinated by Helin, a shy, stocky man whose eyes don't track properly so you're never quite sure if he's looking at you or over your shoulder, the fletchers create the arrow shafts, each nocked and fitted with feather fletchings to enable each arrow to fly true.

Ashur oversees the neophyte knappers who daily knap pieces of flint into new arrowheads.

And then there are the shield makers—big-nosed Bern heads up this group—who are still scrambling to finalize shield designs and prototypes. These will be chiefly for the men; they'll be too heavy for most women. We've never had a need for shields before. Until now.

Since Hari and I are working all the time, not doing the two days on, one day off schedule, Jarmo's best hunters make sure we have some kind of meat daily, and my women friends share liberally with us their supplies of root vegetables, nuts, snails, and mushrooms.

Jarmo has been so self-sufficient and stress-free up to now, we have no inclination to docilely follow any leader who might try to bully villagers into a fear-based dictatorship. Hari wouldn't last a week if he tried a stunt like that in Jarmo. Cooperation is the only way we can survive.

As we walk slowly behind the bowyers, observing them at their tasks, Tarek reminds all of us present, "Remember, archery practice after lunch today. And every couple days, indefinitely. For everyone, except you, of course, Chieftain, until you can all hit stationery and moving targets."

Hari looks at him from under his brows. "Everyone means me too, Tarek. I'll be there. We all will."

Tarek does not reply but nods without a word, stepping sideways to lift something off a series of pegs on his wall.

Suddenly he places what looks like a huge, golden-blond toothpick horizontally into my two hands. "Here, hold it."

I do; it's surprisingly heavy and unwieldy.

It's Tarek's own bow. I attempt to pivot the intimidating assemblage of wood and string into a vertical position, grasping the only place where it looks logical to do so—the leather-wrapped grip or waist at the midpoint on the bow.

Tarek points out its many features as I struggle to keep the bow perpendicular to the ground. "Here! See if you can draw this bow."

Self-consciously, I hold the bow handle in my left hand and attempt to pull back the bowstring, even a little bit, with my right. I struggle mightily, but the damned thing won't budge. It's like trying to move a bolder by tugging on a cord.

"You'll have to use a child's bow for starters, but we'll make yours a little longer since you're tall."

Shit. I've already been measured and found wanting at my first archery test, albeit an informal one.

"See this wood?" Tarek strokes the bow lovingly. "Yew, that is. Best wood anywhere for making a bow, so supple and strong. Yew wood harnesses more energy from the Great Mother than other wood. But it's not so easy to find. Goddess keeps them rare so we won't use them all up thoughtlessly, so we'll appreciate it for the great treasure it is. We'll have to use ash or mahogany instead to make so many bows at once."

He hands the strung bow back to me to observe and admire again.

And I *do* admire it. In the same way I admire Olympic athletes on TV—shining, admirable, meaningful, powerful. But something I could never hope to master.

Feeling suddenly overwhelmed, I start to prop Tarek's bow carefully against the wall.

"Don't!" He reaches for the bow before it touches the ground. "Never prop your bow up-and-down. It'll ruin it. Only place it horizontally up off the ground. Preferably on pegs against a wall."

Another failure on my part. When will I ever learn? Do I have enough innate moxie that'll even permit me to learn something so physical?

"It's a good thing you couldn't pull this bow," Tarek admits. "I didn't think you could, or I'd never have let you try in the first place. Because a bow must only be used by the man—or woman—it is made for. It's alive, this bow, and it knows and loves only its master—or mistress. It soon becomes attuned to the way you pull the bowstring. This bow was measured and made for me and no other. Even as your bow will be."

"But how will I learn if I can't use another person's bow?"

Tarek reassures me. "You'll start with a child's bow. An old, well-worn, but reliable bow used by many before you. When you're ready for your own, grown-up bow, you'll know it. And so will I."

He puts his hand on my shoulder in a semblance of comfort, nothing flirtatious about it. "Don't worry. You'll come to love and revere the power of the bow, even as I do. Great energy is released in each arrow's flight. Speaking of arrows, come along with me now to Helin's place, our master of arrows. After all, a bow is nothing without an arrow. Even as an arrow is nothing without a bow."

CHAPTER 27
The Arrow

Chance favors the prepared mind.
~ Louis Pasteur ~
1822–1895

Stella

W hen a shot arrow hits something alive — I'm guessing humans too — I am told it makes a sound like *th-ooot*. Actually, I know about this *th-ooot* sound for a fact.

I just heard it, and it gives me the willies. But it also gives me an illicit thrill.

But that's nothing compared with the sound of a *volley* of arrows. That's what they call it here in Jarmo, a volley, meaning a bombardment of arrows all coming your way at once. It makes a chilling, hypnotic sound as they pierce the air simultaneously: *Whoosh*.

Whoosh is the last sound before you hear the *th-ooot*, but by then it's too late, because by that time you're screwed.

But I'm getting ahead of myself. Back to Tarek's House of the Bow. Before Tarek packs me off to Helin's house, Hari assures me he'll catch me up before archery practice begins.

Nearby, Helin's place is a smallish, H-shaped dwelling, mud brick with a stone foundation and thatched roof. There's hardly a need for new homes in Jarmo because our tribe's population has a way of staying remarkably stable — unfortunately or fortunately, depending on how you look at it. There's infant mortality, fatal pregnancy problems, childhood illnesses (which are few in number here due to our isolation and small gene pool, but, still, they can appear and quickly turn deadly). Plus there are animal attacks, lightning strikes, rock slides, avalanches in the high country, infected wounds, and just accidents in general. Many, many accidents. That's why every baby in Jarmo is a cause for much celebration and rejoicing. They don't all survive. Nor do all the mothers. Not by a long shot.

I'm fascinated to see that the arrow assembly line at Helin's is even more impressive than the one for bows at Tarek's. Several women, a few men, and a bunch of half-grown children are there today, seated in organized rows, cutting and shaping arrows, then passing them along to the next, um, department.

Absurdly long they are, these arrows. Surely too unwieldy for anyone to readily grab and shoot. I'm no good at estimating inches (and besides, inches won't be invented for several thousands of years yet), but these arrows, if placed tail end on the floor, would probably reach my crotch.

Taking me in hand, metaphorically speaking, Helin starts chattering away to me (even as his wall eye looks disconcertingly over my shoulder) about everything arrows. According to Helin, the arrowheads we make must be "only broadhead flints. For quick killing, you know."

Piles of waterfowl wings — fletching materials — are everywhere. And kids who look like fifth graders from my previous life use stone straighteners, a bone implement with a sharp-edged hole in it, to shape the arrow shafts.

"An arrow must always have feathers attached near the nock. And do you know why, Chieftain's wife?"

Um, no.

"They help each arrow fly true." Helin brings an arrow in close for my inspection. "See, there must always be three feathers around the base of the arrow, just above the nock."

"Why three?" I ask. "Why not two or four?"

Helin looks at me under his thick brows. "Three is the *Goddess* Number, the number of our Great Mother. The chief of the three feathers is this one, called the cock. It's always tied or glued in a straight line with the arrow, then trimmed so it won't come in contact with the bow when the arrow is shot."

Indicating the remaining two fletchings, he adds, "These others are just the hen feathers since they don't do much except help the cock to fly true."

(Just. *Just* the hen feathers.)

I mutter dryly, "Why am I not surprised?" Some things never change, despite the century.

Raising an eyebrow, Helin continues. "And always remember, all fletching feathers must come from the same side of the same bird. We don't know why this must be so; we only know that it *is* so. And if we mix feathers from different sides of the bird, or even take them from different birds, the arrow won't shoot straight. Remember that when you start tying on the fletchings."

I can't help asking. "How do you make the arrowheads stay on? They seem awfully heavy to just be slid into a notch or tied on with a cord."

"That's the part that takes so long in arrow making." Helin shrugs. "We must haft the arrowheads on, and that can take all day. The soaking in water, getting glue from ibex hooves, waiting for it to dry and tighten…" Helin shifts topics. "You're probably hungry. I'll bet folks have brought enough dried meat along for you to have a chew or two. We'll stop now for our meal. Later today, after archery practice, we'll teach you how to select and start shaping the wood for arrows. The girls will show you how to pluck and sort feathers—and whatever you do, *don't* mix up those feathers!"

After the spare meal of water and ibex jerky, other villagers start strolling in. In twos and threes, then larger groups, Hari among them. He slips his arm around my waist and waits expectantly.

"Outside!" Helin claps his hands together briskly with evident anticipation. "Archery practice, everybody. Time to show us what you've got!"

We follow him to the north meadow at the edge of the village. We're a huge crowd by now. I'm guessing two-thirds of Jarmo's population must be here, gathered around.

Here, five targets—big slabs of meat, actually—confront us about twenty yards out on five chest-high piles of rocks. A large mammal, probably a deer, has been segmented into bloody quarters, with the head a separate target in itself.

I hear a women whisper to her child, "Don't worry. It'll be dinner tomorrow night."

Little is ever wasted in Jarmo. What arrows pierce today will be covered with leaves and sand on a bed of coals tonight, then happily ingested by villagers the following day. No doubt with a new, hapless prey taking its place as target species.

Helin calls out to the group. "First we'll practice basic shots, then we'll work on volleys."

Suddenly, I start quivering with apprehension. I'm out of my league here, and don't I know it.

Hari takes some of us aside — four young girls about nine or ten years old, Koral, and me — to begin with the basics. Other archers, also serving as teachers of beginners, gather other neophytes about them.

Hari motions us far enough away from the real archers, and everyone else, to keep us out of trouble. We're far off to one side, with our own groups and our own newbie target, with no one around to snicker at our baby-step efforts.

I see our target — a dog-sized, skinned mammal, possibly a marmot, propped on a rock pile. Life can be the shits sometimes. For some carbon life forms more than others.

We gather around Hari as he sorts bows and other equipment to disseminate among our group. Koral, of course, hovers near his left elbow, leaning in confidentially and giving him a sidelong look. I am quick to lean in just as closely on his right.

Somehow, Koral always manages to weasel herself in between Hari and me. *Always.* And I hate it. She always makes me feel... rumpled. As if she's competing with me. Which she undoubtedly is.

I know she likes Hari far more than she should. I can't help thinking viciously, *Bitch, I wish you'd just...disappear.*

I keep my eye on Koral with more than a little concern.

Today she's wearing her I've-got-a-secret look around Hari. Which is annoying as hell. Thankfully, he doesn't seem to notice anything out of the ordinary.

Where is her own husband, Kern, anyway?

There's a question for you, Squirrelly Girl can't resist informing me. *One without a good answer.*

"First," Hari begins by passing around small leather cylinders. "Finger tabs," he explains, and then holds up his own covered finger to show us. His finger tab looks well worn. "To protect your hand while the bowstring is drawn." I slip it over the first finger of my right hand with a growing sense of unease.

Next he distributes leather arm guards, which are old, weathered, and flat segments of hide, tied on with rawhide strings. "To protect the inside of the bow arm from being hit by the string. And also to prevent your winter long sleeves from catching the bow string."

"Now, then, bows. Children's bows for starters." Hari distributes them from a pile of what looks like oversized toothpicks, up off the ground and resting on a low rock pile — perfectly horizontally. Tarek would approve.

From the corner of my eye, I glimpse the more experienced archers move into place. I hear Tarek's order. "Wait for my signal, now. Ready, set…let fly!"

Holy crap. For the first time, I hear that sound…*th-ooot.* And it's loud. Yet somehow not loud at all. Menacing, yes, but also whistling and somehow silvery. Yet solid. Irresistible.

Th-ooot. That's the sound of five shot arrows simultaneously finding their mark deep in purple flesh.

"Before you shoot the bow, try to warm it up a bit." Hari demonstrates as he speaks. "Pull the string to about half-draw, maybe ten times or so, like this. And use your back muscles, your archery muscles, to do it. Pull the bowstring back quietly and deliberately. Don't yank it. And don't hold it for a long time either. Just draw it back…" He places an arrow, demonstrating for us with effortless, fluid motions. "Nice and easy, slow and relaxed. Hold it for a couple seconds, aim, and then let fly!"

The arrow flies and hits the target with a satisfying reverberation. As he walks over to retrieve the arrow, he looks us over again. "I'm assuming everyone here has a right hand that's stronger than her left?"

We nod.

"The hand that holds the bow is your bow hand, your bow arm. The opposite hand is called the string hand, so hold the bow now with your left hand."

Hari walks down the line, handing us each an arrow. Mine is longer than my arm.

Using our left hands, we each hold the bow out before us. Mine wobbles ominously. I grit my teeth and will it to stay straight.

"Come form a line-up, and we'll take turns shooting. Stand at an angle to the target. Like this. With your feet placed shoulder-width apart."

I shuffle my feet into an approximation of the correct stance.

"To load your arrow, point the bow toward the ground, like this, and place the shaft of the arrow on the arrow rest."

I glimpse Koral out of the corner of my eye. Her face is rapt; she hangs on Hari's every word. As mine would be (should be) too. If I weren't always keeping a weather eye on Koral.

"Now attach the back of your arrow, where the slit is, and fit it to the bow to nock the arrow. Make sure the cock feather is on top, pointing away from the bow."

More bow-wobbling on my part as I comply.

"Use these three fingers to hold the arrow on the bowstring." Hari demonstrates. "The finger with the guard goes here, on top of the arrow, with the next two fingers holding it below.

"Then you raise the bow and pull back on the bowstring. Keep your elbow angled a bit, like this, so the bowstring doesn't hit it. Keep your drawing arm rigid and the bow hand more relaxed. Draw it toward your face where it should rest lightly on your chosen anchor point. That might be the corner of your mouth, or your chin, or ear, or cheekbone. Wherever it feels right. You'll know it after a while."

Tentatively, I tip my bow face down, slot the arrow's nock around the bowstring at the location marked with ochre-colored cording.

"Remember not to fling the arrow or jerk it. Just gently relax and let your fingers go. And that's it. Soon it will all be instinctive."

Hari looks around at us hopefully, and then continues. "Now don't anyone shoot anything or anyone until I tell you personally to let fly. Fedy, you're first."

He smiles at one of the young girls. She blushes crimson as she nocks her arrow, which is entirely too big for her, and pulls back the string with little visible effort until her hand touches her chin.

Squirrelly Girl comes awake in my head and starts in with the snarky editorial comment thing. *See, even little children can do it. Think you can keep up with them?*

"Now aim, with this eye…That's right. And…let fly!"

Fedy's arrow makes an instantaneous *th-ooot* sound that turns into a clank as it strikes a rock.

"Nobody else shoot yet. Now go find your arrow, Fedy, and bring it back. A good first shot. Karn, you're next."

All four of the little girls are eventually able to shoot their arrows adequately, if not gloriously, since none of them comes anywhere near the target. Yet.

Next it's Koral, who says with elaborate casualness, "It's been a while, but I think I remember how. You and I have done this a time or two before, remember?" (News to me.) She inclines her head closer to Hari and imparts this information in a whispered, confidential tone. He looks faintly surprised, then nods.

I can't help noticing she keeps looking deep into his eyes as if to telegraph this news: *We're not like the others. We two have a secret together, you and I.*

Unwillingly, I remember the young wives of Jarmo mentioning to me in an offhand fashion that Hari has slept with each one of them, at least once in turn, as their gesture of community service to the grieving Widower Chieftain.

Until now, I remind myself. That was before, but this is now, and *I* am his now. Aren't I?

Taking the arrow from Hari with confidence and nonchalance, Koral nocks the arrow, holds it between the proper fingers, and pulls back the bowstring with no visible effort.

I hate to admit it, even to myself, but Koral has very shapely arms. Well-muscled (although I don't know how; she scarcely lifts a finger to do anything) with tan, rounded curves.

When Hari gives her the go-ahead, she takes aim, then releases her finger grip on the bowstring, scarcely moving any other part of her body. She remains like a statue as the arrow, still quivering faintly from its journey, materializes instantly at the far left edge of the meat target. Off to one side, but still a hit.

Hari laughs in surprise and pleasure. "Well done! You should be teaching this class, not me. A fine shot."

She looks at him with a lop-sided smile and says, "Oh, I've got my secrets…"

My stomach is roiling by this time. Not with pregnancy pukes, which I still experience occasionally, but with real discomfort. I can't help caressing my small but growing bump as if to protect my Little Bean from a woman who cares less than nothing about me or the fruit of my womb.

The very proximity of Koral makes me glower. I consider the liberties she's taking with my husband. Who seems to be enjoying the scene just fine, or is literally too clueless to notice.

Don't you dare touch his arm confidentially like that, you…you predator.

"Stella?" Hari turns to me, expectantly—and yes, lovingly—as he hands me my arrow. "You're next."

He looks hopeful that I'll rise to the occasion, although he's probably well aware that I probably won't. Hari knows of my short-comings in the athletic arena. So far, I haven't been a quick study at any physical activity. Well, except for one, *that* one, which I've taken to like a duck to water. But otherwise, no.

In a nanosecond, I realize that only Supernatural Aid can help me now. Mentally I gabble a quick prayer: *Dear Mom…God…Professor Vale…all of you…somebody, help!* I pray to them, equally and fervently since they're all equally far removed from me in time and space.

And then I think: *That's no way to pray, all pleading and whiny. Be thankful first, dammit. Thank you for guiding me to hit that target. Thank you, thank you, thank you…*

Tipping the bow down as I've been taught, I nock my arrow. Its slot fits snugly around the bowstring.

Carefully I bring the bow upright. Oddly enough, the bow feels… right. Slowly I pull back on the string. After a momentary flare of panic, when the bowstring feels stuck and motionless, suddenly I feel a *pop,* a release. My arm pulls it back gradually but smoothly, like a hot knife cutting through butter.

Ha! I haven't loosed the arrow yet, but suddenly I feel so relieved and grateful that I feel a lump rise in my throat. *Thankyouthankyou. Oh, I can do this, I* know *I can…and I will…and I thank you that I do.*

I focus my gaze hypnotically on the lump of meat. It's turning purple and sticky, already covered with flies. I narrow my vision, so much so that everything looks fuzzy and gray except for what's in my immediate field of view. I line up the target, down the long shaft, to the arrow rest, to my eye, willing the bow not to wobble. Mystically it complies.

Then Hari cries, "Let fly!" and, without thinking (or seeing or hearing), I loose my fingers from the bowstring, retreat from the gray zone I'd entered, and suddenly Hari and the four little girls start cheering and yelling in approval.

My arrow is dead center in the mass of dead flesh.

Hari looks at me in surprise. And with surprising, sudden lust. "Do that again," he orders me with as secret smile.

And I do. By God and the Great Mother and Harry Vale, I *do!*

Again and again. Holy crap. *Thank you. A million times over.*

The little girls grin in awe, Koral glowers, and Hari looks downright enchanted.

I'm over the moon with joy over my new talent, one I never knew I had any aptitude for, a talent that has got to be innate. How else could I do it? And piss off Koral to no end?

Now I'm filled with new resolve, strength, and even enthusiasm for the many tasks ahead. In my mind, Squirrelly Girl fires back a challenge: *Good thing you've got renewed resolve, because you're going to need it. Especially for the hand-to-hand combat practice coming up soon. Killed anyone lately? 'Cause you're going to need a hefty dose of resolve when you do.*

CHAPTER 28
Build That Wall

How can you prove whether
at this moment we are sleeping,
and all our thoughts are a dream;
Or whether we are awake,
and talking to one another
in the waking state?
— Plato —
428 BCE – 348 BCE

Harry

After class, I drive to the hospital and sit beside my inert Stella, like I do most days, and suddenly I'm tired to death.

I'm tired of sitting here with Stella, tired of her unresponsiveness. Not that there's much I can do about that. Wait it out, hope for the best.

Tired of my classes at the university. Okay, some days I do enjoy it, but today I feel spent.

I'm tired of the hospital and its impersonal routines. Tired of not being able to fasten the bottom button on my blue chambray shirt. *Shit*, I'm getting too fat. I'm tired of that, too.

Not only tired, but I'm also uneasy. Restless. And I don't know why. It nags at me. Something is missing; something is wrong. What is it, and why can't I remember?

I can't stop thinking of Jarmo. Plucky, helpless, hapless Jarmo and its one hundred plus hunter-gatherer residents. Okay, so the people of Jarmo aren't *really* alone out there, but they might as well be. The closest villages are several days' travel away. Metaphorically and literally, they're sitting ducks for anyone who happens to come over the hill.

I keep wondering what's happening out in Jarmo right now. I hope Stella is there, implementing the tricks of the war trade that I crammed her with during her brief period of lucidity. Of course, Stella's anima—the soul that makes her body come alive—could be anywhere now: ancient Greece, Mongolia in the 1700s, New York's Roaring Twenties, or as part of a twisted virtual world on some kid's computer. Or she could also be nowhere, snuffed out like a candle. Or maybe she's like Han Solo in Star Wars, frozen in time, in a big, gray block of carbonite.

As she lies on her hospital bed, Stella's shut-eyed face looks serious. Resolute, even. Every now and then, she makes slight movements—head, hands (now encased in mitts again to prevent the inevitable clawing-up), an aimless arm wave here, then a shuffling of her feet and legs against the waffle-weave hospital blanket. Sometimes she makes faint, audible sounds, an amalgam of a whine, a squeak, and moan. She's breathing quite well on her own and doing A-OK with her feeding tube. She's actually doing great except for one thing—she just won't wake up.

And it's been so many weeks now.

I wonder how Time—Time in the abstract with a capital T—spins itself out in Jarmo. Is it synchronous with our own time, hour for hour, day for day? Or has time sped up or slowed down somehow so that five days in our time might be five months in theirs? Are our two time zones (for want of a better term) consistent with one another? Or does Time have an infinite number of tributaries, each flowing like a river, following its own path of least resistance?

Quantum physicists tell us that Time bends in on itself. They say Time is an artificial construct used to make things simpler for mere mortals like us to understand. Scientists say that nothing really exists at all until we call it into existence in our own minds. Everyone sees and makes his or her own reality. It is we who create all actions, reactions, decisions, and choices.

All things that ever were, that ever exist right now, or that ever will be, all these things we call into existence. Or there's nothingness. World without end, amen.

Nothing is real except the Eternal Now and the Nevertheless. Nothing comes into being until we call it forth.

Hopefully Stella is experiencing her own Jarmo now. I sure hope so. I wish I could be there with her to see the wonder of it all.

What more can I do for the people of Jarmo and their coming struggle? What am I missing here?

I take hold of Stella's hand (orthopedic mitt and all) as footsteps shuffle by in the hall. A nurses' aide enters the room quietly, bringing fresh towels into Stella's small bathroom, then tiptoes out again after flashing a smile my way.

Sitting in the guest chair beside Stella, I drift into a gray fugue, then I sleep. Deeply. Beyond time and space.

And then I'm floating—no, I'm gliding, soaring—over a small village. Square mud-brick and stone cottages topped with thatched roofs huddle together atop a hill. A precipitous cliff drops off along one side: down, and down, and down, to a slow-moving river that bisects a broad valley. Snow-capped, forbidding mountains rise close by, and dramatic wild countryside looms suddenly before me. A stiff wind tugs winter-brown prairie grasses against their will. Skeins of thin winter clouds go scudding by.

Jarmo. It can only be Jarmo.

And I see people. Lots of people. Men, women, children, old and young. Wearing animal skins and loose-weave, homespun winter garb.

All are working together. Doing something on the ground, something…I can't tell what it is.

I'm gliding over Jarmo. Aware that I'm dreaming. A lucid dream: I've always wanted to experience one, and now I am. I hope I don't upchuck; it's very dizzying…

My subconscious self is eager and excited; everything seems so real. It *is* real. Realer than regular waking life can ever be.

I will myself to move in closer to see what the people are doing.

Well-I'll-be-go-to-hell! They're building a wall. A huge, chest-high, rock wall that encircles the entire village and its twenty-five houses (give or take), all except for the sheer cliff side. Everyone works together as a team, fetching, carrying, hauling, and stacking rocks. Even unfinished, the wall looks formidable. Men dig a trench with stone-headed axes along the exterior side of the wall. A dry moat. Not exactly impregnable, but still a challenging impediment to anyone aiming to mess with Jarmo.

My consciousness immediately resounds with a great, unspoken *Yes! This* is what's missing. This is what they must build to help vanquish the foe.

I glide over the lines of workers. I wish I could slow up, even stop, and look around. Their faces come closer and closer in my vision. I see their faces plainly, and then…

Suddenly, my twenty-first century eyes lock onto a pair of eyes that are unusually blue for this ancient time and place. They belong to a sun-browned man about my age, maybe a bit younger, dark beard trimmed close and chin-length brown hair a curly thatch. There's something wrong with one of his eyebrows; they don't quite match.

A beautiful young woman, tall and slim, wavy brown hair to her waist, works beside him. Her blue eyes are Stella's eyes. The rest of her is regal. Beautiful.

Finally it seems like I can slow down and come in for a closer look.

They both look at me in surprise but with little fear. I pause and hover, staring back at them. I want…I want to tell them something. In the dream, my voice rings out, "*Yes,* this is what you must do. Build this wall!"

Next I feel a pulling sensation. I'm being sucked away, first slowly, then faster and faster. Much like what happens when you click on "find an address" on Google Earth. It's taking me away, and I can't stop it. Long after Stella averts her face, the man's smudgy blue eyes continue to stare into mine as I drift away. And I know absolutely that it's Hari. Jarmo Hari. Stella's Hari.

And it's me…in a long-dead incarnation of myself.

Then Jarmo Hari nods at me. Relief floods me like a warm bath.

I'm pulled higher and higher, faster and faster, as I look back at them…

I awake as if I've been shot, sitting bolt upright in my chair. While twenty-first century Stella, she of the close-clipped, red-brown hair and square figure, sleeps on beside me in her hospital bed.

Across the bedside, a PT tech smiles at my disorientation. "Sorry, didn't mean to wake you. It's time for her daily workout."

She quietly releases one of the side rails on Stella's bed. She proceeds to carefully rotate each of Stella's ankles, flexes each of her knees, then starts in on her arms.

Meanwhile, my inner mind is roaring back at me. *Fortified walls! You clueless git, why did you not think of it before?* I saw it happening the way it should be, so they must be doing it on their own…or they soon will be.

"I'll let you have at it, then. Back later." I nod and smile at the PT tech, then leave the room with speed, my laptop tucked under my arm.

In a quiet corner of the hospital coffee shop, I open my laptop and I…what? What is it that I want?

Ah, hell, if I can't *be* there, I just want to *look* at it again: Jarmo.

It all seemed so real in my lucid dream. The faint, pervasive whiff of goat. Fast-moving winter clouds. High altitude air, so breezy and bracing it almost hurts to breathe it in. The gray-blue scent of snow, wafting down from the mountain peaks.

After grabbing a decaf, I boot up the laptop. I click on some old, captioned photos of the famous archaeologist couple, Dr. Robert J. Braidwood and his wife, Linda, in an old scientific journal article about their Jarmo excavations from 1948 to 1955. And I sigh.

As I examine this picture from the early fifties, I can't help thinking, *God, doesn't Jarmo look desolate in the twentieth century!* And it's just as dreary in the twenty-first century too, according to agricultural scientists and Iraqi tourists who've visited the site recently. Nine thousand years separates the dusty desolation of today's Jarmo from the earlier Jarmo that was green and rich with life.

A 1950s magazine sidebar runs in a column beside an old picture of the dig:

Under the auspices of the Oriental Institute at the University of Chicago, Dr. Robert Braidwood and his wife and professional associate, Linda Braidwood, excavated the Jarmo site in northeastern Iraq from March 1948 until June of 1955. Seven meters deep, the levels of habitation at the Jarmo excavation site included the ruins of 25 mud-brick houses that were rebuilt over the centuries at least twelve. When the Jarmo site was first excavated at the foothills of the Zagros Mountains, it was determined to be the oldest settlement yet discovered in Mesopotamia. It showed evidence of a growing agricultural economy, although hunting was believed to still play a major role. Items uncovered among the various levels at Jarmo included flint and obsidian tools, stone mortars, milling stones for grinding grain, stone hoes, bone awls, bone spoons, bone beads, and buttons, as well as unfired clay figurines of animals and female deities. The vessels discovered in the lower levels were of stone (semi-spherical and conical cups) and those from the upper levels of unfired clay (cups and goblets with handles). Since many of their tools were made of obsidian from mineral deposits nearly 300 miles away, some form or early commerce must have existed at that time. It is estimated that approximately 100 to 150 people lived in this village. The inhabitants of Jarmo lived in square, multi-roomed houses built of pressed mud bricks and included firepit areas vented to the outside and built-in clay basins. In early Holocene times (about 7,000 BCE), the climate became more warm and moist, enabling oak forests to grow and flourish, together with pistachio, juniper, mountain maple, and yew. During the time of Jarmo, the fig tree became domesticated, along with grapes, lentils, beans, onions, lettuce, cucumbers, cooking herbs, millet, and both emmer and einkorn wheat. The grasslands around Jarmo bloomed with wild daisy, chicory, purple aster, yellow yarrow, blue bachelor's button, dusty miller, cornflower, daisy ragwort, red poppy, as well as white and lavender wild hollyhocks.

If only I could be with Jarmo Stella. Especially now, at this time of uncertainty and fear. But I'm not there and never will be. I'm here in this hospital, sitting beside a comatose college girl, and grumbling through my lesson plans for the coming week. And spending most every night alone. When will I ever learn to just go out and get my own life?

I think of the Braidwoods, a longtime love-match, at least I hope they were. They'd been married for ten years when they first excavated Jarmo. I think about how intertwined their lives must have been, living with and for each other, for another forty-eight years together.

Years. Until they died together on January 15, 2003. In the same hospital, on the very same day, passing on at ages ninety-five and ninety-three.

And I'm thinking, what a grand and glorious life they must have shared. If only Stella and I can someday do the same.

When I return to Stella's beside to check in before I head home for the day, I wait until no one else is in her room but me. Then, leaning in so close that I'm touching my lips to her good ear, I speak.

"Stella. Stella, darlin'. Listen. I have a better plan for Jarmo. It's a wall, a siege wall. Just like in a dream I had today where I saw you—you and my karmic double—building a siege wall. Stella, I hope you can hear me. It's very important. Build the rock wall around the town, just like you did in the dream." I repeat variations of this to her over and over.

Tiring of the sound of my own voice, I quit for the day and go home. Hoping and praying that Jarmo Hari and Jarmo Stella can hear me and incorporate this critical new element into Jarmo's battle plan.

Stella

I'm in a dream. We both are, Hari and me. But it feels so odd and real. I can feel the cold wind snarling my hair, chilling my fingers. We're both outside, working together with our own people of Jarmo, dozens of them. We're building a rock wall. All the way around the town, except for the side with the cliff.

Gradually in the dream, a misty face starts looming toward me. A man's face, squarish and friendly-looking, short dark brown hair, early thirties, wearing something blue. That's unusual; blue vegetable dye is uncommon in Jarmo.

His eyes look funny, too. Small, dark pieces of wood frame each eye. They're...*they're glasses!* Instantly the twenty-first century word rises to the forefront of my mind, ready for me when I need it.

The face hovers before me. With a sudden crinkle of my heart, I think, *Oh, it's Professor Harry Vale, my professor from my other life where I'm still in a coma.* He's telling me...words...I can't quite make them out at first, but finally I hear him. He tells me we're doing the right thing, building Jarmo a rock wall against the invaders.

Suddenly I feel way too hot as I shake my head from side to side. I wake to find I'm now a sweaty mess with a goat-hair blanket wrapped around my head and neck. It feels about to strangle me.

"Augh!" I cry out sharply and sit up in bed.

On the other side of our bed-for-two, Asher remains deep in dreamland in his small, messy nest.

But Hari is instantly awake. He clutches my arm and asks with excitement, "Did you see him too?"

Dawn isn't far away. There's enough ambient glow in the sky, coming through the bedroom window already, for me to see his eyes gleaming in the darkness.

"See who?"

I know what he's going to say, but I want to be sure first I'm not losing my mind.

"The little fat man in blue. With the strange, dark lines around his eyes. I know I was dreaming, but it was so real!" Hari seems abashed to admit how the dream has obviously affected him. "I…I really can't explain it. Unless the fat man was a messenger from the Great Mother…"

My voice is quiet, and I'm aiming for subtly persuasive in my tone of voice. "Hari, tell me what you saw in your dream, and then I'll tell you what I saw in mine."

"We were…building a rock wall together, you and I and all of us in Jarmo. And this odd-looking man told me yes, *do* build a wall around Jarmo." Hari shrugs. "To keep out the invaders."

"Yes!" I repeat in astonished joy. Too loud. Ashur stirs and groans in his sleep, while Grandmama sighs audibly. Hari puts a finger to his lips—I hadn't realized the universal symbol for *be quiet* was at least nine thousand years old. I giggle softly and press both hands over my mouth.

"The man in the dream told me…told *us*…to keep on building the wall around Jarmo!" Hari gabbles quietly yet excitedly. "He said it's the right thing to do."

He's probably mentally kicking himself for not thinking of this idea first.

Dear Harry. Make that Hari and Harry. I hug my shoulders with foolish love for them both. I hope they don't beat themselves up too much, either of them, for coming so late to this important idea. War is a new concept for us all.

Instead I tell my Jarmo Hari softly, "Yes, the man in blue is right. We *must* build this wall. You see…I know him. And so do you."

I shouldn't have said that, because Hari looks instantly taken aback and uncertain.

"The little fat man? In blue? I'm certain I don't know him."

"Oh, but you do. And so do I." I experience a palpable yearning then, and I explain. "He was…I mean, he still is…*you.*"

"Me." Hari repeats the word flatly. Obviously he thinks I'm temporarily out of my mind. He looks at me with concern.

The words are out of my mouth before I know what I'm saying. "His name is Harry Vale. *Professor* Harry Vale, which is a title that means Great Teacher. He is…was…my teacher, and I believe that he was…still *is*…you. Yes, *you*. In a life you're going to live someday, far, far into the future. Where I used to live before I came to Jarmo."

"Me." He repeats the word again, then looks away. He shakes his head in disbelief. "You think I'm a…little fat man with blue coverings on his chest?"

"*Another* you. A future you. With your same spirit within."

Hari says nothing. He sits motionless, starshine gleaming upon his wavy hair through the open window.

"Yes, you. In another body—not as handsome as *this* body, of course." I plant a lingering kiss on his Adam's apple. "And, yes, he lives in a different time and place. But he's still you, coming to both of us from the Great Mother herself to warn us and teach us and save us…by telling us to build that wall."

He looks at me skeptically, but his voice is soft and tender. "And so…you really think…he's me?"

I shrug, nod, and smile at him tenderly. Hopefully.

"And so…does that mean there's another you out there in the future, too?"

I stop smiling. My face freezes. Please, may this not upset him.

"Yes." I whisper my response.

"And do you look like…this?" His face looks sober as his right hand tucks a lock of my hair behind my good ear.

"No." Another whisper.

Looking faintly encouraged, Hari perks up. A tiny bit. "So, what *do* you look like, then, Future Stella?"

I'm almost twisting my thumb out of its socket; that's how much my brain is churning. "Future Stella looks like…everyone else. Like *no* one else. Future Stella looks like someone you wouldn't remember. She's sick—wounded, actually. In that respect, Future Stella and Professor Harry Vale…complement one another very well."

Hari stares into the darkness for a long time. I remain silent with baited breath.

Finally, he exhales like a buck snorting in rut, then relaxes his shoulders with a visible slump. "Just so *that* Harry and *that* Stella stay where they are and don't come back again to where we are, well, then, it's all right."

Hari exhales deeply. I fling my arms around him and squeeze him tight.

It's a lot for him to take in and swallow on faith. I know this. But apparently Jarmoites have fewer impediments to believing unbelievable things than do we of the twenty-first century.

Then Hari grins in the waning dark—I can see his white teeth against his shadowed face, while Ashur sleeps on—and he rolls his eyes. "Just you watch, though…" He snickers softly. "Yes, it *is* the right plan, and we're definitely going to build the siege wall. But just you watch. Our people will have my man-parts tied in a knot for this."

"What? And why?" I can't figure yet why he's amused.

"Because building a protective wall is yet another job for our people to tackle, a huge, sweaty, filthy job that might take a long time to complete. Plus, there are all those *other* projects, now maybe not as important, that we've already worked on so hard."

Hari sighs, then turns me around and tucks me in close against his body, spoon-fashion. I can tell his mind is still running a mile a minute.

I'm starting to realize the implications of his response. "So, you're saying that taming horses to ride doesn't really matter now? Or the war wagon…the wheat field…or hand-to-hand combat training? We won't need *any* of these things if we build the wall?"

"We should be so lucky if that were true! We're going to need all of our new skills to fight the enemy. Building a protective wall will slow them down some, but still, there *will* be a day of reckoning. It won't keep them out forever."

CHAPTER 29
The Arrangement

Jealousy and Love are sisters.
— Russian proverb —

Stella

Hari was wrong—for once. The people of Jarmo *love* the idea of the defensive wall. Not that they like the work, but at least they're willing to suck it up and start digging in, or I should say piling it on. A wall is something they can understand. And they definitely approve.

We start work on it immediately in shifts from dawn to dusk.

So, what about Jarmo's invention of the wheel? Or the highly promoted "war wagon," a clumsy wooden cart? Not so much. Jarmoites still can't figure out what it's for. And sometimes I can't either. I still don't remember how to make an axle, and without it the wheels won't revolve.

But still, even if our people politely roll their eyes at it and can't imagine it would have much in the way of function, still it's something our people have got to learn. I want them to have a leg-up on the wheel—and the future—before anyone else can invent it.

And the horse-taming? Still going full speed ahead. Although I'm not sure what we're going to do with our five horses and riders yet, tactically speaking. Maidie is still clearly the boss of them all, head and shoulders above the rest in fearlessness, agility, and skill.

Archery practice? One word answers apply here: Yes. Daily. Mandatory. Anyone physically able must successfully shoot at least twenty arrows daily. Arrows must reach the targets from a reasonable distance. And you must stay there and keep shooting, even if you have to move closer to the targets, until you succeed.

Comprised chiefly of upper-middle-agers and little kids, the Wheat Committee now moves forward with speed and surprising success. After a dodgy start, both of our winter wheat strains are knee-high now, nurtured by Jarmo's mild winter temperatures, gentle rains, and plenty of hand-watering when needed.

Until I awoke in Jarmo, I'd known nothing about growing wheat—nothing about wheat at *all* (except for the seven-grain artisan bread at Kowalsky's in Minneapolis and what good toast it makes). I still know precious little about wheat, but even so, I have to admit that young wheat is knock-out gorgeous: fluorescent green, delicate and tender, seeming to flow in any breath of wind. And shooting up so fast you can almost see it grow. Einkorn wheat's cylindrical cones bristle with tiny spikelets, while emmer's small, flat faces are set off by long, dramatic whiskers protruding from each kernel.

I'm well aware that Professor Harry Vale would be distraught at the knowledge that I've introduced agriculture to Jarmo, probably sooner than they would have come to it naturally in earlier times. Oh, dear Harry Vale, my sweet, square-faced professor. So much more than a friend. I sense that Jarmo's days of the hunter-gatherer bands are fleeting now, going fast and accelerating all the time. But what else can we do to keep our people alive? Nothing but start growing our own food, most of it anyway, on the hoof, in the garden, and in the wheat field.

Chieftain Hari and the Wheat Committee decide that the defensive wall will also encircle the small wheat field. Otherwise, what is the point of growing wheat at all if it's not there when we need it? We must have grain close at hand to feed the people of Jarmo. Especially if push comes to shove with the invaders, and they surround us in a siege.

And what of the Death Squad? These men who are supposed to teach us the arts of killing? Truth be told, although the Death Squad guys are feisty and can be lethal in a fight, they're men who have never *seen* a war, let alone fought in one.

But just because Jarmo is generally a peaceful place, that doesn't mean it's not without its own life-or-death crises. An unavoidable, dark part of the human condition. Individual men—and women too, sometimes—are driven by inner demons to steal, to rape, to kill.

And certain male Jarmoites are better at kicking ass than others. Much better.

Even I know that Jarmo isn't so idyllic that there haven't ever been fights over the years, even to the death. Greed, jealousy, and not having enough available women can do that to a man.

And to women, too, when they have to share their man.

This fact is brought home to me in a sudden, searing jolt this morning.

Plain and simple, I just don't like Koral. Most people can figure that out about me pretty fast. I *especially* don't like Koral when she fawns all over Hari. Even on her best days, she's tiresome and petty, doesn't pull her own weight on work projects, and flaunts her beauty (which I think is overstated, although no man ever realizes it) to get her own way.

And, like most beautiful women (even an average woman whom men believe to be beautiful), she usually gets her own way.

The thing is, Jarmo is simply too small for our collective preferences — or pettiness. There just aren't enough people around to be choosy about it. And that is how, and why, Koral married Kern, according to my girlfriends who've told me the whole story.

Like most Jarmo girls, Koral married shortly after her time of First Blood to an unremarkable man of twenty-two seasons. Koral is his second wife. Wife number one died shortly after their wedding of what sounds like an asthma attack; folks tell me she just couldn't catch her breath anymore.

Koral had just come into womanhood around the same time as the first wife's death. One moon cycle after the funeral, with no other available partner possibilities at the time, Kern took Koral for his new wife. Pragmatic Jarmoites rejoiced for them, and life went on.

Kern *is* pretty boring, bless his heart. Although well-intentioned, he's unremarkable in every way with nothing much to say for himself. His scraggly brown beard hides what I suspect to be a receding chin. He reminds me of a frog, with his too-widely-spaced eyes, sloping shoulders, and mottled acne on his back. He's also half a head shorter than his wife. Koral and I are the tallest women in Jarmo, and she's even got me beat by an inch or two.

Koral always treats Kern in a cavalier fashion, bossing him around and snapping at him for the smallest infraction. He takes it phlegmatically like a tail-thumping dog—or a long-suffering frog—and never protests; he grew up expecting no better. Kern and Koral live in an ancient, square house that shares walls on both sides with other homes, right in the heart of the village. For five years, they've lived together as man and wife, and still no sign of babies. Whether this is by Koral's intent, thanks to the purple leaf plant, or due to some lack on Kern's part, no one is saying.

This morning Kern headed off with a gang of men on a hunting trip, like they normally do at least once a week. Hari wasn't along on this excursion. But later today, the hunters, all but one, return to Jarmo. And I hear a great caterwauling arise from the side of the village that slopes gradually toward the cliff. People exclaim, then start wailing in grief and shock.

Carefully setting aside the bow and quiver of arrows I've been practicing with, I race to follow the crowd toward the sound. My greater height provides me a front-row view of the unfolding drama.

Three hunters are carrying Kern, or what's left of him, tied to a pole like today's prey.

Women are crying, men exclaiming, children chattering and shrieking as they follow the gruesome corpse on its journey. Already I hear numerous voices buzzing, "Koral…where is Koral?"

He's dead. Anyone can see that. He's a bloody mess. One arm is missing from the corpse. Huge bite marks glisten crimson on his neck, back, and side. A hunk has been bitten from his neck, which makes his head loll to one side.

Oddly enough, the bitten-off arm doesn't bother me. However, the gory neck, still attaching head to body by a hand's-width of skin, causes bile to rise in my throat. It burns, acrid and sharp. The neck bones protrude from the neck cavity, curving outward and obscenely exposed. I have a sudden thought that the line of attached bones is reaching for me.

Slowly, the group marches up to Kern's house. The same one he'd inherited from his father, grandfather, and unknown ancestors before him.

With great weariness and sorrow, the hunters carefully lower their blood-soaked, dead-weight passenger to the ground, as Jarmoites hover around the cadaver. Men clamor, demanding to learn what happened.

One of the hunters—I can't recall his name, but he always smiles at me in a frisky fashion whenever I see him—steps forward as the unofficial spokesman. "He was jumped by a lion. A short-eared one, not the big-maned kind. Kern was…well, he was off behind a nearby bush, you know, unloading. The lion tried to drag him off, probably to stow his body in a tree for safe-keeping, but we—" he gestures toward his companion hunters "—we yelled at it, waved our arms, and shot it with our bows. The lion took off into the underbrush. Kern…he bled out almost immediately."

At this inopportune but definitely dramatic moment, Koral dashes onto the scene. And sees her mangled husband.

Koral starts to scream. And keeps on screaming. She's still not stopped when I can stand it no longer and slink away home.

This afternoon, many women gather to clean Kern's body and prepare it for burial, but I am not one of them.

I just…cannot. Other women try to comfort Koral, who is still shrieking periodically, although she now seems more energized by the crowd's crooning attention than by grief. While Kerki, Nydre, and Maura help wash Kern's body, Koral cries noisily in a corner of their front room. Others pat her hands, bring her nibbles to eat (which she dramatically waves away), and stroke her hair (when she's not writhing or twisting about in exaggerated agony).

I hover around the edges of this unfolding catastrophe, feeling I should do something but subconsciously rebelling against doing much. Finally, I murmur to the corpse-washers that I'm stepping out to gather a pile of wild flowers to cover the body in the grave at the funeral tonight.

Beyond the village toward the western hills, Jarmo's burial ground reposes in a silence broken only by a low breeze. A rock cairn marks each grave. Recent graves stand tall and symmetrical, while cairns over graves of the long dead are dotted thickly with lichen.

That night, all villagers gather at the grave site, dug earlier this afternoon by a gaggle of reluctantly compliant teenage boys. A huge bonfire paints the scene, and those coming to pay their last respects, with a golden glow. Everything else in blanketed in darkness.

Five Crones and three wise old men conduct the funeral. In shrill, quavering voices that carry clearly across the darkness, they repeat ritual sayings, as old as time, and move in ritual motions, gesturing with small clay Mother figures.

As part of his responsibility as tribal chieftain, Hari calls out respectfully to the Great Mother, asking her to please bid Kern welcome—helpless, hapless Kern, a blameless son of Jarmo if there ever was one—into the next existence.

During the solemnities, Koral continues to wail, moan, and carry on. Obviously she's loving the attention and adores having an audience. But I say nothing and continue to hold my armload of flowers with respectful attention.

Hari turns to look at me then. Lifting his eyebrows at me with a faint nod, he whispers, "It's time." He nods again in encouragement.

Oh. I've not witnessed a Jarmo funeral before. But I remember what Professor Harry told me about early Neanderthal graves and the vestiges of flowers found there. Of course there's a huge chasm between Neanderthal times and Jarmo—nearly two hundred thousand years—but I figure that one can never go wrong, saying goodbye to the dead with flowers.

I move toward the grave and kneel awkwardly beside it, still clutching the flowers. On one side of the open grave, a huge mound of dirt lies waiting, dug out from the hole in the ground, waiting to be shoveled back in over its occupant in eternal sleep.

I hope I'm adhering to correct Jarmo funeral protocol by kneeling beside the grave with my flowers, but no one says anything, so I continue to wing it. I don't know if Kern's grave is actually six feet down as twenty-first century protocol requires. However deep it is, it looks like a long way down to me. I don't know who placed him there this evening, but there he lies nonetheless. Arranged in an approximation of the fetal position. Almost graceful. Very, very restful. Finally with no worries.

I'm struck suddenly with a deep pang of regret and sadness for Kern. *Ah, poor guy, life short-changed you in so many ways here—marital love, smarts, looks, authority, respect. It even took away the rest of your future for good measure.*

I find myself praying silently into to the Great Unknown. *Oh, Kern, may you find more happiness somewhere else.*

I drop the flowers gently, handful by handful, trying to cover as much of the body as I can. Then I stand and resume my place by Hari's side.

The teenage grave diggers then pile new wood onto the bonfire: dried branches of sage and creosote. The bonfire roils in protest as clouds of black smoke and sparks fly up to join the cold stars above. Then the grave diggers start placing many sticks, about as long as my arm, carefully along the edge of the fire so that only one end of the stick will ignite.

The Wise Women come slowly toward Koral and, gently but inexorably, start shoving her none too gently toward the dirt pile. A shovel made of a large mammal scapula hafted onto a stout pole lies waiting atop the dirt.

"No, no! Not yet!" Koral's wail rises to a shriek. She pulls back, protesting. But the Crones embrace her and quietly move her forward.

It is Grandmama who finally takes the shovel, shoves it into the pile of soft earth, and pulls it out with a pile of dirt on its indented surface.

She attempts to place the shovel into Koral's hand.

Koral's narrow face looks fierce and knife-thin in the firelight. Her coarse dark hair whips about her like thick, black spiderwebs as she shakes her head in denial. But Grandmama is inexorable. With her own aging fist of iron, she takes Koral with one hand and maintains the pile of dirt in the shovel with the other. The remaining Crones push Koral with little ceremony from behind. Grandmama manages to "help" Koral dump the first shovelful of dirt onto the body in the open grave. The dirt clods hit with an audible thump.

With a scream of rage and hysteria, Koral flings the shovel aside and starts sobbing. The five Crones lead her away from the grave, out of the firelight, and back to the village.

At this mute signal, the three Graybeards start to sing: a slow, hypnotic funeral dirge in their high, wavering, old man voices. The song is brief and simple, evidently another part of Jarmo's ancient funeral rite.

The song serves to call those in attendance to form a haphazard line at the dirt pile. One by one, each person takes a shovelful of dirt and drops it into the grave. Then the head of the household for each family group carefully pulls out the non-burning end of a stick from the fire—a Neolithic flashlight—using it to light his family's way back to the village.

The song of the Graybeards burrows deep within my head, rendering me temporarily immobile. All of us move in slow motion as if in a dream.

Finally, except for stragglers, everyone has cast their shovelful of dirt into the grave and walked home under the starlight to bed.

Just a few of us remain: the three singing Graybeards, the gang of teenaged grave diggers, Hari and me.

My turn next. I take up a small shovelful of dirt and cast it sideways into the pit. The dirt disperses widely and makes hardly a sound.

I wait for Hari to cast his dirt before we walk home together, the wavering sounds of the old men still on the air. Hari pulls the unburned end of a flaming stick from the bonfire to use as our torch.

I'm freezing in the starry winter darkness. With his free hand, Hari wraps an edge of his ceremonial cloak around me, holding me close as we walk. In the distance, we see dim lights and head toward them. Some of the village windows are still reflecting firelight from within.

"What happens now?" I ask, my teeth chattering.

"The Graybeards will conclude their singing," Hari replies. "And the grave diggers will fill in the rest of the hole, tamp down the fire embers, and cover them with dirt."

That's not what I meant. "What happens now with Koral?"

Hari squeezes my shoulder under the cloak as we amble slowly in the dark. "The wise women will take turns staying with her, five days and five nights, one for each of the Crones. And then…" Hari doesn't elaborate.

"And on the sixth night?" I can't help asking. "What happens on the sixth night? Who is going to…provide…for Koral in the meantime? There are no single men right now. Boys of course, yes; several boys are coming up fast. But they're not yet officially men."

Hari squeezes my shoulder but remains silent. That silence makes me nervous.

I can't help saying it. After all, I've *thought* it for a very long time. "I'm so glad that men don't take second wives in Jarmo," I say and shiver involuntarily. "I don't think I could bear it if they did. If *you* did."

Lights of the village are closer now. The starshine is bright enough for us to see one another's faces, and I see Hari looking at me sideways. He looks sober, somber, even, and full of pity.

He speaks as if reluctant to do so. "There are not enough of us here in Jarmo to take second wives. And lately, as you know, more boys than girls are surviving into adulthood. Some of our boys will have to wait for a wife. Until a girl comes to her time of First Blood, or when a woman is widowed. Like Koral. But, as you said, there are several boys right now on the cusp of fulfilling their requirements for manhood, so it shouldn't be too long before one of them will take her to wife."

This reassures me. A little.

I want to be sure of my facts, so I continue to quiz Hari in my voice made higher than normal by concern.

"And the requirements are—I think I remember?—they must kill a bull auroch all by themselves? Demonstrating that they can provide for a wife and family on their own...and..."

By the light of our flaming stick torch, I see Hari nod. I plow ahead.

"And they, um, also must also learn how to pleasure a woman before they can take one for their own."

Hari doesn't look at me; he just nods. We're close to the village now. Firelight from the open windows gleams, and the darkness is less total. I can see Hari's face clearly, and it looks...sad. And grim. Both.

I've got a bad feeling about this. But I'm afraid to ask.

Something tells me not to ask any more questions tonight. In bed later on, I envelop Hari like an octopus, and what can he do but respond? I feel a creeping desperation but ask him nothing more. And for once, Ashur knows enough not to approach me. Not tonight.

For five days, my Jarmo life goes on as usual. Daily archery practice; helping to build the defensive wall; checking in with bow, arrow, horse, wheat, and wheel committees; helping to hunt and gather whenever I can.

On day six, I wake up with an ominous feeling that oppresses me before I'm even fully awake.

And I'm right. Hari seems uncomfortable and apprehensive when he says to me after breakfast, "Let's take a walk to the round pen to see the horses."

And so we walk, hand in hand. And Hari still says nothing. Yet. But I can he's working up to something. Something I probably don't want to hear.

Finally he speaks. "I'm sure you're aware that this is...the sixth day after Kern's death."

I say nothing. I'm not going to make it easy for him. Whatever it is.

"And the wise women have been staying with Koral during these days, bringing her food, keeping her company. But today that will... cease...and..."

I can't help asking now. Squirrelly Girl is goading me internally, and I can't help myself from sniveling. *Don't let me show it, don't...*

Reluctantly, I speak. "But why does it have to cease? What's going to happen instead?"

Hari looks down at the ground as he speaks, and we continue to saunter toward the horse pen. "You know that because I'm the chieftain, I have certain...responsibilities to our people. Even as the villagers have certain responsibilities to me. The difference is, I have responsibilities to *all* of our people, and that includes providing for widows until new husbands can be found for them. If a widow is beyond child-bearing age, of course, she doesn't need a husband, only someone, usually someone from her own extended family, to take her in and provide for her, even as we do for my late father's mother, our own Grandmama. But for women who can still bear children, it's important to get them married off again as soon as possible."

I exhale and feel a little better at this point. This sounds reasonable. This I can tolerate. I think.

Hari continues his explanation as we walk slowly amid bright sunshine. "The thing is, though, if no new husband is immediately available for a young widow like Koral, and if she has no living male family member to provide for her while we're waiting for a husband to become available, for example an older boy who finally kills his first auroch or an older man whose wife dies unexpectedly, well, then..."

I can't look him in the eye yet. I'm still waiting for the other shoe to drop. Shoe, sandal, whatever. The pit of my stomach is a cold, hard knot above my baby bump.

"Well, then, what?" I want to hear it. Want to hear him say it before I'll believe that it's true.

"Then the chieftain must...step forward and provide for all of the widow's needs until a husband can be found for her."

I hear him swallow audibly. "Stella, before you say anything, let me tell you that it's always been this way in Jarmo. In my family, the sons of the chieftain are always called Hari. First my grandfather, then later my father, and now me. And as chieftain, we all cared for the needs of any young widows and their dependents until such time as new husbands could be found for them. As long as it took..."

There's something he's not telling me...yet.

"You already know, when my previous wife died, how the other wives of Jarmo took care of my needs, once each in turn, until you came to be my wife and share my bed. But now it is my turn, and my responsibility, to show mercy to a widow in need. Just for a little while, until a new husband can be found."

"Meaning that…" I can't finish the sentence yet. My throat is closing up.

Hari looks uncomfortable, even weary. It's clear from the lines on his forehead, the droop of his shoulders: why am I being such an unreasonable wife? He gives my shoulder another reluctant squeeze. "Let's turn around and walk back now. We'll see the horses later. It was just an excuse for a walk anyway."

I can tell Hari is a man with his mind made up. He looks resigned, not happy at all, but still willing to take on whatever responsibility he perceives as his and his alone to fulfill.

"Koral should be stopping by the house later this morning. And I must be there to hear her plea."

Suddenly I'm filled with equal parts rage, desolation, fury at Koral—and guilt about Ashur, even though he was originally Hari's idea.

I have no words. We return to the house. And wait.

Sure enough. Within a short time, an entourage approaches our house — Koral, the five wise women, and the Young Wives Club, followed by many mildly interested children, and more than a few curious men.

Hari and I watch from the threshold as they approach.

Koral no longer sobs or appears to grieve. She tries to look pathetic and helpless, yet only succeeds in looking sexy, wouldn't you just know. She kneels in the dust by our front door, lifts her arms delicately but in a theatrical manner, then speaks in a clear, sweet voice.

"Chieftain, I throw myself upon your mercy. I am a widow, now alone, with no father or brothers to bring food to my fire. Who will hunt for me? Who will take care of me? Who will service me? For without service, we of Jarmo, including myself, will wither and sicken and die."

Service. *That* kind of service.

I feel as if a pitcher of ice water has just been poured over my head. Hari servicing Koral…and being serviced in return? Even "just for a little while"?

Please, no.

Oh, yes.

It's one thing to "know about things" as part of the Greater Culture of Jarmo. It's another thing to be on the enduring end of things. The shit end of the stick.

To be the one who has to suck it up, paste on a smile, and act like everything is all right. When it's so horribly *not*.

The ice ball in my stomach makes its presence known with a shooting pain to my heart and spirit. Inside my head, Squirrelly Girl feels pity for me, a little, but still, she reminds me of one important fact: *You've got to remember, how is this any different from what you're already doing with Ashur? Inviting him in, so to speak, with Hari's urging, blessing, and complete approval? Even as Koral now pleads her case before Hari for him to warm her bed, for as long as it takes to find her a new husband. Only, who knows how long that might take?*

Hari doesn't look at me when he steps forward. In a flat voice that carries clearly over the crowd, he responds to Koral's plea. "As your chieftain and protector, until such time as a new husband can be found for you, I will bring food to your fire…protect you from harm or distress…and will provide the service your body and spirit require."

Koral crosses her arms over her flattish chest, hands to her shoulders. She looks down modestly and replies in a butter-wouldn't-melt-in-her-mouth voice, "It shall be as you ordain, Chieftain. Thank you for so generously caring for me, your lowly hand-maiden."

Nothing more is said. Everyone nods deferentially at Hari, even Koral does, before returning to their own homes and pursuits. Even Grandmama and the other Crones head for the hot pool. Ashur heads for the arrow assembly line. Hari and I are alone in the house.

"Don't hate me, Stella."

I can't believe Hari is saying this. But he is. I still feel…frozen. Horrified frozen. Desolate.

He embraces me with desperate hope and squeezes me into a hug. He doesn't let go. I remain in his hug unresisting, but I can't seem to say anything or even focus my eyes properly.

"Star, dear one, *please* don't. It is my duty, my *job*. Someone has to do it, and I am chieftain. Like it or not, I must provide for our tribe. And this is part of the…providing."

My first rational thought is that it's hell to live in such a small gene pool.

Hari's voice starts to sound like it's coming from deep inside a sea shell. I hope I don't faint.

Before she left our front entryway, and as other women hugged her in support before leading her away, Koral gave me a cool, level look.

With a faint whiff of triumph in it.

That does it. The memory of that look fuels my resolve. *No* one is moving in on my man and me and getting away with it. Somehow, some way, I'll scrounge up a new husband for that bitch before I'm a moon older.

A short time after Koral leaves, Hari says, "I'm going to leave now to go hunting. I'll go with others; you needn't worry."

There's a fresh haunch of venison hanging over our firepit right now, so I know the hunting isn't for us. For me. It's for her.

"When will you be back?" I'm surprised my voice sounds so normal, even to my own ears. I thought it would come out sounding mechanical, unreal.

He comes to me then and kisses me. Deeply. I can't help responding but still I say nothing. I merely look at him. He's going, and there's nothing I can do or say to make him stay.

"I'll return tomorrow morning. Don't worry, wife. It will be all right." He kisses me again, but my lips are cold and stiff. After taking his atl-atl, bow, a quiver of arrows, and bag of spear darts, he's gone.

I haven't moved. Tomorrow, he says.

Tomorrow. I seem to recall Shakespeare saying something about tomorrow. *Tomorrow and tomorrow and tomorrow…*and something about *this petty pace from day to day.* How can I get through today, let alone tomorrow, and yet another tomorrow after that?

All day today and tonight too, Ashur looks at me with sad, puzzled eyes. He observed Koral's infamous visit this morning, so he knows what's going on.

I can't eat. Can't sit down. I don't attend archery practice today. I don't assist with wheels or wheat or horses. I can only pace restlessly.

Grandmama returns from the hot pool and starts roasting a slab of the venison, slowly all day, on a spit over the coals of our fire pit. I hug her tightly for making it for us, Ashur and me, but I can do no more than just taste a morsel at dinner. Then I'm up and pacing again.

And then it's too dark and dangerous to walk alone outside anymore. I work at a small hand loom that Hari had set up for me a while back. I fling the shuttlecock first left, then tamp down the wooden bar to bring the goat-hair threads closer together with a shallow *thump*. And do it again. And again and again, for hours. *Thump*. Staring blankly, looking at nothing. Listening for what, I don't know. *Thump*. Hari's footsteps, maybe, returning home against all logic to the contrary. *Thump*.

I continue to feed the fire with wood so the shadows dance. So I'm not left alone, brooding in the dark. Well, okay, I'm not exactly alone. Although Grandmama's at Maidie's house tonight, Ashur is still here. Finally he starts to approach, looking solemnly at me as if to offer aid and comfort, the only kind he knows how to give.

Yet all I can do is yell at him, poor kid. "Get away from me! I'm sure as hell not in the mood tonight." I can't help speaking to him harshly. Someday I'll apologize, I hope, but I'm in no position to do so just yet.

Ashur slinks away to his sleeping nest, which is currently pulled up snug next to the big bed. He pulls his sleeping furs far back into the corner. Eventually he sinks into a restless slumber, as far as possible from me. Even in sleep, he looks like a whipped puppy.

I sit up most of the night. Hot tears swim in my blank eyes. I lean against the wall by our bed, all pretense of weaving forgotten. I watch the firelight and try not to imagine what's happening in Koral's house near the center of town.

I can't stop thinking of Koral's ivory-tanned skin, sun-kissed but not quite as brown as mine, and Hari, touching that skin, and doing so much more than just touch. Involuntarily, I spasm, fisting my hands against my chest as I emit a tiny moan. And then I do it again. And again and again.

Eventually in the wee hours, as the sky starts to lighten, I fall asleep from sheer exhaustion.

And suddenly Hari is there—Hari, my husband, home again as if nothing out of the ordinary has happened. He enfolds me in a deep embrace, hugging and hugging me tightly as I sob and shudder against him.

All I can do is cry helplessly and hug him even harder. All he says is, "I know…I know…I know…" I don't—I can't—even ask him anything. What would be the use? I don't want to know.

Squirrelly Girl mentally rolls her eyes at me and asks, *Why are you even holding him, caring so much, when he has just come from Koral's bed?*

Her comment makes me cry more quietly, but with even more tears. It makes me hug him even harder, too.

Hari has dark circles under his eyes. I don't want to know how they got there. After a shuddering sigh, all he will say is, "Don't worry, Star Girl. We'll find a husband for Koral soon…somehow."

I look over at Ashur, still asleep in his disheveled corner nest as the morning sun clears the hill. He still looks—and is—so young! Hardly ready to assume the role of head-of-a-household, as bread-winner, or should I say effective hunter.

He's never been much of a good shot, not being raised in a hunting culture. Obsidian knapping was always his trade. His band of traders typically eked out their diet with snared rabbits or woodchucks knocked off by a well-flung bolo, as well as opportunistic gathering of whatever else might be available along their trade routes.

And then I feel it: the first flickering of something positive, a sense that happiness with Hari has not eluded me yet. There's got to be a way out of this mess. And it's up to me to arrange it. I just need to forge Ashur into a successful bull auroch hunter—and soon—whether he likes it or not. I'm sure he's scared shitless of the prospect. Auroch bulls must easily weigh more than three thousand pounds. I have no way of knowing for sure; they all look like boxcars to me. I know for sure that they have quick tempers and can run as fast as a horse.

And so the days continue to flow ever onward.

The defensive wall grows high and strong, thick and formidable. It's high enough for us to shoot arrows over, so long as we stand on a stool or rock pile. It will keep invaders out…for a while. Hopefully long enough for us to mow them down with a rain of arrows.

Most nights Hari is beside me, as affectionate and horny as always, if not more so. Even Ashur snuggles in too, after the fact, so to speak, and I no longer discourage his approach.

Even my precious, growing baby bump quickens with life one night. With great excitement, I press both of my men's hands against my belly to feel the faint kicks, flops, and flutters. Great happiness reigns in our house that night and for many nights to come.

As days and nights pass, I tell myself over and over, *Relax. Relax. It won't be forever, you know. Just until Koral gets a new husband, whether it's Ashur—poor kid!—or somebody else.*

Yes, it's ghastly to think of it, but young women who die in childbirth (not me, God-willing) *will* leave a husband behind. Or perhaps an older woman, already the mother of youngsters, might drown in the river or choke to death on a bone, or *some*thing. But there *will* be a husband for Koral, eventually. Hopefully sooner rather than later. One way or the other, Koral won't be alone for long.

On some days, I can almost forget this strange arrangement is even strange. Squirrelly Girl can't help reminding me. *Hey, your life is already full of strange arrangements! What's one more? After all, think of Ashur…* But then, every few days, Hari will quietly go out hunting again. And be away all day. And all night. Just to keep Koral fed and happy.

I know where he is, but Hari never speaks of it anymore. Nor do I. What would be the use?

True, I don't do a lot of breathing on those nights, either. Hell, I can scarcely breathe just thinking about it. And I don't sleep well, even when I do succumb to exhaustion. But now I *do* take what comfort I can from Ashur. And yes, it helps. The kid — who is only five years younger than I am, after all — continues to gain skill, confidence, and a sense of finesse, more with each time.

I've come to terms with the fact that "folks who live in glass houses ought not throw rocks," and truth be told, somehow that fact comforts me now. It also helps that Ashur is finally sprouting a sparse beard on his narrow cheeks. Although he's still small and skinny, his shoulders are broadening and his voice deepening (when it isn't cracking). Yes, it all helps. *He* helps. I will miss him, more than I care to admit, but I want my husband back, all to myself. I want my Chieftain Hari back, and I want only two of us in our bed. Not three.

If I can just jump-start the process so that Ashur kills an auroch bull all on his own, then Koral can marry Jarmo's newest eligible bachelor, Ashur — whether she likes it or not. And trust me, she won't like it a bit.

CHAPTER 30
To Hunt the Auroch

The true man wants two things: danger and play.
For that reason he wants woman,
the most dangerous plaything.
— Friedrich Nietzsche —
1844–1900

Stella

"Good morning, dear men of mine! Get up, get up. It's time!"
It's a fresh, bright morning, and I'm already wide awake, sitting up in bed. The other part of the L is quiet since Grandmama is spending a few days at Maidie and Timon's place. My men seem loath to submit to the new day as they burrow down in their covers, evidently indicating "not just yet."

I, on the other hand, am tensed with resolve and anticipation.

Once their eyes blink slowly open, I smile at them both. Largely and, I hope, irresistibly.

"Time?" Ashur mutters, still half asleep. "Time for what? Time to get up?"

"Yes! Time to get up, time to move forward." I hurry my case along in case either decides to protest. "I've been thinking about this for a while, so, please, just hear me out."

I sit up even straighter in bed, bare breasts chilly in the morning air as I pull a rabbit-skin coverlet over my shoulders and settle myself into a nest of covers and skins. Hari yawns and stretches beside me.

I talk quickly and cheerfully before either can interrupt. "The defensive wall is nearly complete, the horses are doing well at carrying riders. Well, at least carrying Maidie. The war wagon looks mighty impressive, and we'll soon figure out how to make those wheel axles work. The wheat is flourishing, *and*, most critical of all, the time of the rut is *over* now for auroch bulls. They're not fighting each other anymore, they've bred the cows, and they're as ready as they'll ever be to be hunted. As I said, it's time."

After staring at the opposite wall for a while, thinking deeply, Hari unfolds himself into a sitting position. "Ashur, what say you? Are you ready to show the bull what you're made of? You've practiced enough. Are you ready to become a man at last?"

Ashur doesn't look too sanguine about the possibility. He looks scared shitless instead.

But, to his eternal credit, he just gulps and says, "Maybe. That is, if…if you really think I'm ready."

"Only if *you* think you're ready," Hari qualifies. "Are you? Ready?"

Ashur says nothing, but at least he doesn't say no. I'm sure Ashur likes his life just the way it is, with its none-too-taxing responsibilities and bedtime pleasures. Why change?

But I am adamant. Time to rid Koral from our lives—and to nudge Ashur into adulthood.

"I've been wondering, though. Why must he kill an auroch bull?" I ask. "Wouldn't an ibex or giant elk do just as well?"

"No, it must be an auroch, and *only* an auroch, because that's the one animal sacred to the Great Mother herself," Hari explains.

I'm curious now, so I ask, "How and why did the auroch bull get to be so sacred?"

Hari looks serious, and more than a little reverent just then, as he explains. "It's within the auroch's heart alone the Great Mother has placed the heartstone—an actual bone of power—out of all the animals in the world."

"Mm." I make a small neutral sound, then smile and nod slightly to soften my unspoken editorial skepticism. This all sounds highly dubious to me.

No matter how beloved he is to me, a hunter-gatherer like Hari living four thousand years before the earliest cuneiform writing system, is not one to whom I'd direct a twenty-first century science inquiry.

I can't help protesting gently. "But surely, dearest, surely there are no bones in an animal's heart." Biology is not my specialty, but even *I* know there are no bones in a heart. The heart is a muscle. Period.

"Of course there are no bones in human hearts." He speaks to me in a patient voice as though I'm a small child. "But in the heart of an auroch, it is so; it is true. The Great Mother placed a holy bone there to convey strength and power to all those who possess it. There's one right here in this house."

He rises in a single fluid motion and walks naked over to the altar shelf against the wall. It's a shelf that usually holds a wooden bowl with wildflowers in water, various clay Mother Goddess figurines, and other holy objects. I've never paid close attention before to what was up there, but now I gaze at the dusty object in Hari's hands with interest.

Yes, it definitely looks like, well, a bone. Sort of. Ossified cartilage, maybe? It's shaped like a large, lumpy butterfly and still bears traces of ancient dried blood.

"When I became a man and killed my auroch, this is the very bone I cut out of his heart. A hunter always keeps this bone and puts it in a place of honor so it will bring abundance and protection to his entire household. Just like it will be soon with you, Ashur." Hari looks encouragingly at the last living obsidian trader, and Ashur smiles weakly back.

To which I silently add, *After which time, the boy will officially become a man. And can take a wife. Named Koral.*

"*I* think Ashur is ready now. As ready as he'll ever be. Don't you?" I look from one to another with a brilliant, and I hope not too cheesy, smile.

Don't press your luck, Squirrelly Girl warns from deep in my head.

"Here's what I'm thinking." I take Hari's hand in mine and look into my husband's blue eyes, glancing back at Ashur occasionally to make sure he's still listening. "The battle with the invaders is probably coming sooner than we think. And in this time of trouble, husband, you and I need fewer responsibilities, not more. Please. Let Ashur try for the auroch now. We'll go with him to assist as much as we can. Yes, I *know* he has to kill it by himself. But we'll make sure it happens successfully. After all, as my people used to say, what golden moment are we waiting for? Oh, Ashur, I just *know* you can do it. I know you can."

Hari looks from me to Ashur. "We all have to grow up sometime. Are you ready to do so now?"

Ashur knows he's in for it. His lips form a thin line as he exhales deeply. His only reply: "Yes, Chieftain. I'll do my best."

I'm enormously proud of him. And almost sorry I've been such a nag and a bitch to press the issue. But, still…

"You will *succeed*, Ashur," I correct him, then smile at them both, sensing victory on my side. How does the saying go? *Beautiful women usually get their way.*

After a quick cold breakfast, Hari and Ashur go off together to have their little talk about Ashur marrying Koral. Fortunately there's a rare free moment for them; Jarmo doesn't have many such moments the way it used to. Hari later tells me he stressed the positives of marriage to Ashur, including unlimited sex, a healthy and attractive bed-mate, Koral's substantial house (soon to be his own), and no in-laws around to make trouble or provide for. He even glossed over the negatives: Koral's prickly personality and the endless responsibilities of adulthood.

And they talked about aurochs.

Ashur isn't as familiar with aurochs, be they cows or bulls, in the way that born-and-bred Jarmoites are. Since toddlerhood, Jarmo's local boys view aurochs as just another part of their world. They know that an auroch bull is a huge creature of uncertain temper, bearing within its heart the mystical heartstone, a bone that conveys great powers of stamina and protection when a vulnerable human heart needs it most.

Later today, in the midst of our constant war preparations, Hari directs Ashur to put together a hunting team, "whoever you'd like, seven or eight men, and make ready your weapons." As soon as any villager spots a herd of bachelor bulls nearby, Ashur's hunting troop will head out at first light of the following day before the bulls wander out of reach.

Before nightfall, Ashur's news is telegraphed through the village. No one can quite say how it happens, but it does inevitably. By the next morning, hunters and gatherers alike know to keep an eye out for aurochs for Ashur.

If Koral has heard the news—and she *must* know, how can she not?—she says nothing. Just acts more prickly than usual, if possible.

Fortunately for Koral, men consider her to be good-looking, which is a damned good tool to have in one's feminine toolbox, especially if one's toolbox happens to be skimpy, as Koral's is. A good-looking girl can sometimes get away with murder. Or so the saying goes…

Hari says nothing directly to Koral yet about marrying Ashur, because the kid still has to pass a major test first. Everything depends on that. He's already passed the how-to-pleasure-a-woman test, thank goodness.

Later, Hari tells me privately that he still has trepidations about Ashur going on such a hunt. "You know this is nothing like killing an ibex or elk, don't you?"

Hari's face looks sober when he tells me this, and the worry line appears between his eyes. "An auroch bull is formidable in every way. It takes a strong man to face one and kill it. You've seen them at a distance; you must know what I mean. They're utterly without fear. And they've sent more than one man I know to the next world."

I've been reticent to ask it before, but now I can't help it. "Was it…hard for you, too…when you killed your auroch bull?"

"Yes." He looks and sounds serious as he replies.

"It must have been awful."

"It wasn't easy, I'll tell you that much. I had to climb a tree—fast—in order to get enough arrows into him to put him down. Yes, I had, as you say, moral support from other hunters, and they would have hammered him with arrows if things hadn't gone well on my part. It was scary enough as it was. But to go through the manhood ceremony? Yes, I had to kill the auroch bull myself. And I did. But remember, I was a lot bigger and taller than Ashur." Hari shakes his head. "Ashur's such a runt! It worries me. But we'll do what we can to keep the bull from killing him."

These words keep me shivering and awake for a long time that night. I consider just what it is that I'm setting Ashur up against, just to ease my own—how shall I say?—marital peace of mind.

I'm grateful to remember anything and everything that Professor Harry told me about aurochs, because we're going to need every informational ammunition we can gather if we're going to help Ashur on his hunt.

On my sleepless night of worry, my dear Professor's measured voice flows through my mind as I try, unsuccessfully, to will myself into unconsciousness.

For one thing, they're not just big animals, they're tall. *Their face is on the same level as a man's—a tall man, not a shrimp like me. That's because they have such absurdly long legs, like a chorus girl's.*

The reddish auroch cows are big enough, but they're nothing compared to the bulls. Big black boxcars, that's what they are, with long tails. Even their faces are elongated with funny blond bangs between their eyes. And they weigh a ton—no, more than a ton. Up to three thousand pounds.

And don't forget their horns. Just as impressive as a Texas Longhorn's, only these horns don't veer off to the side; these both point forward, *dead on right at you, the hunter. Ivory-colored with black tips. Sharp and deadly as daggers.*

On a lighter note, though… Yes, Professor Harry's familiar voice, soothing and sonorous, continues to flow through my brain, but on an up-note now; my heart doesn't feel so heavy anymore. *Yes, there is a lighter note concerning aurochs.*

Across time and space, I can see Professor Harry's reassuring smile, clear as day.

Studies of contemporary bovine DNA now show that all domestic taurine cattle—meaning cows with no humps—in the entire world *originated from just eighty wild aurochs who happened to live, you can guess where, right around Jarmo.*

In fact, by the time Jarmo starts to wane, folks there will domesticate the auroch all on their own. But you'd best leave that project for another century and another project manager.

On that somewhat cheerful note, I finally sink into a fitful doze and from there into a dreamless sleep.

Several days pass. No auroch sightings yet. Where's an auroch when you really need one? Things return to Jarmo's new normal: that is, lots of work and low-grade worry leavened by unsubstantiated positive bucking-up. ("We can do it! I *know* we can!")

But the delicate balance between Ashur and me is tipping now. Since the auroch hunt looms in his future, Ashur knows that things are going to change in his life, and one of them is my presence in it.

I want to make sure Ashur realizes this, so I bring up the subject as soon as I can work it into a conversation. Some things just have to be said. Hari took off early to work with the bowyers, so this morning I'm walking alone with Ashur to the arrow assembly line; he's got another batch of arrowheads to deliver to Helin.

"You know that your time of being my…student…will end soon, don't you? Once you kill your bull?"

"Can I put off getting married for little while? Isn't everything good just the way it is?" Ashur looks more than a little crushed. "I thought you kind of liked me. Or at least liked *part* of me."

I have to laugh at that. "I *do* like you, Ashur. More than I ever thought I could. But do you have any idea how hard it is for me, this…situation? Not *you*, of course. That part isn't difficult at all. That part is…pleasing. But when Chieftain Hari goes to Koral as…" The words stick in my throat. "Look. I know there is no logic to this. I just…I just can't do it anymore. I can't endure Chieftain Hari being Koral's temporary husband and mine as well. Koral is a widow now, and she needs a man of her own. Not mine! Not anymore."

Ashur looks at me glumly with a raised eyebrow. He knows that Hari and I are strongly behind the plan for him to take Koral as his wife. "She's way taller than I am, you know."

"Well, so am I, for that matter! But what difference does that make, especially with a wife?"

I try to smooth out the wrinkles in both his mind and our intertwined futures. "At night, the only difference with Koral will be that her feet will extend further down in the bed than yours. But everything else is made by the Great Mother to fit. And it will. Don't you want your own place, your own wife?"

Ashur looks resigned. Frankly afraid of the future and annoyed as well. Too many things are changing too quickly in his life.

His foreign accent sounds very pronounced to me just now, for some reason. "Well, I *would* take a wife. If I could choose for myself. But not *that* one. Too tall and too…grumpy."

"Sometimes, Ashur, sometimes we just have to make do." I thread my fingers through his — reassuringly, I hope — as we stroll together under the slanting winter sunshine. "There *is* no one else for you just now. Not unless some husband dies or a girl comes into womanhood soon. Would you please just think about it, though? A fine house and a wife of your own to service every night? Surely *that* would be worth killing a black cow over, now, wouldn't it?"

Ashur looks a bit brighter. He's considering it at least. "Well, when you put it *that* way…" But now we've arrived at the arrow assembly line, and all talk of marriage is dropped. For the moment.

The next day, several women gathering mushrooms range far afield and happen across a small band of about fifteen auroch males. A typical bachelor herd.

Breathlessly, they return home to tell us of this auspicious happenstance.

Front and center, everyone! Ashur's auroch hunt begins tomorrow.

Ashur, Hari, and I sleep little the night before, so excited and nervous are we in preparing and packing for the hunt.

Day one starts auspiciously enough, a glorious day with the cheers and good-luck wishes of Jarmoites still ringing in our ears. We of The Hunt are nine: Hari and Ashur; Helin, our arrow impresario; Tarek, the preternatural bowman; four other young bowmen. And then there's me, tagging along with the group on the clear understanding I'm to be chief wood gatherer, cook, and camp grunt. I don't mind at all; I'm excited to go. Not only do I want to personally watch Ashur cut out the heartstone—heart bone—myself, I also just want to make sure the deed gets done. Nothing must get in the way of Ashur killing that bull and finally becoming a man in the eyes of all Jarmoites.

We follow the same path as that of the mushroom seekers, but see nothing all day. A little disappointed but still hopeful, we build a good-sized bonfire for cooking dinner, to keep animals away, and frankly to bring light to a little corner of the great darkness for ourselves before we unroll our sleeping skins by the fire. We take turns keeping watch, while nocturnal creatures abroad in the night make mysterious shuffle-and-click sounds at the edge of our consciousness.

Now it's day two, and I'm dejected already. Although none of us will say so aloud, I'm afraid the auroch bulls have ambled off to other pastures. Hari has told me that, after the rut, all the bulls, from young to prime, middle-aged to seniors, readily gather into numerous, small bachelor herds. Guys hanging together, as it were. The cows and yearlings happily congregate in their own herds, far removed from the short-tempered bulls.

After breaking camp, we continue to amble south, following the great river.

The four dogs trot along briskly beside us. One is Hari's—brindled, jackal-like Whitefoot—and the other dogs belong to the young hunters. Shaggy, black-coated Trusty remains behind at home as part of the guard force watching over Jarmo's small, communal band of goats. No sheep; they haven't been domesticated yet. I've been remiss in my duties about enlightening my tribe about that. But goats, yes. They're important critters—another source of milk, crucial to making kefir, and serving as dinner in a pinch.

After walking for about an hour, scanning the hills in all directions for our prey—or for anything that might prey upon us—suddenly all of us see the bulls at the same time. We buzz together in a whispered group exclamation. There on a nearby hill, a handful of black dots. Our prey shows itself plainly. And I'm thinking, thank goodness they don't look *that* big. But I learn soon enough it's just an optical illusion because we're still far away.

Hari, Helin, and Tarek call us into a huddle. "Lay low, keep your heads down, move slowly and quietly—but only when we do." Ashur, the four other young hunters, and I do as we're bid without a murmur.

Moving low and unobtrusively, our group finally approaches the prey. Ashur and I experience a simultaneous, chilling realization that bull aurochs don't look at all small up close.

From this vantage point, I can see that they're huge. And disconcertingly tall.

Ashur shoots me a look of near panic: *Shit, guess I'm in for it now. If I live through today, it'll be a miracle.*

And I return him a look of my own: *I'm sorry I forced you into this, and there's no way I can help you out of it now.*

The bull band is certainly aware of us, but after glancing our way once, they look away, disinterested. We're still on our bellies, obscured by brush. We look small, and we *are* small. Little for them to be concerned about.

We watch from a distance, leashing the dogs and ordering them to stay. We shush them in stern whispers when they whine.

I count fourteen auroch bulls. The ones with smaller horns seem young, not too bad. Others look respectably formidable. Still others look as big as cement trucks.

Still watching on our bellies, we collectively select a likely victim. Hari, Helin, and Tarek point him out to Ashur. He's a medium-sized bull, one who looks spirited enough but certainly not one of the alpha males.

But then Ashur isn't an alpha male either. Hopefully this will be a good match, at least for the young human.

"All right, Ashur? Will this one do?"

Ashur murmurs in a voice as glum and resigned as how he must be feeling right now. "Yes, all right. This one." He exhales explosively. "Let's do it."

Seeing no other way but forward, Ashur starts assembling his weapons. He drops his bow twice and manages to get his quiver twisted, then untwisted, in the process. His hand visibly shakes as he tucks an obsidian-bladed hatchet into his ibex-skin belt. Ready or not, here he comes.

Suddenly Ashur holds up one finger to us. And ducks behind a bush. Hey, bowels made watery by fear will not be denied. After an interminable time, he finally emerges and begins a stealthy approach of the bull.

Hari, Helin, and Tarek ready the hunting dogs. The four scruffy canines wait, sides quivering with excitement, to receive official permission from their masters before they give chase. But not just yet. The moment must be right.

I feel so sorry for both bull and young man—well, he who is almost a man. The hapless young bull seems so quiet and aloof, minding his own business as he tears off grasses and chews with innocent gusto. I feel great anguish about Ashur, too, facing this dangerous ordeal. What a stupid idea, to risk a man's life in such a way. And I'm the one who put him up to this. But Hari says it's got to be done.

I know, I know…Jarmo will have it no other way.

Our hunters nock arrows in their bows, ready to let fly if needed. We're allowed to remain close for moral support with implied permission to save our young manhood candidate in an emergency. But we're not to help him do the actual killing. That he must do all by himself.

If he can. Without getting killed himself.

Sensing our hyper-alertness and furtive movements in the underbrush as we approach more closely, the bulls grow uneasy. They begin a slow amble. Ashur must keep up. He nocks a broadhead arrow as he moves stealthily, bush to bush, seeking cover as he moves closer. Finally he's within shooting range.

Now.

Rising to his knees in the underbrush, Ashur lets fly with his first arrow. It hits the huge animal in its thigh, piercing the surface but lightly, just barely hanging on.

Outraged at this sudden effrontery, the bull roars and kicks out with his hind legs, undecided whether to run or to attack something… anything.

With brazen disloyalty, the other bulls pick up speed as they start moving away from their injured brother. They don't pause until they're at the crest of a small hill, where they turn and observe this negative turn of events.

Standing now, Ashur shoots four arrows in immediate succession. Two find their mark deep in the creature's body; the others do not.

Someone behind me cries the order, "Go!"

Suddenly four dogs gallop onto the scene. So swift they are, their feet scarcely touch the ground. They start barking their heads off immediately. High-pitched yips and growls fill the air.

The bull is crazed with rage by now. He charges each dog in turn, thrashing his great head about with its deadly horns, trying to reach — and gore — the treacherous human. The dogs surround and taunt the auroch, yelping and snapping, while the massive head-and-horns charges them repeatedly.

"Shoot, Ashur, shoot!" we all yell to him. "Quick!"

Some arrows connect with the bull, but many do not because of how the animal twists and thrashes. Also, Ashur is a pretty mediocre archer. A snare is more his speed.

By now the bull knows that the origin of his pain is the small two-legged creature. The dogs are just a diversion.

The bull is spitting fire now and not slowing down a bit. He gallops toward Ashur — and toward us all. We noncombatants scatter in all directions. Black and liberally pierced with arrows, the auroch bull looks like something out of *La Corrida*, the traditional Spanish bullfight.

The bull gallops like thunder, closer with every thud of his hooves. Ashur appears mesmerized as the bull bears down on him. Suddenly, he flings his bow aside — the animal is almost too close to shoot anyway — as he pulls his obsidian-blade axe from his knotted waist-belt.

This tool he knows and trusts with his life.

One dog savagely bites at the bull's left foreleg, distracting the huge beast momentarily from Ashur. The bull's tall, slender legs make a good target for a canine.

Ashur and the bull's legs and belly are within a hand's breadth now. The bull pivots quickly to impale Ashur on his horns and fling him to one side.

Atl-atl readied with a spear, Tarek is about to chuck it into the beleaguered bull at any moment. So are the others. They're not about to let Ashur die today just so he can enter the ranks of men.

But Ashur makes a move of his own. Being so short, he ducks easily under the bull despite danger from the flailing bovine legs.

With courage born of desperation, Ashur drives the axe head deep into the belly of the bull, then pulls the blade up, then up again, like a zipper.

The bull's entrails — voluminous, glistening, and purplish-brown — pour out of his belly like imprisoned snakes set free. Such masses of them! I can't believe that enormous, fleshy organ all came out of one animal.

This latest, and probably fatal, indignity brings the animal to its knees in front, while its backside, improbably, still remains upright over its hind legs.

Ashur's in the middle of the mess; purple-red bovine blood and cow shit cover the ground and the boy. The roaring bull thrashes his head from side to side, bellowing in despair. Futilely, the creature tries to jump and run but slips on his own entrails. This at least brings the bull's hind legs out from under him, causing the entire body to slump to the ground. Even then, the huge head continues to swing from side to side helplessly, open mouth bellowing, deadly horns aiming to impale Ashur if they can.

"Cut his throat! Whack him, Ashur, whack him! Bleed him out!"

All of us yell our own advice. Although not yet dead, the bull is definitely down. We approach closer now for support and sheer curiosity as Ashur finishes him off.

Since he doesn't have a knife handy, just his axe, Ashur starts whacking savagely at the bull's neck and throat, careful to stay out of range of the horns. He chops at the animal's neck as if it's a tree trunk. Bloodied and slimy himself, Ashur doesn't know what else to do, except to keep doing what he's doing like a crazy person.

Hari waves the rest of us back. "Let Ashur do it himself." And we comply.

Finally the great beast slumps over for good. The bellowing ceases. The lethal horns, while continuing to point sideways directly at Ashur, thrash no more.

Everyone cheers, claps and whistles. *You've done it, brother!*

Shakily, I exhale the breath I didn't know I was holding. I can see now why these impressive animals survived in the world as long as they did. And why they came to be worshipped as the Bull of the Moon, sacred to the Great Mother.

Due to the stench of congealing blood and warm shit mixed with severed intestines, Ashur looks almost ready to throw up. Yet he's happy and relieved at the same time: he's *done* it! And he won't ever have to do it again. At least he's officially now a man.

Unsuccessfully, he tries to rise to his feet, but the ground is covered in slippery entrails. "Get me out of this shit, will you?"

Many hands pull him up and out. Congratulations ring out from all directions. "Well done, brother! Welcome to the Brotherhood of Men."

As everyone cheers their assent, I tell Hari, "I'll scrounge up some firewood."

Sexist or not, woman as beast of burden and kitchen slave as part of the natural order, I freaking don't care just now. I'm here to do my part, and this is it. Besides, I'm thrilled to the skies that Ashur killed his bull. The future is starting to look a whole lot brighter to me at last.

As I gather armloads of branches, I observe the hunters carefully slicing the bull's flesh along each leg, exposing the long bones.

Seeing my ignorant look, one of the young hunters explains, "It's to get at the marrow. That's the very best part!"

Evidently, it's no easy task to get at the bone marrow. As I spark the firestones together over tinder and carefully feed the tiny flame with dried grass and small sticks, I watch as the men begin to pound the long bones with large rocks, or with axes if they have them. It looks to me like they're aiming to split each bone lengthwise, and sometimes they succeed.

Hoots, exclamations, and happy moans of anticipation greet the marrow. Our men seem *crazy* about it, and most aren't interested in cooking it. They suck their portion raw, so to speak, and look around hopefully for more.

I watch the men remove lines of raw marrow from the pounded ends of bone after giving each bone a sharp tap, then teasing the marrow out with a knife blade. It comes out in one long, disgusting cylindrical piece.

The bull's bone marrow is whitish pink—that's when most of our men devour it—but it turns brownish if cooked. A few of the men, those with more delicate sensibilities, place their marrow portions on rocks by the fire to at least warm it up. I have to admit that it smells pretty good as it cooks, but I'm happy to give up my portion to the men. I feel like gagging to even think of ingesting such a greasy, gluey substance.

Once the marrow is finished off, and when the consumed wood starts forming coals under subsiding flames, the men carefully cut out each rib. They stir the coals about with a stick and lay the great, meaty bones on them in rows. Everyone is smiling, especially Ashur, who is hugely relieved the much-dreaded ordeal is over.

I've brought a precious little bag of salt—a prized commodity in Jarmo—along on this journey, and our men can't seem to get enough of it: marrow, grilled ribs, and salt. The ribs are tough but mouth-wateringly tasty, especially when well-seasoned. We throw generous tidbits to the quivering dogs who snap them up in mid-air. A communal exhale exudes the air, that of a job well done.

The men carefully and systematically cut the rest of the meat from the bones while I wrap it, at their direction, in hides or tie it with leather thongs around carrying poles. We'll take it home tomorrow.

But we're not yet done with the ceremonial bull killing. Two important steps remain.

Once we're all stuffed with red meat and salt, as well as warm beer, brought carefully from home in clean animal bladders, Hari announces the next order of business.

"Ashur, as killer of the bull, you—and only you—are entitled to cut the yellow hair patch from the beast's head. From it you will make a belt for your new bride to ensure fertility."

Everyone cheers long and loudly at that. I look at the snarl of light-colored bangs, now spotted with blood and dirt, between the creature's dead-fish eyes. Asher cuts the flesh that contains the hair follicles into a careful square, using a borrowed knife. I sigh to think that this innocent giant had to die so a young human might have a new life. But this is not a Disney film, I remind myself. This is just life in Jarmo, just the way it is.

And there's more. Hari announces, "Now you must cut the heart from the bull and take for yourself the blessed heartstone within."

Although it's evident that Ashur isn't eager to muck about in this slippery, odorous carcass any more than he already has, he knows what he must do. With pursed lips and quiet concentration, he begins cutting high on the bull's belly, hacking through layer after layer as he seeks the no-longer-pulsing heart of the beast.

"This heartstone, this bone created by the Great Mother herself, will keep you safe and prosperous all of your days," Hari intones. Perhaps it's part of a ceremony with ritual words; I do not know. "It is the protection given by this bone that makes you fully a man."

With no small difficulty, accompanied by much cutting, grunting, and spilling of blood, Ashur finally pulls out the surprisingly large heart from the chest cavity of the bull.

He uses the blade to cut and clean carefully around the strange, bony object within the heart. When he finally holds it up for public display, the men cheer and offer congratulations.

Yes, it looks much like Hari's heartstone, only much newer and much bloodier, of course. Rather like a tiny, jagged-edged, cross-shaped kite made of what looks like bone.

All of this fuss over one strange little bone, taken from a place where bones aren't supposed to be.

Hari rises to make a benediction of sorts. "Ashur of the obsidian traders, now of Jarmo, receive this heartstone as your own, a sign of power, respect, and love from the Great Mother, to keep with you always in a place of honor in your house."

"May it be so." The men rumble their response respectfully.

I think of long-ago responses in the Lutheran liturgy, words from another life. Ashur wraps the precious bone in a wad of goat wool, then puts it in a little bag, and hangs it around his neck.

In the twilight, we bathe off the blood and gore in the great river—the one Professor Harry says is the mighty Tigris—and later we arrange bedrolls around the fire, despite the relative proximity of the bloody, dismembered carcass. We set up a series of watch posts and times, approximate of course, to keep dangerous wildlife at bay. On the night breeze, the scent of fresh blood perfumes the air, rich and heavy with promise. I remind myself the dogs will bark their heads off first if any danger comes near.

We stay up late, laughing and joking around the fire. We relive the great hunt and Ashur's success, while the men start getting ribald, teasing him about his bride-to-be. From time to time, they look at me. Respectfully, yes, but even so…They smile and wink surreptitiously, since they know that Ashur is no stranger to me in that respect.

"You've been taught well," they tell him. There are no secrets in Jarmo. If we have any, we do not keep them for long.

Ashur gives me a look—a sleepy, private, satiated smile. Happy finally to be a man, but sad that he'll no longer be substitute husband to the likes of me.

As we finally drift to the edge of sleep, Hari folds me in beside him with my backside tucked up close against his front. The night is melodious with crickets, punctuated by the snores, faint groans, belches, and farts from the hunters. Hari murmurs softly to me, "When we get back, I'll inform Koral about her wedding to Ashur. It'll be soon, probably within three days."

Just three days, I think. And I smile. They don't mess around in Jarmo!

"Just as soon as we supplement this meat with a couple of ibex for the wedding feast," Hari adds.

My mind floats dreamily on the black breeze of the wilderness night. I'm so happy right now, I can hardly stand it. I smile even more broadly than before and start drifting off.

I can't help thinking, if I'm ever dragged back to the Land of Google, I'm going to look up heartstone...or heart bone.

Squirrelly Girl's voice pipes up from the depths of my head. *Real or imaginary, the heartstone is working for us now.*

Damn straight, I think, before sleep claims me at last.

CHAPTER 31
A Second Wedding

A woman's life is not perfect or whole
Till she has added herself to a husband.
Nor is a man's life perfect or whole
Till he has added to himself a wife.
≈ Anthony Trollope ≈
1815 – 1882

Stella

The late afternoon sun shines on my closed eyelids. I smell the delicate yet slightly sulfurous scent of warm springs all around me. I slide down until the water reaches my chin, and I feel my hair fanning out like seaweed. The water is just right, not too hot in this corner of the pool. I make sure of that because I want nothing to harm our precious Little Bean.

My belly looks like a ripe melon now — no, not the tiny sweet wild melons around Jarmo, but not like an unwieldy American watermelon either. Probably more like a cantaloupe, which doesn't grow around here. But cantaloupe best describes dear Little Bean's protuberance. I rest my hand on the bump and bask in the sun, radiating happiness.

Many female voices sing, punctuated by laughter and happy chatter, and then they sing some more. Drowsily, I join in here and there, wherever and whenever I can remember the words and tune.

I can't stop smiling: it's wedding time again, and this time, it isn't me but Koral who is the bride.

After the men spend a couple of hours in the pool, finally it's our time at the springs: girl time, woman time. We chase the men up the hill and away, then luxuriate in our favorite hot spots. Now is our time to fix one another's hair, sing old songs and create new ones, and give the bride a constant barrage of good-natured, wedding-night teasing.

An older woman starts another song, obviously familiar to all, and everyone joins in the refrain. The clear tones that rise up toward the blue above sound unbearably sweet.

For a bride, Koral isn't saying much today. After all, she's already been through this before, five years ago. Today, although she loves being the center of attention, she still can't hide a hint of glumness and reluctance. She says little about her diminutive groom.

Just like at Jarmo's big double wedding last year, this wedding commences its festivities with the sex-segregated barbecue. Females on one side of the giant bonfire, males on the other. This time, Hari grins at me broadly from across the crowd. I smile back with a grin just as wide. He knows how happy I am right now…and how disgruntled Koral is.

I couldn't resist eavesdropping on Hari—I hid around the corner from Koral's house and strained my ears—when he tapped on her door, entered the house, and informed Koral she'd be marrying Ashur in three days' time.

"I won't, I tell you. I can't!" Koral's high voice carried clearly to my hiding place. "He's still a child, no bigger than a kid goat. It's just not fitting. *He's* not fit, and I won't have it!"

Swiftly, she switches tactics. From harpy to helpless maiden, pleading her case.

"Oh, please, Revered Chieftain…" Her voice is all honey. "Please allow me to wait, just a little while! For another candidate to come along."

"It's been decided, and it shall be done," Hari says with quiet finality. He looks, and is, implacable on this subject when asked about it, even now. "With war looming, I can no longer provide food for two households, and I will not take a second wife while there are young men of Jarmo, like Ashur, who have none. The taking of multiple wives only leads to disharmony. Multiple wives would fight like wildcats, and trouble would take hold in Jarmo that could never be undone."

Koral interrupts him, speaking passionately. "But you don't know that, not really—"

"It's done. No more discussion." Hari will not be dissuaded. We two girls can assuredly hear the finality in his voice, each unseen to the other. "Prepare your house and yourself to take a new husband in three days' time."

Now at Ashur and Koral's wedding party, the outdoor feast is in full swing. All fingers and lips are greasy and glistening from eating delicious, slow-cooked auroch and ibex, liberally salted, washed down with bladders of warm beer. People seem so happy to just be *happy* again…light-hearted and playful, not thinking, for once, about invaders or fights to the death.

After dinner, the men's and women's concentric circle dances commence around the bonfire. First, men dance alone; then they pull women to their feet to dance counterclockwise within the ring of clockwise-moving men.

Hari grabs my hand and pulls me into the mob of dancers. Female after female gets snapped up, joining the laughing, singing, and clapping celebrants. It's a joyous process, hypnotic too.

But still Koral stands with a scowl, partnerless. It's customary for the bride to be selected last, right before the Graybeards and Crones come to speak the marriage words over them.

At last, Ashur comes to stand before her. As bridegroom, he looks pretty resplendent himself, although a mite abashed and intimidated by the enormity of it all. He extends his right hand to Koral, while his left arm is tucked decorously behind his back.

Koral looks at him under glowering brows. The look that passes between them is unfathomable. The pause grows long…too long… and the guests grow uneasy. *Hey now, kids.*

Finally, Koral puts her hand in Ashur's extended palm. Reluctantly. But the crowd is just relieved that she did it at all. They're happy to sing and clap all the louder.

Our Wise Ones step to the small stone altar nearby. A carved stone image of the Great Mother dominates the altar. The statue is flanked by many smaller spiritual images: small goddess figurines, painted with three downward stripes in blue pigment on each cheek.

A hush falls over the crowd. I move quietly to Hari's side and slip my hand into his, as Jarmoites form a large semi-circle around the Wise Ones.

With a sense of *déjà vu*, I watch, with an unmistakable lump in my throat, as Grandmama's right, gnarled forefinger dips into the black, then paints what looks to be a rough capital H on the foreheads of the two wedding supplicants.

"The symbol of Jarmo," she intones. Her gravelly voice is somehow reassuring. I close my eyes as a feeling of rightness reaffirming itself suffuses me.

Then Betta gestures for the couple to come before her. She dips her thumb into the bowl, bringing out red pigment and pressing a red thumbprint both above and below the horizontal cross line of the H, first to Ashur and then to Koral.

"This is the blood of the marriage bed. Plow her field, plant the seeds. You are now partners together on this journey through Life."

Grinning, Nance comes forward with a thin, leather strap. She binds their wrists together, his left to her right, firmly tied but still allowing sufficient slack for movement. With shocking clarity I remember what I was thinking last year when they tied Hari's wrist to mine: *No one's getting out of this one alive!*

But now, watching this ancient affirmation of life, all I can think are the words *World without end, amen.* Ancient liturgy from a rite as old as time, coming to me now from a different world. My other world.

Everyone starts singing again, loudly rejoicing. As Ashur and Koral take the lead, his hand firmly bound to her wrist, the crowd surges slowly forward in a joyful procession toward Koral's house, a bonus dowry from her late husband, Kern. No other family members are left to share it with them. It will be Ashur and Koral's alone.

The mob stops in front of the house. Looking very embarrassed and quivering with nerves, Ashur pushes open the door and pulls her in reluctantly behind him. The sound of the crossbar coming down across the closed door is evident to all. The crowd cheers raucously.

Oh, yes, I remember this time. Very, very well.

The villagers remain in front of the house, milling about, drinking, and laughing. The crowd is so boisterous, I can't hear a thing going on inside the house. Poor Ashur. I sure hope he's doing *something* in there. Something good and right as it should be. I hope she's not ordering him to get the hell out.

Time passes. Ten, fifteen minutes perhaps. I'm only guessing, because in hourless Jarmo, time is a fluid concept.

Standing next to Hari as I wait, I feel a faint smidgeon of guilt, but mostly of wistful tenderness, as I recall what happened yesterday.

With no prior planning on anyone's part, Ashur and I happen to be alone in our house for a brief time in the midst of wedding preparations. We talk about the wedding, about his new life and adult responsibilities.

"I guess this is goodbye, then," I tell him. I don't mean to sound dramatic, but there's no denying that I am…what, actually? Truth be told, what I am is wistful. I'll miss him a lot in every way that counts. Of course, I'll probably see him around the village most every day. But I can no longer…

That's when I realize the knife indeed cuts both ways. In order to get Koral out of my life and Hari out of her bed, *I* have to give up something too. Something—someone—I've come to count on for enjoyment and reassurance. For friendship.

"Would you…that is, could we…?" Ashur looks up at me, his dark eyes searching mine, hoping-against-hope. "Could we say goodbye, you know, just one more time?"

And then I back him up against the wall. No words. Just a physical goodbye for both of us to remember.

Yes, I feel guilty afterward, but only just a little. Jarmo has got me in its mindset now, with neither room nor time for twenty-first century squeamishness or prudery. Ashur got the goodbye he deserved, and I'll treasure the memory of Ashur the Boy before he becomes somebody else's husband.

Who knows? Perhaps Hari said goodbye to Koral in this same way. Some things it's best not to ask, best never to know.

I'll never go back on my word to Hari. And neither will Hari to me. Last night, we vowed to move forward together as a faithful loving unit, Hari and me and Little Bean. Otherwise, things just get too complicated. I know only too well firsthand.

Suddenly, I'm jolted back to the present moment by cries and cheers. I exhale a sigh of relief to see Ashur open the door and come out grinning like a fool. That appears to be all the proof that's needed at this wedding of a young widow and randy young man.

A great cheer goes up from the crowd. After a moment, Koral steps outside to another resounding cheer. I have to admit she looks far less grumpy than when she went in. She's even smiling a little and looks a bit bemused. Perhaps it *will* work for them. Stranger things have happened.

From a different stone bowl this time, Betta anoints both groom and bride with three blue stripes on each cheek. She then paints the tied wristband with blue pigment too. "You are now husband and wife," Betta announces solemnly, but she can't help smiling. Everyone else is whooping and cheering at the tall elegant bride and diminutive groom as they wave goodbye to the guests and close the door behind them.

"Let's go home now, shall we?" Hari's voice is soft, almost gently pleading. "The rest of these folks'll be here half the night. We don't have to stay."

He looks weary suddenly. Tired of being the Chieftain of Jarmo, tired of being Koral's provider and bedmate, tired of watching a young boy gain sexual confidence practicing on his very own wife.

"Yes, let's do." I reach up on tiptoes then and kiss him. And he pulls me in closer and deepens it. We head for home with speed. Our house is silent; Grandmama will stay with the Crones tonight in front of Koral's house, enjoying the merriment and beer, along with seconds and thirds of barbecued auroch and ibex.

Tonight in our house, as firelight dances against the opposite wall, Hari and I renew our vows without words, but in the only, and very best, way we know how.

CHAPTER 32
We the People

As soon as there is life, there is danger.
~ Ralph Waldo Emerson ~
1803 – 1882

Stella

"But what's it actually *for?*" That's what I'm asked, time and time again, by committee chairman Zene at working sessions of the Wheel Troop. Most Jarmoites still can't fathom why the wheel is such a big deal.

Sure, as an official committee, they're glad and proud that they're working on something critical to our, shall we say, national security. They just can't get their heads around what it can do for us yet.

I wish I'd had some foam board and an craft knife when I first showed the committee what a wheel looked like. But I didn't. All I could do was draw in the dirt with a stick. I thought it was enough, but obviously it wasn't. Oh, it was enough to enable them to construct four wheel prototypes, but still.

How can I get through to them how amazing, how game-changing, the wheel is going to be? Then it comes to me: by appealing to every human's desire, thereby every Jarmoite's desire, for something cool, something mind-boggling, something that they can possess before anyone else. Something like Smartphones are in the twenty-first century.

This morning, I talk to them slowly, moving deliberately about in the designated committee space in one of their homes. I choose my words haltingly but with great passion. They listen with what appears to be dubious hopefulness.

"Look, long ago, before any of you were born, your ancestors had to work very hard just to exist. There were no spears, no bows or arrows, hardly any modern tools at all. Just hand axes—with no clever hafted handles, mind you!—and little else. Your people lived in rough shelters, skins draped over piles of branches. With very little standing between the people and the elements or dangerous animals. *Or* dangerous strangers.

"But now, our lives are so much better, so much easier. Because of what? Because of knowledge."

I look at each one of them and try to look impressive as I do so.

"It's because of knowledge that the Great Mother has given us over time, with each new bit of knowledge building upon what has gone before. She's given us opportunities to invent helpful tools for ourselves. Modern, strong, and clever tools, like the spear and atl-atl, knives and bows and arrows. And fire stones! Very important things, those fire stones."

Everyone chuckles a bit at that. *Obviously!*

"The Great Mother gives us inner knowledge so we can build solid, permanent, comfortable houses, like this one, where we can be safe and warm."

I pivot in my pacing to provide emphasis to my words.

"And now, through knowledge given to me in the life I had before I came here, the Great Mother is bringing, through me, a *new* tool to Jarmo. An amazing tool called the wheel. One that'll allow us to move heavy things from place to place faster and easier. One that'll move *us* around faster and easier, too."

I look at their hopeful yet skeptical faces. Halfway there but not just yet. I continue with my pacing and proselytizing.

"You've done a fantastic job carving and fastening together these four wooden wheels, but let me remind you where the concept of the wheel comes from. I've told you earlier about the sledge, which, where I come from, is called a sled. It's already a useful object here in Jarmo."

So far, so good.

"I know you're all aware of how a sledge works. When you put rounded segments of logs under the two runners of the sledge before you pull it, it moves along much faster. Doesn't it! And you don't need all that many logs, because you can keep moving the log segments forward — log, after log, after log — as you drag the sledge. But still, it's a slow process, and you still need several men to keep bringing the logs forward each time."

Several heads nod in agreement. They're still listening.

"But now your sledges will gain a *huge* improvement with the wheel. And here's how." I take a deep breath before continuing.

"No doubt you've noticed that, after a while, the two bottom runners of the sledge start wearing grooves into the log segments, and *that* makes the sledge move along even faster still. So, we're going to do away with the entire, large log segments and keep only the small grooved portion of the log. And that's what these wheels really are, what they're going to replace: the grooves on the logs. Then we'll attach them to the sledge by this axle — actually there's two of them, one for the back and one for the front of the sledge."

I brandish before them a long, nearly straight, peeled sapling. "We're only going to keep the *concept* of the roller where it's already grooved. It's like we put on these wheels, and then cut away all the rest. We make holes in the sledge and holes in the wheels, as well. Then we'll put on lots of marmot grease to the areas where the wheels, axles, and sledge come together. We'll fit the two axles in, one in front, one behind, and put it all together. And it will move fast, like the wind, when pulled by a man — or by a horse!"

At that, the committee erupts into laughter, scoffing, and good-natured protests to the contrary. I have a horrible feeling that I'm forgetting some essential piece of knowledge to make the whole Rube Goldberg contraption work. But I can't remember what it is, and suddenly I just want to get out of here and lie down with a cold cloth on my forehead.

Although I'm still smiling when I leave, my exit is speedy and abrupt, despite using my always reliable excuse of pregnancy.

Originally, I had ambitious visions of Jarmoites constructing rows of handsome spoke-wheeled chariots, each to be pulled by thunderous-hooved horses. With a sinking feeling, I know now this isn't going to happen.

We've only captured five horses so far — and skittish horses they are, too — and I think that's going to be *it* before the invasion. We can only spare one horse to pull the cart, our so-called War Wagon (I dredged up that name from an old Hollywood movie). No matter how clunky it may look to me, *hopefully* a wheeled cart drawn by a horse will still knock the eyes out of our enemies. Still and all, a glitzy Egyptian war chariot would have had a million times more wow-factor. But who am I kidding? Certainly not Stella Denton of Jarmo.

We — no, make that *I* — can't remember how to coordinate the wheels properly, how to make a higher-tech fixed axle instead of a primitive one that moves along with the wheels. I just freaking can't *remember* any of that from my hospital cram sessions. We'll be lucky to get even a basic wagon constructed and operative before the time comes. Thundering chariots are just a pipe dream.

As chairman of the Wheel Troop, Zene is a smart man, though, and his people are clever. Surely they'll figure it out, even if I cannot. I keep telling myself that, and I will myself to believe it.

Whatever happens with our committees, troops, and squads, at the very least I'll have planted seeds for Jarmo's future. Inventions and new skills that'll help my people not only survive but also thrive. (And, if need be, kick everyone else's ass.)

After lunch, I walk down to check on Jarmo's equine operations. In the round pen, Oren, who will eventually be our cart driver, works patiently with his none-too-enthusiastic horse. The other three horse-men are still cautiously gentling their horses.

Even ever-confident, sunny-faced Maidie gushes about Boss Mare. "She lets me lie across her back, face down, and she carries me around that way with no complaint! I'll be riding upright on her back any day now — and shooting arrows, too. I promise, you'll see!"

Maidie's also gotten Boss Mare so used to having her human mistress scratch between the horse's eyes and rubbing her neck, that the mare now submits to wearing what Professor Harry calls a thong bridle. It's a breathtakingly simple arrangement: a braided leather thong is draped over the gap between the rear teeth of the lower jaw and knotted under the horse's chin, with the trailing ends able to serve as reins.

Surely after inventing such a clever device, actual riding on the back of a horse cannot now be too far behind!

But still, *still*, we'll have to figure out how to hitch a horse to the War Wagon and teach the horse to pull it — holy crap — all in a very short time. Figuring out a workable harness and reins system for the wagon might as well be computer programming, for all I am suited to help figure it out, which I am *not*, let alone anyone from Jarmo figuring it out. What was I thinking?

Every few days, I visit the round pen and observe as unobtrusively as I can. The horses have their pecking order now and don't seem afraid of humans, although they don't seem any too friendly either.

Maidie and her horsemen work their animals every day. It's a good thing her husband is so patient. At least, he started out being patient, but I think it's wearing thin now, poor boy. I don't blame him, but what else can I do? He wants nothing to do with the horse business. Arrow making is more his line.

He probably wishes this horse experiment had never begun. His young wife is down there so much of the time, hanging out with the horses and the horsemen, or else they're out cutting tall grass to bring back for feed. For such a slender little person, she's not a bit afraid to let the horses (and the men) know she's boss. I think of Maidie and Timon and their lives together after the war; I sense a bumpy road ahead.

Using the thong bridle, Maidie works on training Boss Mare to walk calmly beside her, training her when and how to stop, how to back up, and how to be mellow.

Before I leave the round pen for today, I see Maidie looking at me with concern. I guess my face is betraying me. I manage a small half-smile and say only, "I'd really like you to ride on her back tomorrow. I don't think we can wait any longer for additional readiness."

After promising to return in another few days to observe — I need the horses to get used to seeing me, too, even if it's just my head peering over the high wall — I walk slowly home, unseeing of what's around me and heavy of heart.

I try not to notice tiny, new leaves appearing on the trees. Spring. It's coming too fast. I actively ignore the shrinking snowpack on the mountain pass. Warm weather is trying its damndest to arrive. And with it, the invaders. Neither fact can be put off any longer, no matter how hard I try.

Hari comes home to find me slumped in a heap in a corner of the empty house (Grandmama is cooking today for Timon). Soon, I'm in a full-on crying jag. He gathers me up and asks what's wrong.

I can't help gasping amid a second rain of tears. "Oh, Hari! What am I doing? What am I going to do?"

Before he can respond, I rattle on, enumerating my numerous crises. "Things aren't going as they should, none of it. Well, except maybe the archery. Maidie's *still* not yet ridden her Boss Mare, and her four horsemen are even further behind. And the wheat…well, it's growing beautifully but not ripening as quickly as it needs to. There's no way it can ripen and be harvested before the invasion and feed our people!"

I'm really rolling now, wringing every ounce of drama from each setback. I feel nauseated and hopeless. Each drawback seems to increase in biomass until I'm paralyzed by panic.

Do I doubt myself? Utterly. Miserably. Irrefutably.

Hari makes another move to speak, but I'm not yet done venting. Not by a long shot. "And the Wheel Troop, we've reached a blind spot there. Yes, they've constructed four lovely, solid wheels. Yes, they've built a good sledge that'll hold two archers. But now none of us can figure out how to attach wheels to the axles and the axles to the cart and make the wheels go round so the cart can go—"

"Stella," Hari whispers, shaking his head a bit, tender with helplessness.

Despite his embrace, I feel myself sinking into a heap again, heading inexorably toward the floor. I've sobbed so much I wouldn't be surprised if I've, I don't know, damaged my spleen or something. Or permanently marked the baby.

Hari turns his embrace into a bear hug. Immovable, immutable. He murmurs repeated shushings into to my left ear—my infamous left ear—and, while they're loving sounds, they're also brusque. I can tell what he really means: *Enough. Knock it off. Now.*

I turn off the wailing and the waterworks. For the moment.

"Worry not, wife." He caresses my hair with one hand while he holds me close with the other. "It'll either work, or it won't. I It'll either help, or it won't, but either way, it's all right. It won't be from your lack of trying."

Hari continues to hug me tightly, and I feel his goodness and preternatural calm suffuse throughout my body.

I exhale. Deeply. And it feels good.

"All we can do is…all we can do. Nothing more. You are your own fiercest critic. Nobody else."

I quietly leave a residue of tears and mucous on the shoulder of his tunic.

"There's still one thing more you *can* do, though." He tilts my chin back so my blue eyes meet his. "That you *must* do. Something you've been avoiding for some time now, but it's probably the most important bit of knowledge for you to gain—and that you must learn from the Death Troop."

Oh. Them. Instinctively I recoil. But Hari persists.

"You—that is, you and Little Bean—*may* find yourself fighting to the death with another individual. And your chief duty in all of this is to survive, to live, for me and the baby. I don't care how you manage to survive. You must just *do* it."

After a gulp and a watery smile, I make him a promise. "Yes, Hari, I will. I promise. I'll see them yet today."

Before the sun has moved further down the sky, I'm moving purposely toward an unkempt cottage, the house of Boze, one of the three Death Teachers and headquarters for the Death Squad.

Hari is right about me and my ambivalence about this troop, and he's most generally right about these things. The Death Squad has been operating for some time now (I can't bring myself to say Death Committee, it just sounds so wrong). I'm long overdue to check on this…troop, squad, committee…for myself. Although Hari's been doing so religiously, I've continued to hang back, falling back on the excuse of my pregnancy. But I can't put it off any longer. I'll most likely have to kill somebody or many somebodies. Face to face, whether I'm pregnant or not.

Three intimidating men—Boze, Geshur, and Jozen—all tough guys in their prime, run the Death Squad. They've finally gotten their act together, and now, frequently, or when enough people ask them about it, they hold self-defense classes and demonstrations for small groups.

I go toward the house of Boze. The men happen to live near one another at the east end of the village, surrounded by their large, noisy families. But today there's hardly a peep to be heard: no wives, children, dogs, or goats around for some reason. But Boze himself is there.

I see him plainly, sitting on a bench in the sunshine between his front entryway and the ubiquitous, overgrown mint bush by the front door, whittling away on an already sharpened stick. And he's watching me as I move forward on my walk of shame.

"I wondered when we were going to see you. If ever." He doesn't look very approachable as he slides his eyes my way, yet keeps on whittling. He looks like a cross between the future/late John Belushi and Hugo Reyes, the big guy from the TV show *Lost* and *Hawaii Five-O*. (I'm surprised my mind can still make such a tenuous connection, here in Jarmo of all places, but then again, consciousness is a mysterious thing.)

Maybe Boze has been bugged to death by nervous students and is now savoring a rare moment of peace and quiet. Maybe his family is off gathering at the new wild turnip patch my friend Kerki recently discovered. Maybe Boze is pissed that I haven't been over yet to check out his operation. Maybe it's just that his feelings are hurt. I think it's the latter.

"Looks like you're already busy. I'll check back tomorrow." Already I'm making excuses and starting to back down the path.

"So, do you want to learn how to save your own life or not?" He cocks an eyebrow at me and sets aside his knife and stick.

"Oh, yes, please. I really do. Want to. But I can wait till a class has gathered, if you'd rather." Suddenly I'm all mush-mouthed and babbling.

"Come here," he says. And I come.

Sighing deeply, his hands on his hips for a moment, he sizes me up. "You're tall. That'll help."

"But I'm pregnant," I tell him. Although I'm not terribly huge just yet, the bump is clearly evident.

"All the more reason for you to learn how to kill—or avoid being killed." He rubs his face then and sighs deeply. "No time like the present. So, how is your archery? Can you hit the target?"

I'm ridiculously glad to be able to honestly report excellent results on that score.

"All right." He nods, looking pleased at least by that. "So, stick to your archery and use it if at all possible. It keeps a distance between you and the invader, and that's what you want. A safe distance. Just keep shooting, and shooting, and shooting. Make sure you have twice the number of arrows you think you'll ever need. Will you have any problem shooting an arrow into an invading woman's belly—say, a pregnant woman? Or, say, even a child?"

After a moment's quailing, I blurt, "Not if they're trying to shoot me first. No, I really don't think I will. I always *thought* I would, and I never considered myself a warrior. But, to keep Little Bean safe…"

Reflexively, I cover my bump with two hands and narrow my eyes.

"Yes, I'll shoot. No worries about that."

"Good girl." For the first time, Boze grins.

For the next few hours, he works with me—my own private lesson, although others pass by, smiling and watching us. "Don't look at them, look at me. I'm aiming to kill you here, so what are you going to do about it?"

He shows me how use the palm-heel of my hand on an invader's chin or nose, a hammer fist on a man's throat, or a karate chop (although it's not called that yet) on the side of the neck. He directs me toward the body's most vulnerable points: eyes, neck throat, face, gut, groin, ribs, knee, foot, fingers.

"Sometimes it's best to fight from really close in when someone has got you in a front clinch." Boze shows me how to slither my left hand around to grab the back of the attacker's neck and pull it toward me, then strike immediately with the flat of my elbow into the nose or mouth.

"Then rake his eyes." He makes me demonstrate (gently) on him. "See, I instinctively react by raising my free hand to cover my injured eyes, during which time you grab my throat…right here. Remember, attack the eyes first, then go for the throat. Don't just go for the throat alone. Or you can reach onto his back and start pulling his tunic up over his head—if he's wearing any, he may be bare-chested – then slam a hammer fist into the side of his head and ear, followed by a knee in the groin. And when he's down, *you* are off and running. Make it so he can't see, can't breathe, can't fight."

Boze runs me through scenario after scenario, all of them presuming that my supply of arrows is gone. Nearly all scenarios end with me kneeing groins, raking eyes, then grabbing the invader's trachea with a free hand and squeezing until it cracks. Fatally.

"One more thing to remember…" Boze is sweating hard but looks to be enjoying himself thoroughly.

I'm feeling more chipper about things myself. These things that I'm learning—eye raking, groin kneeing, trachea crushing—I now know how to do. I just hope the training will kick in so I *will* do these things. If necessary to save my life. Or Little Bean's.

"If the Bad Guys make it into Jarmo, despite the wall, despite everything, and if you run out of arrows or someone rips the bow out of your hands and puts you in a choke-hold, here's an important thing to remember." Boze touches two spots on the back of my head at the bottom of the hairline, where the skull attaches to the neck, halfway between the back of the ear and the spine.

"If you're fighting on the ground, see, remember these two spots where you can kill somebody using only the side of your hand. First, grab onto the Bad Guy's tunic or pelt. If he's sitting on you and beating away at you, pull him in closer—yes, closer, with your left hand. At the same time, bring your right arm up and over the top of his left arm—the arm that's probably still punching you. Then, when you get your right arm on top of his left, use great force and wham the heel or the side of your hand onto one of these two pressure points where the head meets the neck, and just keep whamming away at him till he's dead."

"Dead. Right. Got it." Reassuringly enough, I believe that I do.

"One more thing: if your attacker attempts to choke you, you've got to respond quickly! Remember to tense your throat and tuck your chin. Sometimes you'll end up on the ground, rolling around, as you try to defend yourself. Just remember, tuck your chin, go through the attacker's arms, and see if you can strike a vital target. If you can't reach any, just strike out at whatever is closest to you until you work your way to the main targets. Attack as hard as you can and then escape."

Boze makes me promise to practice with him every few days or so. I promise, and I walk home in lengthening shadows.

I think deep thoughts but don't feel as desperate or hopeless as I did earlier.

As I walk, I look up toward the mountain pass, which looks even more bereft of snow now than it did a few hours ago. I'll check with Hari and the other troop leaders first, but I think we need to start those round-the-clock lookouts now.

In my mind, I still talk of clocks and hours and dates and months, even though we have none of that in Jarmo, but some habits of a lifetime in the twenty-first century are impossible to break.

All around Jarmo are signs of new life. New leaves, new colors, Spring's relentless forward roll. Even my favorite cherry tree, where

I waited that day for Maidie to bring in the horses last fall, is loaded with buds, ready to erupt into pink blooms at any moment.

When I arrive later at home, the supper fire is already lit. I stir chopped wild turnips and onions together in a stone bowl while Grandmama adds in dried herbs, and I can't help asking Hari a question.

"Hari, have you ever killed a man?"

I'm not sure what to think if he says yes.

The silence grows, and even Grandmama stops sprinkling sage and looks toward her grandson.

"No, I haven't. Not yet." Hari looks down at his fingernails for a moment, then looks up at us, almost shame-faced. "It's always been so...so *safe* here in Jarmo. Before this war. We rarely had anything to fight about. But now, everything's changing. And we've all got to rise to the task of, well, killing them all. No, make that killing *enough* of them so there'll be no question of whose village this is. And who shall rule over Jarmo."

Sudden visions come unbidden to my mind. Power-hungry dictators, terrorists, warlords with twisted ways. Will war change our people forever? Will it change Hari? Into something I fear and hope he never becomes?

I'm still staring at him, with questioning eyes and a quivering chin, when he takes pity on me. He tempers and clarifies his words when he answers. "As chieftain, I'm really just the symbol of our village, our people. *We* shall rule Jarmo, Stella. As we have since time out of mind. We."

"As in We the People?" I can't help asking. A ghostly memory of the Stars and Stripes flashes through my consciousness, then drifts like smoke away.

"As you have said, yes. We, the People."

Slowly I smile and am satisfied. I resume my turnip-stirring and exhale.

CHAPTER 33
The Siege of Jarmo

Life is either a daring adventure or nothing.
～ Helen Keller ～
1880–1968

Stella

T he day we've feared so long has arrived.

It is here; it is now. The invaders stand poised and ready in the field north of town.

Our system of paired scouts is working great—so far. Teams of what I still think of as junior high age kids keep watch in shifts, day and night, from many hidden vantage points.

We've had them stationed at various lookout points to keep watch for the invaders' arrival, with strict orders to return without being observed, giving us advance warning of the Bad Guys' arrival.

Yesterday, two of our youngsters came racing back to Jarmo, chests heaving, sweating and gasping. "We saw them! They're coming! Masses of 'em, making camp for tonight just below the pass."

Further questioning refines the estimate from masses to about ninety men, seventy women, and an indefinite number of children. Their numbers *do* loom larger than ours, but not by much. Still, we were hoping the odds would go the other way.

No one can sleep a wink the night we learn how imminent our war truly is. Women and children sort the last of the gathered root vegetables, mushrooms, and nuts, tote bladders of water up from the stream, and salt down more carcasses of venison. The two remaining open passageways through the defensive wall are feverishly filled up with rocks.

There! For good or ill, we're all buttoned up for the duration.

And then we wait. And worry. And wait some more.

We're all behind the wall now. That is, all but seven of us — Maidie and her three horsemen, Oren, plus two skilled bowmen — who are secretly, under Hari's orders, camping out in the round pen. The invaders probably have little inkling of the round pen and its horses because the pen is situated on the far side of the village, on the downhill slope toward the river.

Tonight, Hari ceaselessly makes the rounds of the village, over and over again. Checking, counting, making sure of things — people, positions, supplies of arrows, food and water, vantage points — one more time before morning. Who knows? Maybe the attack will come in the wee hours, perhaps in the middle of the night.

I'm counting on the fact that the invaders will be lazy. Too complacent. Sure of their strength of numbers, never doubting they'll pull off this coup. Surely people like that wouldn't trouble themselves to stumble about in the dark.

On his rounds, Hari dispenses words of strength, support, and positivity. He even makes sure that the new, temporary, in-town latrine is ready for business so no one will try to leave the enclosure until…well, until it's time.

Last night, he finally slept, but just a little and very restlessly. He's double-checked that the on-duty lookouts will wake him long before sunrise. When Hari doesn't sleep, I don't either. All of us are up and ready — quivering with anticipation, dread, and determination — long before sun-up. But we wait. And we wait. And wait.

Nothing.

We didn't all just dream it, did we? I'm starting to wonder.

It's the Siege of Jarmo: Day One. Mid-morning, as we tensely watch from our positions along the defensive wall, still keeping our weapons hidden at Hari's order, we finally observe a cluster of men coming over the hill above the town. The cluster soon becomes a stream, then a river of humanity that keeps on coming. And coming.

I have to admit that the group who assembles at the foot of the hill can definitely be called a mass by anyone's definition of the word.

An emissary group of about forty men breaks away from the larger mass and starts walking toward us. A tall, stocky man leads the way.

It can only be Vizla, the invaders' leader whom Ashur has told us about.

Vizla! I look with eagerness tempered by dread, at the king of the Bad Guys, the People of the Shield.

Ashur has told us what little he knows about Vizla: that the leader thinks he's pretty hot stuff, that he's cruel, that he likes to intimidate underlings of any kind, and that he's bald.

Vizla and his henchmen approach the wall more closely. Just enough so that his loud voice will carry. But they're not yet within good arrow range.

"People of Jarmo! Well, well, well! I've been looking forward to this for some time!"

Vizla extends both arms wide, as if in welcome. His subjects grin, yell, and roar their own approval.

Vizla smiles hugely, which makes for a daunting first impression on us Jarmoites. Although his accent is thick and strange, we can still make out his words. All too well.

He wears a fine, closely-woven, cream-colored tunic and leather breast-plate. He looks almost Egyptian, even though I know the classic Egyptian look won't come on the scene for another four thousand years yet. Besides, Egypt is almost a thousand miles away, to the south and west of Jarmo.

Speaking with grand gestures, Vizla talks in a voice that would never need a microphone.

"People of Jarmo, we have come to see you, bringing a proposal. Our home, our former home over those mountains, there to the east, has now become…worn out. Water, prey, and easy gatherings have all grown scarce there. We need a new home. We need *this* home."

What a shit! I can't believe what a cheeseball this guy is.

"So, allow me to tell you how it's going to be from now on." Vizla speaks in a clear, unhurried, almost cultured voice. He's taking all the time in the world. Which he probably has.

"You will send out your chief to negotiate with me. I think you'll find me a very generous man, as you will see. I offer you two plans from which to choose. Both provide for a fair and orderly transition. But be aware at the outset that, with either plan, we will be keeping

your young women, women of child-bearing age, but I will generously allow you to keep the rest."

He smiles magnanimously and continues. He knows he's on a roll.

"Plan One. Tomorrow morning all of you, except for your fertile
women, will move out quietly and leave this place forever, taking
nothing. And you will follow the great river south for at least six days'
walk. If you disobey these directives and try to stay around this area,
we'll capture you and sacrifice you to our god, Malik.

"Plan Two. If you do not choose to leave Jarmo, we will happily
accommodate you—*some* of you, that is—as slaves, laborers, and
servants. We won't need all of you, just enough. Everyone else that
we don't need—the grandmothers, grandfathers, little children, the
old and weak and lame—will be sacrificed upon the altar of Malik,
Lord of the Underworld. If you do choose to stay on under our
dominion and are among those selected as slaves, know that these
houses will no longer be yours. You will live apart from us, however
best you can. In a shelter of brush in the fields, perhaps." He waves
one hand dismissively. "This plan should work well for everyone,
and I'm confident you'll agree that an orderly transition is best for
all concerned. Why make it harder on yourselves?"

From my fellow archers along the wall, I hear an audible mutter-
ing which turns to a growl, then develops into an ominous rumble.

My mind blazes with certainty. *NO one is going to come in here
and tell us what we are or aren't going to do!*

We Jarmoites wait, standing on stools and wood piles, behind
the rock wall. Although more than ready to shoot our arrows, we
remember Hari's orders: *Whatever you do, do not let them see your
weapons in the beginning. And men, don't show your heads above the wall.
Let them assume that we're mostly women and children, listening in fear.*

Without a doubt, Vizla and his men *can* see part of us, as head
after head after head of our women and older children peer over our
defensive wall, like the silver heads of pins along a long, low pin-
cushion. Our men crouch down beside us, out of sight behind the wall.

Oh, how I wish Hari were here with me now, beside me. But who
knows where he might be now? Constantly on the move in service
of his people, Hari has to be everywhere at once.

We're going to have to shoot first, Hari has told us. Do what he
calls a pre-emptive maneuver. And many people will be killed. But

we must wait till we hear Hari calling out in the distance, giving us the go-ahead.

We wait.

Vizla looks surprised and a bit put out that the Chieftain of Jarmo has not shown himself, let alone not yet responded to his offers.

His smile is still wide, but now has more of a false look to it. Fewer teeth gleam as he repeats his offer, speaking more loudly and slowly as if to a child.

"Send your chief out now to speak with me. For the well-being of all concerned. I know you to be a sensible people, and life is always better than the…alternative. So, what shall it be, then? Plan One or Plan Two? Perhaps we shall decide it for you!"

He chuckles at that. His henchmen are smart enough to laugh along with him. Vizla smiles a satisfied half-smile then and begins sauntering toward our defensive wall. His men—armed with bows, but none as yet readied with arrows—saunter along behind him, a couple of steps behind.

Suddenly Hari cries out in a loud voice. "We choose Plan Three! Let fly!"

And at the signal, we pin-heads, as well as our men, now no longer crouching beneath the wall, suddenly move ourselves and our bows into position. We're clearly visible with arrows nocked.

We draw back the bowstrings and rain down a torrent of arrows on them all. The bone-chilling *whoosh-thoot* sound whistles in the air from more than eighty arrows let fly.

Screams of rage and pain shatter the air. A third of Vizla's men have fallen, dead or dying. But Vizla is not one of them. Stumbling about in confusion, the henchmen huddle to protect their chieftain as the living run past the dead on the field. A second volley of Jarmo arrows finds their mark in invader flesh, as Vizla's surviving men hustle their leader (and themselves) out of the range of our weapon of mass destruction.

Over the hill they go, Vizla and the men of the First Surge who follow behind him like lemmings. They are soon out of sight.

For all intents and purposes, day one of the Siege of Jarmo is over.

Meanwhile, *we* are drunk on adrenaline and success—of a sort. And we can't understand why they are not coming back yet for a second or third frontal attack. The quiet disturbs us. What can they be doing out there?

I hug Hari over and over when I finally find him amid the crowds. Safe, for now. Then night falls, and suddenly it's even quieter still. *Damn*, what could they be up to out there?

On Day Two of the Siege of Jarmo, many of us are still up from the night before. Keeping watch in shifts along the defensive wall. And the rest of us are still too keyed up to sleep. Since before dawn this morning, we wait, standing on stools and wood piles pressed up anxiously against the wall from the inside, bows and arrows at the ready.

The sun climbs higher. Another sublime late spring day. Birds sing everywhere; it's nesting time. As the sun climbs higher still, the arrow-studded corpses start to draw flies. And magpies, crows, ravens, even foxes and the occasional brazen jackal.

Hours pass. But where are Vizla and his tribe? Why don't they show themselves? Why don't they come out? What are they doing out there?

The sun starts to feel oppressive, especially since we can't easily duck under overhangs to find shade. I watch as a raven pecks the eyes out of a corpse. They seem to go for the eyes first, I notice. The eyes, then the groin and nether regions of the butt. I'm surprised I don't find it disgusting, but I don't. It just seems sensible for an omnivorous bird to go for the softest, easiest meat first.

After a while, we keep watch in shifts and rest when we can. We scrounge about for things to eat, gossip with one another in whispers or low voices, although I don't know why. I'm sure Vizla can't hear us from wherever he is. Finally, we succumb to boredom and snappishness. People start making disparaging comments about the in-town latrine area that has become totally disgusting.

Hari, bless his heart, continues to make the rounds of the village, making sure enough people remain at their posts as look-outs and snipers, that everyone has enough arrows and something to eat and water to drink, making sure (as well as anyone *can* be sure in a siege situation) that we're as prepared as we'll ever be.

I'm so enormously proud of our people; my heart swells with it. Come what may, we'll meet each challenge head-on with courage.

By nightfall, the enemy still has not shown himself. But, hey, if I were Vizla, knowing Jarmo is all bottled up and not going anywhere, I wouldn't be in any hurry either.

On the second night, Hari makes sure that fresh troops—I'm calling us troops, we've certainly earned the title—replace exhausted archers and look-outs. Tonight, most people do fall asleep, frightened and twitchy with nerves and uncertainty.

Why don't they show themselves? What are they plotting?

With both of us wrapped in an auroch hide and huddled against the wall, I sleep in Hari's arms, and he sleeps in mine. Still, I can tell his own sleep is fitful at best. So is mine. Deep in my belly, dear Little Bean, so restless of late, seems quiet. Too quiet and seated too deep, only too ready to be born.

Siege of Jarmo: Day Three. On this, our third morning of war, Jarmoites are itching for a fight. Waiting for something to happen. This waiting is driving everyone mad. The nasty, overflowing latrine brings tempers to the boiling point. Bitchy whispered comments fly back and forth, threatening escalation.

Then a young boy cries shrilly, "They're coming!"

All of us scramble madly to our posts at the wall. We straighten up, look alive—and try to stay that way.

Then I see them too, plain as day. Walking leisurely but with quiet deliberation down from their stronghold in the hills. Some carry piles of wood in their arms. (Now that's strange…) All have bows slung over one shoulder, and each wears a quiver stuffed with arrows—and what looks oddly like old rags.

They're not yet quite within arrow range—them to us or us to them—but they will be soon.

But wait…Now they're coming together and heaping wood onto a pile. Someone has brought fire flints, because soon the woodpile is ablaze.

The bonfire's flames appear oddly pale in the bright sunshine. Why build a bonfire on such a bright spring day? It's already a perfect day for war. A perfect day for somebody to die.

Vizla's men draw arrows from their quivers. The arrowheads look so lumpy. Bulky, even, as if the projectile points are wrapped in dirty cloth bandages.

And they are. Wrapped in oily rags. Each man dips the point of his rag-covered arrow into the fire.

Hairs on the back of my neck stand up. *Holy crap.* Flaming arrows.

Vizla barks his men to attention, and they start assembling into three rows behind the bonfire.

We Jarmoites watch as if in a dream. We're mesmerized by their actions. Not sure what to do. There's no way to stop them until they come into range.

Within Jarmo's wall, even the whispered exchanges, shoving, and nudgings cease. Our people watch and wait, without resisting or protesting, seemingly accepting of what comes next in our destiny.

Vizla's men nock their flaming arrows into their bows. "First line, approach," he orders in loud voice.

They suddenly start running toward Jarmo's wall, all of them, from various directions. Each aiming at a different location along the wall. Then I hear Vizla yelling hoarsely, "Shoot! *Shoot!*"

Our people snap out of their collective trance and start scrambling to nock arrows.

Yes, they're coming within range now. I hear Hari's voice above the sibilant buzz of Jarmo voices as he cries, "Shoot, damn you, *shoot.* Let *fly! Now!*"

Enough of us shoot arrows into the surging invader throng. Because of this, some of the flaming arrows fall harmlessly to the ground, as the men who were about to shoot them are pierced by a plain but effective Jarmo arrow.

But we still don't kill enough. Plenty of men remain alive enough to loose their flaming arrows. Which they aim toward the thatched roofs of many Jarmo dwellings.

Immediately, there's the ominous sound of fire crackling as small plumes of black smoke starts roiling against the sky.

Over the immediate caterwauling—screams, shrieks, ineffectual beating of flames with animal hides, even throwing our precious water—Hari's authoritarian voice rings out above everyone else's.

He pleads, "It's only a *diversion!* Stay at your posts, stay and *shoot!* They'll be back."

Within the walls of Jarmo, we're close to bedlam. Trying to help Hari, I'm screaming too. "Back to your posts, everybody. Back to your posts and *shoot!*"

I watch as Vizla's surviving First Line men regroup, well out of arrow range, then spread out thinly in a semi-circle around the wall. They nock their bows with non-flaming arrows this time. Either way, they're still deadly.

"Charge and shoot!" Vizla orders. They instantly comply.

Suddenly, a rain of arrows rattles down upon our *own* heads with a whoosh and deafening clatter. An arrow narrowly misses my head. A few yards down the wall, I see a Jarmo youngster slump forward, an arrow protruding from his chest.

In fury, we shoot back at the retreating invader surge. We actually *do* manage to cut some of them down. So much adrenaline courses through me, I haven't time to be horrified nor repulsed. I just keep shooting arrows. But too many move out of the range of our arrows to regroup.

Now they're running toward us again, ready to shoot more arrows. Flaming ones again, this time.

"Second line, approach!" Vizla yells as loud as he can.

At his order, a mob of invader women and children flow over the hill.

Suddenly I feel dizzy and sick. I see at least four ladders—hastily constructed but tall and stout—among the throng, each carried by six women or youngsters.

But I don't have *time* to think or be sick or dizzy. I must remain vigilant, because flaming arrows continue to rain on us. And I fear we're starting to lose. Lose heart. Lose momentum. Lose our courage to prevail.

Now all hell breaks loose, and we seem helpless to do anything about it. Invader men and women are running toward us now, flat out. Propping their ladders against the defensive wall with audible thuds. Before we can even shoot enough of them down.

Close to me—too close—I hear the thud-and-crunch sound as a ladder is flung against the wall. Shit, it's right there in front of me! I shoot at close range the first invader to come scrambling over the top.

My first face-to-face kill, I think dully. And I don't feel a damned thing.

None of it seems real. None of it *is* real. I simply react instinctively.

After him, another invader starts to follow. The mob of strangers roils ominously at the bottom of each ladder, jostling one another for a chance to enter the village.

Amid the din and bloody confusion, my mind keeps thinking: Divide and conquer. They're trying to divide us and conquer us, and if we don't do something fast, they'll succeed.

Adrenaline continues to course through me like boiling oil, making me light-headed and trembly with fury and fear. I'm an automaton, with no past and no future. I simply *act*. Managing around my big belly, I nock arrow after arrow, draw, and shoot. Over and over and over. Killing people whose names I'll never know, before they can kill me first.

Acrid smoke rises into the clear sky from several small roof fires. Too many now to count. It's all a blur to me. I have no idea where Hari is. I just keep nocking and shooting arrows.

I even shoot an invader woman who charges up the ladder, preparing to draw her own bow, and I shoot her through the gut before she can pull the string.

Suddenly, my abdomen feels a strong, sympathetic pain. It's like an echo of a pain. But it's sustained, and it's hard. It's a long time before it subsides.

And then I no longer feel like an automaton. I feel like a living, breathing woman—like a mother. It's the baby. I know, I just *know*, the baby is ready to be born.

I try not to think about it now. That's the last thing I need, a baby showing up in the middle of a war.

Then I hear thundering hooves. And something else. Something wonderful.

It's the sounds of ululation. The famous, bone-chilling, spirit-thrilling sound that Middle Eastern women make to express strong emotions. It's a trilling, high-pitched cry made by moving the tongue back-and-forth repetitively in the mouth while producing a sharp, clear, scream.

It's other-worldly, mesmerizing…and something else Professor Harry suggested Jarmo should use in its intimidation arsenal.

And it pretty much stops the invaders in their tracks. For the moment, anyway.

It's Maidie and her three horsemen, galloping the horses madly, and shooting people from horseback with their bows.

The horses look wild and strange, frightening in their black and red war paint (courtesy of numerous Hollywood Westerns I saw as a kid; I'm so glad I thought to require this most effective upgrade). I have to say, they look like evil spirits.

And here comes the war wagon too, on its bumpy, awkward wooden wheels, racketing along like mad. Two archers shoot from behind while the third man drives the harnessed horse via reins. Oh, thank the Great Mother, they *did* figure out the axles after all!

Vizla's people cry out in fear. *Yes,* they do cry out, in shock and in more than a little awe. What kind of creatures are these, a mix of human and horse…led by a woman! Who is actually riding upon the back of a *horse.* A spirit horse, all black and red, shooting arrows, and making that unearthly noise.

The invaders are temporarily pole-axed by these unnatural wonders. They actually pause in their warfare to gasp at such marvels. A wooden box…that can move behind a horse on strange wooden disks!

With an opportune jolt of awareness, we Jarmoites work to get our groove back. We smother the invaders — men, women, and children alike — under another rain of arrows.

The invaders who aren't quite up the ladders yet now back away, retreating in fear. They're afraid and totally thrown off balance. What strange new weapons might Jarmo have, anyway? The retreating women cry shrilly in fear, as do many of Vizla's men. Maidie and her horsemen move in quickly to mow them down.

Suddenly, I hear a sound behind me. It must be one of the few invaders who did breach our walls before the blaze of horsemanship and ululation.

The invader struggles with Tarek, Jarmo's premier bowman. With no preamble and in close range, I shoot the invader in the back with an arrow, adroitly working around my belly bulge. Awkwardly, Tarek scrambles to his feet and gasps with relief.

"See, I always said you're a natural at the bow!"

Then more ululations pierce the air as we of the wall take up the cry. The sound reverberates in my head and hurts my ears, but it's supposed to. The sound is fury and power made audible, the sound of Jarmo recovering its mojo.

Tarek grabs my arm and pulls me up onto the wooden bench next to him. "We're running low on arrows…so many dead…looks like it's all hand-to-hand now, out in the field. I'm going over."

Slipping his bow around his left shoulder and without another word, Tarek vaults over the rock wall and into the thick of battle. I see many other Jarmoites — man after man, and some women too — doing the same: climbing or vaulting over the wall, out of our enclosure and into the thick of things, shooting arrows until they run out, and finally fighting hand-to-hand with Vizla's people using stone blades or anything they can get their hands on.

And another pain grabs my womb and squeezes, long and hard and scary. And I think *Oh shit...*

Oh my God, I've got to...what?...find the midwife or my girlfriends. But they don't have time for me now. Who even knows where they are or if they're alive? Find Hari? He's needed on the battlefield. I can't disturb him for a baby, even his own.

Without at first realizing what I'm doing, running with an arrow still nocked in my bow, subconsciously I make my cautious way toward home. Our own, dear L-shaped house.

I want to go *home*. I *need* to go home...now...

Then I come upon a death struggle right there on the path. Two invaders are grappling fiercely with a couple of Jarmoites, a man and a woman. I know their faces but can't think of their names just now.

Apparently out of arrows, these invaders brandish knives. My arrow-nocked bow is still in my hand. Without thinking twice, I kill first one invader, then the other, both at close range, before the two invaders even realize what's happening. Now they're dead on the ground. Although both beleaguered Jarmoites are hysterically thankful to me to find their opposite numbers permanently vanquished, I cut them off and stammer, "I've...I've got to go..." and stumble away.

Another pain. One that means business. I thought a first baby was supposed to come slowly, take all day. This pain twists within me like an obsidian blade and keeps turning without let-up. I whimper, then cry out in surprise and fear.

Home...I just want to go home...where I'll be safe...

I pass more struggling duos, other people on the run who totally ignore me — both ours and theirs — while another pain elicits from me a deep moan that ends in a squawk.

Home, if I can only get *home*...

Finally, our own beloved doorway.

With, what? A face at the window. I can't quite see whose —

"Stella!" A voice from within the house makes me stop in my tracks.

The voice's owner flings open the door. It's Koral.

"What are *you* doing here?" I say in honest surprise. My voice sounds surprisingly strong, matter-of-fact even.

"Staying safe. And waiting for Hari."

All I can think is, *You cowardly bitch, hiding away from all the action when we need you so badly on the front lines.*

Koral looks shocked to see me too. She's spotted with blood — I don't know whose — and carries no bow or quiver. I don't ask about that either.

"What are *you* doing here, Queen of the Bowmen?" says Koral.

"I'm…I think…I think the baby is coming now." I don't really want to tell her. But I've got to tell somebody. Or do I? Can I deliver it by myself? Oh, Lord, anyone but her…

Outside, I hear footsteps running past in panic, but I can't stop to investigate. They race by without stopping.

Suddenly, the piercing ululation sound stops abruptly. A collective cry of anguish rises up like a wave, then subsides again back into the noise, blood, and confusion of battle. I don't know what it means; I can't look away from Koral's eyes.

Koral's dark eyes are bloodshot. As usual. Especially when they're fixated on me as they are now. She looks at me dismissively.

"Where's Hari? Where's the chieftain?" she demands.

"Don't know…In the battle…" Why am I even answering her? She deserves nothing from me — or from Hari now.

With a kind of satisfied triumph, Koral coughs up a single, harsh laugh. "So, he's left you in the end, has he? Not surprised. *You* never could be a true Chieftain's Woman. What do *you* know? And who are you anyway? A stranger, probably an invader yourself, a secret spy feeding Vizla our plans. Chieftain Hari deserves better than you. He deserves *me.*"

"But what about your own husband, Ashur?" I cry indignantly.

Poor kid, that I have saddled him with such a wife.

She laughs again. "He's a child. Besides, accidents can happen, *or* be arranged, for the likes of you and Ashur."

"You're dog-shit, do you know that?" I have to say it. So juvenile and futile. But I have to say it to her face.

Her smile is quite lovely — I have to admit it, even though my soul's on fire — as she plans out my murder. "What better time than a war to dispose of inconvenient spouses like Ashur...*and* you. No one will ever ask questions. Because no one will ever know."

She leans in close and raises her toned arm. I see the glitter of knapped obsidian in her hand. It's a knife. A big one.

Suddenly she's grappling with me. Trying to bring that big, bright blade somewhere into my body — my neck, my heart, my abdomen, my baby bump.

I hear more footsteps running; several more people pass. They don't stop.

As we struggle, Koral and I, three more individuals approach nearby — ours or theirs, I don't know. Three young men. Two keep running, but the third pauses to peer at us more closely.

We struggle fiercely, and Koral manages to wrestle me to the ground, baby bump and all. She's on top; I'm on the bottom on my back, both of us in the dirt now, right at my front entryway, rolling and grunting and making ugly, subhuman sounds.

From a deep reservoir of power, I summon the strength to knock the knife from her hand with a fortuitous elbow jab. Score one for Boze and his elbow knock-out.

The knife is flung too far for me to reach it, though. Now it's just Koral versus me — and the waning strength of our own arms and hands.

The young man watching us breaks into a run. Toward us.

That Koral is one strong bitch! Deep in my head, Squirrelly Girl utters these words in awe, as the red-eyed predator continues to claw at me with grips like iron.

Tell me something I don't already know, my brain yells back, as I hold off Koral's arm with both my hands to keep her from closing off my trachea.

I hear Boze's self-defense advice as clearly in my head as if his onion-breath were right in front of me. *Keep your chin tucked and down! Don't let her close off your breathing, whatever you do!*

Too late. With Koral on top, it's easy for her to grab my throat in both her hands, bending her elbows in order to force greater power into the squeeze.

Koral grunts herself into a position of greater strength — all the better to choke the life out of me — shifting my head a bit in the process. She shakes my upper torso like a dog worrying a bone so that my head lifts up, just for a moment, off the dirt.

Then I fall back again, sideways and hard, onto one of the stone pavers of our threshold. Right on my skull, just behind my left ear. *Shit!* Where is that young man, whoever he is, when I need him most?

Koral's hands effectively close off my trachea.

Red smoke snakes across my vision. And the pain is so intense I can't even vocalize. I'm seized by its power. Red fades to gray, and I see the indistinct walls of the tunnel closing in around me again.

And I'm going faster and faster, when I —

I open my eyes again and see a hospital room.

And Professor Harry Vale is sitting there beside my bed. Loyal and square-faced as ever. Peacefully working on his laptop.

Loosing a banshee cry, I say the one word that conveys everything I feel. Every pain, every fear, every longing.

"No!"

CHAPTER 34
The Whiff of Death

We must be willing to let go
of the life we have planned,
so as to have the life
that is waiting for us.
~ E.M. Forster ~
1879 – 1970

Harry

I've just placed music ear buds into Stella's ears — both ears, even the bad one. Dr. Montrose finally told me I could, so I'm starting her out with the track "Sacred Road" by David Lanz. This lovely, plaintive tune always elicits a pang in me, a yearning for…hell, I don't know, flint arrowheads and bare-breasted women maybe, set against a backdrop of rugged peaks on the other side of the world.

Yet again, I'm spending a couple of hours in the hospital, keeping my sleeping fiancée company. Day in, day out, I do this. Just like the song says: Same as it always was.

But suddenly, less than thirty seconds into "Sacred Road," everything changes.

I'm in the middle of editing a scholarly paper on my laptop — a real knee-slapper for *Near Eastern Archaeology* about carbon dating and human teeth.

But I almost jump out of my skin, and yell loudly myself, when Stella lets fly with her banshee cry.

Holy *shit!*

She even writhes her shoulders and claws blindly about with both arms, her hands still encased in coma mitts. She shakes her head from side to side, which is highly unusual in a waking coma patient. Such patients usually don't make sense or major movements for days.

Stella's eyes are open now, faintly stained with yellow dye to detect the presence of incipient eye infections. Her eyes are wild and wide. She shimmers with fury at the actual fact of awakening—and rejoining the living.

Filled with a sudden lurch of joy and surprise, all I can think is, *she's back!*

Stella cries out a couple more times, looks around in horror, and then finally brings her gaze around to me. Anguish is evident in the first words she speaks. "Not again!"

After so many weeks in her second coma, my dreamer finally awakes, and it's obvious that's the last thing she wants to do.

Instantly, I'm out of my chair, unceremoniously plopping my laptop onto the bed and, as best I can, cradling my agitated fiancée. "Stella, Stella! I'm here. Welcome back *again,* darlin', welcome back to *this* world."

She looks as if she's been shot out of a cannon. Furious, frightened, and disoriented.

Except for patients in made-for-TV movies, "fast" isn't the way coma patients normally wake up. And I ought to know. She sure didn't wake up fast the first time.

It's different this time. Her yellow-tinged blue eyes are panicked and mutinous. She's panting as if she's run a great distance. Or maybe come out the loser in a fight. She stares at me as if she can't believe her eyes. "I can't believe it. I'm back *again!*"

"Stella! Stella," I embrace and try to reassure her.

I must be dreaming. Can she really be alive, awake, aware? Again? After all she's been through?

"It's me, Harry." I cup both my hands gently against her cheeks. "Oh, Stella…Stel…I'm so glad you've come back to me a second time!" I have the odd feeling I'm in church and should be reverent. I feel huge relief and gratitude. Stella is back. With me. And not with that other guy.

She jerks her hopeful gaze around the room, then back at me again. Then her face droops with weariness that's bone deep. "Oh...it's you."

"Yes, it's me. The other guy." I can't keep a slightly sardonic tone from my voice. "Probably not the one you wanted to see. But it's what you get."

I don't know whether to deepen the embrace or let her be. I decide to wait and take my cues from her.

I find I'm no longer excited about anything just now.

Her face immediately dissolves into weak, gasping sobs. "Oh... *shit!* They're *gone. All* of them. Hari and Ashur and Maidie and even Koral. Everybody. Now I'll never know what happened to them, never know how the battle came out. Did we win? Did we? I'll never know because they're gone forever."

Her voice rises on a note of passion and panic.

Somehow she's levered herself into a sitting position with my arms still around her. Surprising strength and unbelievable lucidity for one just awakened from a coma, even of moderate duration.

"So, the war came after all?" I ask her. "And did it help? All that stuff we learned about the wheel? And horse training? Defensive walls and self-defense? Did it make a difference?"

"Yes." Just the one word from Stella. Then silence.

I'm about to carefully ask for more details when Stella explains in a halting voice. "Yes, the war *did* come, and I was in it." Her voice sounds thick with despair and grief. "We all were."

I don't ask any more questions but allow her to mentally find her own way.

After a long silence, she continues. "We were fighting a great battle...fighting to the death...over who would take Jarmo. Invaders were trying to scale our wall."

She pauses as if summoning the will to go on. It must take a huge effort on her part to go from zero to sixty, so to speak, after so many weeks of being inert and unaware. At least unaware of the twenty-first century world.

She speaks softly now, and I lean in close to hear her words. "During the fighting, another woman, a *friend*—sort of..."

Stella stops her narrative to emit a laugh that sounds rusty with disuse. "This...this *girl*, one of our own people, tried to kill me. First with a knife, but I knocked it out of her hand. Then we struggled on the ground, and she tried to choke me to death. I hit my bad ear on a rock. The last thing I saw was her eyes."

Stella suddenly looks incredulous, then affronted, when she considers that fact. "She...Koral...must have killed me. She *must* have. *Bitch!* That must be why I came back."

Then horror floods her features. "Oh *God,* my *baby!* Where's my baby? I was right in the middle of having a baby, and then all of a sudden I wasn't. I was *here.*"

I attempt to calm her agitation.

She reaches down to palpate her abdomen, frantically seeking something there. And finding nothing but the feeding tube, she tugs at it in growing fear.

I try to stop her, to calm her. "No, darlin', no! Don't pull on that. Now that you're awake, we'll have the doctor take it out. What're you looking for, honey?"

She looks at me as if I'm a total doorknob and rushes on in a panic. "I'm looking for my *baby*, what else? Where is my baby? In Jarmo, I had my baby, my bump, and now it's gone. What did Koral do with my baby? Did she kill it?"

Enormous pity suffuses me then. *Oh, Stella.* What can I say?

I try to break it to her gently. "Dear heart, there isn't any baby. You don't have a baby in this world. Not yet, anyway."

Weak and wordless, Stella cries even harder. Ugly, shuddering sobs that finally summon one nurse, then two, running to her bedside. They page Dr. Montrose in the midst of his grand rounds; he's now on his way to her room.

All I can do is pat Stella's shoulder ineffectually. *Cry, dear heart, cry. To you, they are all now dead. All of them and your baby, too. Buried deeper than the ruins at Pompey, deeper than ancient Egypt, deep in an antediluvian time of no writing, no records. Nothing.*

After Dr. Montrose's first excitement at finding Stella awakened, the doctor observes as she cries herself toward exhaustion. Shaking his head, he injects her with a very mild sedative. Nothing stronger, he tells me in an aside. "We don't want her to slide back into the dark again, but I don't want her so agitated she might start a brain hemorrhage either."

Stella seems to sleep very lightly, but, hey, at least she's stopped sobbing. Her brow is furrowed, and occasionally she makes a whimper like a puppy. Then, nothing. Her breathing becomes regular, but it has a determined, angry sound. After much consultation among doctors and paraprofessionals, they leave me alone at Stella's bedside. Again.

While she sleeps. Again.

About two hours later, I awaken. Can I actually have been dozing, slumped in a chair by her side?

When I rouse, stiff and a bit muzzy-headed, she's already awake and gazing at me. She's not crying any more.

Lucid now, Stella remains calm and quiet. Looking at me, she summons a small, watery smile.

Somehow she looks more mature and also somewhat resigned. As if she's made up her mind to make the best of things, including me.

"Hello, Harry." She's very tired, and she's not going to fight me anymore. Her half-smile deepens. It's still sorrowful and chastened, but even so, it glimmers with faint possibility.

"Yes, I'm back, and I'm very glad to see you again."

I say nothing, but I take her two hands in my own and bring them to my lips.

Before two more hours pass, Stella's feeding tube is removed, and she's up and even starting to stumblingly walk again with assistance.

The medical staff is incredulous. Stella's "instant recovery" is almost unheard of. She responds to questions properly and seems to be actively regaining her twenty-first century normality, much faster than she ever did after her first coma.

But, it also seems to me that Stella is also listening. Listening intently for something from far, far away.

But that's all right. I give myself a pep talk, selfishly calculate the odds, and decide they're in my favor.

And I'm thinking, she's here and *I'm* here. We're already both here together. Eventually, she'll adjust back to twenty-first century life. After all, there's a lot to love here, including me. There's already somebody here who *loves* her: me. When she comes around to that fact, I'll be ready. Right here by her side.

After three more days in the hospital while her feeding tube site starts to close over and heal, Stella comes home.

With me.

For good.

To stay.

Truthfully, she has no other place to go. It's either back to Chicago with stepfather Chuck and his new wife, who would, no doubt, rather move forward on their own, rather than become a threesome with a frail, adult stepdaughter.

Or she comes home with me.

I suppose Chuck could pay for excruciatingly expensive home healthcare aides for several months. Or years, depending on what the future holds for Stella. Or we could go the Medicaid route for her as an indigent independent adult, but the whole idea of that just leaves a bad taste in everyone's mouth.

She's still my fiancée, no matter how she got that way. I still want and love her. And Stella passed her twenty-first birthday during the second coma. She's a free agent now, no longer a dependent on anybody's tax form. It's best that she just comes home with her fiancée, the ever-loyal Professor Harry Vale.

Chuck flies in from Chicago to help Stella's transition from hospital to her new home, and also to welcome her back to the world.

"Look at you, kiddo!" Chuck gives her a tentative, delicate hug as I carefully settle the two of them into the back seat of my ten-year-old Subaru Outback. I serve as chauffer and driver, while heaps of medical supplies and gear occupy the front passenger's seat.

"I always knew you'd come around and come back to us. You're looking great, you know. Hair growing back and everything."

Chuck is a good and generous man, and Stella is lucky to have him in her life. But everything's changing now. Morphing and roiling and stewing and changing. And Stella must morph too. She cannot go back; her only way is forward.

"Now that you're back to real life, kiddo, how does it feel?" Chuck asks. "Harry has told me of your plans. And while I must admit it all seems pretty fast, maybe that's for the best. So, you're both ready to start writing that new chapter in your Book of Life?"

"Yes." Stella just says the one word, but she looks like she means it.

It seems to satisfy Chuck. I echo her sentiment and murmur in the affirmative too.

Stella doesn't say much, but she sends me a meaningful look.

Right then I vow: by God and the Great Mother and John Coltrane, I'll teach Stella to love me for myself. Not as a…a…*placeholder* for somebody else. I'll make it happen if it's the last thing I do.

With Chuck's help, we settle in at home—my home, our home—on that first day out of the hospital. Okay, my place is kind of a dump. Not a dirty wreck or anything, just a slightly dreary bachelor nest, a 1940s fourplex near campus, but one I'd been subconsciously updating for Stella all along, should she awake and deign to stay with me.

And now she has. I still find it astonishing. How that one ridiculous lie I told all those months ago—that Stella and I were engaged—has now taken hold with truth and substance and tangibility.

Which now has become my path into the future.

That night, Chuck sleeps on the hide-a-bed sofa in my—our—living room. And, with her blue (and no longer yellowed) eyes looking at me levelly, Stella comes in that night to share my queen-sized bed without comment or protest.

All throughout the night, even with the bedroom door closed, we don't touch one another. I'm especially careful not to touch her head—still partially bandage-swathed—or any other part of her, even by accident. Stella seems to be waiting. For what I'm not sure.

The following day, after generously buying us heaps of groceries and a new recliner chair for Stella that he arranges to have delivered later today, Chuck flies back to Chicago.

After lunch, he hugs us both, wishes us well, and says, "Call me immediately if you need anything! I mean it." Then he jumps into an airport taxi and is gone.

We're alone together in the house.

God *knows* that men don't like to talk about things, and I'm no different. But I can't go forward with Stella until I know. More.

"Stella, darlin', come here and sit by me on the couch for a while. I want…I want to set your mind at ease. What I mean is, now that you're back in the world again, so to speak, and moving forward into life, I want you to know that you don't have to…*do* anything that you don't want to do. Not with me or with anybody else."

Stella looks into my eyes, but says nothing. Yet. So I natter on.

"I'm here to help you onto the path that *you* want to travel. Whether that includes me or not, that's up to you. Just tell me what you want to do next, whether it's to go back and finish college or get a job, stay here or go somewhere else, whatever you want. Just let me know, and I swear I'll help you do it. Whatever it is."

"A baby," Stella finally says. "I'd like you to make me a baby."

Not exactly what I was expecting. I don't exactly cover myself with glory with my answer. "A baby. I see. Um, and just when did you have this in mind?"

"Now." She looks at me steadily. Not sad, not serious, not playful or joyful either. Just quietly decided.

"Um, now like…tonight?" My eyebrows rise in question.

"Yes. Now."

"But, honey, your brain and body are still healing. Christ, you still have bandages on! Pregnancy can be pretty hard on a body, or so they tell me. Especially a body that's experienced the trauma yours has. Montrose would kill me if I did something like that. Besides, I, um, don't have any condoms in the house."

Stella looks at me and raises her right eyebrow. "You don't need condoms to make a baby."

"Yes. Well, right." I'm playing for time now, not sure what to say or do. "Don't you think we should ask the doctors first, though?"

"My body. My decision." Softly, she amends her words. "*Our* decision. And I'd like it done today. Now, actually."

She doesn't look hopped-up or hyped-out. Everything about her is deliberate. Quiet and centered and very, very sure.

Without warning, she puts her hands on the front of my pants and touches me. Immediately I think, *holy crap!* It seems like she knows what she's doing, but how could that be?

Then I remember that Stella is no longer the inexperienced wall-flower I met over a year ago. She has obviously learned a thing or two—or ten—during her months in Jarmo. Probably more than *I* know, I realize with sudden shame, given my own lackluster sexual history.

As Stella's hands progress, I can't help wondering what I know about *anything*, really. Here I am in my early thirties, and my sex partners can still be counted on one hand—with three fingers still left over. I replay a fleeting vision from college: those bathroom stall quickies with Stacey Gregori. And who could forget the fumbling nights with Susan Armentrude in my twenties? Before she dumped me, that is, to sleep with a pest exterminator.

"But, Stella…Stel…don't you think it's too soon? We should get to know one another better. That is, you'll want to rest…"

But Stella doesn't want to rest. She fumbles at the buttons of my worn chambray shirt, actually popping two in the process, and tugs at my zipper and pants before I can even kick off my loafers.

Stella knows what she wants. How she wants it. And whom she wants to give it to her. Even if I might be a stand-in for somebody else that she wants more but can no longer have.

"No condoms," she says. She's serious. Not playful or timid. Like I say: deliberate.

"Okay," I whisper in response, and suddenly I'm swept away by Stella's unstoppable tide. As I follow her lead, I am lost. And found.

And so our sexual life begins. And there's no more talk of condoms or birth control pills. She won't hear of it. "That horse is already out of the barn," she convinces me repeatedly. "I want your baby. And…you like it this way, skin to skin, don't you." It's not a question. It's a statement. And it's true.

Holy *crap*, is it ever true!

What can I say? I'm extremely easy to convince these days. Total putty in the woman's hands, truth be told. Logic has totally left my body, especially south of the brain—and belt. My typical expression these days is a mush-mouthed smile as I enjoy the gifts of her body. I tell myself, after all, nothing good ever came from too much thinking.

Our time together that first time is kind of messy, more than a little awkward. Although Stella's heart and body have gained experience in Jarmo, her twenty-first century physical body is still virginal. She's tight and bleeds a little, but still she comes, strongly, holding nothing back.

And, wow, so do I.

In the first afterglow, she murmurs in pleased affirmation, "Skin to skin, just as it should be. I *like* it. And I like *you*. And I know that I'll learn to love you too. Very soon."

And before I know what's happening, Stella has straddled me and says, "And here's yet another way to do skin to skin."

Suddenly I'm lost. And I find myself in her body.

Early one morning, five weeks later, we sit together on the edge of the bathtub as Stella reads the instructions for the Clear Blue Easy pregnancy test kit. There are two options with the kit: one, to hold the absorbent test strip in the urine stream for five seconds, or two, to pee into a clean dry container and put the test strip in the urine for twenty seconds. Opting for the latter, Stella has already "caught the first urine of the day" in a clean, dry, empty jelly jar.

I watch as she removes the foil wrapper. After testing, she carefully lays the test stick flat, as directed. The hourglass symbol flashes—like a beating heart—letting us know the device is working. Within three minutes, our test results are supposed to appear: the words "pregnant" or "not pregnant," followed by the number of weeks since the body released the egg.

Almost simultaneously, the words "pregnant, one to two weeks" appears.

Although we'll follow up with another test soon just to make sure, I know it's real. I know it in my bones. And so does Stella.

Oh, baby.

"It's real now. Little Bean is *real* again." Stella is overjoyed. I am still pole-axed, yet happy, by the enormity of it all.

I thought I'd feel trapped by impending fatherhood. Hemmed in by increasing responsibility and the speed with which fatherhood has been thrust upon me.

But instead I just feel happy. I can't help thinking: at last I'm actually *good* for something, *worth* something, part of the Great Mainstream of Life now, and on my way to being a father and husband. This prospect gives me deep joy and hope for the future. Our collective future—Stella's, baby's, and mine.

Two weeks later, Stella stands beside me in HCMC's Spiritual Center, second floor in the Red Building, before a Lutheran chaplain.

The larger main room of the Spiritual Center is just too much for Stella and for me too: too big, too harshly bright, too echoing, despite the attractive mandala design on the floor. We opt to have our brief ceremony in the smaller, more dimly-lit anteroom, the one dominated by a brown, rectangular prayer wall.

In the cracks between the faux bricks of the prayer wall, people have stuffed folded written messages—prayers, hopes, dreams, desperate pleas—on Post-it notes.

A pad of blank three-by-three Post-it notes and a mug stuffed with hospital pens lie ready and waiting atop the chest-high wall.

Stella peels off a blank sheet and writes something too, folding it twice and stuffing into a crack. She doesn't show me what she has written, and I don't ask.

I decide to write a note too. Folding it in half, I tuck it into a crack near the bottom of the wall. On the paper I've written one word: *Please.*

In a minute, we'll be sharing wedding vows that we've written ourselves. We wear the dressiest clothes we've got, barely adequate at best, but we don't want a lot of fuss. Or even an audience.

We tell Stella's stepfather we'll visit him as a married couple sometime this winter in Chicago. We don't want a big wedding and no honeymoon to speak of. Well, okay, I did arrange for one day and one night at the handsome Hotel Ivy, including dinner and breakfast. It's just us and the ceremony, vows and pledges for us two alone. Dr. Montrose and Dr. Fanning join us as witnesses.

Tremulous with anticipation, we take a giant step forward into our future.

CHAPTER 35
Another Life

Life and death are one thread,
The same line viewed from different sides.
❧ Lao Tzu ❧
6th century BCE

Stella

About six weeks before my due date, Harry wins a silent auction item he bid on at the last Near Eastern Archaeology Workshop. Something he knows I'd like: an overnight stay at a self-described historic bed and breakfast in Red Wing, Minnesota. What's not to like about a view of the mighty Mississippi and hot, homemade Czech *kolackys* for breakfast? I'm ready for a little getaway.

My new life with Harry Vale is…a surprise. Good and surprisingly glorious. For all of my continued shock, and grief, and desolation — the sudden loss of my Jarmo husband and unborn baby — I find that I still have the will to *live*.

But it's more than that. Much as I struggle against it, my sacred Jarmo memories *are* receding, ever so gradually but inexorably, into a precious-but-distant place in my mind and heart. I just can't help it. Life continues on, and it's taking me with it.

And there's the baby-to-be. Harry's and mine together. One thing that keeps me sane, keeps me moving forward into life, is the fact that I make myself believe that 'the babies' — my about-to-be-born Jarmo baby and my growing, twenty-first century baby bump — are one and the same. Just as I believe—I *know*—Harry and Hari are two aspects of the same universal soul.

We now live carefully industrious lives, as Harry calls it. Bless his heart, he watches over me like a benevolent hawk, balancing stimulating activities, both mental and physical, together with plenty of healing rest.

Thanks to Harry and his connections on campus which allowed me to make up a lot of the lost college work at home, I've even finished my degree. I only had to finish out that last quarter—the one cut short by the gunshot—and add a couple more credits.

Harry dotes on me, and I thrive on it. We're both grinning like ninnies most of the time. I never knew twenty-first century marriage could be fun, but it is. He takes me to hear live music at our local bar, treats me to movies and dinners out at budget neighborhood cafes. He even arranges for me, at my specific request, a part-time, non-taxing volunteer job at our local food bank.

To please dear Harry, I even go through a small December graduation ceremony at the university. Somehow it feels like more than just a graduation from college. I'm married now, I'm pregnant, and this is my life, now and forevermore.

And I'm horribly guilty, astonished, ashamed, and more than a little abashed to find that I'm actually in love. With Harry Vale.

I thought I'd *never* be as happy with anyone as I was at Jarmo with Hari, but life and time have a way of fooling you. I'm just as happy, here and now, with Harry, his karmic double. Just in a different way.

I find myself waiting and watching for the door to our apartment to open, and for Harry to say, "Honey, I'm *ho-ome!*" (hey, it's just a joke between us) and then to grin at me as he comes swiftly through the door and takes me in his arms.

Both of us have a voracious appetite for affection. I can't seem to get enough of the hugging and kissing and stroking and nibbling. The more I see of Harry, the more *his* face is the one I want most to see, the one I love best.

His blue eyes no longer remind me of Hari's. (Well, a little sometimes, but the poignancy hurts too much. I try never to go there.)

I remind myself that I'm *still Stella*, even if I'm no longer in my glamorous Jarmo body, which I don't miss as much as I thought I would. Each time I glance in a mirror, my face seems happier, brighter, prettier—from love alone.

And Harry? Harry is *still Hari*, even if his body this time around happens to be shorter and with love handles.

Though I'm creating a life for myself again, that doesn't mean I have any desire to be super-social. Not that I ever was. Chattering, joking, squealing bevies of women still intimidate me. They make my head hurt. Literally.

Our quiet life together, just the three of us—Harry, the bump that's Little Bean, and me, with occasional fly-in visits from Chuck—is plenty for me.

Sharing our thoughts, ideas, hopes, dreams; preparing the nursery; our frequent bouts of sweet, sweaty sex…I marvel at it all and gobble it up like a starving person. I feel so unworthy yet so keenly thankful for every moment of this unexpected joy, this undeserved grace, that is love.

We decide not to learn the sex of Little Bean ahead of time. We want to be surprised. By life.

Although I'm considered a high risk pregnancy due to everything that's gone before—and, yes, the doctors *are* furious and rightfully concerned about this pregnancy—I experience each month of this incredible experience with textbook perfection. My blood work is perfect. My urine is perfect. My blood pressure is magnificent. Little Bean's scans are perfect too.

When Little Bean moves lower in my body and stays there, six weeks before my due date, I'm not too worried. Everything has gone perfectly so far, and there's no reason to think it won't keep on that way, right on through the delivery.

It's early May now in the Twin Cities. Flowering crabapple trees burst like popcorn kernels into incredible pink, white, and magenta blooms. I remind myself that there are bound to be blooming crabapple trees somewhere around in Red Wing, too. It'll be great to get out of the cities for a while.

"Let's call the place," I beg Harry. "See if they have room for us this weekend."

Harry looks dubious yet lovingly indulgent with me. As always. Harry is always My Harry to me now, not Hari. I made a conscious decision to no more summon thoughts of Jarmo anymore. My dearest Professor Harry Vale deserves no less.

"Are you sure you feel up to it, honey? It's a bit of a drive, you know. At least an hour away."

"I know, but I feel like going somewhere." I shrug and give Harry a lopsided smile as if to say *it's a pregnancy thing*. "I feel, you know, restless…"

"Okay, Stel. Whatever you want."

Within moments, Harry is giving them a call. Although Friday and Saturday nights are booked, a fortuitous cancellation arises for Sunday night, and Harry doesn't have to work until Tuesday. We snap up the opening.

On Sunday, once away from the megalopolis of The Cities, we drive leisurely down on Highway 10 toward Hastings, then south and east to Red Wing. Actually, it's Harry who does the driving; I'm happy just to go along with him at my side as a glorious day unfolds around us.

I'm feeling especially pretty today, even with a pregnant belly, or possibly because of it. My long, patchwork prairie skirt is filmy and swishy, and my swollen upper parts covered loosely and artistically by a cream-colored, long-sleeved peasant shirt.

During the coma and before the baby, I lost twenty pounds — although I wouldn't recommend the Coma Diet to anyone. Sitting next to Harry in the passenger's seat, I glance at the visor mirror. Not bad. Not bad at all. How and when did I ever come to be so pretty?

The wooded, rolling hills are so fresh in their first light-greenness of spring. No dust, no insect damage, no plant rust yet; that comes in July. Even the farm fields are fluorescent green, so winsome and handsome, like perfect miniature scenery in a model train set-up.

Flowering crabapple trees flank the front door of the Goodhue Arms Bed and Breakfast, just coming into their own now with pink blooms. More flowering trees encircle a little knoll in a park across the street. The trees couldn't be more beautiful here than if they were part of the National Cherry Blossom Festival of Washington, DC.

For some reason I can't fathom, the blossoms make me unreasonably happy. And the word *nevertheless…nevertheless…*keeps repeating itself in my mind, over and over, oddly comforting. I don't know what this means. Maybe it has to do with the turning of the seasons, a new soul about to be born, life prevailing despite everything. And so shall we.

After checking in and exploring our room at the B&B, which is cheesily cheerful in pink gingham and ruffles, Harry and I stroll across the street to the park. We unfold our car blanket under a crabapple tree that's thick with blossoms. We stretch out, our heads in the shade and the rest of us in sunshine.

Harry starts to doze as he half-heartedly peruses an article in *Near Eastern Archaeology*. I affect no such pretense; I just close my eyes and will myself to drift into sleep.

I soak in the warmth. My closed eyelids look red to my covered eyes. And then I think: Little Bean, who is actually a big bean now, has been awfully quiet today. That brings me halfway awake.

The baby pundits—those in the know—say that a baby stops flopping about when it's ready to be born. Partly because there's no room left at the inn. But also because it's getting into position above the birth canal.

But I'm not due for another six weeks yet.

Another thought enters my mind, unbidden. I wish my mother were here. *Oh, I miss you so much, Mom.*

My mother's handsome, Celtic-skinned, perpetually smiling face remains vivid and keenly dear in my mind. It's been nearly three years now since she died. So fast did she slip away that I can scarcely believe it, even now. The only body characteristics I inherited from her are my pale skin and blue eyes, and, yes, my solitary, reclusive nature. Everything else—my unremarkable nose, the squareness of my frame, my hands, even my jaw—must come from that sperm donor I never knew.

Mom never wanted to talk about that stuff with me. She always dismissed it as immaterial, not important, so I never pressed it, but I'm willing to bet he was a one-night stand.

Dear, dear loving Mom, who made one too many ill-advised decisions, how I miss her so! I hope somewhere she's happy and is also happy for me. True, she'd not be crazy about how young I am, and here Harry is in his early thirties. But still, knowing me and my, shall we say, social limitations, I know she'd be glad I've found someone who's worth his weight in gold to care for me, to make a baby with me, and to bring me into the mainstream of life.

I reassure myself by repeating the prayer of St. Julian of Norwich in my mind. It's easy, multi-purpose, and even agnostics can feel good about praying it: *All will be well, and all will be well, and all will indeed be well.*

A calm of sorts descends on me then, and my mind drifts lazily from thought to thought. *We really need a bigger apartment with the baby coming... What careers might I choose that have something to do with medicine...? I need to buy Harry a new coffee maker because his old one leaks something terrible...*

Suddenly, a ripple of unease shimmers over me, followed by the strangest, strongest pain I've ever experienced—and I've experienced a lot pain in my nearly twenty-two years.

"Oh!" I sit up in alarm. Always quick to respond to any discomfort of mine, Harry sits up too.

"What is it, Stel?" He takes my hand and looks at me with concern. "Are you okay? Is it the baby?"

"Not sure. Probably not. It's kind of early."

I feel so weird. Just...off. It can't be the baby already, can it?

Then I feel an ominous, warm roiling in my lower gut. Not exactly a pain, but something is not right. A gush of fluid rushes from between my legs. Can I be peeing and not even know it?

"Holy crap," I mutter and then look over at Harry for an explanation. "What on earth? I've peed all over the blanket, my clothes, *everything!*"

Brave Harry dips a finger into the mystery liquid, raises it to his nose. "That's not pee. Stella, it must be your water has broken!"

"But it's six weeks too early. It can't be already, can it? Dr. Anna says everything been going so well, I can't imagine..."

Harry is already gathering up the soaked blanket, our snacks, and papers. "When your water breaks, the baby usually comes pretty fast. Oh, *fuckin' A*, why did we ever come all this way down here? Against my better judgment. I just knew it."

"Please don't worry me, Harry." My words come out plaintive with worry and fear.

Harry hugs me against his chest then. "I'm sorry, hon. I didn't mean to yell. Let's just *go*. Right now, just to be safe. We'll grab our stuff from the room and blast up to the hospital. It's going to take more than an hour, any way we look at it."

Hastily, Harry informs the B&B manager that we have to leave (baby is coming!) as we forfeit our prepayment (the manager regrets that she can't cut us a refund). We literally throw our stuff into the Outback and start racing west on US 61, then north onto US 52.

On the road, we're blasting at eighty-five miles an hour while Harry calls HCMC on his cell and has them patch him through to Dr. Montrose's message center. He also leaves a message for Dr. Anna at the Birth Center.

Labor pains are coming in earnest now. *Real* ones. Not the feeble imitations I've been dreaming up over the last few weeks.

Shit, the homeward bound traffic is already backed up. Already, the summer rush of weekend folks going forth and back to their cabins at one of Minnesota's ten thousand lakes is in full swing. And it won't let up until the snow flies. Actually Minnesota has 11,842 lakes — I looked it up once. That makes for a lot of traffic on Fridays and Sundays.

We're now on State Highway 55, moving into the thick of the cities, over to West 7th, then Portland Avenue heading north, with a quick left onto Park.

The baby could come at any time. And I've *got* to make that date with destiny — the carefully monitored C-section — before baby decides to make his or her debut.

At last, the overwhelming bulk of HCMC looms before us. Shaped like an amorphous letter H, this hospital has become my second home. It's like it doesn't want to let me go. Finally, yes, yes, we're here: the curving entrance, doors, signs, the banks of windows, the reassuring familiarity.

Oh, dearest Harry, just get me into the ER as fast as you can.

Harry

I've never driven so fast in my life. Swerving, taking chances, even blasting the wrong way down a one-way alley. I'm sweating like a pig, trembling badly, and flooded with adrenaline.

I try, gently and carefully, to ease Stella out of the Outback's front seat and support her back with my right arm, but don't succeed. She's doubling over, then straightening up, over and over, moaning and crying out, "Shit, *shit!*" (Ever her favorite word in a crisis…)

I yell to the ER attendants, who rush toward us with a gurney. "Help me get her out! She's in labor, baby's coming fast, but she's not supposed to deliver vaginally! She's an emergency C-Section — I phoned it in from the road — contact Dr. Obuchowski…Dr. Anna. Tell her we made it, we're here, but I don't know if we can make it up to the Birth Center in time."

One EMT tells me, "We'll take her now," as he pushes me, respectfully but firmly, out of the way, and two strong men manage to get her out of the car and onto a wheeled gurney. Immediately they start rushing her to the ER, and I rush right along with them, one hand on the side of the gurney and the other arm pumping for all its worth to give me the speed that I need to keep up with them.

Our EMTs with their flying gurney (and me, hanging close for dear life) are still a short way from the ER that's been prepared for us. Stella's cries intensify. Her soaking-wet prairie skirt is rucked up to her waist; her underpants hang loose around one leg. The baby's head — dark hair! — is already crowning. I can see it for myself. It's too late for a C-Section. Stella will have to do it on her own and hang the consequences.

Apparently we're at the right ER now, because the doors automatically open, and our troop flies right on through, with me on their heels. One of the EMTs barks at me, "Sorry, sir, you can't come in here. You're not sterile."

"Neither are you!" I yell back. "I'm her husband, and it's our baby."

Dr. Anna and Dr. Montrose are yet to be seen, so I can't plead my case with them.

But just as we enter the ER, Stella decides the matter for us. Suddenly she emits an anguished, prolonged cry. She arches with a gargantuan push, and a tiny baby plops like a greased pig onto the gurney. It's so little, so covered in blood and fluids and curved away from me, I can't tell its sex yet. Even at six weeks early, the little mite has a thick head of dark hair. And it cries. Lustily. Amazing for one who has shown up so early.

Suddenly two nurses burst in from nowhere and start tending to things. "It's a girl!"

They both speak in soothing voices that strive to be reassuring. They tend to both mother and baby with what look like towels and moist squares of flannel. The nurses briskly rub our baby girl with soft moist cloths, removing blood and fluids and what looks like bluish-yellow axle grease. They note the time of birth and weigh our tiny bundle on a digital baby scale. Five pounds, two ounces. A respectable, healthy weight for such an early baby.

Dr. Anna and Dr. Montrose enter the ER at a run. I tell them, "You missed the main event, and she did great! It's a girl."

While the doctors gather round the baby and the business end of Stella's body, I lean down to kiss my wife, then embrace her again. "Oh, Stel, you did *marvelously!* I'm so glad she's a girl, a beautiful baby girl, our daughter, ten toes, ten fingers, everything!"

I'm babbling now, but I don't know when I've ever been so happy.

"She's beautiful, Stel!" I give the new mother another kiss, which she returns in an exhausted but heartfelt fashion. "So much dark hair. Like her dad."

"I want to hold her!" Stella pleads. "Can I please hold her now?"

Dr. Anna answers with a smile. "Sure, just one second. We just need to do one more thing with the placenta—"

Suddenly, Stella's eyes grow huge. Fear, shock, surprise register on her face in quick succession. Then great anguish.

She looks into my eyes. As if memorizing my face. "*Oh, Harry!* They're calling me! I have to go…I love you…"

She tries to repeat the last three words again, but they come out as a soundless whisper.

Then Stella's head slowly pivots until her chin points toward the ceiling. At that moment, she closes her eyes. Her features assume a frightful grimace, and she screams.

Good God, what a cry!

Her entire body quivers as her muscles tighten, contract, then release, again and again. Over and over, causing her to writhe and shudder in a terrible rhythm.

Dr. Anna cries out, too, in her strong Polish accent. Furious and frightened. "*Niech to szlag!* It's eclampsia, sudden onset, grand mal seizure."

Dr. Anna, Dr. Montrose, the EMTs, and nurses gather around closely as they start tending to Stella—and shut me out.

"I'll take the baby," I hear myself saying. A nervous aide actually allows me to take the swaddled tiny bundle, so engrossed are staffers in caring for the critically ill young woman on the gurney.

I can only see a bit of Stella's face, what with all of the bodies in the room gathered round. I see that her eyes have rolled back into her head. Two crescents of white are visible as her eyelids struggle to shut but don't quite succeed.

Then Dr. Montrose is at my side while Dr. Anna and the others continue to tend to Stella.

"We don't *think* she's feeling any pain, but we really don't know." Montrose speaks close to my ear in a hushed voice. "The scream is totally involuntary because, at the beginning of a seizure, the muscles around the vocal cords seize up and force air out in a scream. She's already passed through the tonic phase of the seizure. Now she's in what we call clonic phase. We just have to keep her from hurting herself until she wakes up, which may take a while, especially for someone in Stella's condition."

Nothing seems real. It's all crazy. It cannot be happening. Just twenty minutes ago, we were careening up Portland Avenue.

With my heart racing and body trembling, I hold tight to the baby. *Stella, you're mine now, so what are you doing? Where are you going?*

Stella continues to seize in grotesque bodily contortions. Dr. Anna snaps orders at underlings. "Blood pressure, stat."

There's not much anyone can do for Stella as the seizure continues unabated. Montrose puts his hand on my shoulder: not a good sign. "We think her brain may be hemorrhaging too. Won't know for sure until we do tests." Then Stella's favorite doctor sighs deeply and shakes his head. "We were afraid of something like this."

After another minute or two, Stella's convulsing finally ceases. Although we collectively exhale then, we all continue to look stricken: Dr. Anna, mad at fate and doubtful of any good outcome, and Dr. Montrose, just plumb furious at life.

And then there's me, frozen in time and space, except for a numb questioning feeling: Why…why…*why?* And why *now*, just when everything is so wonderful?

Dr. Anna approaches me as others continue to monitor Stella. Still looking pissed, the Polish obstetrician also now looks dubious. And sorrowful.

"I believe the seizure was brought on by one of two things. Either sudden onset eclampsia, or it could also be an amniotic embolism brought on by the delivery itself."

Dr. Anna looks at me accusingly then. "Well, you both knew she'd be a high-risk pregnancy."

Still numb, I nod. Now is not the time for telling Stella's complex back story nor offering up excuses. "Amniotic embolism," I stammer. "What does that actually mean?"

Dr. Anna explains in a weary, discouraged voice. "It's where amniotic fluid enters the mother's venous blood stream through a tear in the uterus, even a small one that otherwise would cause no problems. This causes amniotic fluid to clog the lungs, which decreases oxygen delivery for the mom. In other words, you get a pulmonary embolism. In Stella's case, even a mild embolism decreasing the oxygen flow to her already-compromised brain is, well, catastrophic. It could easily send her back into a coma. So, let's hope not, eh? And even if the emboli could resolve itself over a few days, Stella could still be comatose for some time. Either way, your wife has also, apparently, suffered a brain hemorrhage. We don't know yet how extensive. We'll start tests as soon as we can."

She reaches for my swaddled baby then, saying, "We'll take her now to see if her lungs are functioning properly. You know, that sort of thing."

"Yes, of course." My lips are numb as I reply. My baby's eyes are open now in her tiny red face. I hand her off to a nurse who stands near me, arms ready to receive the precious bundle. I follow the baby with my eyes and mentally speak her name. *Star.*

Dr. Anna takes pity on me with a hug. I'm too numb to even reciprocate properly. But still I appreciate it.

The hard part—the mystery to unravel, the data to collect—now begins: determining if any recovery at all is possible.

Or if Stella has gone where I cannot yet go.

CHAPTER 36
War's End

Who is the slayer?
Who is the victim?
Speak…
∾ Sophocles ∿
497 BCE – 406 BCE

Stella

I hear myself scream—a strange, loud, choking gag—and, again, feel that inexorable pulling away.

My brain, soul, and being scream along with my body. *No!*

I'm not going. Not this time. Not now. Not ever again.

I won't. I *can't.* Oh, Harry, dearest, *help me!*

From somewhere, an oddly robotic voice keeps calling my name, over and over.

Then all I can think is *God help me,* and I mean it to my very core, as the magnetic pull latches on and takes me with it at warp speed.

Now my journey through the familiar gray tunnel seems faster than light.

My Harry…my baby…my Harry…my baby… I hang tight to these words, refusing to let them go, as I'm transported against my will from one reality to another.

And still the robotic voice continues to yap, more like an annoying dog than anything. "Stella…Stella…*Stella!*"

The gray blur starts coalescing into a pair of eyes above me—almond-shaped brown eyes with slightly bloodshot whites.

With no time yet to mourn, grieve, or gasp, no time to wonder where I am (I *know*), I must act.

Because Koral continues to choke the life out of me.

Again. Still.

In the Eternal Now, the act is still happening.

I only know my pregnant self is fighting for its life and the life of my baby.

And still the annoying voice keeps calling me from a distance: "Stella...*Stella!*" Only it sounds less like a robotic dog now and more like a teenaged boy.

I gag and gasp for breath as we struggle, Koral and I, her strong, bony hands closing around my trachea.

My head hurts terribly behind my left ear. And I remember: Koral gave my head a good whack, a moment or an eternity ago, against the stone threshold of my front door.

Chin tucked and down! Again Boze's self-defense advice comes to me when I need it most.

Then Koral's eyes above mine widen suddenly into glistening jewels. So very, very bright they are above my face—and so surprised.

She falls heavily against me as an arrow protrudes from her throat. It barely misses impaling me as she slumps against my right shoulder. Koral continues to make gurgling sounds for a second or two. Then the sound stops.

"Stella!" The out-of-breath, teenaged-boy voice yelling my name is suddenly near.

Running footsteps approach, and then Ashur is here beside me. Examining the handiwork of his broadhead arrow.

"Holy crap!" he exclaims. (He got that expression from me.) He's sweating profusely and quivering from adrenaline. "The bitch was trying to kill you!"

"No lie." It's all I can muster just now. With little success, I try to shove her dead weight off me.

I'm simultaneously numb with grief and shock, as well as quivering-breathless from my close call with death.

Those three people I heard running a minute ago *(an eternity ago)*, one of them must have been Ashur. Not sure who they were running from—or where they were running to—but the other two men fled while Ashur stayed behind. Because he figured it must be me there, wrestling on the ground with Koral, and he knew he was the only one who could save me.

My piercing grief for Professor Harry and our tiny daughter, while terrible in its immensity, must wait. For now. While death and danger still stalk me.

With revulsion, together with sweat and adrenaline of my own, we manage to push the wide-eyed corpse off me and into a heap off to the side.

Then a labor pain moves over me like a steamroller.

Labor pains…again. Imminent birth…again.

But this time, it's happening in Jarmo, not HCMC. And our child is not Harry's daughter. It's Hari's seed this time. (But even so, one and the same.)

My daughter…my daughter…Little Bean…whom I never got to hold in my arms… My agony over her loss, and the loss of my beloved Harry Vale, is almost unbearable.

But even now, destiny won't give me time to mourn. Not with labor pains coming thick and fast now, one right after another.

I let loose with a deep groan. "Ashur, the baby's coming. *Now.* Please don't leave me, *please!*" My groan deepens into a cry. "I need you to help bring my baby!"

That's good enough for Ashur. "Don't worry," he assures me. "I helped a dog deliver once when her first pup came out the wrong way."

Although this news doesn't exactly inspire confidence, I'm glad for anything at this point.

As the Siege of Jarmo rages on around us—even now, from a distance, I hear the screams, cries, and grunts—Ashur helps me stumble to my own bed (while part of me protests: *But it's not our bed, our own beloved bed with the patchwork coverlet, Harry's and mine*) before the next pain consumes me.

Again, there's that same thrill. But this time, it's of fear, dread, and, yes, excitement.

My twenty-first century grief, my Jarmo worries about unsanitary conditions, unwashed hands, and my own flesh tearing, all are for naught now.

I haven't *time* to worry; things are happening too fast. There's just enough time to make sure Ashur washes his hands in the day-old water in our baked-clay basin. I bid him to scrounge around for a thin leather thong for tying the cord. He'll have to cut the cord, too, with the obsidian-bladed knife in the scabbard at his waist.

The pains are constant now, one flowing seamlessly into the next. No let-up now until the finale.

The knee-length skirt of my tunic is pulled up around my rib cage as I writhe and cry out. The big, bare expanse of me holds no secrets for Ashur. He's seen it all, and more, many times. Thank God for Ashur here by my side.

Finally, after an ear-splitting cry, great pain, and enormous sustained effort on my part, like a gigantic bowel movement, I feel a small, slippery person slide into the world. Crying, even, as soon as the head leaves the birth canal.

"It's a boy!" Ashur seems inordinately proud, as if he arranged the whole thing.

(*But it* can't *be boy. It's a girl! Wasn't it? Isn't it? Harry said we have a daughter…and the doctors did, too…*Somehow I can't remember much very clearly just now.)

With surprising skill and little fuss—maybe not so surprising, he's a man of the world now after all—Ashur cleans blood and fluids off the baby with a square of loose-weave wool. Cleans up the meconium, too—the first poop that comes almost immediately.

I ask Ashur to place a small wedge of sphagnum moss against the baby's backside and wrap him up as best he can, even while the cord is still attached.

He places the baby in my arms, the cord still pulsing but starting to turn flaccid.

So much thick dark hair! Again, I see the same, dear, little red face. The baby looks like the same, tiny, perfect human I just delivered, an eternity ago, in another world.

It…she…no, *he*…looks the very same. And *is* the very same.

The same—yet not.

Some things don't bear thinking about. *Ever.* For that way lies madness and pain.

At my instruction, Ashur ties off the cord in two places—one a short way from the birth canal, the other a little bit beyond that.

Between the ties, he saws his obsidian blade back and forth against the cord — I'm too queasy to watch — until it's severed from my body. Moments later, I yell again, briefly this time, as the afterbirth comes out in a big mess between my legs.

Again, at my instruction, he swaddles the baby tightly — my *son*, Hari's son — in a goat-hair shawl, careful to keep the sphagnum moss in place as his first diaper.

I remember the many hours, many days, before the birth that I'd spent gathering sphagnum moss near the woods — so, so worth it.

Without me asking him to, Ashur gently cleans me off as best he can. Carefully, he straps a wad of sphagnum moss between my own legs to catch any residual blood.

I murmur my deep thanks to him. Over and over and over.

Then he gives me a look.

"What?" I ask.

"I've…I've got to go. In case you haven't noticed, there's still a war going on, and I've got to go back. Things could still go either way."

"Yes, go now, but be so careful!" It's the helpless plea of every woman to every man going to war.

I *know* that every man is needed. Every woman, too. But I'm far too weak and beat up just now to do anything, even grieve or rejoice, but seek out sleep.

Before he leaves, Ashur drags Koral off some distance so her corpse won't be obvious — not that it makes much difference with so many other corpses around, both within and outside of the wall. But still I'm glad. I won't have to look at her just outside my own front door.

Before Ashur dashes away, I call out to him, "Are you sure you're not sad? About Koral, I mean?"

I can't help feeling guilty that this young man was faced with the choice of killing his own new wife or saving me.

He swallows, looks down and then away, then back to me. "No." There's no equivocation in that tone. "She was a…a bad wife, a bad person. Did you know…a few days after the wedding…she told me not to touch her anymore? Unless it was her idea. And it hardly ever *was* her idea. When nobody else was watching, she was cruel and hateful, and I know she was plotting to get rid of me. And you, too. But we won't need to be afraid of her anymore."

"No," I echo. I think of Koral's intention to have Hari all to herself, hang the cost. "Not anymore."

Ashur snatches up his bow and quiver of arrows, preparing to scale the rock wall like a monkey while I watch from the bed with the baby.

I muster strength to call out to him as he exits through the open door. "Ashur, let's not tell anyone about this. She's…just another casualty of war." I look in the distance at the heap of snarled dark hair and rumpled fabric that used to be Koral.

Ashur nods. "Our secret forever." He throws me a crooked smile as he leaves, then scrambles over the wall.

I am alone now. Joy for the new baby fights with grief at the sudden vanishing of my life with Harry.

Suddenly I miss him with a pain so keen it tears my heart out. I just want Harry to hold me again, right now. *Oh, how will I ever find you again?*

Then I hear the voice of Hari. The voice of my Jarmo husband. Yelling from far away. "Everybody, over the wall!"

I hear footsteps pounding closer, then receding, most likely his. Like a desperate town crier, he must be making the rounds of the village along the wall. "Over the wall, come and fight! Everyone onto the battlefield! Now!"

Nestling my son—*our* son—carefully into the blankets, I painfully drag myself to the front door. I call out for Hari, but my voice is as weak as a kitten's. He's long gone by the time I reach the doorway.

I've got to see what's happening with the battle. I've got to see it *now*, no matter what. No matter how exhausted I am, there's no sleeping for me yet.

Thankfully, after his first lusty cries, the baby is sleeping like… a baby.

I clutch him to my chest. Cringing with residual pain, I wobble out of the house and slowly make my way toward the wall. Our house faces the direction of the field where the battle currently rages. The defensive wall isn't ten steps from our house.

Surely I can make it that far.

With baby in my left arm, I drag the wooden stool to the base of the wall. I stagger slowly onto it on unsteady legs.

The sickening, coppery smell of human blood is in the air, overlaid with the stench of human excrement and black smoke from several burning thatched roofs.

In my other life, I'd read that the first thing warriors lose in battle is control of their bowels. Now I know for a fact that's true.

With great caution, I peer over the wall. Still holding my son closely, I exhale and sag my body against the rocks as best I can—just enough so I can still see the battle, yet still take the load off my legs.

God, I hope you don't faint, Squirrelly Girl comments mentally with surprising concern.

I have the unexpected good luck to notice, and inch my way over to, a protuberance on the wall. A large flat rock sticks out where it shouldn't be, but I'm very glad that it is. I wedge myself and baby onto it sideways. My trembling legs thank me, and sitting on a flat rock doesn't hurt my bottom as much as I thought it would. I figure the lack of pain must be due to shock and adrenaline and everything else that comes with it.

I'll feel it all—my grief and joy, pain and sorrow—later.

My rock ledge seat is a perfect vantage point from which to observe the end, or the new beginning, of Jarmo and our people.

Suddenly there's Vizla, king of the invaders, right before me on the field. Big as life, but *not,* I am quick notice, in the thick of battle.

What I can see of the war, it's nothing but chaos and carnage. Bodies litter the field. It smells like hell is supposed to—blood and stink and excrement and smoke.

I can't tell who is winning. Everyone looks the same, exhausted and battered.

Vizla screams at his own troops. "Come on! *Move,* you worthless shits. *Charge!* Charge and *kill 'em,* you assholes!"

Men stagger about, looking for someone to kill, hoping it's not a comrade. There are no generals, no orderly commands or battle plans. There's only King Vizla, working himself into a shouting, gibbering madman.

For all his grandiose claims, Vizla isn't used to warfare either. Nobody really knows what they're doing.

One side had better come out the winner soon, or we'll all be dead from ignorance, incompetence, and loose bowels.

Hari! At last I see him again. There, on the far edge of the battlefield, he struggles with a taller man. My husband tries to get his knife into him; they're too close together now for either to shoot an arrow. Then two other battling duos cover my field of vision, and I don't know what's happening with Hari.

Clearly, exhaustion is overtaking all warriors from both camps.

The remaining invaders look as bad—I'd say worse—than do the people of Jarmo. Bloodied, gasping, sides heaving, no one is sure what to do next. Except keep moving forward and shoot more arrows. Everyone looks like the walking dead.

Finally Vizla loses it. He literally grabs at where his hair would be if he had any and jumps in mindless fury. "Kill them, kill them *all*, you fuckers! You fucking pieces of *shit!*"

Enough.

One of Vizla's own henchmen turns then, looking expressionless at his leader, and shoots an arrow into his own chief.

Vizla manages to turn at the last instant; the arrow pierces his upper right thigh instead of his back.

Screaming in outrage and shock, Vizla jerks, then appears to slip on a detritus of war—probably a patch of excrement or blood—and falls to one knee. The arrow, still deep in his flesh, quivers with his every movement.

In an involuntary movement he's probably embarrassed to make, Vizla tips over sideways, leaving his bare bottom luminous in the sunshine like a fat pale moon. Not pale for long, though. Vizla's bowels escape him, too, oozing with a relentless impetus of their own.

It's simply too much.

Another exhausted invader nocks an arrow, aiming it at the brown patch on King Vizla's lunar surface. *Th-oot.* Another arrow finds its mark there. Then another and another.

Vizla's own men are turning on him.

I see our people—mostly men, but a few women too—looking wildly from one to another: what strange turn is this battle taking now? Who are we supposed to shoot?

The battle slows to a crawl as all fighting stops, and everyone watches, without expression, the humiliation of Vizla.

The invader king still thrashes feebly with rage. He continues to scream as his ass receives assault after assault of the stone broadheads.

The arrows around his asshole make him looks like a wild turkey with tail feathers on display.

Wondrously, to me, anyway, the sight of these depleted invaders shooting their leader in the ass causes our Jarmoites to cautiously approach and do the same. Soon everyone, Jarmoite and invader alike, gathers around Vizla like a swarm of honeybees, pouring all the despair, waste, and regret of this battle into the big man's asshole.

Amazingly, Vizla still lives—for now—and makes a high-pitched keening sound to prove it.

Suddenly, someone shoots an arrow through Vizla's trachea at close range: Hari. Tattered but still resplendent in his chieftain's head gear, he runs onto the scene, gasping for breath, exhausted and bloody as any of them. With the honor of one chief to another, Hari puts his nemesis out of his misery. The keening ceases.

It is said that there are times when you can actually seeing the tide turn in a battle. And I witness that tide turning now.

One invader falls to his knees in front of Hari, flinging aside weapons, bowing his head, and raising his arms in supplication. "Surrender! Surrender!"

Like falling dominos, the remaining invaders—not many are left, truth be told—also fall to their knees before Hari and his not-too-depleted field of Jarmoites.

"Surrender! Surrender! No more, master. No more!"

Our men wait to take their cue from Hari. He just stares at the carnage and weary humans before him.

He's silent for a moment. Then he slowly utters his decision; his voice carries clearly throughout the battlefield. *"Enough.* There will be no more war here today. Or *ever."*

He looks about at the exhausted warriors, theirs and ours, one face to another. He looks more exhausted than any of them, filled with a sorrow beyond words.

"You are now our prisoners." Hari's words make that clear. He speaks slowly. We all hang on his every word. "*But* know this: if your actions remain peaceful, we will temper justice with mercy. Your numbers are now much reduced. *Our* numbers also are reduced. Together we will restore peace to Jarmo. And we will no more make war with one another."

Gradually the adrenaline subsides in my body. I'm now feeling the exhaustion of the delivery, the tenderness, the emotional confusion and pain.

I look down at my son's small, round face and feel an infinite tenderness. "It's going to be all right. Somehow, it will. Your father's making it right."

From my perch on the wall, I watch as Hari directs a squad of our people—all of them with nocked arrows in their bows—to march what's left of the invaders, stripped of their weapons, down to the round pen. Our new temporary jail. The five horses will wander free tonight and will probably show up hungry tomorrow. Or perhaps they'll head for the hills.

Hari directs another group of Jarmoites to start rounding up bodies. Invader corpses—men, women, even a few half-grown children—get thrown onto one great heap. To be burned tomorrow is my guess.

The beloved dead of Jarmo—not so many as there could be, but still enough—are laid out carefully in rows. To be buried soon, after we mourn them and properly send them on their way to the Great Mother.

As Hari works, I see that his actions are quick, decisive, but distracted. He keeps looking around desperately, his face dark with dread, wondering when or where he might find me and Maidie amid the destruction of lives and property.

Grandmama, I hope—I trust—is keeping herself scarce with the other Crones, caring for the babies and toddlers, barricaded behind a door in the heart of the village. I haven't seen her. I can only assume they're all right.

I see Hari questioning person after person, probably asking if anyone has knowledge about his women. The battle veterans shake their heads.

Again and again, I try to call out to Hari, but at that distance, he can't hear me. I'm literally weak as a mouse.

Baby makes mewing noises. I tug on the loose, open-weave material of my tunic to free one breast. He latches on to the nipple, and I feel the strange, pulling sensation of the colostrum being suckled, his first meal on earth.

I start glazing over, then—mentally, spiritually, and physically. I hardly sense where I am or what I'm doing. So weary now I could sleep forever, but I don't dare to yet. In my weakened, disoriented condition, I might drop the baby. I'm still perched up high on the rock ledge, too tired and woozy just now to get down safely by myself.

In answer to my unspoken plea for help, I see Ashur sprinting toward me across the battlefield. Of course, Hari is nowhere to be seen.

Ashur's small athletic self readily scales the rock wall. Soon he stands before me and helps me down from my precarious perch.

"Don't worry. Chieftain is all right," he assures me first thing.

I tell him I know; I've been watching the surrender. But now I just need to go home and lie down.

With his arm around my waist—he can't easily reach my shoulders—he guides me to my house. Where Koral's remains lie not far away in an untidy heap.

Thankfully, neither of us can see her piercing dead gaze just now. "I'll drag her out with the others," Ashur says. "But first, let's get the two of you back to bed; then I'll go find Chieftain."

After bringing me clean bedding off Grandmama's little nest, he settles both mother and baby into bed.

Before he leaves, I hug him long and hard. I can't stem the tears as I tell him repeatedly, "Thank you, thank you, *dearest* Ashur, for saving my life. And baby's too. We'll always be in your debt. I hope…I hope your next wife will be all you deserve and more."

He looks sober then, but eventually turns on a faint smile. "About that…I've already got my eye on a certain invader girl. Of course, she's in the round pen now with the other prisoners. But, when they let her out, I'll be ready."

After a quick kiss on my forehead, he tucks the covers around us and stands abruptly. "I'll go find Chieftain and bring him here if I can. He's been crazy with worry over you. I told him you're all right—both of you! I'll leave the door open so you can watch for him."

And, just like that, he's off and away.

Suddenly it's all just too much for me: Harry and Hari, Jarmo and our fourplex apartment, our daughter, our son…

Too exhausted to make sense of it all, and still grief-stricken, I sleep. With baby in my arms.

An eternity later, a sound awakens me. I wait and wait, hoping that every footstep I hear might be Hari, but not yet. Not yet. It's always someone else passing by, evidently under orders or with an important task. My son sleeps on. I need to see his father. Where can he be?

From the long angle of light outside the front door, it looks to be close to sunset now. And finally a man stands there. Hari.

Carrying the body of a young girl in his arms.

My throat seizes. Literally I cannot draw a breath.

Squirrelly Girl's voice in my head mourns for us both. *Not her. Not our Maidie too...not the bravest of us all...*

Despite my uncertain legs and still painful bottom, I manage to bundle the baby in my arms, stand, and make my way slowly toward my Jarmo husband.

He sees me coming and remains just outside the door with Maidie in his arms.

As I first approach them, she looks unmarred, as if she's sleeping with her eyes sweetly shut and face peaceful. Then I see the snapped-off arrow deep in her side.

There are no words. I just start crying then, softly sobbing over Maidie and this stupid, senseless war. I cry for my lost Harry, for the daughter I never got to hold. I cry for my conflicted feelings. I cry for us all.

Hari looks stone-faced, frozen. His tears will come later.

Finally he speaks. Very slowly, as if all he can do to keep it together, which it probably is. "There was a great cry that rose up from our people — maybe you heard it? — when she was shot and fell from Boss Mare."

Yes, I remember now. "I did hear it," I whisper. "And I wondered what it meant." I sob convulsively. "She looks so beautiful. How can she be...? Does Timon know?"

"They tell me he's looking all over for her." He still sounds frozen-voiced.

Hari looks down at his daughter for a long time, then kisses her forehead. I clutch one of Maidie's small brown hands in my own — it's still so warm! I kiss it and bathe it with my tears.

"I must bring her to him," Hari says. "He will tend to her now. Ashur...Ashur said our baby is a boy." He swallows down emotion and looks almost nervous despite his sorrows. "May I see him?"

He will be called Little Hari. It is the way of our people.

I remove our son from my shoulder and pivot this precious chrysalis of swaddling-and-baby so his father can see him — his only living son.

Hari just stares at him. Great wonder and yearning flit briefly across his face over the underlying grief. Hari's chin quivers then. "He's perfect." That's all he can manage to say just now, and all I can manage is to nod in return. But that's enough.

He turns, still holding Maidie close, and softly orders me, "Go back to bed, dear wife. I must take her to Timon now."

Barely suppressing a sob, I nod again. And I kiss Maidie's fingers one more time.

As the sun sets, the blue hour begins. I watch as Hari slowly makes his way down the lane, clutching Maidie close to his heart.

The only smoke remaining from the burning thatch roofs now consists of a few, thin curls. Fortunately, we'd had much rain in the days before the battle. The fires didn't make too many inroads. Although many roofs must be replaced, most of the houses still stand.

I make a nest for Little Hari in our bed, but I can't sleep. I take a seat, only wincing a little, on the wooden bench outside our front door. I leave the front door open to listen for our son. The fresh, pungent scent from the mint bush almost, but not quite, covers the smell of smoke and shit.

Quiet and still, I sit in the gathering darkness. Utterly spent. Too tired to grieve, too tired even for a coherent thought.

And then, I'm suddenly not thinking at all.

I am no longer Stella of the Two Worlds.

How curious is this…but how right it feels. I'm now a mote of dust, a molecule maybe, in the Mind of the Source.

Time stops.

And there's Nothing.

Nothing exists now but the Infinite Source and my own single cell of being.

I feel that seed — the tiniest idea of myself — now split slowly in two. My last twenty-first century conscious sensation is, "I'm a cell dividing…mitosis…meiosis…"

The essences of Jarmo Stella and Harry's twenty-first century wife now divide into two separate beings. Each with her own history and memories. No longer aware of the other's existence, hopes, fears, and dreams.

The Source sets time in motion again, and I am Stella of Jarmo—to stay. I have always been Stella of Jarmo. There is no other reality but this.

The Source has chosen for me. Or maybe it is I who has chosen for the Source.

Some last vestige of twenty-first century Stella, still within me, whispers her favorite quotation from Jean-Paul Sartre before she vanishes altogether: *Life begins on the other side of despair.*

CHAPTER 37
The Awfully Big Adventure

To die would be an awfully big adventure.
~ J.M. Barrie ~
1860–1937

Harry

"It's time." Dr. Montrose puts his hand on my shoulder.

I'm at the corridor outside Stella's hospital room. Where else?

The Hospital—in capital letters—has always been the Alpha and the Omega of our relationship, Stella's and mine. Where it began. And now where it ends.

Little Star lies in my arms. She wears a newborn sleeper gown decorated with stylized clouds. Her arms and legs are swaddled tightly in a blanket. She looks older to me already, her hair thick and dark like her late paternal grandmother's. And like mine.

I still can scarcely grasp the reality that she's actually here in the world. And that she's mine.

I look into Dr. Montrose's familiar, light-brown eyes, usually so optimistic and full of the wonder of life, and today I see only empathy in them. Empathy, deep sadness, and an overarching weariness. He understands better than anyone—except me—what Stella's flat, post-delivery brain scan means.

He's done all he can. All of the doctors and caregivers have. But now there's nothing left to give. Or prove. Or try.

The flat lines on Stella's latest EEG tests says it all. She continues to breathe and her heart to pump. But she exists only because of the feeding tube.

With no discernible brainwaves, that's simply not living. No one is home.

No one will ever be home there again. Her unique electrical blueprint, so to speak, has moved on.

And so, after consulting with her stepfather, Chuck, and with me, doctors removed Stella's feeding tube three days ago. Today, her fourth day without food or water, is projected to be her last.

I don't wonder where her soul essence might be. I *know.*

Today the strange tale that is—was—our love story finally ends.

And my story, as the single dad of a baby girl, begins.

I'm left alone in Stella's private room with the express purpose of saying goodbye to her.

After dropping the diaper bag onto the bedside roller table, I hold little Star close so as not to drop her as I lean over Stella's bedside.

I hear a deep sigh and a groan. I'm surprised, and not surprised, to realize that these sounds are coming from me. Star and Stella sleep on, oblivious to it all.

"Oh, Stel, it wasn't supposed to end this way."

My voice sounds tight, yet oddly conversational. It doesn't reveal my inner desolation, my chasm of darkness.

With my foot, I nudge the visitor chair closer to the bed and sit, arranging Star more comfortably in my left arm.

My right hand seeks Stella's, and I clasp it as I memorize her familiar freckled fingers.

"You hardly got a chance to even *see* Star before the seizure. And then…you were gone."

Forever.

Still clasping Stella's right hand in mine and cradling Star in my left, I lean down to rest my head against her hipbone and let my vision grow dim.

I hear cheerful voices out in the hall. Someone laughs, then two sets of footsteps move away. *The world goes on.*

I mentally acknowledge that fact, but really I'm just too weary to care.

I gaze at Stella's quiet, expressionless face. I must do what I came here to do. Before I break down.

"You know, we were supposed to grow old together, to love each other more each passing day. And we *were*; we were! My dream came true, and you grew to love me too. But I understand—I *know*—you had feelings for that other Hari too. But that's all right, because he's me too. And I know your love for me, for us, was real."

Any jealousy I've ever felt escapes like hot air from a pin-pricked balloon. I'm just…spent. I hardly have the energy to speak except in low monotones.

I can't suppress a sob. I hope Stella can hear me. I hope she's listening to me. I would have kept on being so *good* to her, kept on loving her. I would have—

Savagely I tell myself to stop already. No more pleading. Don't feed the anguish.

I kiss Stella's hand and gently place it back at her side. It hasn't started to fist up yet which usually happens with coma patients. And now it won't. Ever.

I try to clear my throat around an enormous lump that has somehow lodged there. "Anyway, I just wanted to thank you for…"

I swallow hard, and I'm lost. Tears start to flow, dammit. So does my nose. I'm not a pretty sight. I don't care.

"Thank you for giving me Star. The most precious gift anyone could ever give another. Thank you."

I touch my hand to Stella's again. There's no response. I rest my head upon her hand. And I cry silently. And cry some more. And more still.

Then I can take no more.

Enough.

This final chapter concludes now.

I stand abruptly, sling the diaper bag over one shoulder, and try vainly to wipe tears away with the palm of my hand. *Aw, shit!* Tears keep coming. Sighing, I switch Star to a more secure, two-armed embrace.

I look down at Stella's pale face. Her eyes are closed. Her breathing is noisier now, and the length of the pauses between breaths increases with each exhale.

I memorize her lips. They are actually quite beautiful. Many people wouldn't take the time to look at her closely, get close enough to realize just how beautiful she really is. Inside and out.

My voice sounds froggy to me now when I speak aloud, thick with mucous, salinity, and deep devotion. "Thank you, Stella, for being the making of me. For molding me, one way or another, into a man who matters to somebody—a husband and a father. Just...thank you...for this precious opportunity to love and care for her always."

Still clutching Star, I bend down and touch Stella's lips with mine. They're still soft but just barely warm.

It's a long time now between breaths. In fact, I haven't heard one in a long time.

"I'll always love you, Stella Denton. May you find lasting love with my...chieftain self." I bark out a brief, watery laugh, then sigh. "May he love you enough for both of us."

I take a last look. There are no breaths now. Stella looks severe, waxlike. Gone. Unable to evade this last journey. But I don't think she wanted to. She knew she had to go.

"Goodbye, darlin'," I whisper. "Goodbye."

As if in a trance and breathing unevenly, I exit the room with speed and move down the hall. Dr. Montrose and three nurses encounter me in the hall on their way to check Stella's vital signs. Each stops to give me a huge hug, reaching carefully around Star in my arms. Some have unshed tears; most cannot meet my eyes.

"Do you want to come in while we ascertain that she's—" Dr. Montrose can't finish his sentence, but still he makes me this last offer.

I shake my head and stare off into the distance. "No. Thank you—that is, I mean, I couldn't. Star and I have already said goodbye."

Then I lift my head and look from face to face. "Thank you, all of you, for trying so hard to help us make a life."

I turn around and keep going before anyone can hug me again. I'll absolutely lose it if they do.

Unseeing, I walk down the hall toward the large bank of windows at the end of the corridor. The sound of medical staff's footsteps going into Stella's room grows muffled. Then they close the door, and I hear nothing more.

I approach the tall windows and stop. Sunshine pours over us both, Star and me. Below me near the street, a flowering crabapple tree is lush with pink blooms. Spring. The start of new life, The Time of Nevertheless.

I look down at my baby. Star's eyes are open now, blinking at me solemnly. Life goes on. Star is my Nevertheless.

A thought comes to me then: perhaps someday I'll have another chance at happiness. I must. For Star, if not for me.

But maybe, maybe for me, too. Nevertheless…nevertheless… life goes on forevermore.

Nevertheless and forevermore. Said by some to be the two most beautiful words in the English language.

I walk the short distance to the elevator and press the down button. I'm going to show Star the new spring promise of the crabapple tree.

EPILOGUE

You're something between a dream and a miracle.
⌒ Elizabeth Barrett Browning ⌒
1806–1861

Stella

Last night turned out *not* to be a night for sleeping. Probably not for Grandmama either. She stayed with new widower, Timon, so he wouldn't be alone. Certainly no sleeping for Hari, still grieving the loss of his daughter, still trembling with battle exhaustion, still rejoicing over the new life born in our midst. A new life amid so much death.

Little Hari awakened to cry at intervals last night, then suckled greedily and made a fresh mess in the pile of sphagnum moss tucked around his bottom. In the wee hours, as quietly as I could, I replaced the soiled moss with a fresh handful.

But on the night when a war ends, no one sleeps. Not really.

Who could sleep after a day of endless blood, much destruction, and severed relationships? Not me, and certainly not Hari. Not with so many of our own beloved ones dead. Not with death moving stealthily amid our own family and taking our Maidie.

As night moves on toward morning, Hari opens the shutters of the window over the bed. He stares into the darkness for the longest time. He's standing there now. I see faint stars still glimmering in the predawn sky.

Carefully arranging Little Hari into a nest of blankets and furs, I tiptoe to the window myself and embrace Big Hari from behind, my head against his shoulder.

He turns in my arms to face me and sobs uncontrollably. I just hold him and hold him — hard — crying quietly myself.

We mourn Hari's lovely, lion-hearted daughter, now gone from us forever. And so many, many more. The grumpy but lovable self-defense teacher Boze, my girlfriends Kerki and Maura, Oren the cart driver, so very many archers, even Koral —

Koral. Suddenly, I can't bear to think about death anymore.

Hari grasps my shoulders then, positioning me so he can look into my eyes. His eyes are visible in the starlight, glittering with tears; mine are as well.

"Did we do the right thing, Stella? Did we do right by fighting to the death here, instead of giving in and assimilating as slaves? Did we do right by using, you know, your special knowledge of the future to help us vanquish them?"

I am…confused. What is he talking about? Dear Hari must be grieving so keenly he's losing his mind. What special knowledge? I have no special knowledge of *anything* that I know of.

"What do you mean? What could I possibly know about the future?"

"Because it's where you're from, of course. Not from around here. Not from over the mountains either." He's starting to get a handle on his grief now, acting more like himself. "You've admitted it to me before, time and time again."

Our voices awaken Little Hari, who suddenly emits a high-pitched wail, his tiny hands jerking aimlessly about. Hari beats me to him, leaning down to lift his son into his arms.

He studies the tiny face in the starlight for a moment, then announces in a soft voice, "In this one lies the future." Then he bends to kiss his son's head and holds him close.

Hari's tears have subsided. For now.

The baby continues to fret in his search for a nipple, and Hari hands him over to me to rectify the situation.

Hari's confusion about my past concerns me. I have to set him straight.

"Dear husband, I don't know what you're talking about. Jarmo is my home. With you. It's *always* been my home, ever since I can remember. And it always will be."

"But —" Hari looks more weary and confused than I've ever seen him. "What about when you said that —"

I just shush him gently and lean up to kiss him, Little Hari still at my breast. "Never mind. It doesn't matter."

Too grief-stricken and confused just now to worry about my supposed exotic past, Hari confronts me with a more immediate worry.

"But what about our people? Can we ever come back from something like this? Will Jarmo ever be the same?"

Somehow I know the answer to this. I don't know *how* I know it, but I do, as sure as the Great Mother watches over us all.

"No." The negative that I speak, though hushed, is hard with finality. "Jarmo will never be the same again. There won't be any going back to the paradise of days of old. But Jarmo *will* come back from this. Sooner than you think. And it will be stronger and, yes, even good again. Jarmo will be a different place, but it will be a *happy* place. I just...know."

I look down at our tiny son as his cheeks pulse greedily as he suckles. "It will be a good place for him to grow up in. You'll see."

Although still hollow-eyed, Hari finally looks, just a little bit, at peace.

I rest my head on Hari's shoulder. He slips his arm around my waist as we both watch the stars fade in the east. And I tell him, "Don't worry too much about our people. They will go on. The people of Jarmo will be all right."

And together we watch as a new day dawns over the land of Jarmo.

Yes, I am happy.
Things are as they are,
and I am a part of them.

Earth Abides, 1949

❧ George R. Stewart ☙

1895 – 1980

The End

ACKNOWLEDGMENTS

Birthing a book is much like birthing a baby. Quick conception, long gestation. Many months in which to work, worry, and wonder while often feeling pukey and exhausted. And always, *always* you yearn to hold The Final Product — beautiful, miraculous, and finally tangible at last — in your arms.

Yes, book-birthing can be painful, scary, thrilling, and overwhelming. And that's why it helps a debut author when she metaphorically follows the beacons of light that shine from authors who have traveled this road before, including authors like the matchless Diana Gabaldon. Diana and her sumptuous *Outlander* series continue to help guide the rest of us in the right direction.

Author of the best-selling *Chosen by a Horse* trilogy, Susan Richards sent me writing advice and positive juju while I was at a pretty low ebb. I was, and still am, deeply grateful to Susan whose way with words is nothing short of astonishing.

The intuitive and tender Amy Espeseth, Australia-based author of *Sufficient Grace*, also wrapped me in kind words and encouragement.

I'm eternally grateful to Omnific Publishing LLC and its Publisher/President Elizabeth Riley for taking a chance on me, pretty much an unknown quantity. I thank you and am grateful — more than you'll ever know.

Head Editor, Colleen Keough Wagner, was — and still is — a pearl of great price, patiently addressing each of my round-the-clock bombardment of emails. Colleen's helpfulness, kindness, and upbeat attitude remain invaluable to me, as well as her excellent editing skills.

My Developmental Editor, Kathy Teel, remains a wise, approachable, patient, and inexhaustible source of knowledge about…well, *everything*. Thank goodness, and thank *you*, Kathy, for your skill at carefully shaping the book into the best it can be.

I *hugely* appreciate the work of talented Publicist Traci Olsen on behalf of this book. Without her directing the midwives during delivery, this newborn book would scarcely see the light of day.

Thank you, Coreen Montagna, for your classy interior book design featuring the matchless Adobe Garamond Pro font. Love its striking, easy-to-read style. Micha Stone and Amy Brokaw, you've beautifully captured the essence of Stella's upside down life where a kiss is her 'open sesame' to simultaneous lives in two different centuries. The look and feel of it is terrific. Special thanks also to designer Gina Gibson of Melbourne, Australia, for finding and adapting the original Stella cover design in such a beautiful way. My website designer, MK McClintock, remains the epitome of patience, skill, and style; thanks, MK, for your excellent work.

Many thanks to beta reader Larry Temple for serving as the initial eagle eye for any errors of spelling and punctuation. Anne Hubbard's Women's Reading Group and Betty Connell's Women Writers' Group continue to send positive vibes my way.

Mom and Dad, Jim and Jessie Stahl, I know you're sending me an atta-girl from the etheric realm. Your love and support sustain me always, even from the beyond.

Both medical professionals, my younger sisters, Rebecca Karnes and Corinne Bolser, contributed reams of medical data and fact-checking for this book. How lucky am I to have such experts right in my very own family! Any medical mistakes that managed to sneak into the book are totally my own.

And most importantly, my immediate family.

I thank my children—daughter and cardiac nurse Mindy Mac-Carter Mangel, her husband, Zac, and their sons, Jake and Ben, as well as our Australia-based son and published poet, Kent MacCarter, and his editor wife, Penny, and son, Auden—all of whom have supported me with unflagging love and relentless literary cheerleading throughout the years.

My husband, Don ("Buzz") MacCarter, continues to be my rock of support and constant source of encouragement, support, and love—essential to me since I tend to beat myself up a lot.

Betty Smith, author of the classic coming-of-age novel *A Tree Grows in Brooklyn*, said in 1947 what I'd like to say now to everyone connect with *Twice Upon a Kiss*: "Thanks! Thanks a *whole* lot."

ABOUT THE AUTHOR

Jane Susann MacCarter is a Montana-based writer who was once peed upon by 850,000 bats as she (and the bats) simultaneously exited Carlsbad Caverns at dusk via a seldom-used egress. (Later, she swore it felt and smelled like being misted with lemon-scented perfume—really.) Originally from Minnesota, MacCarter came into her own once she moved to New Mexico. There, she hobnobbed with psychic channelers and endangered species biologists, billionaires and game wardens, once cooked pasta with a famous filmstar, was jumped on by a mountain lion, and finished a half-eaten sandwich that was originally Ted Turner's.

www.janesusannmaccarter.com

New Adult Romance

Three Daves by Nicki Elson
Streamline by Jennifer Lane
The Shades series: *Shades of Atlantis* & *Shades of Avalon* by Carol Oates
The Heart series: *Beside Your Heart, Disclosure of the Heart* & *Forever Your Heart*
by Mary Whitney
Romancing the Bookworm by Kate Evangelista
Flirting with Chaos by Kenya Wright
The Vice, Virtue & Video series: *Revealed, Captured, Desired* & *Devoted*
by Bianca Giovanni
Granton University series: *Loving Lies* by Linda Kage
Missing Pieces by Meredith Tate

Paranormal & Fantasy Romance

The Light series: *Seers of Light, Whisper of Light* & *Circle of Light* by Jennifer DeLucy
The Hanaford Park series: *Eve of Samhain* & *Pleasures Untold* by Lisa Sanchez
Immortal Awakening by KC Randall
The Seraphim series: *Crushed Seraphim* & *Bittersweet Seraphim* by Debra
Anastasia
The Guardian's Wild Child by Feather Stone
Grave Refrain by Sarah M. Glover
The Divinity series: *Divinity* & *Entity* by Patricia Leever
The Blood Vine series: *Blood Vine, Blood Entangled* & *Blood Reunited* by Amber
Belldene
Divine Temptation by Nicki Elson
The Dead Rapture series: *Love in the Time of the Dead, Love at the End of Days*
& *Love Starts with Z* by Tera Shanley
The Hidden Races series: *Incandescent* & *Illumination* by M.V. Freeman
Something Wicked by Carol Oates
Chronicles of Midvalen: *Command the Tides* (book 1) by Wren Handman
Saving Evangeline by Nancee Cain
Twice upon a Kiss by Jane Susann MacCarter

Romantic Suspense

Whirlwind by Robin DeJarnett
The CONduct series: *With Good Behavior, Bad Behavior* & *On Best Behavior*
by Jennifer Lane
Indivisible by Jessica McQuinn
Between the Lies by Alison Oburia
Blind Man's Bargain by Tracy Winegar

Historical Romance

Cat O' Nine Tails by Patricia Leever
Burning Embers by Hannah Fielding
Seven for a Secret by Rumer Haven
The Counterfeit by Tracy Winegar

Erotic Romance

The Keyhole series: *Becoming sage* (book 1) by Kasi Alexander
The Keyhole series: *Saving sunni* (book 2) by Kasi & Reggie Alexander
The Winemaker's Dinner: *Appetizers* & *Entrée* by Dr. Ivan Rusilko & Everly Drummond
The Winemaker's Dinner: *Dessert* by Dr. Ivan Rusilko
Client N° 5 by Joy Fulcher
The Enclave series: *Closer and Closer* (book 1) by Jenna Barton
The Adventures of Clarissa Hardy by Chloe Gillis
The Ground Rules by Roya Carmen

Anthologies

A Valentine Anthology including short stories by
Alice Clayton ("With a Double Oven"),
Jennifer DeLucy ("Magnus of Pfelt, Conquering Viking Lord"),
Nicki Elson ("I Don't Do Valentine's Day"),
Jessica McQuinn ("Better Than One Dead Rose and a Monkey Card"),
Victoria Michaels ("Home to Jackson"), and
Alison Oburia ("The Bridge")

Taking Liberties including an introduction by Tiffany Reisz and short stories by
Mina Vaughn ("John Hancock-Blocked"),
Linda Cunningham ("A Boston Marriage"),
Joy Fulcher ("Tea for Two"),
KC Holly ("The British Are Coming!"),
Kimberly Jensen & Scott Stark ("E. Pluribus Threesome"), and
Vivian Rider ("M'Lady's Secret Service")

Sets

The Heart Series Box Set (*Beside Your Heart, Disclosure of the Heart* &
Forever Your Heart) by Mary Whitney
The CONduct Series Box Set (*With Good Behavior, Bad Behavior* &
On Best Behavior) by Jennifer Lane
The Light Series Box Set (*Seers of Light, Whisper of Light, Circle of Light* &
Glimpse of Light) by Jennifer DeLucy
The Blood Vine Series Box Set (*Blood Vine, Blood Entangled, Blood Reunited* &
Blood Eternal) by Amber Belldene

Singles, Novellas & Special Editions

It's Only Kinky the First Time (A Keyhole series single) by Kasi Alexander
Learning the Ropes (A Keyhole series single) by Kasi & Reggie Alexander
The Winemaker's Dinner: RSVP by Dr. Ivan Rusilko
The Winemaker's Dinner: No Reservations by Everly Drummond
Big Guns by Jessica McQuinn
Concessions by Robin DeJarnett
Starstruck by Lisa Sanchez
New Flame by BJ Thornton
Shackled by Debra Anastasia
Swim Recruit by Jennifer Lane
Sway by Nicki Elson
Full Speed Ahead by Susan Kaye Quinn
The Second Sunrise by Hannah Downing
The Summer Prince by Carol Oates
Whatever it Takes by Sarah M. Glover
Clarity (A *Divinity* prequel single) by Patricia Leever
A Christmas Wish (A *Cocktails & Dreams* single) by Autumn Markus
Late Night with Andres by Debra Anastasia
Poughkeepsie (enhanced iPad app collector's edition) by Debra Anastasia
Poughkeepsie (audio book edition) by Debra Anastasia
Blood Eternal (A Blood Vine series single, epilogue to series) by Amber Belldene
Carnaval de Amor (*The Winemaker's Dinner*, Spanish edition)
by Dr. Ivan Rusilko & Everly Drummond

coming soon from
OMNIFIC PUBLISHING

The Keyhole series: *Keyhole Kinklets* (short story anthology)
by Kasi & Reggie Alexander
A Nightingale in Winter by Margart Johnson
True Gold by Kathryn Barrett
Finding Parker by Scott Hildreth
Guardian of the Stone by Amity Grays
The Revenger by Debra Anastasia
Subject X by Emma G. Hunter